17 FEB 2010

08 JUN 2013

E

22/6/12   11 AUG 2017   06 SEP 2021

27/6/12.   25 MAY 2018

10 AUG 2012

                 10 AUG 2019

12 MAR 2013   23 OCT 2019

27 JAN 2014

-5 JUN 2017

14 JUN 2018

2 FEB 2019

BASIC

Please return this book on or before the date shown above. To
renew go to www.essex.gov.uk/libraries, ring 0845 603 7628 or
go to any Essex library.

R

Essex County Council

D1391924

NO CURE FOR LOVE

The East End brought them together ... and tore them apart.

Widowed Ellen O'Casey is struggling to support her ailing mother, her teenage daughter and herself, while saving for their passage to a better life with their extended family in New York. Danny Donovan, a local gangster, is determined to make her his mistress, though she doggedly resists his advances. When Ellen catches the eye of the new doctor, Robert Munroe, an intense rivalry is formed between him and Danny. As Ellen and Robert become closer and aim to bring an end to Danny's reign of terror, their own chance at happiness seems suddenly to be at stake.

NO CURE FOR LOVE

NO CURE FOR LOVE

by

Jean Fullerton

Magna Large Print Books
Long Preston, North Yorkshire,
BD23 4ND, England.

British Library Cataloguing in Publication Data.

Fullerton, Jean
    No cure for love.

    A catalogue record of this book is
    available from the British Library

    ISBN   978-0-7505-3043-9

First published in Great Britain in 2008 by Orion
an imprint of the Orion Publishing Group Ltd.

Copyright © Jean Fullerton 2008

Cover illustration © Rod Ashford

Published in Large Print 2009 by arrangement with
Orion Publishing Group

Magna Large Print is an imprint of Library Magna Books Ltd.

Printed and bound in Great Britain by
T.J. (International) Ltd., Cornwall, PL28 8RW

*To Kelvin, my dear husband, for all his love
and unwavering support.*

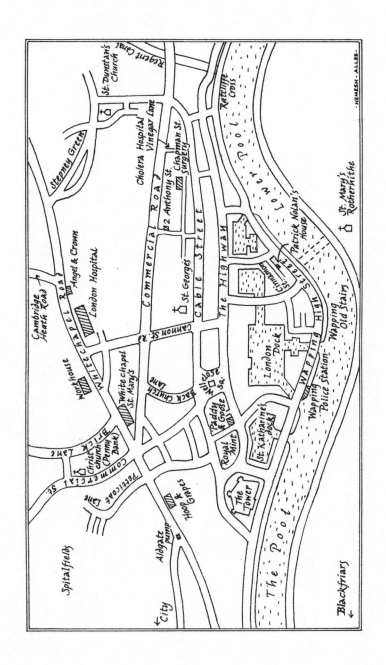

One

On an April evening in 1832, with her shawl wrapped tightly over her abundant auburn hair, Ellen O'Casey ducked out of the cold on the Whitechapel Road in East London, and into the tradesman's entrance of the Angel and Crown.

Thank goodness she had bought a half-hundredweight of coal from the merchant. Even now, in March, the two rooms in Anthony Street she shared with her mother and her daughter, Josie, could be cold, and her mother was still low from the last bout of chest ague.

Through the door that led to the public bar and supper rooms Ellen could hear the familiar buzz of customers enjoying their evening meal. She was late, but the staff area at the back of the public house was deserted and she hoped that she could get to the minute dressing room that she shared with Kitty Henry without being noticed.

Dashing down the narrow corridor, Ellen had almost reached the door with the faded brown paint when someone caught her arm.

'You're late,' the voice of Danny Donovan, owner of the Angel and Crown, snarled in her ear. 'Kitty has already sent word she is sick.'

Trying not to show the pain from the dirty nails digging into her, Ellen turned and faced the huge Irishman beside her.

'Josephine was sick. I couldn't leave her until

me Mammy came back,' she said, trying to free herself. Danny held her fast.

'I don't pay you to look after your brat. I pay you to sing.'

Danny Donovan was dressed in his usual flamboyant manner. He wore a mustard frock coat over a multi-coloured silk waistcoat, and a thick gold chain was strung across his paunch. A shiver of disdain ran down Ellen's spine as he glanced over her, and she wrenched her arm away. 'Then, if you'll be unhanding me, I'll go and do just that,' she said.

He blocked her path. 'You look well tonight, Ellen,' he said.

Her outer shawl had fallen away and Danny's eyes ran momentarily over the simple cotton dress she wore. It suited her more than the satins and feathers the other girls in the Angel wore. It set her apart and Ellen wanted to keep it that way.

Danny snatched the chewed cigar from his mouth, shot his arm around her waist and pulled her violently against him.

'Come and warm me bed and you won't have to sing for your supper,' he said, his large hand making free with one of her breasts. His rancid breath and his body odour of sweat and tobacco hit her in the face and her stomach lurched. 'I'll give you money to look after that old mother of yours, and young Josephine. What do you say?'

Using all her might Ellen pushed him away. 'The same thing I said last time you asked. No,' she spat, gathering her shawl from the floor and dashing past him to her dressing room.

'You can play the respectable widow all you

like, Ellen O'Casey, but I'll have you in the end,' he called after her as she slammed the door.

Ellen leaned with her back to the door in an effort to still her wildly beating heart. She shut her eyes and took measured breaths as panic threatened to engulf her. Every part of her wanted to flee from the Angel and Crown, never to return, but she couldn't. She needed the money. She had worked here a little over a year and Danny had been after her from the moment she had arrived. He would force her if he ever got the chance, but she was determined never to give him that chance.

'Come on, Ellen, it won't be for much longer,' she told herself firmly as her breathing began to slow.

Three months, four months at most, then she would have the money to buy passages for her mother, Josie and herself to New York to join her brother and his family. With trembling hands, Ellen hung the shawl on the nail behind the door and started to get ready.

Looking in the cracked mirror behind the small dressing table, she contemplated her reflection. She pulled a small curl down and over her shoulder. Her hands slid down to her waist. It had been a gruelling ten years since Michael had died, leaving her with a small child to support, but to look at her, none would have known that she was just shy of twenty-eight and mother to a leggy thirteen-year-old.

Ellen frowned. Her breasts were too visible over the narrow lace of her neckline, and she tugged it up. She didn't want any of the men in the audience to get ideas.

15

There was a faint rap on the door. Ellen turned from the mirror and went out. Tommy was standing by the curtain rope when she took her place at the side of the stage. Adjusting the lace around her neckline again, she asked, 'What's the house like, Tom?'

'A bit busier than the usual Friday night.' Tommy wiped his nose with the back of his hand. 'Your fame must be spreading.'

The low hum of the supper room reached Ellen's ears. For a Friday it was quite lively, and she would be fortunate if she got away before midnight.

Peering through the little peephole in the curtain, she glanced across the heads of the diners in the cheap seats in front of the stage, her eyes rested on the raised gallery where the wealthier patrons of the Angel's supper room sat and ate. Danny Donovan was now lounging in his usual place in the corner against the oak handrail that separated the rooms. He was entertaining loudly.

Ellen caught the conductor's eye. He winked in acknowledgement over his half-rimmed spectacles and called the small group of musicians to order. The opening bars of 'In Ireland's Fair Hills' drifted across the room and the rumble of conversation stopped.

Tommy pulled energetically on the winding rope and the velvet curtains swished back releasing dust particles into the footlights at the edge of the small wooden stage. With a deep intake of breath, Ellen fixed a smile on her face and stepped out on to the stage.

Doctor Robert Munroe sat alone under the hanging oil lamp that illuminated the main medical laboratory in the London Hospital. For the third time he began reading the letter in his hand. It was from Miss Caroline Sinclair, daughter of Henry Sinclair, owner of Edinburgh's most successful brewery company, and the young woman with whom – or so his mother insisted on telling her circle of friends – he had an understanding. As he slid the pages under each other, Robert's lips formed a grim line. Understanding! After reading the contents of the letter through yet again, he reflected that misunderstanding might describe their relationship better.

After a cursory enquiry about his health, Caroline's letter contained a full page of complaints as to why he was staying so long in London, and demanded that he return to Edinburgh before the Spring Ball and the assemblies which began in May. It finished by telling him about the new captain of the town garrison who was accompanying her family to the opera next week.

Robert raked his hand through his mop of light-brown hair and let out an oath. Why couldn't Caroline appreciate that in order to continue his studies and make his professional name he had to be in London? He had told her all this when he had left not three months ago.

He let the letter fall from his hands onto the bench and looked up at the laboratory shelves, stocked with various jars containing twisted body parts immersed in jaundice fluid.

I'm supposed to be documenting the day's findings, not reading Caroline's letter, Robert thought, firmly putting aside a mental picture of Edinburgh's foremost beauty standing up beside a heroic, red-coated captain for a country reel.

The smoke from the lamps was beginning to sting his eyes. After all, he had been in the laboratory these past three hours studying the various specimens from the Black Ditch, the foul trickle of what was once a free-flowing stream that passed through much of East London.

He pinched the inside corners of his eyes with his finger and thumb and resumed peering into his newly acquired brass microscope. A few seconds later his attention was broken again as the door creaked open. He looked up to see William Chafford, his friend and colleague enter the laboratory. William was a would-be surgeon, and the son of Henry Chafford, physician to the rich and indolent in Bath and the surrounding county.

'There you are, old man. What keeps you so late?' William asked, closing the door sharply behind him and making the glass rattle. The draft from the door disturbed the various waxed dissection charts that hung around the walls.

'I'm just finishing recording my day's findings,' Robert answered, trying to slide Caroline's letter into his waistcoat pocket without his friend seeing it. But William was too quick.

'Findings, be blowed,' he said with a wink. 'You've been sitting here daydreaming over that love letter from your long-suffering fiancée in Scotland.'

'Miss Sinclair is not yet my fiancée. Although my mother's every letter presses me to make her so,' Robert answered. Then he relaxed his stance and pulled the folded paper out of his pocket. 'I did happen to glance at her letter, but I certainly would not describe this,' he held the paper aloft, 'as a love letter.'

William gave him a sympathetic look. 'Munroe, you must find yourself some better company than these dull fellows,' he said, sweeping his hand around to include the petrified specimens stored in the coloured glass bottles.

'Take a look at these, Chafford,' Robert said, indicating the microscope.

With one eye closed, William peeked down at the worm-like entities as they squirmed and multiplied in the droplet of water.

'Ugh. Where did you get these nasty-looking brutes, Rob?' he said, pulling a face. Robert's usually sober expression changed to an open smile.

'From the Black Ditch this morning,' he replied. 'And if you ingest enough of them they'll make your bowels turn to water. No wonder sickness is rife amongst the poor souls who live in the dark alleys of Wapping.'

'Gad, whatever gives you that idea? You can't even see them without the 'scope.' William straightened up, pulled down the front of his silk waistcoat and adjusted his cravat. 'I can't understand why you are so fascinated with the water worms,' he continued, as he strolled past the grinning, bleached skeleton that hung patiently awaiting the next day's lecture.

Robert let out a rumbling laugh. 'That's why I'll be the chief physician in Edinburgh while you're still learning to amputate a leg without taking your assistant's finger along with it.'

William shrugged and gave Robert a generous grin. 'So you will, my dear fellow.' He hopped onto the bench and sat between the saucer-shaped glass dishes.

'I have seen twenty patients over the past four days from the streets around Mill Yard, all with the same stomach cramps and vomiting. One old woman has already died and some of the children were just lying around like rag dolls when I visited this morning,' Robert said, running his hands through his hair, which flopped forward again as soon as it was released.

'You went there?' William said, clearly astonished, as if just informed that Robert had voluntarily put both hands in an open fire.

'Aye. How else can I see my patients? As the sick cannot come to me, I must go to the sick. I am a doctor after all.' Robert stood up, scraping the stool across the polished floorboards. He towered over his friend, who was himself hardly short by usual standards. 'It's by linking the disease to those nasty-looking brutes, as you rightly call them, that I will be able to treat the sick more effectively.'

'And make your reputation,' William commented.

Robert smacked one fist into the palm of the other hand. 'We are on the brink of new discoveries, William, and I am determined to be in the vanguard of this new science. But I have to be in London, at the heart of medicine, to accomplish that.' He waved Caroline's letter aloft and gave it a sideward glance. 'I just wish that I could convince Miss Sinclair,' he exclaimed, as a growl sounded from his middle region. His serious expression changed instantaneously. Lifting out a gold hunter from his breast pocket he glanced at it. 'Well, this watch and my stomach tell me it's past supper. Have you eaten, Chafford?'

'That's precisely why I've come by.' He put his arm around Robert's broad shoulders in a comradely gesture. 'I deem it my Christian duty to save you from your serious nature and insist that you accompany me to the Angel and Crown for supper.'

Turning to the part-glazed door Robert grabbed his dark navy frock coat from where he had thrown it absent-mindedly across the professor's chair and shrugged it on.

'Will I do for the Angel and Crown?' he asked, setting his top hat at a jaunty angle.

William shook his head dolefully. 'That you will.' He handed Robert his cane. 'You really should think about getting a practice in a fashionable resort like Brighton or Weymouth instead of burying yourself and your talents in East London.' He nudged Robert in the ribs and his friend bent at the waist and gave an exaggerated bow. 'The widows and dowagers with the vapours would pay readily to have a tall, well-favoured physician like you to cure their ills, Munroe.'

Robert let out a great rumble of a laugh and slapped William on the back, making the other man stagger.

'I'll leave the widows to you, Chafford, if you leave the water worms to me.'

After a brisk walk to the Angel and Crown Robert and William entered at the side of the establishment and gave their hats and coats to a lad before making their way to a table. The alehouse was already packed with men drinking and talking, many with flamboyantly attired women by their side. Small spirals of smoke made their way above the crowd, drifting into the rafters and among the hanging lamps.

Robert had visited the Angel and Crown before but had found it full of rowdy apprentice physicians and so often walked the mile or so to the City for more restrained eating establishments. William, with his more outgoing personality, dined more regularly at the Angel and Crown.

Pushing his way through, William spotted an empty table at the corner of the balustrade that separated the two parts of the supper room. Robert stood back to let a blonde barmaid past.

'Gawd, you're a fine young gentleman and no mistake,' she said to him with a saucy smile. 'I'm Lizzy, if you need a bit of company later, if you understand me like.' She winked at Robert and squeezed past him, pressing her hip firmly into his groin as she went.

'I see Lizzy has taken a fancy to you,' William said as they reached the table.

Robert smiled, but said nothing. He had become accustomed to such boldness since arriving in London.

'Mr Chafford,' a voice boomed across the room. 'Won't you and your friend do me the honour of joining me for a mouthful of supper?' asked a large man with a broad Irish brogue.

He beamed at William, his round face shining like a polished apple under the soft light of the oil lamps. He waved at them with one of his massive hands. 'Make way there for Mr Doctor Chafford, the renowned surgeon, and his friend, fine fellows both of them.'

With his black eyebrows and his curly hair hanging in an unruly twirl in the middle of his brow, the Irishman's face had a boyish look about it that was at odds with his powerful frame. The expensive clothes he wore fitted snugly – a little too snugly. The huge meal on the plate before him showed why that would be.

A path to the Irishman appeared, as if a scythe had cut a path through the press of bodies. William turned to accept the invitation and Robert followed.

The Irishman untucked his large linen napkin from his collar and stood up as Robert and William reached the table. He grabbed William's hand, pumping it so hard that his whole body shook.

'Honoured, I am, honoured, to have you join me,' he said.

William reclaimed his hand. 'May I introduce Doctor Robert Munroe, a colleague of mine and the author of *Observations on the Diseases Manifest Amongst the Poor,* which *The Times* called "the most comprehensive scientific work published in the past decade".' The Irishman raised his eyebrows.

'Doctor Munroe has recently come from Edinburgh Royal Infirmary,' William continued, as Robert shot him an embarrassed look. 'Munroe, this is Mr Danny Donovan, owner of the Angel, and local businessman.' Robert stepped forward and offered his hand for pummelling. He was not disappointed. His hand was clenched in a painful grip and subjected to the same treatment as William's had been. The potman pulled back chairs for William and Robert, then stood waiting.

A disarming smile spread across Donovan's face. 'Two plates of your mutton stew,' Danny said to the potman. 'And make sure there's some mutton in it or I'll be wanting to know why.'

The man shot away and Danny fixed Robert with an inscrutable stare.

'Doctor Munroe. Would that be the same Doctor Munroe who bought the lease on number thirty Chapman Street to open a dispensary?'

'I am,' Robert said, registering some surprise. He had only signed the agreement two days before. 'I must say, Mr Donovan, you are very well informed.'

Danny tapped the right side of his nose twice with a stubby finger. 'I always make it me business to know who's doing what around here.' He pushed the bottle of brandy towards Robert, who poured himself a glass of the amber liquid. He sipped a mouthful.

'Very good,' he said, pressing his lips together and passing the bottle to William.

'They keep it for me, special like,' Danny said, his gaze still fixed on Robert. 'You're a Scot then, Dr Munroe?' He drained the last of the brandy and raised the bottle for another to be brought.

'Aye, I am,' Robert answered, declining the newly opened bottle.

'And would your father be a doctor too?' Danny asked, as William poured another brandy.

'My father's a minister in the Church of

Scotland,' Robert replied, briefly thinking of the large, cold churches where he seemed to have spent most of his childhood.

'A *minister!* God love him,' Danny said, as two bowls of steaming mutton stew arrived.

After a mouthful of the surprisingly good stew, Robert eyed his host. 'Apart from the Angel, what are your other business interests, Mr Donovan?' he asked, his eyes resting briefly on the musicians taking their places in the small orchestra.

'Mr Donovan is the owner of the Angel, the Town of Ramsgate in Wapping and the White Swan in Shadwell,' William said, before Danny could answer. 'Plus a barge or two in the docks. Is that not so?'

The large Irishman inclined his head. 'The Blessed Virgin has rewarded most generously my small efforts to make a crust or two,' he said, his humble attitude countered by a sudden inflation of his chest.

'He is too modest to mention it,' William said, 'but Mr Donovan is also a benefactor to a number of charities hereabouts and on the governing board of the workhouse.'

'Very commendable, Mr Donovan,' Robert said. 'However, the people here don't need charity. They need better housing and clean water.'

For a second Danny's small eyes narrowed and his lips pursed together. Then the genial expression returned. 'The people here are blessed by the Queen of Heaven herself, so they are, to have fine gentlemen such as yourselves to doctor to them.'

'Aye, no doubt that helps, but better living conditions would help more,' Robert replied with a frown, thinking of the poor wretches he had left to God in his mercy that morning in Mill Yard.

Leaving Danny Donovan to talk to William, Robert turned towards the small stage where the worn velvet curtain moved with the activity behind it. The small band of musicians struck a chord, and conversation around the tables ceased as the plush red curtains squeaked back into the wings.

Into the footlights stepped a young woman. In contrast to most of the other women in the Angel and Crown the woman on the stage wore a simple cotton gown. She swayed in time to the music, her head to one side and a wistful expression on her face as she sang about the beauty of the hills of Galway. The song finished and the singer took a small bow and smiled. She signalled for the leader of the musicians to start the next tune, then let her gaze sweep over the audience until her eyes alighted on Robert.

Robert leant forward and studied her.

Caroline had a passable voice for a house party recital, but the woman now entertaining them had a strong, clear voice that was very different. She was completely unsophisticated with her undressed hair and her fresh, unpowdered and flawless complexion, which glowed under the merciless lights. He had thought at first glance that her hair was the same colour as Caroline's, a dark brown, but as she tilted her head jauntily towards the light he saw its shimmering red tone and her clear eyes.

She had a fuller figure than Caroline's, too, more rounded. Under the table his foot started to tap soundlessly against the table leg. As the woman on the stage swayed she invited the audience to join her in the chorus of the song with a wide smile and an arc of her arm. It was an abandoned movement, artless but sensual in its graceful execution.

The song ended and Robert applauded as enthusiastically as any in the room. The singer nodded her head to the maestro and the atmosphere changed from jolly to haunting. In two chords, the woman on the stage changed from vibrant to wistful as she started to sing of a home far away across the sea. Robert was mesmerised.

As she swept her gaze back to him she sent him the echo of a shy smile from under her lashes and Robert forgot all about Caroline, Danny Donovan, William and his mutton stew.

Ellen surveyed the audience to include them in her next song, 'The Run to the Fair'. Once the audience was focused on her there was less background noise. She was intrigued by the man sitting opposite Danny and her gaze returned to him.

Danny's guest was wearing a dark navy frock coat of some quality. Next to her boss's garish outfit it looked positively sombre, but he was elegant in a way that Danny never would be. The light from the candelabra above fell on the angular planes of his face, highlighting the strong jaw and chin. His mop of light-brown hair, showing almost blond in the soft light, was trimmed neatly, but an unruly lock tumbled over his forehead. He leant back in his chair in a casual manner with his arm on the handrail, his strong, sculptured hand resting on the polished oak.

His large frame all but blocked the man sitting behind him and to Danny's right, yet he wasn't stout like Danny, but muscular, with long legs that extended under the table to the edge of the raised platform.

As her eyes came back to his face, his dark eyes rooted her to the spot. Reuben struck the chord again and Ellen jumped out of her daze.

She smiled broadly and tried to slow her pounding heart. The man leant forward, putting his elbow on the rail and resting his chin on his hand.

Forcing herself to break free from his gaze, she started the song. Within moments the people in the supper room had picked up the tune and were swaying and singing along with her.

She stole a glance at Danny's guest. He was still staring intently, a small smile on his lips.

Suddenly Ellen's heart took flight. This man, whoever he was, approved of her, his expression told her so. He was handsome and he was looking at her. She was enjoying a man's admiration in a way she hadn't allowed herself to for a very long time.

The song was exuberant, so Ellen took advantage and jigged a little herself. Roars of approval rose from the floor. She finished with a quick swirl and swept her audience a bow, then gave the crowd two more songs in quick succession. She didn't look at Danny's guest again, but she was singing for him.

She caught Reuben's eye and he smiled at her with a toothless grin. She signalled for him to slow the pace. The violin sent out a melancholy note and then started to play the haunting bars of

28

another Irish tune. The audience quietened as the tempo of the music slowed.

Ellen usually finished with a sentimental song. 'The Soft, Soft Rain of Morning' was one of her favourites. It was a ballad, set to a well-known Irish folk tune, about the heartache of being exiled from the home one loved. It would mellow the audience, many of whom were indeed a long way from the land of their birth.

She could hear her voice tremble a little as she glanced around the room, knowing all the while that the stranger had his eyes fixed on her. Thankfully, only she noticed the lapse and soon women could be seen wiping the corners of their eyes as she sang the sorrowful ballad.

Unexpectedly, the sober mood caught Ellen's emotions. The gaiety of the past moments was suddenly lost as the reality of her life came back to her – a life which could never include a man such as the one who hadn't taken his eyes from her all the time she was on stage.

Disappointment settled on her. She had met the type before. Danny often entertained them. Rich young men who came east for drink and women.

He had introduced her to men like the one looking at her now, and she had seen their eyes light up in the hope of pleasures to come. Ellen had always dashed those hopes smartly. She might have to sing for her supper, but she didn't have to entertain unwanted attentions for it. She bowed, and left the stage to rapturous applause.

Without speaking, she shot to her small room and slammed the door behind her. She sat in front of the mirror and found her hands were trembling.

There was a light knock on the door and Tom's head popped around the door. 'Beggin' your pardon, Mrs O'Casey, but Mr Donovan says you're to join 'im and 'is party for a drink.'

Two

The sweet notes of 'The Soft, Soft Rain of Morning' drifted over them as Danny studied Robert Munroe from under his ebony brows. He chewed the inside of his mouth thoughtfully.

To Danny's mind Robert Munroe looked a mite young to be a doctor, and with his well-tailored appearance Danny would have thought him more at home in a ballroom or at the races than in a bloodstained hospital ward.

'Sings like one of the celestial choir, does she not, Doctor Munroe?' he said, studying the other man's face intently.

Doctor Munroe was still looking towards the stage, although Ellen had already left and the curtains were closed. He turned and pulled the front of his waistcoat down.

'She does,' he smiled, 'she does indeed.'

He picked up his glass and downed a mouthful of brandy.

'Striking too,' Danny continued, watching Robert's eyes for a hint of his feelings.

'Quite,' Robert replied coolly, but Danny saw what he was looking for. Just for a split second there was a flicker of interest in the doctor's brown eyes, then it was gone.

He didn't blame Robert. Ellen *was* striking. There were prettier women who worked in the Angel but none caught hold of a man's attention like Ellen.

'Our Ellen has admirers from all over the city who come to hear her sing,' he said, trying to see if he could spark Robert Munroe's interest again.

'I have no doubt of it,' Robert replied in a bored tone, but his eyes were still warm.

Danny's mouth drew into a leer. Educated doctor he might be, a man of letters even, but in his trousers Robert Munroe was just the same as any other man.

On the pretext of greeting some customers behind him, Danny turned away from the table, but out of the corner of his eye saw Chafford lean towards Munroe.

'I see you think our Ellen a tempting armful, Robert,' William said in a low voice.

A chair scraped on the floor. 'I think Miss Ellen is a fine singer,' he heard Robert reply. There was a change in his voice. 'And she is fair on the eye.'

William gave a chuckle. 'Don't give me that, Munroe. Dash it, man, she's a looker and no mistake.'

Danny spun back to the table just in time to see Robert smile broadly in agreement. 'I've asked Mrs O'Casey to join us for a glass of port, gentlemen,' he said.

'Mrs O'Casey?' Robert said.

Danny winked. 'There ain't a Mr O'Casey, if that's what you're wondering.' Danny pointed with his fork to Robert's abandoned dinner. 'Eat up, Doctor Munroe, your dinner grows cold.'

As if she knew she was the topic of their conversation, Ellen appeared from the side of the stage and made her way around the tables towards them. Robert's dinner remained untouched.

As she snaked around the table she smiled and greeted the regular patrons, Danny watched Robert study her. She hadn't changed after her performance and still wore the simple cotton dress, its folds clinging to her as she moved. She laughed a couple of times, sending the soft curls of her dark auburn hair rippling around her shoulders.

Her rich throaty chuckle caught Danny deep within. Fury rose in him. Smile at others, would she, but too fine a lady to give him a jig? He should ignore her. He had other women – Kitty and Red Top Molly in Cable Street – but Ellen's rejection of him only made him hanker after her more. When he had first taken her on in the Angel and Crown he thought her refusal was just her way of raising her price. Others had tried the same thing and, as anyone would tell you, he was a generous man who didn't mind putting his hand in his pocket for his pleasure. But after a month or two he realised that she wasn't greedy but respectable: well, as respectable as any woman singing for money in a public house could be.

His gaze flicked back to Robert, who had risen from his chair and awaited her arrival. Anger rumbled around inside Danny as Ellen reached the table.

The tall and soberly dressed doctor and the impoverished supper-room singer stood for a long moment gazing at each other. Danny remained seated and slowly explored his front teeth with a silver toothpick.

'Ellie, my dear, you have a new admirer,' he said at length. 'Doctor Munroe, may I introduce Mrs Ellen O'Casey?' With a swift movement Danny grabbed her hand and kissed it loudly. She tried to draw her hand from his grasp, but he held on tighter. 'Ellen, this is Doctor Munroe, a man of letters, and a celebrated doctor from the hospital who has come to cure us of all our ills. And you know Dr Chafford already.'

Ignoring Danny, Robert bowed. 'It is my great pleasure to meet you, Mrs O'Casey.'

'Doctor Munroe is *wild* to meet you, me darling,' Danny said, his kindly expression not reaching his eyes.

Alarm flashed across Ellen's face for a second. Then she wiped the back of her hand against the tablecloth and offered it to Robert.

'I am pleased to meet you, Doctor Munroe,' she said in a clipped tone.

Her manner at the table was like that of a rabbit caught in the yard by the house dogs. Taking her small hand, Robert bowed over it again. He gazed down on soft, clean fingers and noticed her short, ragged nails. Mrs O'Casey did more than just sing for her living.

'You sang most wonderfully. So clear and such a range,' he said, smiling reassuringly at her.

'You have a musical ear, Doctor Munroe,' Ellen said.

Robert found that he was looking at the fluid movement of her mouth and thinking how Caroline's was more often than not drawn together in a sulky pout. Despite her friendly manner Ellen O'Casey was ill at ease. Was it him, William or Danny? Robert didn't know, but he wanted to dispel the feeling and see Ellen O'Casey smile at him with her eyes.

'My mother doesna' think so,' he said with a light laugh. 'Five years of music lessons and I could barely whistle a tune. My music teacher suggested that I take up the most traditional of Scottish instruments, the bagpipes, because no one could tell if I was in tune or not.'

Robert laughed, and Ellen and William joined in, her tension vanishing as merriment rose up. He wanted to make her laugh again.

'No,' he continued. 'I am afraid I must leave music to those who have the talent for it. I have a more scientific mind, not at all given to fanciful thoughts,' he said, trying to look grave and serious. The small twitch of his lips gave him away.

'As would befit a doctor, and a man of letters,' she said, taking the seat between him and William.

Danny handed her a glass of port. She placed it on the table untouched.

'You brought a tear to our eyes singing about the "Old Country",' Danny said, flourishing a none-too-clean handkerchief and dabbing the corner of his eye. His hand slipped under the table.

The tension returned to Ellen's shoulders and she gave him a tight smile. 'Thank you, Danny.'

'You know how much I *admire* you, Ellen dear,' Danny said as his hand came back into sight. He drummed his fingers lightly on the table and cocked his head towards Robert. 'As does Doctor Munroe.'

The mask that had just lifted from Ellen's face snapped back down. Robert silently cursed the Irishman.

'As do we all,' added William.

Robert leaned forward and let his eyes settle on her face. He saw her eyes open a little wider under his admiring gaze.

'The green of your gown suits your colouring, Mrs O'Casey,' he said, wanting to coax that smile back.

'Ho, ho,' Danny snorted, shoving her hard from the side and towards Robert. 'Admire! I'd say the good doctor here was good and smitten with you, sweet Ellen. No wonder he wants to know you better. Am I right, Doctor Munroe?'

Ellen placed the glass of port on the table carefully and glanced up him. 'I'd be thinking that for a gentleman with a *scientific* mind, who is not at all given to *fanciful* thoughts, that's powerful poetic, Doctor Munroe,' she said in a broad Irish accent. 'You must have practised that line on many a poor girl to turn her head.'

She was wrong. He doubted he had ever remarked on the colour of a woman's eyes before, not even Caroline's.

He felt Danny Donovan's glance on him, mocking him for her rebuff. Anger shot through him. How dare she? A respectable young woman was supposed to thank one for a compliment.

Respectable! Robert almost laughed. Ellen O'Casey was no respectable woman. She was a supper-room singer, only a step up from the garishly clothed women who plied their trade in the Angel. Whatever was he thinking of?

'You have to watch our Ellen, Doctor Munroe. She might have the look of an angel, but she has the bite of the devil,' Danny said, flexing his hand a couple of times.

'I must be off home,' Ellen said, standing up swiftly. William and Robert rose to their feet.

A sly expression crept over Danny's face and he looked across at Robert. 'But will you be disappointing the good Doctor Munroe here? And him just saying he wants to get to know you better, my dear.'

A tight smile fixed on Ellen's face as she looked back at them. 'I'm sure there are other women you could introduce him to in the Angel who would be more accommodating company than me.'

Three

Ellen and her mother, Bridget, rose as the first rays of light pierced the bedroom curtains. Silently they gathered their things and left Josie to sleep in the cast-iron bed that the three of them shared. They made their way down the bareboard stairs to their small living room. Kneeling at the blackened range, Ellen coaxed the kindling to flames while Bridget collected the buckets and yokes from the yard.

'You look tired, Ellie,' Bridget said, as her daughter threw a shovelful of coal chips on the fire.

Ellen forced a cheery smile and looped the yoke through two of the buckets. 'I didn't sleep much.'

Her mother shouldered her two zinc buckets and struggled to stand. Ellen bit her lip. Although Bridget would have cut her own tongue out before admitting it, the daily trip to the pump at the end of the street was getting too much for her. It needed both of them to fetch the water for the laundry they took in daily or they would never get it finished in a day, but seeing the blue hue around her mother's lips, Ellen wondered how much longer she would be able to make the journey.

Worry about tomorrow's woes tomorrow, she told herself. She opened the door to the street, letting in the pale morning light. It had rained overnight and the dirt outside was now mud and mingled with a small stream of pungent fluid meandering towards the bottom of the street. Although it was barely an hour after dawn, the pavements were already alive with people. Widow Rosser was already scooping up her harvest of dog dirt from the surrounding streets to sell to tanneries on the Southwark side of the river. Ellen and Bridget waited until she reached of the street then stepped out.

'That devil Danny been after you again?' Bridget asked, crossing herself swiftly.

'It's not Danny. I'm just out of sorts, that's all,' Ellen said.

As they made their way to the pump Ellen and Bridget were nearly knocked over by five or six small boys dressed in rags. Despite being barefoot, the mudlarks joked with each other about the rich pickings to be had in the low-tide slurry.

Ellen lapsed into her own thoughts as Bridget greeted her friends who were on the same early morning errand. Danny she could deal with. Disturbing thoughts of Doctor Munroe she could not.

Was he going to call on her, take her to the ball, invite her to take tea with his mother? Of course not! How could she have let herself dream such a thing? But when his eyes had settled on her that was exactly what she had dreamed. For a brief moment she had allowed herself to imagine a man like the doctor wanting and loving her for life, not just for a night or two for the price of a couple of shillings.

All around them the men of the area trudged towards the docks and waterfront to queue in the hope of a ticket to work. Ellen and Bridget stopped and waited at the pump. Bridget looked around swiftly and then said in a low voice, 'Hard as it is for us, I bless the day Michael O'Casey was taken.' She spat on the ground. 'The devil take his rotten soul. You wouldn't have survived his fist much longer, my precious.'

Ellen's tongue went to the side of her mouth and the space where two teeth once sat.

'When Michael's drunken fist knocked the child from you, I thought I was going to lose you, Ellie.'

Bridget ran her calloused fingers gently along her daughter's face. Then she started coughing. Ellen put her arm around her, but her mother waved her away. 'I'm fine,' she wheezed, then punched her chest. 'Just the early morning dust shifting.'

A dull ache settled on Ellen's own chest. She thought of the poor infant, born before its time. Her mother was right. If Michael hadn't died

38

when he did she would have been in her grave by now. How would Josie and Bridget have fared then?

Forcing her mind back to the present, she stepped forward and put her hand to the pump, working the iron handle until a stream of brown water gushed out. She filled the four buckets and they started back to the house.

Ellen glanced at her mother. There were beads of sweat on Bridget's brow and upper lip. She looked old and grey, like many of the other women who lived in the squalid conditions around the docks.

'A few more months and we will be off, you, me and Josie,' Ellen said, with a too-bright smile. We'll see Joe and his wee 'uns in America, so we will.'

Bridget smiled, but didn't answer. She was concentrating on carrying the buckets of water without spilling them.

Entering the house, they found Josie already washed and dressed in her dark serge dress with a white apron over it. Her bright, reddish-brown hair was tied back in two neat plaits that swished across her back as she moved. She grinned at her mother and grandmother as they entered the room. Ellen frowned. Josie, like the young Ellen, was maturing early. Thankfully, the shapeless dress she wore disguised her burgeoning figure.

'Morning to you, Gran,' she said, giving Bridget a noisy kiss. The older woman's stern expression melted as she gazed on the leggy thirteen-year-old bouncing around the room.

Maybe we will have enough to go to America in three months, Ellen thought. *If I did a Thursday night at the Town of Ramsgate and Mammy took a couple more bundles of washing we could be on a ship by October.*

Bridget started coughing again and Ellen's brows drew together.

'Have a bowl of porridge, Mammy, before you and Josie set out,' Ellen said, leading her mother to the chair and table by the window.

''Tis Josephine who is your child, Ellen Marie, not me,' she said sharply. But she flopped into the chair and made no complaint when Josie placed a bowl of steaming porridge and a mug of tea before her.

Ellen gathered up her coat and slipped on her day shoes. 'You stay here and watch the copper, Mammy, I'll go and fetch the linen.'

'I'm not ready for to be left by the fire while others work,' her mother said. She leant back in the chair and hugged the mug of hot tea to her. 'I'll catch you up presently.'

Robert wiped the blood from his hands and arms, then headed for the sluice room to clean up properly. It had been a difficult operation.

The locals had brought Bobby Reilly in straight from the docks, his crushed arm hanging in ribbons from his shoulder. After he had been lashed down on the operating table, Robert, as the physician on duty and William, his surgical counterpart, had been summoned.

Although Reilly had been made near insensible by the drink poured down his throat, he still had some fight left in him. It took the strength of four orderlies to hold him down while William, assisted by Robert, amputated his arm with a hacksaw.

Robert went into the tiled area with its deep sinks. He grabbed the coal-tar soap and scrubbed at the blood on his arm before it dried. William followed him in.

'Bad business, a young man in his prime losing an arm like that,' William said, taking the soap from Robert.

'Bad business for his family,' Robert snapped. 'He has four young children and a sickly wife. They'll be lucky if they avoid the workhouse.'

He threw down the towel, ran his fingers sharply through his hair and frowned at the dirty water in the porcelain bowl.

'You seem less than yourself today, Munroe,' William remarked dropping the towel in the washing basket.

Robert scowled out of the window. 'I didn't sleep very well. Too much noise.'

That was a barefaced lie. He hadn't slept very well because his mind was full of that sharp-tongued Ellen O'Casey. He had spent a futile hour staring at the ceiling and thinking of her rude response to his compliment. Then another hour remonstrating with himself for being such a fool as to care.

'Are you coming to the mess for a coffee, Rob?' William asked. It was their habit after an operation.

He shook his head. 'I thought I might take a stroll along to Backchurch Lane while I have a free moment.'

'Going to see your lady love then, are you?' Chafford asked, glancing to the foot-long, brown

41

package that had delivered to the theatre while they operated.

Robert grinned.

'I'll see you at dinner,' he said, rebuttoning his cuffs and slipping on his jacket.

Stepping out of the hospital, Robert stood under the classical portico for a moment and surveyed the scene. He tucked the package under his arm, drew a deep breath, and made his way down the white stone steps to the market. The noon stage-coach to Colchester passed just as he reached the bottom, its driver whipping the horses into a steady trot towards the open expanse of Bow Common and the Old Ford across Lea River.

Recognising him as one of the doctors from the hospital, a number of the stallholders touched their forelocks as they cried 'pippin, luverly pippin', 'new water fresh' or 'three a penny Yarmouth Bloaters'. The salty smell of fish mingled with the sweet scent of early flowers, while the meaty aroma from the tray balanced precariously on the top of the pieman's head made Robert's stomach rumble.

He turned west towards Aldgate. As he made his way past the stalls his mind settled. He relegated Ellen O'Casey and her cynical opinions to their rightful place in the grand scheme of things. He had even begun to see the whole incident in an amusing light.

Then he saw her.

She was standing by a fruit and vegetable stall dressed in a homespun, brick-red day dress and a short black jacket with worn elbows. Her face was shielded from the sun by a narrow-brimmed straw bonnet secured with a tie to one side. The whole ensemble was probably second- or even third-hand. As she stood, the wind billowed her skirt, then flattened it against her body, giving Robert a new image to turn over in his mind. She and the rotund stallholder were deep in conversation. He stood for a moment watching her, then walked towards her.

Ellen scratched the skin of the new potato to reveal its white flesh beneath.

'Are you going to buy that, missis, or are you just making it 'appy by giving it a feel?' asked a rasping voice beside her.

'I'll have it and two of its friends, if you please, Jimmy Flaherty, and knock the mud off before you weigh them. I'm not paying for dirt I can get free on my boot,' Ellen answered.

After collecting the sacks of washing from the regular houses, Ellen was relieved to find her mother almost her old self when they returned. She had left Bridget and Josie scrubbing in the backyard.

She had decided to walk to the Waste, as the scrub land between the city and the Essex countryside proper was called, to get dinner and a bit of something for tea. Watney Street was a nearer market but the stall near the white chapel of St Mary's often had fresher fruit and vegetables. Many of the journeymen from Essex skimmed goods from their loads and sold them to the stallholders as they passed by on their way to the City.

Ellen eyed a couple of cooking apples. They were old stock and had probably been kept over from the last harvest but they looked whole enough. If she baked them, they'd do for tea.

'I'll have those three as well,' she said, pointing at the apples, 'and an onion, two carrots and half a swede.'

Jimmy grinned at her as he hung the apples in the scales, 'Ow's yer mother?'

'You know my mammy.'

'And that pretty Josephine?'

Ellen smiled. 'Growing like a flower in an Irish meadow.'

Jimmy turned his round, jovial face to the sky. 'Spring's round the corner, wouldn't you say, Ellen?'

Copying Jimmy's movement Ellen too tilted her face to the sun and took a deep breath in. 'I certainly would,' she said, and caught him looking beyond her. Wondering what the stallholder was staring at, she turned.

'Good day to you, Mrs O'Casey.'

Having tried – and failed – to remove the image of Doctor Munroe from her mind all night, seeing him standing in the fresh morning sunlight not two foot from her was more than a little disconcerting.

'Doctor Munroe,' she said, hoping only she could hear the tightness in her voice. She gathered up her basket from the cobbles and balanced it on her hip. 'Are you buying your su ... supper like the rest of us?'

A smile spread across the doctor's face.

'No, just a small gift. Two Seville oranges, if you please,' he said to Jimmy. He smiled broadly at Ellen. 'Oranges are very good for you, you know,

44

if you've been poorly.'

The stallholder wrapped the oranges and handed them over. Adjusting the package under his arm Doctor Munroe paid for his purchase and turned back to her. His eyes flicked down to the basket she held. Ellen turned towards the City.

'I see you are going in the same direction as I am, so please let me carry that for you,' he said, taking hold of the basket handle.

'But you already have your hands full,' she replied watching him manoeuvre the long, flat package he was carrying.

'Nonsense. If I put my fruit on top of your vegetables I can carry it without any trouble.' He took firm hold of the basket handle.

To her joy or consternation, she wasn't sure which, Doctor Munroe turned with her. His hands touched hers for a brief instant. He cleared his throat.

'I did enjoy your singing last night. You truly have a lovely voice. Are you singing at the Angel again tonight, Mrs O'Casey?'

'No. Not until next week, but I am singing next Tuesday at the Town of Ramsgate by the river at Wapping.'

Robert's brows pulled together. 'You don't walk home from there alone, do you? It's a particularly rough area.'

The concern in his voice was genuine. Other than Bridget no one had ever worried about her safety. Maybe his compliment last night had been genuine too. They walked on. Ellen let her gaze fall on his hand holding her basket. They turned to cross the street, letting two loaded wagons pass on their way to the City. Robert held her elbow lightly to guide her. She could feel the strength of his grasp through the thin fabric of her coat.

'I suppose you have been cutting people up all morning, Doctor Munroe,' she said, as her brain could find nothing else sensible to say.

A smile crept across his face. 'I am a physician, Mrs O'Casey, not a surgeon. But, as it happens, I have been "cutting people up" all morning. Or rather one person, a poor stevedore whose arm was crushed between a ship and the dock.' His brows drew together severely. 'The working conditions in the docks are truly barbaric.'

'You don't blame the man for his accident?'

'Indeed, no. I can see the plain truth that Reilly and many like him are forced to take any work they can, even dangerous work.'

Warning bells rang. Just because Doctor Munroe held the dock owners to account didn't mean that he was any different from all the other well-heeled men who were often Danny's guests.

'Do you plan to open a practice up west after your time at the hospital?' she asked as they waited for two hay wagons to pass.

'I'm not planning to. I'm getting very fond of the sights and sounds around the hospital and by the docks. I'm think about staying in the area.'

'But the money is up west.'

Doctor Munroe regarded her steadily. 'But the sick are to the east, Mrs O'Casey. I am a doctor and I am needed by the sick, not the rich.' He smiled down at her.

Holy Mother, but he's handsome when he smiles.

They had reached the far end of the hospital.

'Unfortunately, I have to leave you here,' he said, giving no indication that he was going to relinquish her basket. His amused look had changed to one of speculation. He looked as if he was about to say something.

'You have a thought to say, Doctor Munroe?'

'I have, Mrs O'Casey. But am I brave enough to say it?'

Ellen folded her arms. 'Let's hear it then.'

'I was going to say that the pink ribbon on the bonnet suited you.'

Ellen put her hand to the third-hand straw bonnet that she had trimmed with pink petersham just to hold the brim together. She snatched her hand away and stared at the pavement.

'That's why I had to be brave,' he said softly. 'Because, having coaxed you out of your shell, I didn't want you to retreat again.'

Ellen couldn't help smiling at the doctor's contrite expression. The shock of light brown hair, that never seemed to remain where it was combed, sat over his eyes adding to the appeal of his expression. She smiled.

'That's better.' He beamed at her. 'The artists of this world may think they alone know of beauty, but we scientists could teach them a thing or two about observation.'

They crossed the main thoroughfare and stopped at the corner of the hospital. She took the basket from him. 'Thank you, Doctor Munroe, for carrying the basket and ... and for your compliments.'

'I spoke the truth. Nothing more.'

Maybe she had been wrong about him last night.

Maybe he hadn't come to the Angel looking for a bit of quick company.

She pressed her lips together. She didn't want to let him think that she was a woman of loose morals, but–

She put her head on one side. 'In particular your compliment last night. I am sorry. I was a mite too sharp in my taking of it.'

Robert sat back in the chair and watched as Polly Ellis swayed back and forth in the light from the window. She threw her hands over her head, smiled at him and then spun around. Robert clapped his hands softly.

'You are the loveliest dancer I have ever seen,' he said, signalling for her to come to him.

'It's all thanks to you that she can dance at all,' Mrs Ellis said, as her daughter teetered towards him.

Polly stood before Robert regarding him with a solemnity that only a five-year-old child can muster. She had been one of his first patients. He had been the physician on duty when her mother and father rushed her into the hospital, limp and barely breathing. That was three months ago.

'How does it feel?' he asked.

'It's a bit diggy here,' she indicated where the strap held her new leg brace to the top of her thigh.

Robert moved her dress aside. The brace had been fashioned out of metal by a gunsmith who had a workshop in Spitalfields and made the occasional implement for the hospital.

'The brace has to rest here.' He drew Mrs Ellis's

attention to where the soft kid padding sat at the apex of Polly's thigh and groin. 'And then be anchored by these straps. It might be sore for a few days but it will help to stabilise Polly's knee joint while the muscles of her leg strengthen. These buckles need to be tight to hold the sides firm when she is walking.' He pointed to the strap above Polly's thin knee and ankle. 'It has been designed to lengthen here, at the sides,' he showed her where small screws held the two lengths of metal on either side, 'And the strap that goes under the sole of her shoe also has to be tight over her instep.'

'Will those shoes do? Because if not the pawnbroker said we can swap them for another pair,' Mr Ellis asked, looking anxiously at him.

'They are fine. And you have to remember to keep the brace joints greased, otherwise if they get wet they'll seize up and rust.'

'You can depend on it.' Mr Ellis bent down to inspect the metalwork that encased his daughter's right leg.

Polly studied her brown boots and stamped her feet. 'Shoes feel funny.'

Robert watched her start to master the brace that she would have to wear for some considerable time. She was fortunate to be the Ellises' only child. On the meagre wages her father earned as a dock porter Robert doubted that he could have afforded the shoes necessary to fit the brace if there had been more than one young mouth to feed. Mrs Ellis did the best she could, but the room in the eaves of a once grand house where they lived was sparsely furnished and shabby.

Although the family was clean, their clothes had more darned patches than original cloth.

'Can I offer you a dish of tea?' Mrs Ellis asked.

Robert eyed the lazy bluebottle circling the milk jug on the table. 'Thank you, no.'

Mr Ellis stood up. 'It's a fine piece of work is that. We are very grateful to you for all your trouble. Ain't we, Mrs Ellis?'

'That we are. We are very lucky that you know about such things,' she said, coming forward to stand beside her husband.

'You're lucky that a damaged leg is all Polly has from her brush with poliomyelitis,' Robert told them, as they all watched the little girl test her brace again by marching across the small room.

The wind rattled the window and the curtain drifted up with the draught. Robert's gaze rested on the child. He noted how very frail she was. So small. Too small in fact. No bigger than a child of three, with barely any flesh beneath the pale skin of her arms and legs. She might have survived polio, just, but she would still be very lucky to see her tenth birthday. The innocent spark of life that was Polly Ellis could be wiped out in a day by any of the childhood illnesses rife in the area. A small lump lodged in Robert's throat.

He coughed. 'Now, Miss Dancing-feet, come here.' When she was within arm's reach Robert lifted her effortlessly onto his lap.

Mrs Ellis grew alarmed. 'Polly, you sit still. Don't you crease the doctor's trousers now. Mind her shoe, sir. Keep your feet still, girl.'

Robert ignored Mrs Ellis's fussing and fished around in the seat behind him.

'As you are the best dancer I think you should have a prize.' He pulled out the two oranges and held them up. Polly's eyes opened wide in wonder. 'One for today and one for tomorrow,' Robert told her.

'Oh, Doctor,' Mrs Ellis said taking her husband's arm. 'You shouldn't have.'

'They were left over from breakfast, they would only have been thrown away,' Robert lied as he handed the fruit to Mrs Ellis and set Polly back on her feet. 'I know it's hard, but if you can buy Polly an apple or a pear once or twice a week it will help her muscles grow strong.'

Mr Ellis touched his forehead. 'I'll try.'

Polly turned and faced him. 'I like you, Doctor Munroe, and I'm going to marry you when I grow up.'

'I don't know where she gets such ideas!' Mrs Ellis said, looking from Robert to her husband.

Robert laughed. 'When you grow up, young lady—' the lump in his throat returned '—you will want to marry a young lad who buys you violets, not some dull old man like me.'

Polly's brows drew together and she stuck out her lower lip. 'Well, if I'm not going to marry you then you will have to marry someone very, very pretty and nice, because you're nice.'

Robert laughed again.

'Polly, that's enough,' Mrs Ellis said, taking hold of her daughter's arm.

Robert stood up and Mrs Ellis handed him his hat.

Mr Ellis opened the door that led onto the tenement landing. 'It is very good of you to take

51

such trouble.'

'If you bring your daughter to the dispensary in a week or two, I'll check the brace.' He gazed down at Polly. 'Goodbye for now.'

As he reached the top step Mr Ellis caught up with him and pressed a coin into Robert's hand. 'It's not much, Doctor, but I want you to take it.'

Robert glanced down at the half-crown on his gloved palm. It was three days' wages for Mr Ellis. Robert knew he could ill afford to part with the money, but although it would have been better spent on fruit or fresh milk from the Whitechapel dairy for Polly, Robert knew he had to take it. People like the Ellises didn't have much, but they did have their pride.

'Thank you.'

Mr Ellis nodded and went back into the room. Robert slipped the coin in his pocket.

Somewhere below a baby was crying fitfully, a woman's voice shouted and then the noise of a hacking cough sounded through a partition wall. Robert's mouth drew into a hard line. He settled his hat on his head and descended the stairs.

Placing the mug of hot sugary tea on the table beside her, Bridget sank into the horsehair upholstery of the chair. She closed her eyes for a second and let her bones find their own rest. The pain across her chest and down her left arm receded. She picked up the mug, holding it against her bony chest, and sniffed its sweet steam. She had stirred in three spoonfuls, which was far too much, considering the price of an ounce of sugar these days. But she needed it.

Through the small back window that looked out onto their yard sheets flapped back and forth in the stiff breeze.

Praise be, it isn't raining, she thought, then chuckled to herself. That had to be the prayer of every washer-woman on God's earth. She let her head fall back.

Although the sharp chest pain of earlier was now just a dull ache, Bridget knew that it would awaken again as soon as she stood up and started the ironing. Every day it tightened its grip on her. That morning she had had black spots in her vision on the way back from the pump, but she didn't dare tell Ellen. She had enough to concern herself with raising Josie and avoiding that brute Danny Donovan's groping hands without having her mother as a burden.

Bridget felt her eyes start to flutter down. She yawned. She would just take five minutes, then put the iron on the range.

She was jolted awake half an hour later by the front door banging. Tidying her hair back into place she stood up, guilty at having been found idling while there was work to be done. Ellen breezed in and snatched off her bonnet, sending it flying onto the table.

She beamed at Bridget. 'Stay where you are, Mammy. I'll put the kettle on. We have an hour or two before we have to start pressing.'

Ellen danced over to the stove humming to herself. Although she had no idea what had lightened her step, Bridget was mighty glad that something had. Ellen was too young, too lovely not to enjoy life occasionally. Without her sacrifice, she and

Josie would have been in the workhouse long ago.

Ellen started to sing softly as she arranged the cups on the table and uncovered the milk jug. She sniffed it and, finding the milk sound, poured it into both cups.

Bridget caught the refrain Ellen was singing and a lump formed itself in her throat.

'Your pappy used to sing "The Sweet, Sweet Dawn" to me.'

Ellen smiled at her and poured out the tea, then came and sat on the stool beside her as she used to do when she was a little girl.

'Tell me stories about Pappy,' Ellen said.

Bridget settled into the chair. 'You've heard them.'

'Tell them again,' Ellen pleaded, her eyes sparkling in the reflection from the window. 'Tell me how Pappy courted you.'

'We lived in farms across the valley from each other. He came from a large family, ten boys and eight girls, although six of them were awaiting resurrection day in the churchyard when I started to court your father.' Ellen sat, hugging her knees.

Images of past days swam into Bridget's mind. Days when the new life in England had held more promise and less heartache. 'The Shannahan family was well known in the county for their argumentative way of being. It was said a Shannahan would have argued with the sainted Patrick himself about keeping the snakes had they ever chanced to meet him.'

Ellen smiled. 'I see where Josie gets her contrary ways now.'

'And not just Josie!'

Ellen pulled a face. They should be gathering in the washing not sitting around chattering. But Ellen was merrier than she had been for many months. Bridget reached out a hand and smoothed a stray lock of hair from Ellen's face.

God grant her a better life than she's seen so far.

'Joseph Shannahan walked ten miles across the county every Sunday to come courting. I used to stand on my bed in the loft of our house to see him coming across the field then run down to be ready when he arrived.'

'Did you think him handsome? Did you notice something special about him, like maybe his hands?' Ellen asked.

Bridget gave her a sharp look. 'Hands?'

The blush of Ellen's cheeks deepened. 'Or something.'

A smile crept across Bridget's face. 'Well, his eyes were sea-green like Josie's, if that's what you mean,' Bridget said, willing Ellen to say more. She didn't, so Bridget continued her tale.

'My father was very strict with me and my sisters. He frightened most of the young men away with his blustering ways, but not your father, no. He was made of sterner stuff. He finally wore my pappy down and we were married a week after I turned seventeen.' She paused for a moment and Ellen waited. 'We were given a cottage on the estate,' she scoffed. 'Cottage. That's a grand English name for a cowshed. It had weed in the thatch and mice in the foundations. But your pappy set to and made it sound.'

A picture of the cottage with its bare white walls floated into her mind. She saw herself as a young bride, eager and frightened in equal parts. She remembered herself and Joseph in that old rickety bed, loving each other. They had both been so young, so strong, back then. Where had those years gone? The loneliness of the years since he had died, a broken man with coal dust clogging his lungs, swept over her.

'I just remember that cottage,' Ellen said, cutting into her memories. 'Me and Joe used to chase the chickens in the yard.'

'That you did, and we would have had more eggs had you not,' Bridget replied.

'I remember how the roof slanted at one end and the rain would come under the door if the wind was in the East. Pappy would shout at the wind to turn around. I remember one day it did and I was afraid that God would punish him for ordering his wind about. And how I swung on the gate waiting for Pappy to come home after market day and he always asked, 'Where's my smiley angel' although I was right in front of him.'

Both women sat silently with their thoughts for a few moments, then Bridget placed her empty cup down.

'You look a bit of a smiley angel today, Ellie.'

'Do I?' Ellen gazed at her fingers.

'What's he like?'

Ellen stood up and started to collect their cups together. 'Who?'

'The man who's put the sun in your smile.'

Ellen gave a forced laugh. 'Man? What man?'

'That's what I asked you.'

'I'm just...' She shrugged and raised her hands palms up on either side of her. 'I'm full of the joys

56

of spring. That's all.'

'Oh, that must be what's making you sing, skip around the room and be talking about "noticing hands".'

Ellen's hand went to her hair. She pulled out a couple of pins and held them in her mouth, then, twisting her hair around, she jabbed the pins back. She glanced at the window and snatched up the basket from the table.

'It's past midday, I'd better get the washing in and ironed.'

A smile spread across Bridget's face. She hauled herself out of the chair, took up the other basket and followed her daughter. As she reached the back door the grinding pain returned to her left arm.

Four

Danny tapped the open book in his hand and shook his head slowly. Black Mike, his giant right-hand man with fists the size of hams, standing behind him, did the same. Both of them looked at Peter Petersen, the chandler. Stood on the shelves were tins of various shapes and sizes, sealed at their rims with wax and sporting nautical scenes. Behind the chandler, coils of rope hung from hooks from the rafters. Danny fixed Petersen with a steely stare.

'My book here,' Danny jabbed at the pages, 'says you have been short of coin for me for three weeks now.'

Petersen pulled out a crumpled handkerchief and mopped his broad brow. He shoved it back in his inside pocket and smiled apologetically.

'Times is very hard, yar, Mr Donovan,' said Petersen, his oiled hair shining in the light from the lamp above.

'That they are,' Danny agreed, his face a picture of concern. After a second his expression changed to a perplexed one. He pulled a fragile-looking chair over, turned it around and sat on it, legs astride. 'But, as I take me morning stroll by the docks, the ships are fighting each other to get a berth.'

Petersen ran his finger around his collar and stretched his neck out. 'That they are. But, Mr Donovan, sir, the prices are low. Why, only yesterday I heard that some ships' masters are carrying tea and sugar as ballast, so low is the price vot they get in port.' Beads of sweat sprang up on the fair bristles of his upper lip.

'Is that so?' Danny asked.

'Yar, yar.' Petersen shrugged expressively at Danny and Mike. 'They are practically giving away their goods.' He gave a forced laugh. 'Only dis morning I was saying to my good Hilda, that as things go, I have barely enough to put food in my children's mouths.'

Danny shook his head again. 'Do you hear that, Mike?'

'I do, guv'nor,' Mike said, casting his gaze around the overcrowded interior of the ship's chandler's.

Danny's eyes rested on a stack of coal shovels

leaning in the corner, their unused blades gleaming in the light from the window. His gaze moved on to a dozen or so pristine cork floats then came back to the chandler.

He rose from the chair and circled around the counter. 'Now, I'm just a simple man. Made my way in this old world, did me and Mike, without the benefit of much schooling, so put me straight if I am astray. If these poor seamen are out of pocket after sailing to the corners of the earth, why would you be stocking up with all manner of seafaring goods?'

Danny placed a heavy hand on Petersen's narrow shoulders and looked him squarely in the eye. He was so close he could smell Petersen's fear.

Petersen shot an anxious glance at his newly purchased goods. 'Na, those are old–'

Danny put one arm around the shopkeeper like a old friend and walked him around to the middle of the shop. The curtain to the back of the shop moved again and Danny saw the face of Petersen's wife through the crack.

He continued toward the bowed window, casually knocking over boxes of ship's biscuits as he crossed the floor. With his free hand Danny tapped the dimpled window pane. The ping of his garnet signet ring on the glass echoed around the small space.

'Do you know why you pay me safety money?' he asked. Petersen's mouth started to move but no sound came out. 'Let me remind you. See this?' He tapped the glass a little harder.

A fine glaze of sweat had appeared on Petersen's forehead.

'If this lot gets stoved in,' Danny said, and punched the glass. There was a snap, and a crack snaked its way across the rectangular pane.

'Or if this' – he let Petersen go and lifted the lamp illuminating the shop's interior from its ceiling peg –'caught onto the sawdust and oil you keep here, you wouldn't have to put food in their mouths because they'll all be in the workhouse.'

He tossed the burning lamp upwards and Petersen jumped forward. He let out a cry as he caught the hot metal bowl of the lamp just before it crashed onto a barrel of turpentine.

Danny rubbed his hands against each other and set his lapels straight. 'Get me my money by to-morrow or you'd better get you and your scurvy brats back to Swedeland,' he told Petersen as he set the lamp back where it belonged.

There was a whoosh as the curtains to the living quarters were thrown back. A small woman, her almost white blonde hair scraped back from her face, and her figure swathed in a long shawl, bustled into the shop. She thrust a small leather pouch into Danny's face.

'There you are, Mr Donovan, now let my Peter up. Please.'

Danny studied the drawn face of Hilda Petersen. She was tall for a woman and he guessed she must have had a pretty face at some point. Just for a split second her pale green eyes caught his attention. They took him back to a time he could barely remember, to a mother whose image he had almost forgotten. He hesitated.

'It's all dere,' she said in a strong Scandinavian accent, thrusting the pouch at him again. The memory evaporated. He let Petersen go and took the proffered money in the same movement.

'Doesn't it take a woman to see the resolving of a situation?' Danny asked, his face taking on its usual jovial expression. 'What would we do without the fair sex to guide us?'

'The blessed Almighty knew what he was about when he created Eve,' Mike agreed as he opened the door for his boss.

'Good day, to you, Petersen, Mrs Petersen,' Danny said, sliding the pouch into his pocket. 'A pleasure doing business with you.' He jabbed a finger at Petersen and looked at him hard. 'When my boy visits next week, be sure to listen to the little woman.'

The bell above the door jingled as Danny and Mike strode back into the street.

Two boys ran past them chasing each other. As they did the smaller of the two, a lad of about nine or ten, tripped up on the uneven pavement and collided with Danny's leg.

Quick as lightning Danny's hand shot out and grabbed the unfortunate boy, hauling him up into the air by the scruff of his neck.

'Watch where you're going, you little bastard,' Danny shouted at the boy, who now dangled in the air.

'I'm sorry, Mr Donovan, sir,' the boy choked out. Danny shook him vigorously and set him on his feet, but held him still.

'Sorry, are you?' he said scowling at the lad hanging from his grip.

'Please, Mister, Charlie didn't mean no 'arm,' the captured boy's playmate pleaded.

Danny's scowl deepened. 'Were you after the contents of me pocket?'

Charlie and his friend denied the accusation in unison.

'No, mister. I ain't no thief, honest. Tell him, Sammy,' the boy assured him as he twisted back and forth.

Sammy added his voice to his friend's plea. 'We're not pickpockets.'

Danny stood unmoved, Mike beside him. 'What's to be done with them, Mike?' he asked, still eyeing the boys menacingly.

'Give them to the magistrate,' Mike suggested.

Charlie and Sammy looked terrified. A trip to the magistrate was a guaranteed trip to Newgate or the Fleet prison and from there transportation to Botany Bay.

'No, I've a punishment more fitting for these whippersnappers.'

Danny reached into his inside pocket. Both boys went white with fear. They watched his hand wide-eyed as he drew it out again and twisted a silver threepenny piece between his finger and thumb. Two sets of eyes focused on the shining object. Danny tossed it in the air. It arched up-wards and then fell on the floor. He let go of his captive who fell on the coin.

'Off with you both, and get yourself a pie. You've got legs like starved pigeons, both of you,' Danny said, as the boys dusted themselves down.

'Thank you, Mr Donovan, sir,' Charlie said beaming at Danny and Mike.

Danny tipped his head to one side and studied the boy who had collided with him. 'You're 'Arry

Tugman's boy, aren't you?'

'Yes, sir, Mr Donovan,' Charlie replied.

'Give your pa me best and tell him I'll see him in the Prospect. Now be off with you,' Danny told them. 'And if you've got nothing better to do, follow the wagons along Whitechapel High Street. They often have the odd apple or pear on the back of the cart that the driver won't miss. You might even lift something to sell up town.'

The boys touched their foreheads and shot off down the street.

'That's what I like to see,' Danny said as they disappeared from sight. 'Respect.'

Black Mike's face took on a mellow expression as his eyes followed Charlie and Sammy disappearing into the crowd.

'Put me in mind of you and me at that age, Danno,' he said.

Danny slapped him sharply on the shoulder. 'We weren't as fortunate as those two. At their age we were grubbing our food in the dirt around St Katharine with all the other poor Paddy bastards fresh off the boat.'

Images came to him of he and Mike as boys, huddled in a cold loft gnawing at stale bread, chilled to the bone and wet through. If they didn't swipe something to sell they starved, and they risked the rope every time they picked a pocket or lifted some goods from a barrow. Danny pushed the memories aside. He wasn't partial to getting maudlin over the past. It made a man soft, and if a man wanted to survive in this world he couldn't afford to be that.

He thrust his hand inside his breast pocket, drew

out the leather-bound ledger again and flicked through the pages. He had money to collect.

'Mahaffy, Mead, Meadows, Malley, Mungo,' Danny said, running his finger down the page. 'There we are, Mike, Mungo. The bastard owes me three shillings for parish safety.' He grinned at Black Mike. 'That is, Mungo had better give me three shillings if he wants to live safely in the parish.'

He noticed that Mike was looking over his shoulder and down the street. Turning slowly, a grin spread across his face.

'Well, Mike, this is turning into a rare morning.'

Ellen turned into Cable Street and heartily wished that she hadn't. On the corner of Mercer Row was Danny Donovan, flanked by Black Mike.

Before she had time to retrace her steps, Danny spotted her.

Holding her head high and adjusting the bundle of washing on her left hip, Ellen walked towards him across the muddy street.

Danny stepped out before her, blocking her way. 'Look who it is, Mike, our very own linnet, Ellie.'

She sidestepped and Danny did the same. His face took on an ingenuous expression.

'You seem to be in a mighty hurry this morning, me darling. Can you not see it as a kindness to me, and to Mike here, to spare us a couple of moments to light up our day?' He took hold of her arm and ran his hand up and down it.

Ellen suppressed a shudder. 'Even if you've time to idle away, I have things to do,' she said, pulling her arm away and readjusting the bundle on her hip.

'Now, you didn't seem too busy to spend the time of day with young Doctor Munroe on Friday, did you?'

Ellen's heart thumped in her chest, but she managed to look puzzled.

She knew, of course, that hardly an apple fell from a barrow without Danny having knowledge of it, but even so... Who would have thought it worthwhile to tell him of her stroll with Doctor Munroe? Unless it wasn't her they were watching but Doctor Munroe.

'Doctor who?' She pulled her brows together then let them relax. 'Oh, Doctor Munroe. The doctor with Mr Chafford in the Angel last week.'

Danny's eyes narrowed. 'The poor man would be heartbroken if he knew that he had slipped your mind so easily.' His gaze ran boldly over her, lingering on her breasts. He took hold of her arm again, his fingers pressing painfully into her flesh.

Ellen met his eye. 'We happened to meet by chance and he accompanied me along the road.'

Danny leant towards her and a waft of stale sweat rose up. 'Did the fine doctor *accompanying you along the road* sweet-talk you, eh, Ellen? Told you that he would look after you, did he?'

With an almighty wrench Ellen freed herself from Danny's grip and put some distance between them. 'Not that it is of any business of yours, but Doctor Munroe was telling me of his plans to stay in the area,' Ellen said.

Danny glanced down at the bundle of washing hooked over her arm.

'What do you want to wash and scrub for,

65

woman, when you could earn a deal more money swivelling on my lap?'

Danny reached up and traced his chubby finger down the side of her face. His bitter breath wafted over her and she almost gagged.

Her arm ached with the bundle she held. It was only some shirts and a few petticoats, but it was becoming heavy.

As his jagged nail scratched along her cheekbone Danny gave a low chuckle.

'Ellen O'Casey thinks she's too grand for the likes of us,' he said to Black Mike but keeping his gaze on Ellen. 'She's forgotten how grateful she was when she was offered a chance to earn a bob or two singing for my customers.'

Ellen's head snapped around. 'I bring in custom and coin from all over the city for you and you still pay me short of my worth,' she told him, glaring up at him.

'See what I mean, Mike, too grand she is now that Doctor Munroe's turned her head,' Danny spat out.

'You must have been drinking your own foul brandy to imagine such a thing,' Ellen said, trying to keep her voice steady.

'Don't play the respectable widow with me, Ellen O'Casey. You were flirting with him, so you were.'

Danny had let go of her, but before she could put any distance between them his left arm shot around her waist. His other hand went to her skirt and he grabbed at her private parts.

'It's been over ten years since you had a man, you must be like a she-cat on the tiles by now. Let me ease you.'

Ellen shoved his hand away and dropped the washing. Danny laughed and Mike joined in. She gave them a contemptuous glare and stooped to retrieved her bundle, which had landed square on a pile of rotting fish heads. It would take her a good hour to scrub the smell out of the shirts.

Trembling with anger she spun around and faced Danny. He remained astride the pavement with his fists balled on his hips, grinning down at her.

'Let me past, Danny Donovan, or by the Holy Mother Mary and Joseph, I'll curse your devil soul where you stand,' she said through clenched teeth.

At last, with a hard laugh, he stepped aside. Ellen swept past him, her eyes blinded by tears of rage and frustration.

Five

Robert and his student doctors had strolled through the wards for the past two hours and seen everything from a sailor with scurvy to a young lad who had cut his foot on a spike of metal in the Thames mud the day before.

Unfortunately, there was one illness his trainee doctors did not see because the damn fool hospital trustees wouldn't allow patients suffering from it to be admitted.

They were now back in the laboratory.

With his hand lightly resting on the microscope, Robert looked at the four students who sat around the scrubbed bench. 'Now, tell me what you know about cholera, St John.'

'It comes from the East, India,' St John answered.

'Benthan.'

Benthan adjusted his cravat. 'The first sign is fever followed by nausea and watery bowels.'

'What then, Maltravers?' Robert asked, seeing Bulmer, the hospital manservant, entering the room.

'Cramps in the guts and thirst, often followed by death in twenty-four to forty-eight hours,' Maltravers answered.

Robert gave them all a broad smile and their shoulders relaxed. 'Good, good. Now, what causes it? Young?'

'I believe the current understanding is that it is carried in foul air,' Young answered.

Robert pursed his lips and clasped his hands behind his back.

'I believe the majority of my peers would agree with you,' he said. Young looked smug. 'I, on the other hand, do not. I believe cholera is carried in the water, by invisible entities or germs.' All four students looked sceptical. 'You must have read Needham's work on *infusoria animalcules*. Or Spallanzani on killing these "germs" by boiling so that no decomposition occurs?'

The students shuffled under Robert's challenging gaze, then Maltravers spoke. 'How so, sir?'

Gripping the microscope Robert leant forward. 'Because I believe, through reasoning and deduction, there are organisms smaller than the eye can see at present, even with this.' He lifted the microscope in his hand. 'I believe that a minute organism, or germ, is the cause of cholera, and many other diseases besides. It is only a matter of time until we can prove it.'

Bulmer was signalling to him but Robert continued. 'Jenner's work pointed to it, when he observed the spread of cowpox. Many now are looking seriously at the germ theory.'

Bulmer was now staring at him with his hands behind his back. Robert sighed. 'I'll leave you gentlemen to think on these matters while I go and see what has sent Bulmer to find me.'

Rinsing and drying his hands under the pump in the corner Robert made his way over to Bulmer.

'Sorry to interrupt you, Doctor Munroe, but Doctor Davies asked to see you in his study when you have a moment,' said the manservant, handing Robert his jacket.

Robert's footsteps echoed through the corridor until he reached the half-glass partition of Doctor Davies's door. He knocked and, after the briefest of pauses, it was opened by Davies's assistant.

The chief physician of the hospital sat behind his mahogany desk and peered at Robert from between two mountains of paper. To one side were an inkwell, several quills, a large blotter and a glass of clear liquid. Around the wall were shelves stacked with books, and more papers.

Thomas Davies was six or seven inches shorter than Robert. He was in his late forties with a receding hairline which he disguised by combing his parting low on the left side.

'Good of you to come,' he said as Robert took a seat. 'Our hospital chairman, Lord Bowden, tells me you are filling the heads of our student physicians with science.'

'I am.'

Davies leant forward and his face creased in a smile which made him look ten years younger.

'Good.'

Robert's shoulders relaxed. 'I knew I could count on your support. Although, I must confess I am surprised that His Lordship knows my name.'

Davies pulled out two letters from the pile on his desk. 'You are too modest, Munroe. Your name is known to a great number of people.' He tapped the papers. 'I have letters here from Lord Ashley and Sir Malcolm Dyer, both of whom praise your work. Do you know these gentlemen?'

'I know Lord Ashley by reputation. He is a member of the Parliamentary Commission on Factory Conditions. Sir Malcolm I know very well. He has worked with my father and is the parliamentary representative of the Women's Society for Moral Improvement.'

'Of which your mother is chairwoman.'

'Indeed.'

'They both urge me to appoint you as the chairman of the Emergency Committee for St George's parish to investigate the cholera outbreak.'

'I would have thought Sir Charles Huntly would be the obvious choice,' Robert said, trying to contain his excitement at the prospect now opening before him.

'Not according to Lord Ashley or Sir Malcolm,

who urges me to' – he adjusted his glasses – 'and I quote, "recognise a gifted young man, who has an incisive mind and exceptional talents".'

Robert felt his face grow red.

'Would you accept the post if I offered it to you?'

What he could only do in such a position! He could force the parish street committees to clear the filth from the gutters as they should. He could compel landlords to provide adequate water and sanitation for their tenants. He might even be able to persuade the parish to open a small cottage hospital to care for those suffering from cholera, as had been done in other cities.

'Not if you offered me the post because of political pressure,' he replied firmly.

'That's just what I expected you to say. I am offering you the post because you are the only doctor I know with a thorough knowledge of the medical and social issues that surround cholera.' Davies raised his hand to his mouth and coughed. 'There is a small remuneration attached to the post.'

Although Robert would have taken the chairmanship without any financial reward, London prices were eating up his modest wages of one hundred and fifty pounds, and the seventy pounds dividend from his shares in the new Manchester to Liverpool railway, at an alarming rate. His private practice in Chapel Street generated an income but it wasn't large, and was less than it could have been because in many cases he charged only the cost of the medicine.

Robert grasped Davies's hand in a firm handshake. 'Thank you, sir. I am honoured.'

71

Six

Josie watched the muscles of her mother's arms grow taut as she lifted the large copper from the hook over the fire then, in a swift move, pour the steaming water into the tin hip bath in front of the fire. She stepped back as the steam rose upwards and wiped the back of her hand across her forehead.

For as long as Josie could remember, this had been the Shannahan women's Friday night ritual: a shared bath in front of the fire, followed by a cup of tea and the rare treat of a sugary bun. The bought bun with its currants and glazing of sugar was terribly expensive, a farthing each. It was the one luxury they allowed themselves. As her gran always said, if anyone in the whole city of London deserved a bit of spoiling on a Friday night it was them, and Josie agreed.

One thing her mother and grandmother both did, day in and day out, was work. As a child, sitting on a blanket on the beaten earth floor, she could remember them bent over a large tub full of soapy washing. As she grew, Josie had joined them in their daily toil. It had always been that way, just the three of them, since her father had met his untimely end at the bottom of the London docks.

Josie couldn't remember her father. She had still been barely able to stand when he was carried home by three fellow dockers. She had gleaned snippets about him from friends and neighbours and, of course, from her mother and grandmother, and knew that he had had dark curly hair and been admired by the women of the area. She knew that he had worked in the docks – when there was work – and that before marrying her mother he had sailed the coal barges between Newcastle and the Port of London. She also knew that Michael O'Casey had been popular around the streets of Wapping and even now, ten years after his death, she would be told by an old mate of his that 'your father was always ready to stand his round'.

This had satisfied her as a small child, imagining that her father, had he lived, would have taken her to the fair and treated her to toffee apples and ribbons. She had always assumed that after he died her mother was too heartbroken to think of putting another man in his place.

Not that she had questioned the lack of men in their lives. She wasn't the only child in the streets around without a father, but most of them had had a couple of stepfathers and the occasional live-in uncle whereas no man had ever put his feet under their table.

Josie hadn't given this matter a second thought until she overheard a chance remark in the market the day before. One of the stallholders, thinking she was out of earshot, had referred to her mother as a 'choice armful' and several around him agreed heartily. It had given the girl pause for thought.

'Come on, Josie, jump in,' her mother called, snatching the towel from the rail over the fire and shaking it at her playfully. With a smile on her face, her mother looked like a girl only a few years older than herself. The apron she always wore when in the house was tied tight around her waist, and Josie noted that its circumference had not expanded like some other women's around and about. Why had no man sought her mother out?

Josie half turned and stripped off her clothes. Although they all lived closely together and even shared a bed, she had become shy of standing naked before her mother and gran. She had noticed a month or so ago that her breasts had budded, making her bodice sit tight across her chest. A number of the boys in the area had noticed the changes, and Josie had started to wonder if they thought her a choice armful too.

'Stop dallying,' her gran said in an indulgent voice, looking better than she had earlier. On her return from school Josie had found Gran clutching her chest in the yard. She had tried to brush away Josie's concern, saying she was just catching her breath.

Josie stepped gingerly into the tin bath. Ellen lifted a pitcher of warm water and poured it carefully over her. She took in a breath as the water flowed over her face. Her mother handed her some soap and Josie set to lathering it over herself. She had to be quick because the water she stood in would chill fast and there were still her mother and grandmother to make use of it. Ellen's hands were on her hair rubbing in the sage cream to ward off head lice. Josie's eyes felt as if they were being shaken out of their sockets as her mother applied the pungent ointment vigorously. She didn't believe there would be any head lice lurking in her hair, not after the painful daily tweak with

the small tooth comb that her mother adminis-
tered before braiding her hair for school. The
water fell over her face in a curtain again, rinsing
the sage paste into the water around her feet.

Hunching down in the tub Josie rinsed off the
remaining soap and stepped out to be enveloped
in a large towel by Ellen, who hugged her and
kissed her on the forehead, drying her rigorously
all the while. When she was satisfied that every last
drop of water had been dried off, Ellen handed
Josie her long nightdress and swathed her in a
crocheted shawl. She then picked up a comb and
started to untangled her daughter's long tresses.

'Ma?'

'Mm?'

'Why haven't you got married again?' Josie
asked.

Ellen's eyes opened wide. 'Whatever put such a
notion into your head?' she replied, bustling to
separate strands of hair and not meeting Josie's
gaze. 'And haven't I got enough to do looking
after you?'

'Why not?' Josie persisted.

An exasperated look crossed Ellen's face.

'I never met a man I wanted to marry.' There
was a long pause. 'I was very young when I met
your father and not much older when I lost him,'
she shrugged her shoulders. 'So I've got used to
being alone.'

There was something wistful in her mother's
tone that caught Josie's attention.

'Don't you miss me pa?'

For an instant Josie thought her question would
be pushed aside, but then Ellen sighed. 'I haven't

told you this before but you're a grown girl now and understand how things are between men and women.' She paused. 'Times were hard, and although your father did the best he could work was scarce. Then you arrived and your father, well, your father...' She stopped and spread out her hands and looked squarely at Josie. 'A man was entitled to a drink after a long day heaving goods from a ship's hold, but the truth of the matter is your father thought he could find the answers to his problems at the bottom of a glass.'

'Don't tell me Pa was like Tiddly Tooley?' Josie asked, thinking about the unkempt Irishman who could be found dead drunk in the gutter at any hour of the day.

'No, he was not, Josephine Bridget. He was a good man who worked hard for his family. He just liked an ale or two, that's all.' Ellen folded her arms across her chest shutting off further discussion

It wasn't all. Exasperation sprang up in Josie. Did her mother think she was a child? Did she think that she didn't notice that whenever her father's name was mentioned her grandmother crossed herself quietly in a corner? Did her mother not think she might have heard that before he fell to his death Michael O' Casey had been drinking for two days in the Prospect of Whitby?

Josie scowled up at her mother, who was teasing out a knot from her hair, her arched brows pulled tightly together in concentration.

Her mother treated her like a child because she loved her. Her mother scrubbed her fingers raw with extra washing so Josie could go to school.

Her mother had made do with her old repaired boots so that Josie could have a new pair with stout leather soles. After a long day up to her elbows in suds, she sang in the Angel for that fat Danny Donovan, so they could go to join Uncle Joe in America. Everything her mother did, from the moment she got up in the morning to the moment she laid her head on the pillow beside Josie at night, was done because she loved her.

'Ma,' Josie said looking up at her mother's face. Ellen gazed down at her with bright eyes. 'I'm sorry.'

'That's fine,' Ellen replied in a clipped voice.

Josie threw herself into her mother's embrace and hugged her. The feeling of safety that she had known all her life and had taken for granted swamped her, catching in her throat and bringing tears to her eyes.

'Love you, Ma,' she said.

Ellen ran her hand lightly around her daughter's face and smiled. 'Love you, too. Now, get yourself your bun, while me and Grandma have our bath.'

'She's a sharp one is our Josie,' Bridget said, finally as Josie moved out of earshot and Ellen stripped off, ready for her wash down. 'I'd say the fivepence a week on Josie's schooling is money well spent.'

'A bit too sharp if you ask me,' Ellen replied as she stepped into the bath. 'She was asking me about Michael.'

'I hope you told her the truth,' Bridget said as she poured the water over Ellen.

'Not yet. Not until she's a year or two older.'

'It won't make the story any prettier,' Bridget

said, looking at her daughter's body in the glow of the firelight as she began washing herself with the rough flannel. 'None would know you'd had a child, Ellie.'

Ellen shrugged, and her mind went to Doctor Munroe. After admitting that she had been sharp with him, Ellen had expected to see him in the Angel, but he hadn't come.

But why would he? A physician and a gentleman would never look at her, a poor singer, and to some no better than a streetwalker. But he had looked at her and she liked it, she liked it a great deal. Ellen's musing was brought to an abrupt end when Bridget smacked her playfully on her bare bottom as she stepped out of the tub.

'Away with you, woman,' Bridget said to Ellen's startled expression. 'Every woman wants to feel a strong man love her.'

'Ma,' Ellen said, glancing at Josie snuggled in the armchair and engrossed in her book. 'What do you know of such things?'

'I know plenty, I tell you,' Bridget said with a wistful sigh in her voice. The kettle on the range whistled and Bridget poured it over the tea leaves. She swilled it around for a moment or two then poured it into two cups through a strainer. She sat at the small kitchen table opposite Ellen.

'You still miss him,' Ellen said, as her mother drank deeply from the cup.

'Aye,' Bridget said softly. 'Loved your father, I did,' and a sentimental expression stole over the older woman's face. 'It was coming here that killed him. He brought us to London for a better life, but no one would give him a job as a clerk,

78

so he had to take what he could get. Whipping coal was no job for a man like your father.' Bridget smiled a bittersweet smile. 'But I'll tell you, Ellie, I loved that man so fierce it still hurts.'

As she looked at her work-worn mother, Ellen envied her. To love and be loved by someone that deeply happened only once in a lifetime to some – and never to most. No matter what life threw at her mother, she had that love deep in her heart and no one, but no one, could take it from her.

Once again, Ellen's mind conjured up Doctor Munroe, standing tall in his dark frock coat, and tears suddenly stung the back of her eyes.

A chorus of coughing greeted Robert as the workhouse superintendent, the unbelievably thin Mr Trundle, and his wife, the unbelievably wide Mrs Trundle, bowed respectfully.

Arranged around the wall of the bleak ward were narrow cots in which sallow inmates languished. Although he was used to the various smells associated with sick humanity, the stench of the ward caught Robert in the back of his throat. Putting his clean handkerchief over his mouth he turned and glared at the two who had followed him in. They shrugged their shoulders.

'As I say, Doctor Munroe, it is funds that do keep us from providing as we would like. Is that not so, my dear?' he appealed to his wife.

She nodded vigorously, setting the frill around her cap flapping, and said, 'Indeed, Mr Trundle, funds are always in short supply.' She fixed Robert with a defiant look and crossed her short arms across her bosom.

'Emptying a slop bucket requires very little funds.' Robert indicated several buckets brimming with stale urine by the beds.

Mr Trundle's eyebrows drew upwards at the centre as his face took on a contrite expression. 'But funds are needed to pay those who empty buckets.'

Robert spied a young woman in what looked like a dirty maid's uniform sitting at the other end of the room. Her head had dropped onto her chest. He strode towards her, Trundle and his wife scurrying along behind him. As he reached the woman, Robert heard soft snoring. Leaning forward he smelt gin, and cleared his throat loudly. The young woman woke up and peered around her.

'What's the crack,' she slurred, then hiccuped.

Not trusting himself to speak, Robert spun on his heels and headed for Mr and Mrs Trundle's private quarters. On reaching the warm parlour, crammed with furniture and garish china ornaments, he held out his hand.

'Your accounts, if you please,' he demanded sternly.

Mrs Trundle glared at him. 'You have no right to–'

'Now, now, my dear,' Mr Trundle interrupted with a deferential expression and placed a hand on his wife's fuzzy forearm. 'We have nothing to hide and Doctor Munroe is the appointed chairman of the Parish Emergency Committee.'

His wife pressed her lips together and glared at Robert, reminding him of a kettle on the point of boiling.

'Doctor Munroe,' Mr Trundle said, handing over a greasy red ledger.

Taking the ledger to the table, Robert opened it and began perusing its columns. He glanced up at the superintendent and his wife, who stood watching him like hungry dogs.

'I'll send for you once I have reviewed the entries,' he told them. For a second or two Mr and Mrs Trundle hovered uncertainly, then the superintendent grabbed his wife's elbow and all but dragged her from the room.

As he flicked through the pages of the workhouse accounts, Robert's face grew grim. After an hour of making notes he called the superintendent back. Mr Trundle returned, minus his stout wife.

'I trust that everything is in order, Doctor Munroe?' Mr Trundle asked.

'It certainly is not.' He tapped the page of the ledger. 'From the extortionate prices you pay for the workhouse provisions, the inmates should be living like kings, not lying half-starved in urine-soaked beds.'

'My wife is in charge of the purchase of food for the workhouse,' the superintendent told him, twisting his hands together.

'Where is your wife?'

'She had to go on an errand. I am expecting her back shortly.'

'Very well. Now about the wages for–'

The door of the parlour burst open and a red-faced Mrs Trundle puffed into the room.

'Oh! Doctor Munroe,' she said in a friendly voice that had been absent so far from her conversation. 'You'll not credit it, but I just turned the corner

81

into Angel Gardens when I happened on Mr Donovan, er, taking the air,' she said, looking coyly at Danny Donovan, who stepped into the room. 'I mentioned that you were paying us a visit and nothing could stop him coming to bid you good day.'

The Trundles exchanged a quick look then stood back, letting Danny Donovan take centre stage. Robert regarded him coolly.

He had seen Danny a couple of times as he made his way around the streets and alleyways that ran off Ratcliffe Highway. He had always been greeted by the ebullient Irishman as if he were a long lost brother, and pressed to take supper at the Angel again. Eventually taking up the invitation, Robert persuaded himself that he was not going there to see Ellen in particular, but found himself bitterly disappointed that she was not singing that night.

Danny Donovan now swaggered towards him, snatched up his hand and subjected it to the usual abuse. 'Now, here is a fortuitous coming together.'

'How so?' Robert said, noting another glance between the superintendent and his wife.

Danny drew up a chair and sat down, the checked fabric of his trousers straining across his thick thighs.

'Mrs Trundle tells me you are not familiar with the arrangement of the workhouse. Is there anything I can be helping you with, Doctor?' He nodded at the open book in front of Robert.

'There are some matters between Mr Trundle and myself that are not altogether clear, but I can't think how you could be of assistance. There seems to be some discrepancy between the quality of goods purchased and the rotting vegetables and mouldy bread that appear to be the daily diet of the poor wretches I have seen this morning,' Robert said, watching Donovan's face closely.

'Discrepancy?' Donovan boomed as he turned to the man and his wife huddled in the corner. 'As a member of the workhouse governors I take a very dim view of such things.'

A shrewd expression crossed Robert's face. 'Quite so. But can you explain how "Supplied by Messrs Donovan & Ass." described here as' – he peered at the open page and ran his index finger under an entry – '"best cut beef shin" only yesterday shows no evidence of it ever having been in the grubby kitchen?'

'I showed you the meat, Doctor, hanging in the larder,' Mrs Trundle said with a puff of indignation.

'The couple of dry, scraggy pieces of meat I saw hanging on hooks in the pantry are hardly what I would call prime shin,' Robert replied, fixing his eyes on Donovan. The Irishman held his gaze, Robert looked back to the ledger. 'There is also the matter of the delivery of three sacks of newly dug potatoes two days ago.'

'They were in the pantry too,' Mrs Trundle interjected.

'Those potatoes you showed me may have been "newly dug" a month ago, but are now green and sprouting.'

'There must be some mistake. My man at the yard must have sent the wrong supplies,' Danny said after a second.

'Is that so?'

'What else could it be?'

Leaning forward and resting on his elbows on the table, Robert steepled his fingers. 'It could be that the workhouse was being charged high prices for poor supplies.'

Danny's eyes narrowed and his mouth started to tighten. 'Are you accusing me?'

'No, but you're right. This is a fortuitous meeting. Now you know of the discrepancies, I have no need to take the matter to the committee immediately, I will wait until you have looked into it first.'

For one second Robert thought that Donovan was about to lunge at him, then the familiar expression of jovial good humour returned.

He slapped his thigh and winked at Robert. 'I said to my Ellie you were a powerful clever man, and that you are, sir.'

With a great deal of effort Robert forced himself to remain composed. He stood up.

'Do you see Mrs O'Casey a great deal?' Robert asked, the question springing from his lips of its own volition.

'Come, Doctor. You're a man of the world.' Danny gave him a mocking glance. 'God love you, sir, Ellen and I are intimate friends.'

With a satisfied grin on his face, Danny took up his top hat from the table. 'I'll have a word with my man at the yard.' He flipped the hat on his head and tapped it down. 'And I'll give Ellen your regards when I see her later.'

Stifling the urge to smash Danny Donovan in his puffy face, Robert forced out a 'thank you'.

Robert stood motionless for a good minute or two after the door closed on Donovan and the Trundles. He sat back down at the ledger, picked up his quill and tried to resume his study of the figures. He jotted down a couple of notes, then stopped and stared blankly at the paper.

There was a loud crack. Ink splattered the crisp, white page. The pen in Robert's hand was now snapped in half.

Kitty lifted her blonde head as Ellen supported her back to her chair and sat her down. It was only half an hour before the entertainment was due to start and Kitty had been vomiting without cease for the past three-quarters of an hour.

'You can't go on like that, Kitty,' Ellen said, giving her friend a glass of water.

'I have to. Danny will sack me if I'm sick again,' Kitty said, her bright blue eyes staring helplessly. She swallowed, then retched again into the bucket on the floor.

Ellen watched, concerned and sympathetic. She and Kitty had started at the Angel within a week of each other and had shared the dressing room ever since. Kitty was willowy and ethereal and danced like a nymph over the water, but unfortunately Kitty had given in to Danny. Not that it did her any good. She still had to earn her wages like the rest of them, although she did get the occasional extra florin or two when she kept Danny company. For having Danny heave and grunt on her, Ellen thought she deserved every penny of it and more. But now Kitty was sick and she knew why.

'What did you take?' Ellen asked, as Kitty sipped the water.

'I got this.' Kitty reached into her pocket and pulled out a small green glass bottle. Ellen peered at the label. Someone had written 'Gentlewoman's Restorative' on it in a scrawling hand. She uncorked the bottle and sniffed, then drew back and waved her hand over the opening.

'How much of this have you taken?' she asked, as Kitty leant over the bucket again.

'Old Annie said to take a mouthful on rising, one midday and again as I goes to bed,' Kitty said.

Old Annie was a loud and quarrelsome woman. It was rumoured that in her younger days she had been a high-class whore up west. It might have been true, but around these streets Old Annie was known for one thing, and that was the flushing out of unwanted infants. Women came from miles around to seek the abortionist's skills – and not all of them poor single girls like Kitty. Old Annie had a steady stream of married women who could not face the thought of another mouth to feed.

'For the love of Mary, there is white vitriol in this brew. You're poisoning yourself, Kitty,' Ellen said hotly, then put her arm around her friend. 'Why did you go to that old hag?'

'The boiling in the bath and bottle of gin didn't work this time,' Kitty said, as her shoulders slumped.

Ellen said nothing. What else could Kitty do? Danny wouldn't help her. One of his women had been dragged from the Thames when she couldn't get a child to budge, and Ellen was determined not to see her friend suffer the same fate.

She stood up and got hold of Kitty's cape. Putting it snugly around her friend she stood Kitty up.

'You're going home,' she said, walking Kitty towards the door.

'But what about Danny? He'll be mad as the devil when he hears,' Kitty protested weakly.

'He'll be madder still if you walk onto his stage and spew over the audience. No buts. Leave Danny Donovan to me,' Ellen said with more bravado than she felt.

'You're so good to me,' Kitty said.

Ellen gave her a mock frown. 'That I am. Giving myself more work tonight while you sit snug by the fire.'

A ghost of a smile crossed Kitty's face. 'You won't mind when you see who I spotted taking his supper here tonight again.'

Ellen's heart started to pound.

'You're blushing, Ellen O'Casey,' Kitty said with a trace of her old spirit. 'Doctor Munroe's fair enough on the eye, I suppose.'

'Tom,' Ellen called and the youthful stagehand came running. 'Take Miss Henry home. She's unwell. Tell Reuben I'll sing two extra to make up her time.'

'Right you are, Miss Ellen,' Tom said, and offered Kitty his arm. 'It'll be fine and smart tonight. It's a quiet crowd, intent on their victuals, and Mr Donovan's gone to the Prospect to sup.'

Despite her assurances to Kitty, Ellen felt mighty relieved to hear this piece of news. As she handed Kitty over into Tom's care she gave her friend a sideways glance.

'"Fair enough on the eye"?' Ellen said in a low

87

voice. 'I say he's powerful handsome is Doctor Munroe and no mistake.'

As Ellen stepped out on the stage her eyes immediately sought out Doctor Munroe. She found him sitting in the far corner, his back against the wall and his head turned away. William Chafford was with him and both were intent on the plates before them.

Disappointed but not over-perturbed, Ellen signalled for Reuben to strike up her first song. She expected that once Munroe knew that she was singing he would turn around as he usually did. As Ellen finished her fourth song and he still had his back to her, her heart was starting to sink.

His attention and compliments had led her to dream that she and he might bridge the gap of status that divided them like a yawning chasm. Now he was pointedly ignoring her, and she wanted to know why.

Taking her last bow and blowing a kiss to the applauding audience, Ellen sped back to her dressing room and wiped her face. She never went into the bar unless Danny forced her to. Why'd she start now? She chewed her lip hard. Then she combed and repinned her hair and adjusted her dress. With a deep breath she left the dressing room and headed for the small door into the auditorium.

The smoke drifted around the barroom in heavy clouds as Ellen came in. A couple of the regulars stared as she emerged, but after a sharp look they resumed their drinking. Doctor Munroe sat drinking with Doctor Chafford and three other gentlemen who had joined them. Ellen cast her eyes over the five men sitting around the scrubbed oak table.

Doctor Chafford spotted her and stood up. 'What a pleasure.' She smiled at him, but watched Doctor Munroe out of the corner of her eye. He sat motionless.

The three newcomers sprang to their feet and Doctor Munroe turned. Ellen forced herself not to look at him.

Doctor Chafford continued. 'May I introduce you to Doctors St John, Young and Benthan.' The three young men bowed while Munroe threw back the remainder of his brandy and signalled for another.

'We don't often see you this side of the stage without Danny Donovan, Mrs O'Casey,' Robert said with a drawl, as Ellen's eyes rested on the face that haunted her day and night. On every other occasion that Robert had looked at her, his eyes had been warm and caressing, but not tonight. Now they were flint-hard and his mouth was turned up in a bitter smile as he spoke. 'Are you sure he wouldn't object to you walking between the tables like the other women in here?'

He waved his hand to where Lizzy and Mo were chatting and flirting with the men.

William Chafford shot his friend a furious look. Ellen felt her face burning. She resisted the urge to turn and run and forced a smile.

'I ... I came to wish you a good evening before I left,' she said, looking at William Chafford. She inclined her head and turned to leave.

'Your pardon, Miss, you're not venturing out on the streets alone?' Benthan asked in a serious tone.

'She'll be quite safe,' Doctor Munroe told the young man with a faint slur to his voice. 'She has Danny Donovan's protection. Do you not, Mrs O'Casey?'

Ellen rounded on Robert. 'I'm thinking, Doctor Munroe, that I'm mighty surprised to find that you are such an intimate acquaintance of Mr Danny Donovan's.'

Doctor Munroe rose slowly to his feet and towered over her. 'And I'm thinking,' he said, mimicking her accent, 'that for all your show of respectability, I am mighty surprised that you are an intimate acquaintance of Danny Donovan too, madam.'

Ellen's hand itched to slap his mocking face. She held her hands together in front of her and gave him the iciest of looks. She turned to the others, who stood open-mouthed around the table looking at her and the doctor.

'Gentlemen, I bid you goodnight,' she said, sweeping past Robert and towards the door just before tears made their presence known. It would seem that men, be they doctors or dockers, were all the same.

Seven

Josie walked beside her mother to Raine's school in Charles Street. She carried her satchel with her lunch and books; Ellen held a large basket on one arm and a pint flask in the other. As they crossed Commercial Road into Sutton Street, Josie gave her a questioning look.

'Have you been crying, Ma?' Josie asked.

'No. Whatever put such a thought into your head, child?' Ellen asked.

Josie wasn't fooled. She had heard her mother weeping softly for over an hour after she slid into the bed last night.

'Oh, your red eyes and the way I felt you shaking in bed last night,' she replied.

Ellen turned to the basket over her arm and shifted its weight. 'If you must know, I was, because ... because I'm worried about Kitty. She was sick last night.'

'Is she in the family way?'

'Josie! What do you know of such matters?' They sidestepped the remains of a dead rat. The cat, whose kill it was, returned to the half-eaten rodent as they passed.

'For goodness' sake, Ma. I know about these things. I know she went to see Old Annie a few months ago when her monthly stopped. I heard you and Gran whispering about it.'

Behind them a wagon's wheels rattled over the cobbles. The driver gave a shrill whistle.

'Morning to you, sweet ladies,' he said, whipping off his worn leather cap, the lad beside him following suit. It was Patrick Nolan.

Josie felt her cheeks glow. She lowered her head, but not before she saw her mother's eyes on her. She glanced back up to the wagon to find Patrick smiling at her. Josie raised her eyes and smiled back at him, noting his curly black hair, and sea-blue eyes as she did so.

'That's Patrick Nolan, Ma, my friend Matte Nolan's brother,' she said, with a soft lilt in her voice. 'He's grand handsome, don't you think?'

Her mother gave her a surprised look, but couldn't hide a small smile. 'He's a good-looking lad, I'll grant you, but you'd better be looking at your books, not grand handsome young men, Josephine Bridget O'Casey.'

Josie grinned at her mother. 'See you later, Ma.' She gave her a loud kiss on her cheek as she turned towards Clark Street. 'Give Kitty my love.'

Even though she was used to the stench of decomposing refuse, Ellen wrinkled her nose as she entered Thomas Court. The cobbles beneath her feet disappeared and were replaced by slippery mud. In the centre of the narrow court was a large lake of stagnant water in which could be seen the contents of emptied night buckets. As she made her way, Josie's words remained in her mind.

Yes, Patrick was a handsome lad. Michael had been, too... Thank God she was only a pound or two short of the passage money. They would be gone by Christmas.

Lifting her skirt and stepping carefully around the foul water, Ellen made her way to the end of the alley and number thirty. Giving the sow and three piglets in an improvised sty in front of the small house a wide berth, Ellen entered the front door and made her way up the dark stairs to Kitty's room. A baby cried and a man's voice cursed from below as she knocked on Kitty's door. On hearing a feeble 'Come in' Ellen opened it.

Kitty gave her a warm smile. She was sitting by

the small kitchen range sipping a mug of tea and, to Ellen's relief, she looked a great deal better than she had the night before. She put her basket on the table, and asked, 'Have you eaten this morning?' Kitty shook her head. 'I thought not. That's why I brought you some oats and bread.'

'Oh, Ellen,' Kitty said with a croak in her voice as Ellen unpacked a pot of porridge and a small fresh loaf.

'Tush,' Ellen said, and held up a waxed paper package. 'There's a bit of best dripping too and, although I spoil you and I shouldn't, I brought you one of these to help you on.' She held up a fat orange. 'They're good for you, you know, if you're poorly.'

'Saint, you are,' Kitty said as Ellen handed her the porridge and poured on a quantity of milk.

Ellen poured herself a mug of tea and sat opposite her friend. 'Did it work?'

Kitty shook her head dolefully. 'No.' They sat in silence for a moment. 'I'll have to go to Old Annie again and see if she'll set me right.'

'Have you lost your wits? That old bitch will kill you.'

'What can I do?' Kitty looked around the room with its damp walls and bare furnishings. 'I can barely support myself, let alone a baby.'

'Devil take Danny Donovan's black soul,' Ellen said fervently. ''Tis he who should have his innards poked with Old Annie's hook, not you.'

'I dare say,' Kitty said wearily as she put down the empty bowl.

'Come and stay with me and Mammy for a while and then come with us to America. It's only three pounds for stowage passage in winter.'

'Three pounds! I couldn't lay my hands on three shillings.'

'You could put some by each week in the Thrift bank like I do. We'll be leaving before Christmas, God willing, to join my brother Joe in New York.' She put her arm round Kitty and gave her an affectionate squeeze. 'What do you say, Kit?'

'Maybe,' Kitty answered listlessly.

Ellen took hold of her shoulders and made her friend look at her. 'Promise me you'll not go to see Old Annie,' she said The girl nodded her head very slightly and Ellen let her go. 'I have to get back to Mammy, but before I go I'll peel you this,' she picked up the orange.

Kitty smiled. 'How's that dear heart child, Josie?'

'She sends her love and is noticing young men with wild curly hair,' Ellen answered, peeling back the orange to reveal the soft juicy segments beneath.

'As you were at her age,' Kitty said, popping a piece of orange in her mouth.

'That I did. I noticed Michael O'Casey's wild curly hair when I was fourteen and was heavy with his child at fifteen,' Ellen said. 'That's not the life I want for my Josie.'

She wiped the orange juice on her hands down her skirt and stood up. 'I'll have to go, but I'll call after Mass on Saturday.'

'Saint you are, Ellen,' Kitty said again, her blue eyes soft as they rested on Ellen. 'And give my love to yer Mammy and Josie.'

Ellen wagged her finger at her with a mock frown on her face. 'Eat your orange, drink your tea and I'll see you on Saturday.'

The sewage that ran down the centre of the narrow passageway crept over the welts of Robert's shoes. Beside him he could hear Mr Dawson, clerk of works for St George's parish, gag. Watching them from out of the doors and windows that fronted the alleyway were the sunken-eyed residents of Anchor and Hope Passage. Robert took in the appalling scene and then stepped forward towards the communal pump.

'Surely you're not going down there, Doctor,' Dawson asked in a horrified tone.

'Of course,' Robert replied.

Dawson signalled to the two men lounging against the warehouse on the other side of Tench Street. They stood away from the wall, pulled the front of their short jackets down and straightened their half-crown hats. In Robert's view it was totally unnecessary to have two parish constables accompany him as he inspected the parish but Dawson had insisted. After a short discussion Robert had agreed. Flanked by Dawson and the constables, Robert entered Anchor and Hope passage.

Although the day was bright the narrow alley, the sides of which could be touched by a man with outstretched arms standing in its centre, was in almost total shadow. The houses had been built a century ago as fine, three-storey terraces, but had long since lapsed into crumbling dosshouses.

Robert unfolded the leather wallet in his hand and scribbled a few notes.

As the inhabitants of the surrounding houses watched them, Robert and his small entourage continued further down the airless alley. They stopped at the hand pump, the sole water supply to the houses of the area. It looked as if it had been adapted from an old cannon and sat six inches or so off the upright. The handle dangled listlessly.

Robert took hold of the handle and wrenched it up. There was a loud creak and after some resistance it moved. Having got it to its full height, he pushed it back down. There was another creak and a small spurt of discoloured water fell on the cobbles.

He turned to Dawson, who at least had the decency to look embarrassed. Robert opened the leather file again.

'According to my records, this pump was replaced six months ago.' He fixed Dawson with an iron stare.

'That was my understanding too, sir,' Dawson replied.

'Didn't you check the work before you paid the bill?'

Dawson looked indignant. 'We have dealt with Mr Cashman for many years and I have never had cause to query his work.'

'Well, I shall have to do so on behalf of the emergency committee,' Robert told him, and noticed the two constables shoot a look at each other.

Dawson's indignation turned to alarm. 'I am sure there is some mistake,' he said.

Mr and Mrs Trundle flashed into Robert's mind. Some mistake. That was Danny Donovan's explanation for the discrepancies in the work-house accounts.

The two constables had been introduced to Robert on his arrival at St George's that morning but, other than acknowledging their presence on his morning's walk, he hadn't given them much thought. Now he studied them more closely. Both were big men, clean-shaven, with hands like shovels. They were neatly dressed – dapper, as the locals would put it – and looked as if they had been fashioned from the same mould. He turned away from the pump and walked to the end of the alley.

At the far end the stench from the rotting vege-tation and human excrement was overpowering. He felt his eyes sting with the vapours drifting up from the floor.

God have mercy.

He had seen enough. He strode back to Dawson and the constables. They had remained at the pump and he could understand why. Even he was having problems with the contents of his stomach now.

Dawson looked visibly relieved when he saw Robert making his way back and took up his place behind him as they walked back up the alley. Half hidden in one of the doorways, a man watched them. Robert changed direction and marched over to him. Neither Dawson nor the constable followed.

The man regarding Robert from the low door-way stood at about five foot three or four. He wore a threadbare waistcoat over a stained shirt and breeches of an indeterminate dark colour, with bare legs and feet. He eyed Robert suspiciously.

'Who are you?' he asked before Robert could speak.

'I'm Doctor Munroe,' Robert told him, trying not to look at the lice crawling around the collar of the man's shirt. 'I am looking into the public works in the parish.'

The man's face lost its belligerence. 'Doctor Munroe, from Chapman Street?' Robert nodded. The man snatched the hat from his head and touched his forelock. 'Fergus Ryan's me name and begging your pardon, sir.' A grin spread across his face revealing a few lopsided yellow teeth. 'We have all 'eard of how you have been fixing up the folks around 'ere, like.' He screwed the hat in his hand. 'And right pleased I am to meet you.'

'Have you seen anyone come to fix the pump?' Robert asked Ryan.

'Me, sir? No, I ain't seen no one. That old pump been like that since I came to live here three year ago.' Ryan looked around and added quietly. 'You're a good man, sir, so I'll tell you this and no more. There are a lot of people around here who say they are going to do this and that. But does any of it come our way? No. Because before the crumbs have fallen on the floor some fat Irish bird has swooped it away.'

Robert felt the two constables draw up behind him. Ryan gave them both a furtive look and stepped back into the house.

'As I said, sir, I don't know nothing,' he said slamming the door.

Robert turned to face the two men standing behind him. They stood, as they had all morning,

98

with impassive expressions on their freshly shaved faces.

Some fat Irish bird! As a prominent member of St George's Parish Council, Danny Donovan would have had a say on any man appointed as a constable. It was a lucrative post in any parish and greatly sought after. He studied the constables again. It occurred to Robert that it might not have been only Dawson who was keen that he have the St George's parish constables accompany him on his investigations.

The door creaked as Kitty pushed it open with a trembling hand. Inside the gloomy room, two small children sat together on the bare earth floor in front of the fire while an older child of about six or seven tried to feed them putty-coloured gruel. All three of them looked her way with wide-eyed wonder but didn't utter a sound.

Holding her breath against the stench of stale beer, Kitty glanced around the room. Her room in Thomas Court was lavishly furnished compared to the one she was now standing in. Apart from the unlit fire, over which hung a pot on a chain, there was a small table barely sufficient for two people. In its centre was a bowl of what looked like three-day-old stew with a couple of flies darting around it. The floor was without the comfort of a rag rug which was the standard feature of even the poorest homes in the area. At the far end of the room was a old iron-framed bed with a striped ticking mattress on which Old Annie was taking her afternoon nap.

Kitty paused. Guilt gnawed at her. She had promised Ellen she would not seek Old Annie out but what else could she do? Danny's child refused to budge. She had even drunk the last of the Gentlewoman's Restorative, but she had nothing to show from it but an acid stomach and cramping bowels.

Nervously she clutched the two shillings in her hand and listened as a faint snoring came from the huddled form on the bed.

After Ellen left her she had dreamed of the possibility of going to America with her unborn child, making a new life in a new land. But in the cold light of day it was clear that the child inside her was determined to stay put and she would have to seek out Old Annie to persuade it otherwise.

'Missus,' the young child called in the direction of the bed.

Old Annie stirred and looked around her. She spotted Kitty and heaved herself off the bed.

The old woman, who was almost as wide as she was tall, scratched through her greasy hair and yawned. Discovering a nit, she cracked it between her finger and thumb then discarded it behind her.

The rumour around the streets was that Annie had been a beauty once but if that were so, Kitty could see no evidence of it now under the layer of grime that covered the older woman's face. In an attempt to revive her youth Annie had daubed French rouge on both cheeks, but it only served to highlight the jaundice hue of her complexion. Kitty judged that the old, high-waisted dress stretched around the abortionist's substantial frame was of some quality, but the delicate pink and blue of the pattern was hardly distinguishable amongst the stains of beer and food spattered down the front.

'What can I do for you today, Kitty my love?' Annie asked, pushing back a tangled strand of hair from her face. 'Is it still your little inconvenience?'

Not able to speak, Kitty nodded.

'Have you got the required?'

Kitty opened her hand and held out the two shillings. Annie took the coins, scraping Kitty's palm with her overgrown nails. She slid her fee into her clothing and smiled, displaying a yellowing set of teeth. Close to her now, Kitty could smell gin.

Annie took her elbow and led her towards the bed. The urge to snatch her arm away and flee from the squalid house swept over Kitty.

Leave, leave, her mind shouted, but her feet continued to follow the older woman. Halfway across the room Annie stopped and turned her attention to the children on the floor.

'Take the babies in next door to Rose for an hour,' she told the older child. 'Tell her I have a bit of business and I'll see her right for her help.'

Without a word the child gathered up the babies and carried them out of the room. Annie watched her go then turned back to Kitty.

'Let us begin to solve your little problem, eh? It won't take but a minute.' She pushed Kitty back on the bed.

Kitty's heart was galloping and her mouth was dry. She stared at the bare plaster wall beside the bed. From somewhere in her clothing Annie produced a bottle and thrust it at Kitty.

'Have a mouthful of this,' she commanded. 'It'll steady your nerves.'

Kitty did as she was told and swallowed a burning mouthful of cheap brandy.

Other women do this all the time. Belle told me she had seen Annie on three occasions and was none the worse for it, Kitty argued with herself as she heard Annie open the cupboard. The brandy was already swimming though her brain, so she stole a quick glance.

Annie had pulled out an enamel bowl and placed it on the top. Beside it was a china jug. Kitty swallowed and looked.

After this I swear I'll not let Danny have his way with me any more, she vowed at the sound of Annie pouring water into the jug.

Annie knocked her arm with the bottle of brandy. 'Take another.'

Kitty did. Again it burnt on the way down but now it joined its predecessor. It was making her thoughts swim. Her head rolled towards where Annie was preparing her equipment.

There was a flash of metal as she wiped a strangely curved blade with an almost clean rag. Kitty watched.

Carefully covering the bowl containing her implements Annie turned to Kitty.

'Now, my sweet,' she sniffed, and wiped her nose on the back of her hand. 'It's going to hurt like your monthlies but worse, that's what the brandy's for. And you won't be able to do much until the child falls away but you should be as right as rain in a week. Do you understand?'

Kitty nodded.

'Right then, lift your skirts, open your legs and let me get on with it.'

Kitty nodded and, pulling up her skirt, positioned herself so Annie had access. Turning her head away and staring at the wall, again she heard the scrape of metal on enamel.

‘

Eight

The woman in the bed looked as white as the sheet she was lying on. Her blue eyes had smudgy dark rings around them and were sunk deep in her head. Her almost-white blonde hair was plastered to her skull with sweat. She stared up at Robert.

‘I’m done for ain’t I, sir.’ It was a statement rather than a question.

‘I am afraid you are, Miss Henry,’ he agreed. ‘Who did this to you?’

‘Call me Kitty,’ she said, in a whisper of a voice. ‘I did it to myself when I let that pig Danny at me again.’

‘I mean who helped you abort the child?’ Robert said, moved by the stoical manner in which the young woman on the bed approached her death.

‘I don’t know her name, sir.’

‘What did she use?’ Robert asked in a tender voice.

Kitty gulped. ‘A small hook on a long stick-like thing.’

‘Have you been to her before?’

‘All the girls go to her from time to time if the mother’s ruin and a bath don’t work,’ Kitty said.

He had seen the result of too many mismanaged efforts to be rid of an unwanted child. Most women got away with it, for a time, but for some, like Kitty, a trip to the local old woman was a trip to the grave and a painful trip at that. For one awful second a picture of Ellen under the hand of this abortionist came into Robert's mind.

Kitty's face contorted in agony and she grabbed hold of her stomach, drawing up her legs. Robert left his uneasy thoughts and beckoned the nurse.

'Sister Perry, if you please, a measure of laudanum for Miss Henry every three hours.'

'Yes, Doctor Munroe.' Sister Perry made her way to the chest in the corner of the room and took her keys from under her white apron.

Robert sighed and placed a hand on Kitty's clammy forehead. She shivered as a rigor swept over her and her teeth chattered. Sister Perry bustled back and spooned in a measure of syrup, then adjusted the covers. Kitty settled and Robert stepped back to consult with the two medical students. He shook his head and glanced back at the now quiet young woman.

'Poor woman,' he said, almost to himself.

'But surely the wom–' Maltravers started.

'Surely what?' interrupted Robert. 'Surely she knows it's an offence to procure the death of her child? I'm sure she does. Surely it's her own fault for getting herself with child? I doubt it was her choice,' Robert said harshly.

'Surely it is a consequence of her loose morals?'

Robert's eyes went back to the woman on the bed and saw Ellen instead of Kitty lying there struggling for breath. 'Kitty Henry is probably no more than twenty-five and now she is dying.'

'I was just looking to the justice of the situa–' Maltravers said.

'Justice!' Robert's head snapped around. 'What of the man, Maltravers? Where is his justice in this?'

'A man is a man, sir. This Danny fellow Miss Henry mentioned...'

Danny! It was a common enough name, but...

Robert shot back to the bed. 'Miss Henry.' She turned dimming eyes to him. 'Danny *who?*' he asked.

She didn't answer, just looked calmly at him, then her eyes started to flicker as she began to slip into unconsciousness. He had to know.

'Who, Kitty? Danny who?'

Her lips moved and Robert lowered his head to catch what she was saying.

'Danny Donovan,' Kitty whispered with a sigh. Robert drew back slightly, a cold hand over his heart.

Danny Donovan was not content with ruining Ellen, he had pressed his attentions on Kitty as well. Did Ellen know? Did she care?

Robert was pulled back from his thoughts by a knocking at the door, and the ward orderly stepped into the room. 'Excuse me, Doctor, but Miss Henry's sister is asking to come in.'

'Yes, of course, she's just in time,' Robert said. 'Gentlemen, there is nothing more to be done here, I suggest we–' The words died on his lips as the door opened and Ellen, soberly dressed and with tears in her eyes, walked in.

She stopped dead when she saw him. For a brief second delight registered, then it was gone.

105

She turned to Kitty, who was now breathing very shallowly, and dashed over to the bed. She knelt down beside Kitty and gently smoothed the hair off the dying woman's face.

Young and Maltravers were waiting by the door for him, but Robert just stood staring down at Ellen, who now wept softly holding Kitty's hand.

The soft sheen of Ellen's hair glowed auburn in the light from the window.

'I'll join you presently, gentlemen,' he said, then drew up a chair next to where Ellen knelt.

'Oh, Kitty, you promised not to go to see...' Ellen stopped as she felt Robert move next to her. 'See who?' Robert asked gently.

'I thank you for what you've done for Kitty, but don't let me keep you, Doctor Munroe,' Ellen said with a catch in her voice.

'Who?' Robert persisted.

'Some ... some old woman Kitty was told about,' Ellen said, not meeting his eye.'

'Why are you protecting the person who did this to your sister?' Robert asked.

Ellen sat back on her heels and rubbed her eyes with the back of her hand. 'The person who did this to Kitty has dangerous friends, Doctor Munroe.'

'But surely–'

'*Dangerous friends,*' she repeated.

She gave Kitty, who was now lying peacefully, a small, brave smile which made his heart melt. 'I'm not actually her kin, but I'm the nearest thing to a sister that Kitty has and I had to see her before...' Ellen trailed off.

A feeling of protectiveness swept over Robert.

He wanted to take Ellen in his arms and tell her he was sorry for his abominable treatment of her in the Angel. To have her cry on his chest and for him to hold her safe, safe from everything.

What *was* he thinking of?

He stood up so abruptly that both Ellen and Sister Perry started. 'I'll leave you, Mrs O'Casey. I have...'

'Yes, of course.'

Robert had to go, but still he stood staring at Ellen kneeling on the floor beside the bed.

'If there is anything you need, just ask Sister Perry and she will attend to it I am sure,' he said, still not moving.

'Thank you, Doctor Munroe.'

'And I'm truly sorry, Mrs O'Casey, for Kitty and' – the nurse moved closer to them and put her hand on Kitty's pasty cheek, Robert bit his lip – 'and for the other night at the Angel.'

For a second, Ellen's eyes softened as they rested on his face, then her reserved expression returned. She inclined her head as elegantly as a duchess, but said nothing.

Go, his brain shouted at his feet and reluctantly they responded. As he reached the door he turned to see Ellen on her knees, head down and a small string of rosary beads moving through her fingers as she prayed over the dying young woman.

Bridget awoke with a start as the front door slammed. She rubbed her eyes and glanced at the window. The light was almost gone. It must be nearly seven. Standing up she went to the range and moved the simmering kettle back onto the full flame.

Ellen almost fell into the room and threw herself onto the spindle-leg chair. She buried her head in her arms and sobbed loudly.

'Good heavens, child, you're soaking,' said Bridget, crossing the room and placing a hand on Ellen's shaking shoulders. 'Take off that coat and warm yourself by the fire before you catch your death.'

Ellen rose and stumbled to the fire as Bridget stripped the sodden jacket from her back.

'Whatever has happened?'

Ellen turned a tear-stained face to her. 'Kitty's dead.'

'Dead! How dead?'

Ellen's eyes darted around the room. 'Where is Josie?'

'She's with Mrs Nolan helping with the twins. Patrick said he'd bring her back. Now tell me what's happened.'

Ellen sobbed out the story then threw her head down on her arms. Bridget put her arms around Ellen and hugged her close.

After fifteen minutes or so Ellen looked up. 'Kitty and the baby could have come to Joe's in America and met someone better than Danny. Someone to love her and who would treat her right, not blame her for being caught in the family way.' She looked mournfully at her. 'And Josie asks me why I haven't married again.'

'Did Kitty know you? At the end I mean,' Bridget asked.

Ellen nodded. 'She did. When I got there she was in a side ward. There was a physician and some of his students looking into her case. The physician, Doctor Munroe, had ordered her to be given a draught of laudanum so she wasn't in too much pain.' A tear skidded down Ellen's cheek and she wiped it away. She looked up at Bridget. 'You should have seen her lying there, as white as a sheet with her breath hardly making it past her lips.'

'Did she know you were there?' Bridget asked, thinking of the poor young woman who now lay on a cold mortuary slab.

Ellen nodded. 'She watched me as I prayed through my beads. Her lips moved but she never said a word, and finally she drifted off into a deep sleep and then slipped away without any fuss. I sat with her for a while then left.' She glanced up. 'I'm so thankful that it was Doctor Munroe on duty when Kitty was brought in,' Ellen said in a softer voice. 'He was very gentle with her and actually looked as if he cared, whereas I could see that some of the others thought that Kitty got no more than she deserved.'

'You knew the doctor?' Bridget asked studying her daughter closely across the table.

'I met him in the Angel a few weeks ago,' Ellen told her, not meeting her eye. 'Danny introduced him.'

Bridget clucked her tongue and jerked her head back. 'He's one of those in Danny's pockets then, is he?'

Ellen's gaze rested on her hands as her expression became thoughtful. 'I thought so, but I hear that he got the sewage cart to clean in Wapping Dock Street.'

There was something again in Ellen's expression that caused Bridget to pause. Then tears welled up in Ellen's eyes.

'He was good to poor Kitty.'

Both women lapsed into silence, the only sound in the room the tapping of the rain on the window. Ellen took a deep breath and stood up. She rubbed the remaining tears from her eyes and smoothed her hair back into the bun at the nape of her neck.

'I told the ward orderly that I was Kitty's sister, that's how they let me in. So that means the wake will be here then.'

Danny handed his hat and cane to the clerk as he walked into the main office of Cashman & Son, builders. The half-glazed door closed behind him as he took a seat. The other side of the desk from him sat Herbert Cashman, owner of one of the most lucrative building companies in East London.

Herbert Cashman was about Danny's own age, but without his abundance of hair. Unlike many who tried to cover their baldness by combing what remained across the head, Cashman had dealt with his by shaving his whole head closely. Although it had been many years since he had wielded a pick or shovel himself, his hands were still deeply calloused, with a faint rim of grime under the nails. He looked up from the account book on his desk as Danny took his seat.

The chair creaked as Cashman leant back and gave Danny a long look.

'I gave Black Mike my insurance last week.'

Danny reached out and took a cigarette from a silver box in the centre of the desk. Casually, he struck the flint lighter and drew on the cigarette, his eyes never leaving Cashman's face.

'How is the little woman? And those darling children of yours?' Danny asked, crossing one leg over the other with difficulty.

'Edith's well. Charlotte is attending Barnsbury College for Young Ladies and young Bert is down in the yard learning the business the hard way like I did from my father.'

Danny took a handkerchief out of his pockets and blew his nose loudly. 'You're a blessed man, so you are, Bert.' Another loud blow. 'Two children and a loving wife to come home to.'

Cashman's weatherbeaten face cracked in a smile. 'From what I hear you've a nipper or two running the streets and *several* wives to go home to if you fancy.'

'Well, you know how it is.' He drew long on the cigarette again. 'How's Cissy?'

Cashman shot a nervous glance at the door then gave Danny a nonchalant look. 'The same as ever.'

'She was a sad loss to the Angel. She sang like a linnet,' Danny said, thinking of the fiery red-head who used to draw drinkers from miles around before she clapped eyes on Cashman and cajoled him into setting her up.

'Well, you've got Ellen O'Casey now to take her place.'

Danny's eyes narrowed a fraction. Ellen had taken Cissy's place on the stage but not where Danny really wanted her, underneath him. The familiar rumbling rage that was ever present

111

when Ellen's name was mentioned started in his gut. Pushing her from his mind, he returned to the man on the other side of the desk.

'You've done well for yourself,' he said, sweeping his hand around the oak-lined office.

Cashman took a cigarette himself and lit it. 'What do you want, Danny?'

Danny leant forward and stubbed out the cigarette on the desk blotter. Cashman glared at him.

'I'm guessing you've heard about Doctor Munroe who's been appointed to the Parish Emergency Board.'

Cashman relaxed back into his chair. 'I did. So?'

'It seems that Doctor Munroe has been asking around about a few things.'

'That's his job. But what's it to me? I'm a builder.'

'The builder who was contracted to refurbish the dwelling houses in King Street and to replace the pumps in the parish.'

A sheen of sweat appeared on Cashman's forehead. 'I let the work out to your boys, and paid you for it.'

Danny leaned back and tucked his thumbs into the armholes of his waistcoat. 'Maybe you did and maybe you didn't.'

Cashman stood up and slammed his hands flat on the table, red-faced and glowering. Danny also rose to his feet. He saw Cashman's gaze falter for a second and smiled.

'Because, Bert, when our good doctor comes to ask about the parish repairs it'll only be your name he'll be finding on the dockets.'

'But we shook hands!' Cashman told him.

Now it was Danny's turn to slam his hands on the desk. He did so, making the inkwell and quill jump with the force. 'Get them fixed.'

'Seventy guineas I paid your men to do the work,' Cashman said. He jabbed his index finger at Danny. 'There may be no papers to show but someone will tell him.'

'Make sure it's not you,' Danny said. 'I don't care how you do it. Solder patches on the pumps, shove some plaster on the walls. As you said, you're the builder. But know this, Bert.' Danny balled his hand into a fist and held it at Cashman. 'If the repairs don't get done then Munroe will go poking around in all our businesses, believe you me, he will. There'll be no young ladies' colleges, no more of your old lady playing at being gentry and no business for young Bert to learn, because that bastard Munroe will finish the lot of us.'

Danny stood up, straightened the front of his striped jacket sharply, walked to the door and grabbed the worn brass handle. Then he turned back to the builder. 'Oh, and will you be giving my warmest regards to Cissy, when you see her.'

Nine

Emptying the water from the jug into the china basin, Robert picked up the tar soap and washed his hands thoroughly. Many of his colleagues thought his excessive use of soap and water to be something of an eccentricity but, as he pointed out to his students, if one decaying apple can spoil a whole barrel, cannot debris from one putrid wound contaminate another?

It had been a long afternoon. Over twenty people and their families had arrived since Thomas had opened the door at one-thirty. This was not unusual.

Robert had seen a variety of cases in the last four hours. Sickly infants with loose motions, for whom he prescribed a mild binding mixture of ground chalk and syrup, others with colic who were given carminative powders, with strict instructions to their mothers about dosage, and a coal merchant with a foul-smelling wound for which he instructed Thomas to mix tincture of myrrh and aloes. He had grappled with tooth pincers as he pulled rotting teeth from both children and adults with gum boils and then packed the cavities with brandy and marigold paste to stem the bleeding. Ten or so children with worms all received a dose of purging worm powder. One poor trollop with the cartilage in her nose eaten away by syphilis was told to present herself at the hospital's medical school on Friday so that his students could see one of the more uncommon effects of the illness. Lastly, a mother of six with a canker in her breast was sent away with vinegar of squill in cinnamon water.

Robert was glad to be finished. He hadn't been sleeping at all well and he *still* had Caroline's letter to finish.

He settled down to complete his notes and observations when the door bell jingled. Closing the

114

ledger, he got up and walked back into the dispensary.

A slight woman in her middle to late forties with a work-worn face was standing there. Although her dress was old, the threadbare patches had been neatly darned by a skilled hand. Her face and hands were clean and under the tartan shawl that swathed her head, her thick grey hair was tied back in a neat knot. She looked familiar. She rushed over to him.

'Please, sir,' she said, stopping at a respectable distance.

Robert could hear her wheezing. He glanced at her ankles. They were swollen.

'What is it, Mr...?' he said, studying her closely.

'Mrs Shannahan, sir. Oh, it's not me,' she said, putting the flat of her hand on her chest as if to slow her breathing. 'It's my granddaughter. She's sick in her throat like, and burning up with fever, so she is. We only live in Anthony Street. 'Tis but a short stroll from here.'

Robert scratched his chin thoughtfully. There had been a number of cases of typhus in the workhouse. That often started with a raw throat and burning temperature.

'Anthony Street, you say?' Robert took his coat from Thomas.

The woman nodded. 'Number two, at the corner.'

'I'm leaving for the hospital in ten minutes or so, I'll call on my way.'

Fifteen minutes later Robert made his way along Chapman Street, then turned right into Anthony Street. The cobbled road and piles of rotting

115

rubbish in the street didn't distinguish it from any one of the other dirty streets in the parish, and he wondered in passing what conditions he would find in Mrs Shannahan's house.

To his surprise, when he stopped in front of number two, he was confronted by a white scrubbed step and polished wooden knocker. Before he could make use of it Mrs Shannahan appeared at the door.

'Thank you for coming,' she said, as he squeezed past her into the small downstairs room.

The cottage, like the rest in the street, comprised one room downstairs and another above it, the access to which was via a flight of narrow stairs boxed in by a thin partition at one side of the room. He looked around. The furniture in the room, though poor, was well maintained. There were two armchairs with threadbare upholstery, but both had patchwork covers over them, giving the room a cheerful appearance, as did the glowing kitchen range. The floor, although made of beaten earth, was swept and a large rag rug covered the centre of it. A faint smell of meat emanated from the pot simmering on the back of the range, while cups sparkled on hooks from the mantelshelf above. There were faded pictures around the walls of what Robert guessed must be Irish country scenes.

'If you please, Doctor, my granddaughter is this way,' Mrs Shannahan said, leading him towards the stairs. Robert left the cosy living room and ascended the stairs after her.

He found the same degree of order and tidiness in the bedroom. There was a large bed in the middle of which lay a young girl of about twelve, covered with clean sheets and a large eiderdown. She clutched an old rag doll. Robert walked over the rag rug and gazed down at his patient.

'I fetched the doctor to see you, Josie,' the older woman said, resting an affectionate hand on her granddaughter's forehead.

Josie swallowed visibly and winced. 'It hurts, Gran,' she said.

'*Aroon, aroon,* my angel,' the older woman said, sitting down on the bed beside her. 'Yer Mammy'll be back soon, I'm sure.'

'Who's this then?' Robert said, smiling widely at his young patient and pointing to the doll clutched to her.

'It's Waisy,' Josie said, swallowing and grimacing as she did.

'Waisey? I've never heard that name before. Is it Irish?' Robert asked, laying his hands on her forehead lightly. It was hot but not dangerously so.

Josie looked up at him with bright green eyes and gave him a wide smile. 'It's not Irish. I just couldn't say Daisy when I got her.'

Robert saw a smile hover around the young girl's mouth and smiled down at her.

'Now, Josie, let me look at your throat.'

Under the anxious eye of her grandmother, Robert looked down Josie's throat and felt her pulse. Then he opened his bag and listened to her chest with his newly acquired stethoscope of polished cow's horn and leather. He stood up.

'I'm pleased to tell you, Mrs Shannahan, that your granddaughter has no more than the quinsy,' Robert said, to the obvious relief of the older

117

woman. 'Call in tomorrow and I'll get my assistant to mix you up a gargle and some Peruvian willow powder for her. Until then give her plenty to drink and keep her cool.' He turned to the girl on the bed. 'You'll be up and around by the end of the week, Josie, or I'm not a Scotsman.'

'Thank you, Doctor,' she croaked, putting on a brave smile.

He followed Bridget down into the snug living room, thankful that the last patient he would see that day would make a speedy recovery.

'Can I offer you a dish of tea before you go?' Mr Shannahan asked, turning her motherly instincts on him.

A polite refusal sprang to Robert's lips, but it stayed there. He was weary and, comfortable though his rooms at the hospital were, they were not a home. Although the room he now stood in was poor, it was a home, and a loving home at that. He dropped his bag onto the table and smiled at Bridget.

'That would be most kind of you, Mrs Shannahan.'

As his hostess collected the cups and arranged them on the table Robert took the opportunity to look around the room more closely. His eyes fell on a stack of books on the mantelshelf. There was a Bible, a couple of almanacs, and three or four copies of the *Penny Magazine* amongst others. He reached up and took down a book. It was a much-mangled copy of *Pride and Prejudice*. The cover was missing and there was a brown stain that ran though the first few pages, but after that the text was clear. He placed it back beside

Munster Village, Thaddeus of Warsaw and *The Mysteries of Udolpho.*

'You enjoy reading, Mrs Shannahan,' he said, holding up the slim volume and trying not to look surprised that she could read at all.

'God bless you, Doctor, I can make out my name but no more. Those,' she indicated the books on the shelf with her head as she poured the boiling water into the teapot, 'are my daughter Ellie's. It's her that's the reader. Like her father is my Ellie, clever like,' Bridget glanced at the window. 'I'm surprised she's not back by now.'

She handed Robert the cup of tea. He sat down, weariness stealing over him as he sank back into the bright patchwork. 'She only went out to deliver the done laundry. I wonder what could be keeping her.'

'It's just the three of you living here?' he asked. She nodded. He noticed that the family food was not left out as in most poor homes he had visited. Even the milk that had been used to whiten his tea was taken from a covered jug. 'You and your daughter take in washing then, Mrs Shannahan?'

'Indeed, sir. We wash in the morning, iron and return in the afternoon and sew in the evening. Josie helps, as she goes to school twice a week to learn her letters. Ellie insists on it, she does.'

Robert's eyebrows nearly disappeared under the rebellious hair on his forehead at this piece of news. It all came together. Mrs Shannahan and her educated daughter were obviously of respectable Irish stock who had fallen on hard times. The neat clean house, the washing that gave the family its income without asking for parish relief.

Mrs Shannahan's genteel Irish accent, and spending money on what most of the neighbourhood would consider unnecessary – schooling – all pointed to that conclusion. He drained the last of the tea.

The front door opened.

'Here's Ellie now, Doctor,' Bridget said.

Robert stood up and found himself face to face with Ellen O'Casey.

It was just twilight as Ellen crossed over from Katharine Street and saw the light already in the window of her home. Thank God she didn't have to sing tonight and could spend the time with Josie. With a quick wave at the rat-catcher, with his day's work dangling head down from his pole and his terrier at his heels, Ellen put her hand to the door and walked in.

Her breath fled her body and her head spun as she found herself staring into the equally astonished face of Robert Munroe. She looked to her mother then back to the doctor.

'Josie,' she shouted, dropping her basket. Its contents spilled on the floor as she fled to the stairs. Doctor Munroe caught her arm.

'There is no need for alarm. Josie is quite well, Mrs O'Casey,' he said, as she turned to him. His eyes were tired but as they rested on her they were warm and tender. She melted for a second, then she snatched her arm away and glared at him.

'You know my Ellie?' Bridget said to the doctor as she gathered up the shopping from off the floor.

'I have had the pleasure of hearing her sing on

several occasions in the Angel and Crown,' he said, still looking at her with an unreadable expression on his face. Ellen strode over to the corner kitchen range and whipped open the ash grate underneath. Picking up a set of fire tongs from the hearth she fished around for a moment or two, then pulled out a battered tin box. Flipping the lid back carefully she reached in and retrieved something then closed the box and shoved it back into the ashes.

'Sixpence is the usual fee for a physician's time, is it not?' Ellen said, thrusting a still hot coin at him.

'That's quite all right, Mrs O'Casey.' Ellen thrust it at him again.

'We may be poor but we don't have to take charity yet, thank you,' she said, daring him to refuse the payment again. He took it and slipped the coin into the breast pocket of his waistcoat.

She could barely spare the coin from her funds but Ellen wasn't going to be indebted to Robert Munroe.

He looked around the room, a friendly, open smile crossing his face and crinkling the corners of his eyes. She reminded herself that he wasn't to be trusted.

'You have a cosy and welcoming home, Mrs O'Casey,' he said. Ellen saw her mother simper at the compliment. 'But I am surprised to find you live here.'

'Surprised? Why so? Where did you think I lived, Brighton Pavilion?' she snapped back tartly.

'Ellen Marie,' her mother said, in a voice that she hadn't used with Ellen since she was a child.

'I thought you lived with...' He trailed off.

Her mother gave her a sharp look. 'Doctor Munroe is as tired as a pony pulling slate. He has been good enough to come by to see Josie on his way back from the dispensary.'

Ellen could feel her mouth drop open. 'You are the Chapman Street doctor?' she said.

When she heard that a parish dispensary had opened in Chapman Street she didn't think for one moment that Doctor Munroe was the new doctor.

'I am,' he answered, then a puzzled look crossed his face. 'Didn't Mr Donovan tell you?'

'Mr Donovan? What has he got to do with this?'

'In view of your relationship, I thought...'

Anger surged up in Ellen. 'Relationship!' Under her blistering gaze Doctor Munroe shifted uneasily. 'Tell me, if you please, Doctor Munroe, what *relationship* would that be?'

He hooked his finger into his collar and stretched his neck. 'Aren't you his...?'

Realisation washed over her like a bucket of cold water. 'How dare you assume that I am Danny Donovan's mistress!'

'I didn't assume anything. He told me,' he said glaring at her in turn.

Ellen drew herself up to her full five foot five. 'What? He told you that I was his bit of slap?'

Shock registered on both Doctor Munroe's and her mother's face.

'Mr Donovan did not use that express—'

Ellen jabbed her index finger at the doctor.

'Don't you give me *Mr* Donovan,' she said through gritted teeth. 'That scum Irishman, God

122

rot him, with the breath of a sow and a belly to match, told you I was his mistress?'

'Not in so many wor–'

Ellen drew in a breath and gave Robert a furious look. 'And *you*, Doctor Munroe, *believed* him?'

'Why should I not?' he said.

'*Pardon me*. Why should you not?' Her voice was razor-sharp with sarcasm. 'I am, after all, just a supper-room singer, a woman who walks the boards for money, who puts herself up for men to gawp at and one of those who, everyone knows, are no better than common *whores*.' She saw Robert Munroe wince and his mouth take on a hard line.

'I did not say that,' Robert said, coming towards her.

'I'm sure that most of the fine society women of your acquaintance, Doctor Munroe, don't take in washing and sing in public supper rooms as part of their daily social rounds.' She took a step towards him, but this time he stood his ground. 'But nor are they two steps away from the workhouse, are they?'

'But he told me–' he stopped.

'He may have done the *telling*, but you, Doctor Munroe,' she jabbed her finger at him again, 'did the *believing*.'

Deep in Robert's gaze Ellen saw rage, and something else, something most unsettling. The doctor's mouth changed subtly as did his eyes. For one heady moment, she thought he was going to take hold of her. Then he pressed his shoulders back and tugged at the front of his waistcoat.

'I'll tell you this, Doctor Munroe,' she spat.

'Although God only knows, it is none of your business. There's been only one man who has ever known me and he was my husband and he's been in his grave these ten years. I never have been and never will be Danny Donovan's mistress or any other man's for that matter. So if that shit–'

'Ellen!' shouted Bridget.

Ellen's eyes flickered to her mother. 'Sorry, Mammy.' She looked back at Robert Munroe giving him her coldest stare. 'So if Danny Donovan tells you different, you can now put him right.'

Ten

Picking up the wax-sealed jar, Robert applied the new label with his thumb. He placed it alongside the others on the shelf and stood back admiringly. Sections of guts taken from patients, suspended in formaldehyde and catalogued by age, sex and street wouldn't be considered by most people as something to prize, but what those jars contained could be as valuable as an Old Master if it helped him unlock the secret of what caused cholera. Over his desk in the outer office was a wall chart plotting the new cases. The good news was that there were fewer cases among those people around the newly repaired pumps.

He took the duster off the shelf and wiped his hands on it. The pumps had been hastily repaired before he had been able to question the builder contracted to do the job months ago. Herbert

Cashman had managed to dodge his first two visits and was the model of hospitality on his third, after the swift completion of the long overdue work. Robert wasn't fooled. He had already heard more than a few whispers that it was Danny Donovan's navvies who had been paid long ago for the work.

He returned to the workbench and was about to put his microscope into its case when the door opened and Bulmer entered.

'I am sorry to disturb you, sir, but there is a Mrs O'Casey to see you.'

Ellen O'Casey here?

'I told her that the casual ward was still open but she insisted on seeing you in person. I'll send her away if you wish.'

'No! No, thank you, Bulmer.' Robert hastily rolled down his sleeves and refastened the cuffs. 'Show her in.'

As Ellen entered she stopped and gazed, wide-eyed, around the airy laboratory.

Standing unnoticed in his corner, Robert let his eyes run over her. Ellen was wearing a faded cotton day dress, with a bright stripe of the original fabric a few inches above the hem revealing that it had been made for a shorter woman. Over this she wore a short velvet jacket which, in its time, had been of some quality. The pile was now worn clean from the elbows and cuffs, but the richness of the jacket's deep russet colour might have been made for Ellen's earthy tones. Her hair was held back in a tight bun at the nape of her neck but several strands had escaped and curled around her face. Robert's gaze slowly traced the curve of her neck. How could a woman dressed in cast-off seconds look so elegant?

Although it shouldn't have mattered to him at all, seeing Ellen O'Casey again gave Robert a moment of uncertainty. That she had sought him out after their last meeting gave him a thrill of unexpected pleasure, but it also caused him a problem. He couldn't ignore the fact that he was very attracted to her. As a doctor he knew that these things were physical in nature and often transient, and while he believed her to be Danny's mistress it had protected him from acting on that attraction.

Ellen O'Casey is a pub singer, he reminded himself, but it did no good. He might be a scientist but he was also a man.

The floorboard creaked under his foot and Ellen spun around. He saw her eyes open wide on seeing him and in an unguarded moment a look of joy crossed her face.

'Mrs O'Casey. What a pleasure to see you.' It was.

She matched his smile. 'I am sorry if I am disturbing you. I know you are a busy man.'

'Never too busy too spend time with a pretty woman,' he heard himself say.

Ellen blushed and lowered her eyes, but not before he saw a spark of alarm in them.

'I'm sorry,' he said stretching his hands out palms up and shrugging his shoulders. 'I seem to have an extraordinary talent for saying the wrong thing to you.'

Much to his relief, Ellen's shoulders relaxed and she smiled up at him. 'I have a talent for rip-

ping the ears off your head every time you do.'
She laughed and he joined in.

'It's for that reason that I've come to see you,
Doctor Munroe,' she said. 'I want to thank you
properly for your kindness towards Kitty.'

'There is no need.'

'There is every need,' she told him. 'I begged
her not to rid herself of the child.' There was a
momentary quiver in her voice, then she said,
looking at him directly, 'You treated her with
consideration and for that I thank you.'

'I am a doctor and my concern is for the sick.
How is Josie?'

A broad, unreservedly maternal smile, the type
that his mother never could quite manage, lit up
Ellen's face.

'She's grand. Her ears are too big and she has
too much to say for a young woman of her age,'
she told him, pride belying her words, 'but she is
fit and well, thanks to your medicine.'

'I owe *you* an apology,' he said, noting how the
things in the laboratory fascinated her. He wondered if she had spotted Napoleon the skeleton.

He had taken Caroline to his laboratory in
Edinburgh some time ago, hoping that showing
her his work might help her to understand its
importance to him. It had been a vain hope. She
had only been in the room a few moments when
she spotted a preserved heart in a jar, screamed
so loudly that the orderlies had rushed in from
the next ward, and stormed out. She had berated
him for his unnatural fascination with dead
things for the whole of the journey home.

So far Ellen hadn't screamed, even though she

had noticed William's collection of eyes.

'I accept your apology,' she replied, and held out her hand.

Robert took it. 'Friends?'

Had he known the effect it would have on him Robert would not have been so quick to grasp her hand. As she pressed it against his palm, a fire ignited within him. He took a step forward, but she snatched her hand away, put it to her hair and tied a couple of strands back.

Then she turned her eyes away from him and glanced at the dishes on the bench. 'What on earth are the squiggly things in these saucers?'

If anyone had asked her at that moment, Ellen could have told them truthfully that she knew what it was like to feel the earth move under her feet. Because the whole world had shifted to one side and then back again as she placed her hand in Doctor Munroe's. So much so that she was in real danger of reaching her hand up and running it over his clean-shaven face just to see what the bristles felt like on her palm.

She should leave. She had thanked him for Kitty and he had apologised. They were friends. That could have been an end to it.

If she had any sense in her head she would leave now but she couldn't. If the room had been on fire she would have looked for an excuse to stay until the flames licked her ankles, just to be near him. As he stood there, his work surrounding him, she was seeing a whole new side to Robert Munroe and she wanted to know more. She wanted to know what made him laugh and why he was so passionate about his work. She wanted to know ... well ... everything.

His face came alive. 'These are specimens of gut from people who have died of cholera in the last five days.' She drew back sharply. Robert caught hold of her arm. 'They are quite safe as long as you don't touch them.'

'Why do you keep them?' she asked.

He beckoned her nearer to the dishes, splaying the hand that had just held hers so firmly towards them, and Ellen was mesmerised by its form. She studied the way the line of small hairs tracked up from his wrist towards his little finger, noticed the clean, square-trimmed nails, and the way the thumb above the joint sat at a right angle.

All the while he was bent forwards, telling her his ideas about the invisible things that caused diseases, Ellen studied his profile, examining the texture of his skin, the contrast of rough beard with his smoother upper cheek.

'I hope to prove they are the same things that make meat rancid,' he said.

'I'm sorry.' Ellen had been too busy staring at the shape of Doctor Munroe's mouth as he spoke to actually hear what he was saying.

'I'm boring you.' He looked deflated and made to move away. Ellen caught hold of his arm.

'Not at all,' she said. She stepped over to the charts on the wall. 'Is this to do with blood?' she asked, pointing at the detailed prints.

He followed, and smiled at her in a way that made a joyous laugh start deep within her. He started to explain how the heart moved the blood around the body.

How did he know all those things? He moved over to the cabinets of specimens and pulled out a shallow drawer with what looked like dried leaves all carefully pinned on top of blotting paper. He described to her how he catalogued all his specimens and kept detailed notes, explaining that it was vital because he never knew where a link between one illness and another might be found.

Following him around the spotless laboratory, Ellen found herself caught up by his passion. She enjoyed seeing how his eyes sparkled and the corners crinkled up. As he leant forward she found herself staring at his ear and wondering how his beard knew to make an orderly line alongside it.

Robert guided her over to the tall shelves.

'Now this,' he said pointing to a jar in the centre of the shelves, 'is a section of duodenum and this a section of colon. I took both from a docker who had been complaining for weeks of stomach cramps before he died. See where the organ wall has been eaten through?' He jabbed at the jar.

Ellen screwed up her eyes and followed the line of his finger. The names he spoke were alien to her but the pale flesh Robert pointed to looked just like the tripe in the butcher's shop. He moved to the next jar.

'Here are the lungs of a coal heaver. See how the dust has settled on the surface.' Ellen dutifully stared at the spongy objects. 'And these are–'

'Kidneys,' Ellen interrupted, recognising the half-moon shapes in the next container. She gave him a crooked smile. 'I must say, Doctor Munroe, it's more like a slaughterhouse than a hospital.'

He threw back his head and laughed. Ellen joined in.

'Once I start on my work it is hard to stop me,' he said, his eyes happy as he looked at her. 'I'm sorry.'

'I am interested,' she said, actually finding she was. 'But I have a question.'

He pulled a mock serious face. 'I always get very worried when a student says that to me, but go on, ask away.'

She looked around at the disembodied organs and then her gaze fell on the bleached bones of the skeleton grinning across at them. Her hand went up and she made a swift sign of the cross on her chest.

'If these specimens are from dead people, does that mean on Judgement Day they will appear before God incomplete? And don't you worry that God might not like you taking something he made in his own image to use for yourself?'

For one moment Ellen wished she had held her tongue. Whatever would he think of her questioning him in such a manner?

'That is a very interesting question,' he replied, after a long – a very long – pause. Ellen's shoulders relaxed. 'I believe that the Almighty doesn't take any pleasure in seeing His creation suffer and that He will not judge me too harshly for trying to alleviate suffering. As for taking specimens from those who have died, in my view it puts them in no different a position than those who have lost a limb or an eye due to disease or accident.' An apologetic smile crossed his face. 'If you want a more theological explanation, then you'll have to ask my father. He is a minister.'

'Your father's a priest?'

She knew that priests in the English church were allowed to marry, but she had never come so close to the son of a priest before.

'Er ... um ... the Church of Scotland doesn't use the term priest,' he told her flatly.

'You didn't want to enter the church?' she asked, desperate to move the conversation on but not sure where it would be safe to lead it.

'No. Too many cold churches.' There was a hollowness in his voice, an echo of the boy he must have been.

'I'm afraid I am a bit of a disappointment to my family. Mother wanted me to follow her family and go into the army and my father wanted me to inherit his fervour for winning souls. But I was more interested in the here and now than the hereafter, so, in the end, my parents and I agreed to disagree. Even as a boy I was fascinated with living things, much to my mother's horror. Try as she might, Mother couldn't stop me collecting animals and insects to study. In the end she let me keep my collection in the stables, well away from the main part of the house.'

An image of a vast house with surrounding buildings, like the houses she collected daily washing from, came into Ellen's mind. Those houses didn't have one ten-by-ten-foot room downstairs and one the same size upstairs, or rag rugs on the floor; nor did their owners have to brew second-hand tea. They had well-sprung carriages, and servants, and chocolate to drink, and of course daily skivvies who were paid tuppence a bundle to take away their laundry.

'It was Mr McKay, my housemaster at the Stirling Academy, who nurtured my interest in medicine and finally persuaded my parents that doctoring was as respectable a career as the army or the church.'

Behind him, the orderly had completed his task and was coming towards them.

'Thank you for your time, Doctor Munroe, but I have stayed too long. You have things to do,' she said, thinking how much the moss-green tone of his waistcoat softened the brown of his eyes.

She should have headed for the door, but her feet were rooted to the spot. They stood staring at each other, the space between them seeming to shrink as the seconds passed. The orderly cleared his throat softly and looked towards the windows.

'Would you like me to inform Mr Chafford you'll be late for afternoon surgery, sir?' he asked.

Doctor Munroe half-turned his head, but kept his eyes on her. 'No, I'll be there presently, Bulmer.'

'I'm singing in the Angel on Thursday, so maybe I'll see you then,' Ellen told him.

A look of regret passed over his face. 'I am afraid it will not be this week. My mother is in London on her yearly visit from Edinburgh.'

'She is coming all that way alone?'

'She travels with her maid, but this year she is bringing Miss Sinclair, an acquaintance of mine, with her.'

Ellen's stomach lurched. *Miss Sinclair? An acquaintance? Bloody fool yer are, Ellen O'Casey. Why wouldn't he have a respectable young woman ready to*

133

marry him?

She gathered herself together and started to
leave. Robert moved a second after her and was
beside the door when she reached it. He held the
brass handle but didn't open it.

'Please give my regards to your mother and
Josie,' he said in a low voice. He was so close to
her that she could smell the faint lingering scent
of bay rum from his morning shave.

Unable to force out any words, she inclined her
head and he opened the door. She hastened into
the echoing corridor and, taking a deep breath,
squared her shoulders and headed for the heavy
doors that led to the Whitechapel Road.

Bloody fool yer are, and no mistake.

As the hotel butler opened the door to admit
Robert, Mrs Munroe pulled her shoulders back
and fixed a smile on her face. After four days in
the coach to London every bone in her body
screamed. Robert sent her a fleeting smile as he
entered and she adjusted her position to ease the
stabbing pain running down her left leg.

'Robert,' she said, as he reached her. Casting
her eyes over him she conceded that he looked
none the worse for moving to London. If anything, he looked jaunty and more relaxed than she
had seen him for a long time. She caught her
breath: he so resembled her brother, his namesake. The same broad stature, the mop of unruly
brown hair. Even his eyes had that same intense
dark colour. The years had not lessened the
sorrow she felt at the loss of her much loved older
brother, crushed under the hooves of a cavalry

charge. Wellington might have won a decisive victory but she could never hear the word *Waterloo* without coming close to tears. Robert, her son, in a red military coat, would look just like dear Rob.

She offered him a cheek, which he kissed lightly. 'Mama, you look well.'

'So do you. I want to hear all about your work, but let us wait until Caroline joins us.'

She indicated that he should sit opposite her. The buttoned leather chair sighed as it took his weight.

'How long will she be?'

Her shoulders relaxed, thankful that it *had* been worth suffering Caroline's wearisome chatter on the long journey. 'I am glad to find you enthusiastic about seeing her,' she said as the butler brought in tea.

'Of course I am. Why wouldn't I be?'

There was something in his tone that made her pause. She sent her son a sharp look, but he seemed relaxed, an untroubled smile on his face. She opened the tea caddy and measured out several spoonfuls and added them to the pot.

'She's gone to Bond Street with Mrs Manners,' she told him. She picked up a smaller caddy and spooned two teaspoons of the black leaves into the teapot.

'To buy a French ball gown to knock out the eyes of Edinburgh society,' he said, as she scalded the leaves then rattled the spoon around.

'Girls today have too much freedom,' she said, as she offered him a dish of tea. She caught the hint of an amused smile.

'I know I've said it before, but in my day we

135

were grateful for one new gown to start the season. And it was white, or at least a demure pastel shade. But now.' She took a sip of tea. 'Red! Can you believe it? A red ball gown for a girl not yet twenty-two. I ask you.' She shook her head as if the ball gown had been fashioned in hell itself. 'I don't blame dear Caroline, she is a sweet girl, but a young woman's reputation is so easily tarnished by a thoughtless action or an unsuitable acquaintance that a mother should always be vigilant and ready with a loving hand.'

Her own daughters, Hermione and Margot, sprang to mind. A loving hand was not always easy to apply and caused no end of nervy tears and hysterical tantrums. There was barely a day in the Munroe household without the smelling salts being called for, but it was her duty to raise them godly, dutiful and unblemished.

'I am surprised you offered to bring her to London with you, Mama,' Robert said, finishing his tea and offering his cup for more.

She sighed loudly. 'My dear Robert, I brought her to London because you are almost thirty and she has been the only woman you have ever raised your eyes from your studies long enough to notice.'

'Of course I noticed her. It would be hard not to, she's very pretty,' Robert said. Mrs Munroe caught then same tight tone as before.

'I am glad you think so. She is the right age and social status, and she is the apple of her father's eye. He will not stint at spending whatever is necessary to keep her happy. She is a fine young woman and would make you the perfect wife.

Don't you think?'

For all her religious scruples, Mrs Munroe was not blind to the advantages of having Caroline Sinclair as a daughter-in-law. It was not only her father's largesse that would benefit Robert, but a pretty wife to care for might persuade him to reside in a more suitable neighbourhood. Goodness knows there wasn't anyone with more of a heart for the poor than herself, but that didn't mean challenging God's ordering of society and making them your neighbours.

Robert didn't answer. He just stared at a point above her head. 'Robert!'

'Mama?'

'I was saying that Caroline would make a perfect wife for you.'

'I agree.'

He didn't sound as if he did and she had her reservations. Caroline Sinclair was pretty enough, with the charm of youth, but she was rather flighty. Before Robert began paying attention to Caroline, she had tried to steer him towards the Smyth sisters, both of whom were accomplished, if a little plain. But she couldn't blame him for being attracted to Caroline. After all, even the most serious and scholarly man is still a man.

'She will be a great help to you in London society. Her mother might not have taught her much, but she has imparted to her the rudiments of being a hostess. She would be quite capable of holding soirees and the like and inviting men of influence.'

'I think you are forgetting that I practise in East London,' he told her. 'There are very few men of influence there.'

Just like Robert to look for obstacles, thought Mrs Munroe. She gave him the same look she had given him at twelve years old when she found him dissecting rats in the summer house.

'You will, however, need to show her a masterful hand because of her tender age. Your father agrees with me wholeheartedly that you should get on with matters. You know how he hates indecisiveness.' She pursed her lips together. 'In short, Robert, if you don't make her an offer soon some other man with his wits about him will.' She fixed him with a steely gaze. 'I am sure your outgoings are considerable in London.'

'I live modestly in my two rooms at the hospital, and have been appointed the chairman of the Parish Emergency Committee,' he replied. 'There is no need for me to rush into marriage. Besides, Caroline has already told me in her letters that she has no desire to settle in London,' he said, stretching out his arm across the back of the chair.

Irritation started to bubble within her. What on earth was the matter with him? Any man in his position, with a limited income, would run Caroline down the aisle. She was not going to leave London without ensuring that Robert secured the young woman – and her father's fortune. She drew in a deep breath.

'Even so, marriage to Caroline would allow–' she stopped mid-sentence as the door opened and the subject of their conversation glided into the room, followed by a hotel porter struggling with a variety of boxes. She spotted Robert and made her way towards him. 'Doctor Munroe,' she said, executing a perfectly balanced curtsy.

Robert bowed and Mrs Munroe was gratified to see his expression soften. 'Miss Sinclair. What a pleasure to see you.'

Mrs Munroe patted the seat next to her. 'Come and sit by me, Caroline. I am sure you are eager to hear all about Robert's important work amongst the poor. He is well thought of even in government circles.'

Caroline did as she was bid and sat on the edge of the sofa. Carefully she arranged her skirt around her legs and assumed a polite expression of interest.

Robert started to tell them about the hospital and his work there. His mother listened avidly, but it all seemed very familiar. She had heard much the same from the ministers working among the dregs of humanity in Edinburgh's Old Town. Of course, as a doctor, Robert wasn't as much concerned with the moral wellbeing of the poor as she was and was apt to make excuses for their idleness. Caroline was evidently less engrossed by Robert's tale. Several times Mrs Munroe caught the young woman out of the corner of her eye stifling a yawn. Each time she blinked to stop the stretching of her face and gave Robert the sweetest smile, but thankfully he didn't seem to notice.

She sent Caroline a stern look, but the girl didn't see it because she was gazing out of the window.

'Is that not interesting, Caroline?' Caroline gracefully turned her head and her face grew attentive again. 'What do you think of Robert's ideas on illness?'

Robert looked at the young woman sitting beside his mother. Studying him for a few moments while Caroline collected her thoughts, Mrs Munroe noticed a tension in him. She had the impression that he was doing what was expected, but that his attention was elsewhere. Then it occurred to her that he had been much the same since he had arrived. There was something that she couldn't quite put her finger on.

Caroline's finely arched eyebrows drew together just enough to indicate thoughtfulness but not so much as to wrinkle her forehead. 'Robert knows I am always amazed at his understanding of such complex things. But' – she sighed, and smiled adoringly at him – 'you expect too much of our sex if you think us able to understand such things.'

Mrs Munroe snorted. 'What nonsense. Women are perfectly able to understand such things, if they put their minds to it,' she said. 'Don't you agree, Robert?'

'I do.'

Caroline gave a tinkling laugh. 'Oh really, you do tease. I doubt you could find one woman who could understand all the things you find so fascinating.'

'I already have, a Mrs O'Casey,' Robert replied. 'I explained all my experiments in detail and she understood perfectly.'

There was that tone again, but even stronger this time. Several questions fired themselves into Mrs Munroe's mind, but Caroline asked the most pressing one.

'Who is Mrs O'Casey?' Caroline's voice was conversational but Mrs Munroe heard an underlying sharpness. Caroline was suddenly taking a keener interest in Robert's work.

'Just a widow who came to the hospital a few days ago to thank me,' he said casually, but there was a new alertness in his expression. Mrs Munroe scrutinised her son more closely.

'Thank you?' Caroline asked. 'For what?'

'For caring for her daughter and a close friend. She took an interest in the laboratory and I showed her around,' he explained in a matter-of-fact tone. Caroline was appeased, Mrs Munroe was not. Robert hadn't lied but there was more to be said, and it occurred to her that it might not be something that Caroline needed to hear.

'Caroline has joined the Society for the Moral Improvement of Distressed Women,' she said, steering the conversation into safer waters. Whoever Mrs O'Casey was, she warranted no further consideration.

Robert's eyebrows shot upwards. He might well look surprised. It had taken her a month of cajoling to get Caroline to agree. She hoped that socialising with women whose thoughts weren't only about lace and silk would help her improve her mind.

'I have.' Caroline lowered her eyes, then swept them up flirtatiously at Robert. A dimple appeared on her left cheek. 'I am going to the next meeting, aren't I?' She looked to Mrs Munroe, who nodded, keeping her eyes on her son. Caroline started to pluck absentmindedly at the fabric of her dress. 'I must confess, I don't know much about it all.' Her face grew very serious. 'But I think that if we had a subscription ball we could raise money to help the poor.'

At that moment Mrs Munroe knew that, whatever she did, her quest to develop Caroline's social sensibilities was doomed. Although she might have wished that Robert had entered a more lucrative and prestigious occupation than medicine, he was a gifted doctor and the right wife could make him a rich one.

There was no denying that on all counts Caroline had the right attributes that Robert needed in a wife – but!

There was a knock on the door and the hotel valet entered. Moving silently over the carpet he handed her a note on a silver tray, bowed and left the room. She opened it, looked at the lines she had scribbled that morning and frowned. She rose to her feet.

'It's from Lord Effingham,' she said, sending up a silent prayer for forgiveness. 'I will have to answer it immediately.' Robert rose to his feet, but she waved at him. 'Sit, Robert, and keep Caroline company. Manners will chaperone.'

She caught her maid's eye, and Manners picked up a book and settled herself in the far corner of the room.

'Will you dine with us on Monday?' she asked Robert as she leant towards him.

'Of course,' he replied, kissing her again on the cheek.

Taking up the bogus letter she let Robert take her place on the sofa. As she left the room she sent another fervent prayer heavenward asking that Robert might take the opportunity given him and do what was expected of him.

As his mother left the room Robert cursed Lord Effingham's letter.

Beside him Caroline rustled and gave him a shy look. 'How fortunate that Lord Effingham's letter needed immediate attention.'

Robert smiled. 'Just so.'

And it was. There, gazing up at him with breathless admiration, was Edinburgh's foremost beauty. Her pale lilac ensemble with delicate pearls and bead embroidery scattered over it highlighted her hazel eyes. As she looked at him, her small red mouth was pulled together as if waiting for a kiss. She looked absolutely lovely.

Whatever madness had possessed him to put off making an offer to her? It was his unhealthy obsession with Ellen O'Casey, of course, he knew that. But now he *had* to put that aside.

His mother was right. Caroline was everything a man with a position in life could want in a wife. True, she was, as his mother so quaintly put it, excitable and frivolous, but he was sure that was nothing more than youthful enthusiasm. It was to be expected. She had led a sheltered life, as was proper for a gently born woman.

Robert gave Caroline the warmest smile he could muster. She fidgeted, and the springy brown ringlets at the crown of her head bounced. A vision of Ellen's dark auburn hair curling around her neck flashed into Robert's mind. He shoved it aside and concentrated on his prospective fiancée.

'I was so pleased that you decided to come to London with Mother.' He half moved to take hold of her hand but stopped.

What would be so terrible, he thought. After all, there was an expectation that they would soon become engaged. It had been the talk of Edinburgh throughout the winter.

Marry Caroline. Robert felt his heart start to thunder in his chest. That was why he'd come here after all. To propose.

With a quick look at the redoubtable Manners at the end of the room he took hold of Caroline's hand. She smiled up at him, but there was an emptiness in her gaze that quite suddenly irritated him.

'Caroline.' She gazed up at him expectantly. He started again. 'Caroline, I ... I wish you could be a little more interested in my work.'

She looked disgruntled, as well she might. A young woman anticipating a proposal of marriage didn't expect to be quizzed about her attitude towards her future husband's career. Her eyebrows pulled together.

'I don't think your mother left us alone so you could talk about your work,' she said, her lower lip jutting out.

'I just want to know why it is so difficult for you to take an interest in what I do,' he persisted. A picture of Ellen listening as he explained his experiments sprang into his mind.

'I am very proud of you and your work but I just don't find it as enthralling as you do.' She gave him an apologetic smile. 'I'm sorry.'

And she was. He could see it in her eyes. Caroline was truly sorry, but there was nothing she could do about it. A chasm opened at Robert's feet. A pretty chasm, but a chasm nonetheless.

144

Her eyes narrowed. 'It's that widow woman, isn't it?'

Caroline might not understand logical science but she certainly understood her instincts.

'I—'

'What's her name? O' something?' she asked through tight lips.

'Mrs O'Casey,' he answered and wished he hadn't. The sound of Ellen's name fell like a stone between them and was totally out of place in the plush hotel room. Ellen belonged in his other life, his real life. Not in this lavish chamber with Caroline's Bond Street purchases stacked up in the corner, but in the life of hollow-eyed children with rickets and women, not yet out of their twenties, wasted and old before their time. His eyes fell on the pile of brightly coloured boxes. What she had spent that morning on frippery could keep a street in Wapping for a year and probably longer.

Caroline shuffled away from him and folded her arms. 'What is Mrs O'Casey to you?'

It was a fair question. What exactly was Ellen O'Casey to him? The answer had to be 'Nothing.' What else could it be?

'I told you she was a widow whose child I tended to.' He took Caroline's hand again. 'That's all,' he said, as much to convince himself as her. 'Now let's forget about her.'

Caroline regarded him for a long moment and then started to talk about her shopping trip and the most recent assembly ball, and his mind drifted off into a world of its own. Ellen came back to him. Ellen singing, Ellen talking and laughing, Ellen giving him a roasting. Caroline's voice drew his conscious mind reluctantly back from its pleasant wandering.

'And I told Ruth Dalrymple that you would be back in Edinburgh before the summer was out.'

She smiled up at him, waiting for him to agree. He tried, but he couldn't. People, not only in London, but in Edinburgh and other large towns, lived like animals, in filth, starvation and poverty and all she could do was propose a ball to raise charity money. As he had said to Danny Donovan, the poor didn't need charity, they needed a decent place to live and food to eat. But Caroline would never see that. Trying to open her eyes to the suffering of others was a lost cause. And so was this courtship.

Sitting next to Caroline watching her refined prettiness he realised that he felt absolutely nothing. No expansion in his chest at the sight of her, no stirring in his loins, no quickening of his pulse – nothing beyond an appreciation of her prettiness. Even holding her hand was barely registering with his senses.

Until he spoke Ellen's name out loud he had been quite willing to marry Caroline because it was the sensible and expected thing to do. But not now.

He eyed the large French clock on the mantelshelf.

'I fear it is time for me to leave,' he said, disengaging his hand from hers. She looked extremely vexed. He didn't blame her. He had given her every indication that he was about to propose and had not done so.

'But you have only been here half an hour,' she

146

said, thrusting her clasped hands into her lap.

He managed a regretful smile. 'I'm sorry.' He stood up and so did Caroline.

'You're not angry with me, are you?' she asked in a little forlorn voice.

'No, I'm not,' he said truthfully. He wasn't. How could he be? It wasn't Caroline's fault that she wasn't Ellen. He bowed.

'Miss Sinclair.'

She must have heard the sincerity in his voice because she brightened a little. 'It's been a pleasure to see you, Doctor Munroe. I look forward to dinner with you on Monday.' She sent him a sideways glance that caused a dimple to form at the corner of her mouth. 'Maybe your mother will have another letter from Lord Effingham that will require her immediate attention.'

Robert didn't answer, just bowed again, collected his hat from the table and left.

Eleven

Josie jumped up and down as she held Ellen's arm. They had been up early that morning and packed a small lunch, then walked the best part of three miles until they reached a small field just by Bow church where the annual May fair was in full swing.

Around them flapped the brightly coloured awnings of stalls and booths, all of which had vendors vying for the attention of passers-by.

There were wonders abounding to entice the visitors to part with their hard-earned pennies. Ellen and Josie stopped to watch some swarthy-looking men and sloe-eyed women tumble and leap in the air while, high above them on a suspended rope, a diminutive young woman in a scanty costume walked back and forth.

Ellen smiled as her daughter stood in wide-eyed wonder. 'She'll need a good bone-setter if she falls,' observed Josie and set Ellen off on a train of thought that she tried to stay away from as much as she could.

Since the day she had visited Doctor Munroe at the hospital and he had apologised for his behaviour she had tried to avoid him, mainly for her own peace of mind. But as if fate knew her intention, she kept running into him. Thankfully, this was mostly in the street so she could get away with a hurried acknowledgement that only disturbed her for about an hour, but from time to time he came into the Angel for supper. On every occasion she found him looking at her with an intense gaze that seeped into her heart and soul.

He has a fiancée, she told herself, as Josie sped over to buy an aniseed twist from a candy booth. *What else would this Miss Sinclair be? After all, she had travelled to London with the doctor's mother.*

Josie was on her way back, dodging a clown on stilts who had a small dog in a ruff hopping on its back legs between the long poles.

'This is such fun. It's a pity that Gran couldn't come,' Josie said, sucking on the twisted cane in her hand.

I think she will be better for a day's rest,' Ellen

148

said, careful not to let Josie see her concern. Bridget's breathlessness was becoming worse and the cough that was never far away had come back with a vengeance after she was caught in the rain.

Josie looked above Ellen's head and dropped a small curtsy.

'Doctor Munroe,' Josie said.

The flesh at the back of Ellen's neck tingled. She turned slowly round to find herself looking directly into Robert Munroe's dark eyes.

He took her hand and bowed respectfully. 'I can't tell you what a pleasure it is to see you, Mrs O'Casey. That cream gown suits your colouring perfectly.' He turned to Josie. 'And Miss Josie O'Casey. I see you're fully recovered from the quinsy. How is Waisey?'

'I am well, thank you, Doctor, and Waisey, well, she is at home looking after Gran,' she said. Ellen saw the beginning of a simper as Josie fluttered her eyelashes at him.

'Are you enjoying the fair?' he asked, still looking at Josie, but stepping closer to Ellen.

While his attention was on Josie, Ellen let her eyes enjoy the sight of Doctor Munroe's features. Although his hair was light brown with the occasional blond streak, the bristles of his beard were dark, just visible even though he must have shaved not five hours ago.

'Isn't it, Ma?' Josie's voice filtered through her thoughts.

'I'm sorry, Josie, my mind was elsewhere. What did you say?'

'I said the fair is better than last year,' Josie replied as Ellen tore her eyes away from the man

149

beside her and back to her daughter.

'Oh, yes ... yes, there are more – er – booths, and the acrobats are certainly finer,' Ellen said, conscious that Doctor Munroe was staring at her with an unsettling expression in his eyes.

'May I accompany you in your enjoyment of the fair?' Robert asked, as he held his arm out for Ellen.

'Are you alone?' Ellen asked.

'I came with Chafford and Maltravers, but they have gone off to see the All-Comers' fight.' With a wry smile, he added, 'You'd think a surgeon would see enough blood and broken teeth in the usual way of things without looking for it on his day off.'

Ellen's head warned her not to let down her carefully built defences, but her heart didn't listen. That look and that smile washing over her were too much. She laughed and laid her hand on his arm.

They walked on, stopping at a booth which invited people to throw a wooden ball at a stand full of plates for a prize. Josie had a couple of throws that wobbled a plate or two, but did no real damage. Then Doctor Munroe took three balls and sent the plates crashing to the ground, earning Josie a length of pink ribbon.

'Did Gran take you to the fair, Ma, when you were a child?' Josie asked, as they watched a juggler in a garish costume toss clubs in the air.

'That she did. Every May Day we would be off to Munster town for the largest fair in the county. Me, me Mammy and Pappy, along with Joe and Sean,' Ellen said aware that Robert was listening as intently as Josie.

'You were born in Ireland?' he asked.

'I was. We all were. Joe was first, then Marie who died when she was four,' Ellen explained, 'then Sean, and lastly me. We came to London when I was seven.'

'Were the fairs like this one, Ma?' Josie asked, as they stopped in front of a booth selling lace-covered buttons and other lacy trimmings.

Ellen smiled, remembering. 'In some ways. There were tinkers and peddlers, just like here, but there were more cattle as it was a market too. We would be up before the sun was in the sky to be scrubbed and dressed in our best clothes for the fair. Mammy would comb and braid my hair so tight it would hurt.' Robert seemed enthralled by her reminiscence, and wondered if he had ever been to a fair when he was a boy in Scotland. 'Me, Joe and Sean had to squeeze in the back of a dog cart pulled by our old donkey, while Mammy and Pappy rode on the board in front. Pappy would always take his fiddle and join the men in the pub, singing and playing songs that were old when Moses was a boy.'

'It is from your father that you must get your ear for music, Mrs O'Casey?' Doctor Munroe asked.

'I would say so, and some of the old songs I now sing,' she said, thinking of the man who sat her on his knee and traced the words in their old family Bible with his finger. 'It's a pity I don't have his saintly patience as well.'

'A grand day, is it not, Mrs O'Casey?' a youthful voice said from behind them. Ellen turned to find Patrick Nolan twisting his cap in his hand.

151

The brawny young lad was smiling at Josie and she was smiling back. 'And that Miss Josie looks as sweet as a flower in a Kerry meadow.'

Josie lowered her eyes and stared at her hands.

'How's your mother, Pat?' Ellen asked, noting that Robert was watching the two young people with barely suppressed amusement.

'She's grand, so she is, Mrs O,' Patrick answered, his eyes still glued to Josie. 'Would you like to see the mermaid, Josie?'

'Can I, Ma?' Josie asked.

'I don't know. You might get lost.'

Josie looked dismayed.

'I'm sure this young lad will take care of Miss O'Casey,' Robert said, and earned a look of pure hero worship from Patrick.

'Say yes, Ma, pleeeese,' Josie implored, holding on to Ellen's hands and bobbing up and down.

Why not?

'Oh, very well, but see she comes to no harm, Patrick Nolan, or you'll have me to answer to,' Ellen said sternly.

'Don't you worry, Mrs O, I'll guard her like me own,' Patrick shouted over his shoulder.

'What are you laughing at, Doctor Munroe?' Ellen said, turning on him with a stern expression.

'You, Mrs O'Casey,' he said, still smiling at her. 'She's only gone to see a mermaid, not to the other side of the globe. Let me buy you a lemonade.'

He led her over to the trestle table where various cool drinks, such as soda water, ginger beer and homebrew were being offered. She should have been annoyed with him for interfering, but instead she found she was glad that Josie had gone with Patrick because now she had him to herself.

He found them a couple of chairs and they sat down across the way from the striped puppet booth of the Punch and Judy. They sipped their lemonade and the curtain opened for the show, Punch appearing with his big stick.

'I'm sure young Patrick will look after Josie,' Robert said, giving her a reassuring smile. 'He seems an amiable type of fellow.'

Punch's wife appeared with the baby in her arms and a sad smile crept across Ellen's face. She turned to Robert. 'They all are 'til they wed.'

Robert heard the echo of the past in Ellen O'Casey's voice as she softly answered him. Behind her, Punch felled his puppet wife with his stick and the children sitting on the grass roared. Robert moved nearer to her.

He had argued strenuously with William and Maltravers when they had dragged him from his rooms that morning, saying that he had a report for the Emergency Committee to complete. They would have none of it, saying he would turn into a very dull egg and it was their duty as gentlemen to take him to the fair in Bow.

Now he was glad that they had ignored his protestations and insisted on him accompanying them. He had been enjoying the sights and sounds of the fair alone when he spotted Ellen. He had stood leaning against a tent pole for some time just watching her as she walked through the holiday throng. He loved every minute of it. Watching her laughing in the spring sunshine, all

153

of the battles that had raged in him from the moment he had seen Ellen were over.

He realised that his own heart had stopped him from the folly of proposing to Caroline. How could he have been so blind? With a sudden clarity of vision Robert knew that he loved Ellen. He didn't know how or why, or what he could actually do about it, if anything, but he did know that he would never be able to pay court to another while she filled his thoughts. No argument about society, profession, class or suitability came into it. He was captivated by her and couldn't escape. And now he wasn't even sure he wanted to.

'I'm sure that Pat Nolan is no worse than any other young lad,' Ellen said, a hint of bitterness in her tone, her eyes still fixed on the Punch and Judy booth where the devil had made his entrance. 'He is no worse than Michael O'Casey when I first laid eyes on him.'

Dozens of questions spun around in Robert's mind. What was this Michael like? How did he die? What kind of husband was he? Had she loved him? Did she love him still?

'I hear you've been busy looking into drains and sewers in the neighbourhood,' Ellen said, changing the subject before he could ask any of them. He raised an eyebrow in surprise. 'There are no secrets in these streets, Doctor Munroe. I'm forever hearing about the handsome doctor who's inspecting the water pumps in Ratcliffe Highway.' She gave him a flirtatious smile that sent Robert's heart racing.

He stood up and straightened the front of his waistcoat. 'Handsome, you say?' he said, with an

154

exaggerated swell of his chest.

'I do not,' she replied, raising her eyebrows, 'I merely repeat others' opinions.' Despite Ellen's disdainful reply Robert could see that the warmth in her eyes belied her words.

'Well, your sources are only half correct, because it's not just drains I'm looking into but also the repair and provision of housing and sanitary conditions.' He stopped and a frown crossed his face. 'Although the Board's findings were only just beginning to be analysed, I can already see' – he stopped.

Ellen put her tumbler down and stood up next to him. He felt the light pressure of her hand on his arm as she pulled him to face her. 'What is it?'

He gave her half a smile. 'I'm sorry,' he said, as they moved on, stopping under the shade of a plane tree at the edge of the fair. 'It is as Chafford said. I *am* turning into a dull egg if on a day such as today and in the company of such a beautiful woman I am talking about sewers and drains.'

Ellen laughed. It was a deep throaty laugh. He took a step nearer to her, took hold of her hand and brought it to his lips, kissing it hard. Then, looking deep into Ellen's eyes, he dropped his voice a tone.

'With you to myself, I should be talking of flowers and love, not drainage and sewers,' he said, as her eyes widened, and Robert caught an unmistakable flash of desire as she ran her glance over his face in an unhurried fashion, taking in every line.

'Ellen,' he said, as he drew her to him. She didn't move away but continued gazing up at him

155

with the assured look of a woman who knows she is desired. Her thumb caressed his knuckles.

'Beautiful, you say, Doctor Munroe?' she asked as he leant over her.

He wanted to kiss her.

'Beautiful, *I* do say,' he replied, in a low, resonant tone.

'Ma, there you are,' Josie's voice came between them. 'I've been looking an age for you.' Robert felt Ellen tense and push him away. He cursed silently.

Although he was actually quite fond of Ellen's bubbly daughter, at that moment he could have wished Josie anywhere else on earth but at the Bow fair. Couldn't Patrick Nolan find some other curiosity to keep the girl occupied for a minute or two longer?

He dropped his arms to his sides and turned to face the two young people coming towards them. Josie was hanging onto Patrick's arm and the young man looked as if he had found the crock of gold at the end of an Irish rainbow.

'Here she is, Mrs O,' Patrick said to Ellen, giving her a speculative look. 'All safe and sound.'

'Er – thank you, Patrick,' Ellen said, giving the young man a melting smile. Robert saw Patrick's surprise.

'Have you got something in your eye?' Josie asked as she looked into Ellen's flushed face.

'No,' Ellen said, putting her hand to the bun at the nape of her neck and patting it in place. 'Whatever makes you think that, child?'

'Just the way Doctor Munroe was standing over you. It seemed as if he was looking into your eye,'

Josie said with a shrug. Patrick covered his mouth and forced a dry cough.

Ellen's back snapped upright and she patted her hair again. Swinging out the folds of her skirts she cleared her throat. 'Doctor Munroe was just ... looking to ... that is to say...' She took a smart step forward. 'Shall we walk on then?'

It wasn't often that Josie got the better of her mother, but today at the fair would rank as one of her most memorable victories. She almost laughed out loud at her ma's confusion. It was clear as the nose on her face that Doctor Munroe was extremely interested in her mother.

As they walked towards the Hall of a Thousand Mysteries she felt Patrick take her arm and they fell in step behind her mother and the doctor.

'There's a thing and no mistake,' he said to her out of the corner of his mouth. 'Your ma and Doctor Munroe canoodling with each other.' He was grinning from ear to ear.

He put his arm around Josie's waist and pulled her to him. 'She wouldn't be able to tick you off for having me as your fella.' He pursed his lips and leant towards her.

She shoved him aside roughly but sent him a saucy smile. He blew a silent kiss into the air and she felt her cheeks grow hot.

'Who says you're my fella?'

'I guessed I was from the way you were kissing me behind the refreshment tent.'

'Shh. Do you want to be getting me an ear-bashing, Patrick Nolan?' She cast an anxious glance at her mother's back but there was no danger of

Ellen overhearing them. She was engrossed in something Doctor Munroe was telling her.

Josie's gaze fixed on Doctor Munroe. He looked just right standing next to her mother, their heads bent towards each other. She'd liked him on their first meeting. He wasn't stuffy like old Doctor Crichton, who used to own the surgery. Not that she'd seen him often because the elderly doctor was most particular about his sixpence fee, and he had been gruff with her and smelt of drink.

Doctor Munroe was quite the opposite. He didn't take his handkerchief out and hold it to his nose as he entered her room or jab her painfully during his examination. For that alone she'd liked him, but when he had laughed at her mention of Waisy, he went to the top of her list of nice people along with Ma, Gran and, of course, Patrick. And she knew about poor Kitty and how it had been Doctor Munroe who had eased her last hours.

'I don't think yer ma could have you by the ear, not with Doctor Munroe wanting to be stepping out with her,' Patrick countered, tucking his thumbs in the arms of his waistcoat.

'Ma's not interested in getting herself a fella,' Josie told him, remembering her previous conversation with her mother on the subject.

'It doesn't look that way to me,' Patrick said, cocking his head to where Ellen and Robert stood, supposedly enjoying the antics of a troupe of dancing dogs, but in fact gazing intensely at each other.

Patrick stepped aside to greet a friend for a moment, leaving Josie studying Robert more closely.

He was old of course, probably almost thirty, just a little older than her mother, but he still had a full head of light-brown hair. Not like Tubby Fenton, the cat's-meat man, who was as bald as an egg, although he was only just twenty. And Doctor Munroe caught your eye. Not in a flash way like Patrick, who liked to puff his chest out and wear his cap as if it was about to slide off his head, but he had a way of moving and standing that made you stop and look. In fact he was quite handsome in a serious, grown-up sort of way, and Josie could see why her mother was taken with him.

But what if Ma did step out with Doctor Munroe? What would Gran say? Josie gave a little laugh. Gran wouldn't say a thing. She often said how Ma deserved a better life, and marriage to Doctor Munroe would certainly give her that. A warm glow spread over Josie. It was just like one of those stories in the books Ma read about a handsome prince sweeping a young girl off her feet. Well, the doctor wasn't a prince and her ma wasn't a young girl, but it was the same anyhow.

'Mrs O,' Patrick said, as he rejoined Josie. Her mother turned and so did Doctor Munroe.

'The strong man is starting his act in a few moments. Can I take Josie to see?' he asked, taking hold of Josie's arm in a proprietary manner. Josie held her breath and waited for her mother's reaction to Patrick's boldness.

To her total surprise her mother didn't seem to notice. She just smiled at them then turned her face up to the man beside her.

'If Patrick takes Josie to the sideshow, would you mind keeping me company for another turn around the fair, Doctor Munroe?' she asked, looking up at him teasingly.

Josie's mouth fell open.

Doctor Munroe's mouth lifted at one corner. 'I can think of nothing on earth that would give me greater pleasure,' he said in a low tone, not taking his eyes off her mother's face.

What would it be like to have a stepfather? She wondered, then felt Patrick pull at her arm.

'Come on, Josie, if we run we'll get front seats,' he said as she turned towards him. Just as the crowd surrounded them, Josie turned her head and saw Doctor Munroe put out his arm and her mother curl hers around it.

Twelve

Robert looked around the well-dressed men of various backgrounds who sat at the large polished oak table in the doctors' mess of the hospital. A couple were medical men like himself; others were clergy of both the established and the free churches, along with a philanthropic merchant or two from the City.

'I take it, gentlemen, you agree that my report into the condition in the Whitechapel workhouse should be sent with all speed to the Home Secretary,' Robert said, raising a sheaf of bound papers. All around the table murmured their assent.

Robert moved on. 'And we also agree that the two houses that back onto Vinegar Lane should be acquired and set up as the parish cholera hospital.' The company nodded. 'And that I should arrange to be equipped, as I have specified, care for sixteen cholera victims at the parish's expense?'

'Yes, but on the understanding that only those who can call on parish relief or who are already a charge on the parish can be admitted to the hospital,' Murphy, the verger from St George's and drinking companion of Danny Donovan, said.

Again all heads agreed.

'Good. Now I have your agreement on the funds for the project, I can assure you that it will be ready for its first patient by the end of the month.' Robert looked around the table and drew in a breath. 'Now to the last item of business today: the enforcement order against St George's Parish Council for failing to repair the drains in Chapman Street and the surrounding area. The order to include allowing the accumulation of foul and noxious rubbish in the streets of the parish, and' – he could see a number of his fellow committee members shifting in their seats – 'for the failure, after many requests, to fix the water pumps in Upper Chapman Street, Upper St James Street, the south pump in Cannon Street by the toll booth and Fenton Street and the two in Back Church Lane, to the detriment of the many persons who have to draw their water from these pumps.'

There was a low buzz in the room and Captain Merton, senior superintendent of the East India Company in Wapping and St Katharine's Dock, cleared his throat.

'While I and my fellow members applaud your

efforts and diligence in the way you have high-lighted the serious health problems of the area, I … that is…' He looked around him for support and six or so members urged him to speak. 'That is … you don't think we are being too hasty? Shouldn't we wait for further direction from the government?'

Robert's brow lowered. 'We act with *haste* because cholera does.'

'But to act with such force against the parish council and its officers is tantamount to saying they are negligent,' Murphy said, pulling a colourful handkerchief from his top pocket and wiping his damp forehead.

Robert folded his arms and regarded the company with a steady eye. 'The parish council of St George's in the east has been asked on three occasions in the past year to effect these repairs and nothing, nothing, has been done.'

'But there are certain interests in the parish that will take exception to this,' Mr Ridley from the Worshipful Company of Drapers said, and several heads nodded vigorously in agreement.

'It is such *interests* that have let the situation become such as we find it now. Workhouses full of mattresses with no straw, accommodating starved, whey-faced men and women. A children's wing with double the death rate of even the poorest streets of the area, and the whole place infested with rats and fleas.'

'Even so, seven pumps–' started Ridley, but Robert cut across him.

'The pumps in question are by no means the only ones in need of attention. I count on your support in this matter or else I will take a vote against these measures as a vote of no confidence in my chairing of this board.'

'I agree with the enforcement order,' Mr Cooper, the elderly Quaker minister, said. 'It is no more than our Christian duty.'

Robert gave him a small nod of thanks.

There was a silence. Then Murphy spoke again. 'We have no quarrel with your chairmanship of the board, Doctor Munroe, and,' he looked around at the table and a number gave him a quick nod, 'we will support the enforcement order.'

'Thank you, gentlemen,' Robert said, tapping his papers into a neat set on the table. 'Our next meeting will be on 25th June at the same time. I wish you a good day.'

Members left and Mr Cooper made his way along the side of the table towards Robert.

The clergyman extended his hand. 'Well done, Doctor Munroe.' Robert took the minister's hand and was surprised by his strong grasp.

'Can I offer you some refreshment in my rooms, Mr Cooper, before you walk back to Wellclose Square?' Robert asked.

After Bulmer had furnished them with two cups of steaming tea and a couple of small cakes, Mr Cooper gave Robert a considered look.

'You know, of course, that Danny Donovan won't like being forced to dip into the parish purse to carry out the committee's order,' he said, picking up a slice of cherry cake from the neatly laid tray on the table.

'I guessed as much,' Robert said. 'Donovan has his hands deep in the parish finances.'

163

'But some work has been done. The pump and houses in Anchor and Hope passage have been repaired,' Cooper said.

Robert put his cup down with a clatter. 'I have it on good authority that although Cashman & Sons were paid by the parish to fix the Anchor and Hope dwellings, it was Donovan's navvies who originally got the money, although no work was done. It was only after I visited the area that Cashman's men hurried down there with picks and shovels. Even now, I'm not impressed with the so-called repairs.'

'Can you prove that?' the older man asked, crossing his legs and sinking further back into the studded leather armchair.

'No, and we both know why. Even the committee was reluctant to cross Donovan. If they, the rich and influential of the area, are afraid of him how much more so are the vulnerable poor?'

Mr Cooper nodded. 'Danny Donovan is a villain of the worst kind.'

Robert gave a hard laugh. 'He is, but until today I didn't fully appreciate just how far his threatening shadow fell.'

'Inspector Jackson at Wapping Police Station, is trying to gather evidence of Donovan's illegal activities.'

'I'll have to pay Inspector Jackson a visit,' Robert said. Kitty Henry came to his mind. 'What do you know of a woman called Old Annie?'

'If it's the same Old Annie that I know, she lives around the corner from the mission in Dock Street. She minds children for some of the prostitutes. Why do you ask?'

'I have had two women in the last month come to me with botched abortions. One we managed to save, the other was not so fortunate.'

'You think it was Old Annie.'

Robert nodded. 'I have heard the name whispered but I am not sure. Inspector Jackson may know more.'

'I thank God for you, Doctor Munroe.' The older man leant forward and looked earnestly at Robert. 'You are the only person, so far, to challenge the corruption in the streets and alleys of the East End. If the poor souls whom we care for in our respective professions are ever to be set free from the squalor they live in, they will need men like you to stand up for their principles and beliefs.' He stood up and retrieved his hat. 'Now I must go. Thank you for my tea, and if you ever need my help in anything you know where to find me.'

When her turn came, Ellen took her place at the beech table and pulled out a small pouch from under her skirt. Josie came and stood next to her. Mr Armond, the vicar of Christ Church Spitalfields, ran his finger down the names in the ledger.

'How much this week?'

Ellen handed over three shillings and with a steady hand Mr Armond wrote the amount next to her name.

'A goodly sum,' he said beaming at her over his half-rimmed spectacles.

It was the weavers who had first set up the penny bank in the church into which Ellen was now depositing her hard-earned shillings, but the area their industry had once made prosperous was now a rookery of destitution.

Mr Almond leant over the table. 'You'll soon have your passage money,' he whispered. Ellen looked furtively around. 'Don't worry, my dear, I'll not tell a soul.'

Although a few people knew that she planned to take passage to New York, she didn't want it to become common knowledge – not that she really minded who knew as long as it was kept from Danny Donovan.

'Thank you,' Ellen said to the kindly Reverend and turned to leave. Josie waved to Sarah Nolan, Patrick's mother, who had just arrived. Ellen retied her bonnet.

'Sarah,' she said, embracing her long-time friend.

'And a good morning to you, Ellen, and to you, Josie,' Sarah said, leaving Ellen's embrace and looking Josie up and down. 'Why, as I live and breathe, my Pat said you were turning into a pretty young woman, Josie, but he told only half of it. You have the look of your mother about you and that's no bad thing, I'll tell you.' Josie blushed and looked at her feet. 'You'll make some man a good wife someday soon I'm sure,' she said crossing her arms over her substantial bosom and looking at Ellen. 'My Pat's got his own cart and rounds now, Ellen,' she said slowly.

'I thought he wanted to take up with the ships?' Josie said.

Sarah waved away the statement. 'A boy's dream, no more. Having your own dray round with the taverns is where the money is, not slipping about in the mid-Atlantic in all weathers.'

'But he said only last week th–'

Josie saw Patrick Nolan last week?

Josie waited for her mother to speak for the whole length of Wentworth Street. Ellen said nothing, but as they passed the Aldgate Pump and the Saracen's Head coaching inn she cleared her throat.

'You didn't mention that you saw Patrick Nolan last week,' she said, in a matter-of-fact voice.

It was too much to hope for that her mother had missed her slip of the tongue. She shot Ellen a sharp look. It wasn't fair. She would be fourteen in August and there were lots of girls her age with special fellas.

'Didn't I?' Josie said, hoping she sounded uninterested. 'I met him on the way back from school. He ... he gave me a ride home on his cart.'

'Did he?' Ellen said, tight-lipped.

'There is nothing wrong with Pat Nolan, Ma,' Josie said, her bottom lip jutting out.

In fact there was everything right about him, with his dark curly hair and ready smile. There was many a girl down the highway mad to have him single her out as he had Josie. There was nothing wrong with him at all. She fixed her mother with a challenging stare.

'No, he is a fine boy,' Ellen conceded. 'Patrick is a credit to Sarah. It's just that you're too young to be thinking of young men in that way.'

'Ma, I met Patrick on the way home. There is nothing wrong in that, is there?'

'No, but–'

167

'The same as there's nothing wrong with your meeting Doctor Munroe when you're out walking, is there?'

Her mother's cheeks flushed crimson and that told Josie a great deal.

'Of course not,' Ellen said, not meeting her gaze.

Josie really didn't want to lie to her mother but she didn't want to stop meeting Patrick either. She waited.

'Patrick Nolan is a great deal better than most of the young men around here. He's seldom out of work, turning his hand to most things to put money on the table. I suppose if you have to be sweet on a young man, Josie, you could pick a lot worse than him,' Ellen conceded with a sigh.

A huge weight of guilt lifted off Josie's shoulders.

Josie threw herself at her mother and hugged her around the neck planting a noisy kiss on her cheek. Ellen hugged her back, and then set her back on her feet. Her face grew stern.

'You can tell Patrick that he can meet you from school, but he must bring you straight home. You've been brought up properly and he had better respect that or I'll be after him,' Ellen told her. Josie hugged her mother again until Ellen protested that she couldn't catch her breath.

'He will. We just hold hands.' Well, that was just a tiny lie, but the odd kiss wouldn't do any harm, would it?

'I know his ma says otherwise, but Pat is going to sign on a merchant ship in a month or two when they sail for the Indies. He says he's going to make his fortune shipping raw cane back to

168

England, then in three or four years he'll be able to take a wife,' Josie said, wondering if she had given too much away. Patrick had told her he couldn't marry yet but when he did he wanted her for a wife. He had told her that as they kissed and cuddled in one of the wharf doorways in the Highway. But it was supposed to be their secret.

Ellen laughed, her eyes twinkling as she said, 'So I'll not be losing you to Patrick as his wife for a few years yet.'

Josie giggled. 'Who knows? I might be losing you to Doctor Munroe as *his* wife before then.'

Ellen's face fell and a haunted look came into her eyes. 'Doctor Munroe? Whatever gave you that idea?'

'Oh, the way he looks at you and you at him,' Josie said. Why did her mother deny it? She had seen the way they stared at each other, and so had Patrick.

'Doctor Munroe and I are–'

'It's all right, Ma. I like Doctor Munroe, so does Gran. You deserve a man like him to look after you so you don't have to scrub people's dirty linen or sing in Danny Donovan's pubs any more.' She took hold of her mother's hands and felt them trembling. 'You can have a proper house with lace curtains and new clothes, not darned and repaired ones.' In her mind a vivid picture of her, her mother and her grandmother living one of the big houses in Stepney formed itself. 'Who knows? In time I might even have a little brother or sister.'

'That could never be,' Ellen said walking resolutely on.

Josie ran in front of her and blocked her path.

169

'Why not? If you love him and he–'

'Enough!' Ellen snapped. Josie stopped dead in her tracks, her face crumpling. 'I'm sorry. I didn't mean to snap at you, my love,' Ellen told her, slipping her arm through Josie's and squeezing it affectionately. 'But you must see. Even if Doctor Munroe and' – she paused for a second – 'and I did have feelings for each other, we could never marry. It would ruin him. His family would see me, an Irish Catholic immigrant who sings for money in a tavern, as little better than the girls who keep sailors company on the Ratcliffe Highway. They would cut him dead for marrying so far beneath him.'

'But Doctor Munroe's not a lord or an earl or something, is he?' said Josie, struggling to understand.

Ellen gave a short laugh. 'No, he's not a earl, as rich as some, but the few pounds I have in the penny bank wouldn't pay for the clothes he stands up in. And even if he asked me to marry him, which will not happen, I wouldn't.'

'Why?' asked Josie. 'If you love him and he loves you, then surely nothing else can matter.'

Ellen gave a heavy sigh. 'I thought the same at your age, but believe me, if I truly lo – loved him...' her voice cracked for a second, 'I would love him enough not to destroy him.'

'But Doctor Munroe isn't like that,' Josie protested. 'He doesn't look at you as ... as ... you...'

'I know but... You don't understand,' Ellen said. She stopped, tears beginning to form in her eyes.

Josie wanted to ask why it mattered that Ellen was Irish and a Catholic. Everybody went to a

170

church of one sort or another, but because of the raw pain on her mother's face she couldn't. She just stood forlornly, thinking that life was so complicated and unfair.

The smell of beeswax polish wafted up as Robert entered Wapping Police Station. No sooner had he been shown into a tidy office at the back of the station when Inspector Jackson entered. Jackson was a man about ten years older than him, dressed in his regulation dark-blue, swallow-tail police coat. The gold braid on the coat entwined to make a frog around a number fifty-eight on the stiff upright collar, and buff-coloured trousers and stout boots completed his uniform.

'Doctor Munroe.' Jackson took Robert's hand in a firm grip. "It is good to meet you at last,' Jackson said, indicating that Robert should resume his seat. 'What can I do for you?'

Robert sat down. 'I understand that you are interested in the activities of Mr Danny Donovan.'

Jackson put his finger to his lips and pulled up a chair alongside Robert. 'Let's keep our voices low.' He glanced at the door. 'The news of your visit to me will be with Donovan before sunset; we don't want him to know the contents of our conversation as well.'

Robert looked aghast. 'Your men?'

'Most are as keen as I am to see Donovan swing, but I am ashamed to say there are rotten apples in any barrel. Now, how can we help each other?'

'During my investigation into the living conditions in St George's Parish it's become clear that much of the money that should have gone into

171

repair works got *lost* somewhere in the accounts.'

'I'm not surprised,' Jackson said wearily.

'I have already spoken to Murray, the church-warden, but he says he has nothing to do with the parish accounts,' Robert told him, thinking of the frustrating hours spent in the gloomy vestry with the account books.

'Of course he can't help you, not unless he wants to make his old lady a widow,' Jackson told him. 'I've already rooted through the books myself and found Murray just as helpful. But the parish funds only scratch the surface of Donovan's dealings.'

'Mr Cooper from the Wellclose Square mission told me that you have a dossier on Donovan.'

Jackson fished out a key on a chain around his neck and went to the large safe in the corner of his office. He opened it and took out a large, buff-coloured file tied with a faded blue tape, and placed it on the desk.

'This is the file on Danny Donovan I have been accumulating since I came into the post three years ago, although some of the statements stretch back before that. It's all here. Every beating, every missing cargo, every body found floating in the river that has a link to Danny Donovan. It's known he has a hand in who is taken on at the docks. Those who "see him right" are offered the first ticket. And if a ship's officer has a perishable cargo, he would be wise to send his "regards" to Danny in coin if he doesn't want it to rot in the hold.'

'Why haven't you prosecuted Donovan long ago?'

'It is *known*, Munroe, but not yet provable.'

Jackson let out a colourful oath. 'If a body is dragged from the Thames, it's a pound to a penny that the poor soul has fallen foul of Donovan in some way. If a shopkeeper is found with the life near battered out of him, it's the same odds that he hasn't paid Donovan his protection money. And most of the stolen cargo from the ships and bonded wharves passes through Donovan's dirty hands on its way inland. I was in the army for ten years before joining the force. I've seen men cut to ribbons in battle but they look as if they have nicked themselves shaving compared with the sort of slicing Donovan and his bully boys dish out. I have a great deal of hearsay evidence against Donovan, but witnesses are too scared to testify against the bastard in open court.'

Robert gazed at the file for a moment. 'Do you have anything in there about a woman called Old Annie? I believe she lives in Dock Street.'

Jackson flipped through the pages.

'Here,' he jabbed a finger at one of the entries. 'Anne Bunton, 23 Dock Street. According to this she's an old moll, but has long since given that up. She's been before the beak for a couple of affrays outside public houses and been bound over. What's your interest?'

Robert told him about Kitty Henry.

Jackson whistled though his teeth. 'Procuring the death of a child is a hanging offence. If we could get Annie on that she might turn King's evidence on Danny, and who knows where that might lead? I'll send a couple of constables to visit her.' An astute smile crept across the inspector's face. 'You never know what we might turn up.'

The chandelier above Danny's head sent tiny points of light over the bleached white tablecloth and the remains of the East London Business Association lunch. All around the table the self-made men of the area and the local dignitaries scraped their chairs back and headed for the drawing room. Leaning forward and lighting his cigar from the candle nearest him, Danny watched them.

He was alone tonight. He couldn't very well bring Mike to a function like this, God bless him. He would have been like a bull at a ball here. Not that Mike minded. Besides Danny had slipped him a guinea to buy himself a bit of classy company after the Angel shut.

Thinking of the man who was like a brother to him set Danny off on an unusually maudlin path. If they could see him now, those barefoot sons of the old country like himself who were once known as the Flower and Dean Street gang! Most of them had long since ended their days at the end of a rope. In fact, as far as he knew, only he and Mike still had the sun on their faces.

Over by the side table stood several men whom Danny knew very well. Alderman Cotton, John Ridley, Captain Merton and Marcus Millstone, a wholesale tea merchant. Danny rose to his feet and sauntered over to their table.

'Good to see you here, Danny,' Alderman Cotton said, the heat from the overhead lights causing his forehead to glisten with sweat.

'So, how's trade?' he asked Captain Merton.

'Brisk, very brisk. I can't unload the ships fast

enough. They're queuing way out to Barking Creek,' the weatherbeaten captain replied.

'Then me boys'll have plenty of work,' Danny said winking.

Merton's face became troubled. 'Times are changing, Donovan. There are Polish gangs working the docks now, and it's a competitive world...' he trailed off.

Danny fixed him with a piercing stare. Merton smiled at him genially, but there was a small tremor in his right eyelid.

'Are the provisions on the dockside when your ships sail?' Danny asked innocently.

'They are,' Merton replied, looking uneasy.

Danny's face creased in a crafty smile. 'I'm pleased to hear it. With ships queuing right back to Barking Creek I wouldn't want there to be any delay in getting your ships off the wharfside, now. I mean, a delay could bring a senior officer from the Company down to see what the problem was.'

Merton shot a glance at Ridley who re-crossed his spindly legs.

'I am sure you heard about the Emergency Committee meeting last week,' Ridley said, his voice a notch higher in pitch than was usual.

Of course he'd fecking heard.

Fury started to bubble in his chest. Even though Cashman had patched up Hope and Anchor Passage, he had refused to foot the bill for the further repairs that Munroe had demanded through the enforcement order. That cost would have to be borne by the parish funds. Even a veiled threat about telling his wife about Cissy hadn't made the builder change his mind. The devil himself take the man. Danny ground the cigar between his teeth. Cashman had been too sure of himself for his liking when he visited the builder again in his yard. It was as if he actually thought Munroe would get the better of him, Danny Donovan.

Danny blew a long stream of cigar smoke above the men's heads. 'I heard about the meeting.'

'There was nothing we could do,' Merton explained. 'Even Murphy, your own verger, argued against the enforcement order.'

'Then why was it passed?' Danny asked in a chilling voice.

A few months ago, such a challenge to his authority would have brought forth swift retribution, but now, with Munroe watching his every move, retribution was not so simple. Munroe had paid a visit to Inspector Jackson. Not for the first time, Danny silently cursed the fact that the one senior officer who refused to have his palm greased was in charge of the local police.

He saw the men look anxiously at each other, then Millstone spoke. 'I wasn't at the meeting, so I don't know why Ridley and Merton were outvoted, but the outbreak of cholera has everyone panicky. The government itself has appointed us, men of substance in the area, to see what can be done to halt its progress. It's our civic duty, if you will. You have to understand that Doctor Munroe is reporting back to the Home Secretary.'

'So?'

Cotton drew himself up tall and stepped forward. 'We're businessmen, Donovan, and leaders in the community.' Those around preened a little and nodded. Buoyed by their support he continued. 'How would it look if we interfered with Munroe's attempts to stop the outbreak? The press and those godly reformers would be all over us.'

Merton nodded his head. 'Munroe's a doctor and trained to be thorough. I think that it is in our best interest to cooperate with him.'

Danny's eyes narrowed. These puffed-up idiots, who did they think they were? Had they forgotten the little favours he did them? Did they think about their place in the community when they were enjoying the entertainment in one of his whorehouses at no cost, or when their wives had expensive silks on their backs because of his arrangement with the wharfmen?

If he went down because of Munroe's investigation, he would not be alone.

'Thorough is it?' he said, his mouth pulled back in a chilling grin, and the men around him looked alarmed. 'Oh, yes, Munroe's thorough. Will you still be telling me of his *thoroughness* when he starts to look into the scales in the East India Company shop and the amount of sawdust there is in the flour?' Ridley blanched.

Alderman Cotton flushed scarlet. 'Now, look here...'

'And will you still be fretting about the Home Secretary when the Revenue start to look into what goes into certain warehouses and compare it to duty paid?' Danny cut in, jabbing a finger in their direction.

There was silence.

'I am surprised that you, with all the different comforts you have to offer, haven't advised our good doctor to be more prudent in how he goes about his enquiries,' Merton said with a sneer.

In any other company Danny would have changed such an expression with his fists. But this was the upper room in the Hoop and Grapes, not Paddy's Goose. He shrugged.

'Such as? He doesn't need money. He's not a drinker or a gambler and has no interest in investments. All he's interested in is shit and water.'

Millstone laughed and the other three glared at him.

Cotton stubbed out his cigar violently in the glass ashtray beside him. 'Surely he must have some weakness, something he's interested in other than drains.'

'He sounds more like a saint than a man,' Ridley interjected, waving to the waiter for another brandy.

Millstone snickered. 'Munroe's a man all right, he's in the Angel often enough. I saw him there myself last week, and he seemed mighty interested in your singer, Ellen.' He nudged Merton beside him. 'Can't say as how I blame him though.'

Ellen. Yes, Munroe was interested in Ellen, but Danny was hardly in a position to offer her to him. And even if he were able to bribe Munroe with her favours, he wouldn't because he was going to have Ellen for himself.

With slow deliberation Danny sank back in the buttoned leather chair. He rolled the glass around in his hand, watching the dark spirit swish back and forth. 'Let me put it like this, gentlemen. You just take care of your business and leave me to take care of mine.'

178

Robert looked up at the large clock with Roman numerals that sat high on the cream-painted wall of his office in the new Cholera Hospital. Four twenty-five. Jabbing his nib into the inkwell on the desk, he returned to the papers spread out before him.

He could just hear the chink of enamel bowls being emptied and the regular tapping of the nurses' heels as they went about their business.

To the committee's credit the cholera hospital had been set up just as Robert had specified. It had sixteen beds, new linen and heating from steam pipes. There were four nurses during the day and two at night to care for the sick. There was even a litter to bring the sick to the hospital if they were unable to make their own way there. He had ordered a controversial regime that included as much fluid as the person wanted, clean privies and no bleeding of the patients. So far, those who had survived the disease with this treatment were greater than the number succumbing to it. Robert made his usual meticulous notes.

The clock struck the half hour melodiously. Pinching the corners of his eyes Robert forced himself to concentrate on the task at hand.

The numbers in the neatly written column danced before his eyes but he continued nonetheless. He had to. He was very near to linking the incidence of cholera with where people drew their water. If he could prove the link then he would be able to prevent the spread of the disease.

He heard the hospital door and the noise from the room outside ceased abruptly. Robert stood up to investigate what could have caused such a silence and came face to face with Danny Donovan, dressed in his usual gaudy fashion finished off with a gold watch, cravat pin and cuff clips. Black Mike trotted behind him. Robert's gaze travelled over Danny's bloated features as he stood in the centre of the ward.

'Doctor Munroe,' Danny said pleasantly. 'Meself and Mike, we thought we might drop by and have a word, with you. Private like.' Danny swept his gaze around the ward.

Robert led them into his office and closed the door.

Resuming his seat, he waited until the two men had settled into their chairs on the other side of his desk.

'What is it, Donovan?'

Danny's face lost its pretence of friendliness. 'You've been making some powerful enemies, so you have, Doctor Munroe, with your enforcement orders and bringing in inspectors to look into parish affairs,' he said, picking up the crystal inkwell and turning it over in his hand.

'I am surprised. Most folk seem mighty thankful that their streets are at last clean and their pumps working. If I've made enemies, it's not of the ordinary folk hereabouts but of those who rob and cheat them to line their own pockets.'

Danny's hand closed around the inkwell. 'The folk around here are ignorant and don't know what's good for them. They're too busy drinking and fecking.'

'And you profit from both, don't you? Dealing in both drink and prostitution as you do. And of

180

course making good use of them yourself at the same time. I believe the late Kitty Henry was an intimate friend of yours. That is before she bled to death after some butcher cut your child from her.'

Danny's face became a jigsaw of red and purple blotches and there was a crack of bones as his hand gripped the crystal inkwell tighter. Black Mike laid a hand on Danny's arm. He shrugged it off and sprang to his feet. He drew the fist holding the inkwell back but Robert didn't flinch. Black Mike took hold of Danny's raised arm, more forcibly this time, and stopped it from completing its arc. Robert's cool eyes locked on Danny's and the men stood, the hatred palpable between them, for several seconds. Then Danny tossed the inkwell onto the desk. It landed on Robert's research papers spilling the indigo ink across them.

'I'll be warning you, Doctor,' Danny ground out.

Robert went to his office door and threw it open. 'Out!'

His gaze didn't waver. Then in a swift move for one of his size Danny spun on his heels and headed for the door. Black Mike, as always, was a step behind. Danny stopped as he came abreast of Robert and jabbed his finger at him. 'You've been warned.'

Holding her lace handkerchief up to her mouth Caroline feigned a cough to hide a yawn. Beside her Mrs Munroe sat calm and serene and the hotel butler stood ready to open the door. For the third time the older woman's glance went to the clock on the mantelshelf. Caroline followed the glance.

181

Seven twenty-five.

Before she could stop it, a long sigh escaped her. As if it wasn't boring enough to have to dine privately with Robert in his mother's apartments rather than taking a table at the one of the Covent Garden dining houses frequented by London society, she had to wait under the disapproving eye of Mrs Munroe for Robert to arrive. In fact, after their last meeting when he'd quizzed her about his work and been so beastly, if they had actually been engaged she would have seriously considered breaking with him. But she couldn't even have that satisfaction as she had yet to receive his proposal.

Caroline stole a glance at Robert's mother and her shoulders slumped as she slid down in the chair.

When her mother had read out Mrs Munroe's invitation to 'take the season' with her she had imagined balls in Whitehall, regimental parades at Brighton, and being seen in the Pump Room at Bath, not churches in Cheapside, promenading in Weymouth and taking the waters at Tunbridge.

Mrs Munroe was dull enough when she called on Mama and droned on for hours about how the poor should attend Sunday service to improve their morals, so why on earth did she ever agree to accompany her south on her yearly visit? Robert, of course. It was only because she had been so sure that Robert was going to make her an offer of marriage. But he hadn't, and now what?

It wasn't as if he hadn't had an opportunity. If he'd wanted to he could have joined them for their stroll in St James's Park. Then he couldn't join them for the recital of the *Messiah* because he had to supervise some hospital thing. Then, just as they were getting ready to take tea with him in his rooms, he sent a note telling them he was too busy, and now they were leaving the day after tomorrow. But there was still time. If his mother would absent herself tonight, if only for twenty minutes, Robert could do as he should and all would be well.

Caroline put her elbow on the table and rested her cheek in her cupped hand. Mrs Munroe's eyes fixed on her sharply. Caroline resumed her upright position and placed her hands on her lap.

'Robert will be here any moment now,' Mrs Munroe told her.

'Doctor Munroe should really live close to town,' Caroline sighed.

Mrs Munroe's expression changed into the exasperated one she had worn almost every time Caroline ventured an opinion. 'As I have explained to you on more than one occasion, my son is a *hospital* physician, and *hospital* physicians live near to their work.'

'Well, why can't he work in a hospital in a more fashionable part of London?' she asked. 'If he worked in Mayfair or Piccadilly, for instance, then I–' she cast a swift glance at the woman beside her. 'Then if Doctor Munroe took a wife she could call on other respectable hostesses in their neighbourhood while he was at the hospital. She might even be invited to tea with an earl's wife or even a duchess. If Doctor Munroe treated someone in the government she might get presented at court.'

Mrs Munroe's gaze was steely as it rested on

her. 'Might she?'

'Indeed. Although it is a pity that we have King William now, because it would have been such fun to meet the dashing Prince of Wales.'

Mrs Munroe's eyes rested on her for a long second, then she turned back to the clock. 'I hope he caught a hackney carriage from the hospital and didn't walk to the city. I understand that Whitechapel is a rough area full of beggars and pickpockets.'

A picture of Robert as she had seen him the week before came into Caroline's mind.

'I think Doctor Munroe's stature would make even the most desperate vagrant think twice about attacking him,' she said, thinking how Robert was at least a hand taller than Captain Miller and broader in the shoulders.

The tight-mouth expression left Mrs Munroe's face. 'My son has an athletic build and boxed at Stirling. He favours my dead brother.' Inwardly Caroline groaned. 'I had hoped that Robert, like his namesake, would choose a career in the Army. Have I told you about my brother's part in Wellington's victory?'

Caroline fixed the polite expression that her mother taught her on her face. 'You have. And please do not distress yourself by reliving again your brother's tragic death,' she said, hoping to avoid the twenty-minute monologue about how Captain Robert held the flank of the field against Napoleon's attack and died just as the Russians were sighted over the crest.

A quiver passed over Mrs Munroe's downy cheek. 'On the morning of the eighteenth, dear

184

Rob was entrusted by Wellington to–'

There was a sharp rap on the door and the butler sprang to life. Robert entered and handed his coat and hat to the man. He had obviously been hurrying as his hair was windswept and his eyes bright. He was dressed formally in a charcoal grey frock coat with lighter grey trousers. He crossed the distance to the table in three strides.

'Mama, I am so sorry for my lateness,' he said kissing her briefly on the cheek. He turned to Caroline and inclined his head in her direction. 'Miss Sinclair.'

Caroline widened her smile. With the turned-out wings of his shirt collar and his cravat framing his square jawline, she remembered why she had been so eager to suffer his mother's company for the long ride to London. Tucking her chin and tilting her head slightly to one side, better to catch the light from the lamp to her right, she lowered her eyelashes slowly so he could appreciate their fullness and then raised them, only to find he was no longer looking at her.

'You look as if you've been running,' Mrs Munroe said, the worried lines from her forehead smooth now.

'I only just got away from the hospital on time. I was tending a woman in labour. The child, a large one, was attempting to enter the world feet first and it took me two hours to turn him.'

Caroline gave a shudder and straightened one of the bows on her dress that had twisted.

'Well, you're here now,' Mrs Munroe said, and indicated that he should take the empty chair.

Robert arranged his coat and sat down, whereupon two tall servants, immaculately dressed in the hotel livery, appeared with the dinner trolleys.

'Have you been shopping again, Miss Sinclair?' Robert asked, smiling at her.

'Well, I so liked the pale cream day dress I procured from Bond Street the other day that I thought it just *had* to have a new hat to show it off to best advantage. I'd seen an absolutely ravishing one in the window of Magasin des Modes, with Belgian lace and a great number of ostrich feathers curling around its crown, so I just had to go back and buy it.'

'How nice,' Robert said. He glanced over to the dinner and rubbed his hands together. 'I am ravenously hungry. Are you all ready for your trip to Tunbridge?'

Caroline's nostrils flared. He was supposed tell her how well he thought she would look in her new outfit, not say how hungry he was.

Elspeth Munroe signalled and the two servants came forward with the soup tureen.

'We are. My sister is expecting us on the Saturday coach and she is sending her steward to meet us. We are to spend a month with her and Mr Turner.'

'Give Aunt Turner my love,' Robert said, beaming good-naturedly at his mother. Caroline coughed lightly and his eyes flickered on her for a second.

'Naturally.' Mrs Munroe leant towards her son. 'We are then going on to the sea, are we not, Caroline?'

Robert's eyes rested on her with mild interest.

'Indeed, we are – to Weymouth,' Caroline told

him with a little throaty giggle. 'Which I hear is quite as jolly as Brighton.'

Robert smiled. 'So I am led to believe.'

Mrs Munroe's face formed itself into what Caroline called her Doing-God's-Will face. 'I told you that Mr Palfrey was called to glory in February.' Robert nodded. His mother shook her head dolefully and the lace of her cap flapped against her temples. 'Well, he was eighty-three, but I have extended our visit to Mrs Palfrey for a full six weeks to offer what comfort I can.'

Caroline's heart sank. When Mrs Munroe had told her their itinerary included six weeks in Weymouth, she hadn't envisaged it being to comfort an elderly widow.

'Then we are to York for three weeks and from there back to Edinburgh. I expect to be home by September.' Mrs Munroe opened her napkin, tucking it under her chin and into the neck of her black dress. 'I have ordered only a simple dinner: soup, one course each of fish and fowl, followed by a cutlet of lamb and then fruit.'

'It sounds delicious,' Robert said, smiling broadly at his mother and not even glancing at Caroline. She drew her fair eyebrows together.

Picking up her spoon, Mrs Munroe gave her son a reproving look. 'You wouldn't have had to wait so long if you had come as we originally arranged, on Tuesday.'

'I'm sorry. I had given my word to dine with Mr Chafford on Tuesday.'

Caroline glanced down at the thin soup in her bowl. It had small circles of fat floating on the surface and the odd pea bobbing underneath.

'Where was that?' she asked, rustling her skirt and playing with the lace cuffs of her new ivory dress. He had been there a full half-hour and not yet remarked on how well it suited her.

'At the Angel and Crown, a supper room near to the hospital. We often dine there on a Tuesday. There is entertainment most nights at the Angel,' he told them, concentrating on scooping up the last of his soup.

'Entertainment!' Mrs Munroe asked pursing her lips together tight. 'What sort of entertainment?'

'Nothing scandalous, Mama. Music mostly, but on Tuesdays there is a particularly fine singer.' He reached across and placed his hand over his mother's. 'As you know, I have always had an ear for music.' Mrs Munroe laughed and Robert joined in. 'And of course both Chafford and I have to stay within the sound of the hospital bell,' he explained, smiling at his mother. Caroline rustled her skirts again.

Robert glanced at her. 'That's a pretty gown.'

Caroline smiled and arched her neck. 'It's from Madame Grandemille. She dresses Lady Houghton and the Marchioness of Stretford.'

'It's charming,' he told her. 'I am sure it will be the talk of Edinburgh when you return.'

'As you like it so much, I will wear it when you return to Edinburgh, Doctor Munroe,' Caroline said, sending him what some would call a scandalously seductive look.

He smiled politely and the servants brought the fish course. Robert asked his mother how his sisters were and conversation moved on to family matters. Caroline tried to join in, telling Robert that she had bought his sister Hermione a new muff and Margot some ribbon for her bonnet, but he responded only with a brief smile.

From under her lashes, Caroline studied him as they consumed the red mullet with Cardinal sauce. She tried to catch his eye, to send him an invitation to admire her, to flirt with her. He was supposed to. That's what men did. That's what Captain Miller did, and he tried to kiss her, which of course she hadn't allowed, but at least he tried. But what did Robert do when they were alone? She gripped the knife and fork tightly and glared at Robert's averted face. Instead of telling her of his undying affection and begging her to marry him, all he could do was talk about his work. Her eyes narrowed and she gave him her displeased look, which he failed to see because he was staring at the window. The empty plates of the fish course were removed and the warm tableware for the following course was being set before them.

'Did the mother you were attending earlier survive?' Mrs Munroe asked, as the waiter withdrew having set the poultry before them.

Robert's face cracked into a broad smile and Caroline forgave him his earlier lack of attention. 'She did, and when I left both mother and child were doing well.'

Caroline stared at his hands holding the knife and fork.

'You *actually* delivered this child yourself?' Caroline asked, picturing the same hand thrust in between some woman's thighs to deliver the infant.

The untidy wedge of hair on his forehead settled across his brow. Robert moved it aside but

189

it returned instantly. 'Of course.'

'But couldn't you have left one of your under-doctors to do the actual delivery? After all, as your mother keeps reminding me, you are one of the chief physicians.' Caroline felt rather than saw Mrs Munroe's sharp look, but she had Robert's attention now. 'Couldn't you just tell them what to do and let them get on with it?'

A patient, almost weary expression settled on Robert's face.

'I could have, but then the mother and, most likely the child too, would have died,' he told her. 'My apprentices are very clever men, all of them, and had the delivery been straightforward I would have left without a second thought, but it wasn't.' Robert put down his cutlery and cupped his hands in front of him. 'Being a doctor is more than just knowing how a body works, it is a skill perfected over long years.' He splayed his hands and flexed his fingers as he talked. 'Knowing how a child should sit in the womb is not the same as feeling its angle and nudging it into the right path. Do you understand what I am saying, Miss Sinclair?'

He was looking at her now and talking with passion about his wretched work again, about these poor people who seemed to be more important to him than she was. It was all wrong. Did he want to marry her or not? Did he think that she hadn't had other men, officers no less, asking to call on her? And how could she face Ruth Dalrymple if she returned to Edinburgh without becoming engaged?

She would have to do something. They were leaving in two days, and who knew how long it would be before Robert returned to Scotland?

She put on her sweetest smile, the one that caused the dimple to appear at the corner of her mouth.

'Captain Miller,' she ran her eyes slowly over Robert's face, 'the officer I wrote to you about who shared our family box at the opera and who danced with me at the Castle ball, is in charge of a whole company.' Beside her she could feel the tension shoot though Mrs Munroe. She slowly smoothed the ivory silk of her skirt and smiled across the table at Robert. 'He is one of the most accomplished officers in the regiment and knows all about soldiering, but he doesn't set up the tents or groom the horses, he orders the lower ranks to do the actual work.' She hooked a tendril of hair from her shoulder and twirled it around her finger.

Robert picked up his knife and fork. 'You seem very fond of this Captain Miller, Miss Sinclair.'

A satisfied glow spread through Caroline. She set her head on one side and raised an eyebrow, as if considering her words. 'He was introduced to us when his regiment took up residence in the garrison in November. He is a very fine officer and a most personable gentlemen. He can converse in any company and has an appreciation of the arts, which is why Papa invited him to join us at the opera. His father owns land in Essex and has interests in the Indies. He was educated at Charterhouse before entering the army.' She lowered her eyelashes and let a shy smile cross her lips. 'And many predict that he will rise through the ranks with speed.' She glanced back up to find Robert staring at her. She was now the centre of his attention, as she should have been from the moment he walked in.

191

Robert's brows drew together and his face grew sombre. 'You seem to know a great deal about Captain Miller after such a short acquaintance.'

Caroline lowered her eyes and extended her shy smile. 'Captain Miller has a commanding presence and an easy way about him.' She raised her eyes and looked fully at Robert. 'He has been most attentive,' she told him firmly.

There was a long silence and then Robert smiled across at her warmly, more warmly than he had all evening.

'Captain Miller sounds a fine young man. I am sure he will be pleased to renew his acquaintance with you when you return home in September.'

He turned to his mother. 'What time does your coach leave for Tunbridge on Saturday?'

Thirteen

Robert sat with his feet up on the fender. It had been a long hard day, like many others recently. He had spent all morning supervising the staff at the Vinegar Lane hospital.

He sighed and loosened his cravat, raking his fingers wearily through his hair. William had called by earlier to invite him to supper, but he had declined. Bulmer had already fetched him a supper while he worked and, besides, it was Thursday and Ellen didn't sing at the Angel that day.

Robert looked up as St Mary's church clock struck eleven o'clock. Goodness, had he really been scribbling for three hours? He pulled out his gold watch and checked. As he slipped it back there was a light rap on the door and Bulmer's cheery face appeared.

'Begging your pardon, Doctor Munroe,' he said respectfully, 'but there is a young lady to see you.'

'A young lady?'

'A very young lady,' Bulmer confirmed. 'I told her that you had retired for the night but she was most insistent. She said her name was Miss Josephine O'Casey.'

Panic swept over Robert. Ellen! Was she ill?

'Show her in, Bulmer, and fetch her a cup of tea, if you please,' Robert said.

Josie burst into the room. She had obviously been crying. She was shrouded in a large coat, which Robert suspected was Ellen's, and was wearing a dark bonnet which she ripped off her head as she entered the study. Seeing Robert standing at the end of the room she dashed over to him and grabbed his hands with a remarkably strong grip.

'It's Gran,' Josie said between sobs. Robert led her over to the large winged chair and sat her down. Bulmer brought the tea and Robert indicated that he should stay.

'Calm down, Josie. Now tell me what is wrong with Mrs Shannahan.'

'After Ma went out, Gran said she had a headache and was going to bed early,' Josie said. 'I didn't think anything of it. Gran's very tired most nights and can only manage an hour or two sewing before her eyes start to drop.' Josie drew in a breath and fixed her gaze on Robert. 'She had not been up there an hour when I heard her retching like into the night bucket. I dashed up the stairs to find her covered in sweat and being sick. She asked for some tea which I got her and she threw that up too. Then the gripes started.'

Robert had heard enough. What Josie was describing were the classic symptoms of cholera. If caught at this stage, there was a good chance that the victim would recover. But if Mrs Shannahan did have cholera, it would not be that straightforward.

'You finish your tea while I get my coat and bag. Where is Ell – your mother?'

'She is singing at Paddy's Goose tonight.' Josie hugged the teacup with both hands and slurped another mouthful.

My God!

Feeling the sweat on the nape of his neck, Robert pictured Ellen in the White Swan, commonly referred to as Paddy's Goose. The White Swan was, in truth, little more than a brothel. Sailors stumbling off their ships would make it their first destination once their feet hit dry land. A vision of Ellen being mistaken by some drunken Scandinavian or German sailor for one of the girls who plied their trade there sprang into Robert's mind.

He snatched up his stethoscope and shoved it in his leather case. Why on earth would she put herself in such danger for a few pennies? As he reached for his patella hammer he paused. You arrogant fool, he said to himself, a few pennies to you is staying out of the workhouse for Ellen. He turned back to find that Josie had already put on her outer coat and bonnet.

'Bulmer, go to the hospital and tell Mr Pierce to bring the litter around to number two, Anthony Street immediately.'

Minutes later Robert, Josie and Bulmer stepped out into the chilly night air. All three walked swiftly to Commercial Road. Leaving Bulmer at Cannon Street Road, Robert and Josie struck east towards Josie's home.

Pushing open the front door Robert smelt the sickness. He had smelt it too often in the last three months ever to forget it. He didn't have to see Bridget upstairs to know that cholera was in the house.

He took the narrow wooden stairs two at a time. He went over to the bed where Bridget Shannahan lay without making any real indentation in the mattress. Beside her on the floor was a washing pail with vomit in it and a full night-soil pot.

Quickly casting his eye over both, he turned to his patient. He said a prayer of thanks when he saw she still breathed. To be sure it was laboured, but it was still breathing. Taking his stethoscope out, he knelt carefully beside her to avoid upsetting the foul containers on the floor. Bridget's eyes flickered open, bright with fever.

'Doctor Munroe,' she whispered.

'Is it too early to say top of the morning to you, Mrs Shannahan?' he said with a smile as he felt her pulse. It was weak, irregular and thready. She didn't answer, just smiled back and closed her eyes again. He laid the broad end of his stethoscope against her chest over her nightdress, put his ear to the other end and listened.

There was the same irregularity he had felt in

195

her pulse, with the odd half beat, but with an occasional squeak between beats. He stood up and put his hand on her forehead. It was hot against his palm. Bridget opened her eyes again and looked up at him.

'What have you eaten today?' he asked.

'The usual, same as Josie and Ellie,' Bridget answered.

'Have you eaten anywhere else in the last couple of days?'

Bridget shook her head very slightly. 'Not that I can think of. I visited old Ma Grady two days ago, in Jane Street, poor soul, and had a cup of tea with her.'

Jane Street was the street next to Katharine Street. Robert didn't need to enquire further. Josie came by the side of him and took hold of the washing pail.

'I'll come back up for that in a moment,' she said nodding towards the tin pot to the left of Robert.

'Have you got some tar soap?' he asked as she lugged the pail to the top of the stairs. Josie nodded. 'Then wash your hands well once you've emptied it. The same when you empty the night pot.' He turned back to Bridget.

'Josie's a fine girl, like her mother,' Bridget whispered, as her gaze followed her granddaughter. 'Do you know, I have seven grandsons, three in America and four in Ireland, along with six granddaughters, four in America, and two in Ireland, and so many nieces and nephews in Liverpool, Bristol and Manchester, that I couldn't even begin to count, but I've never seen them. So I only have Josie, but she's as good as a dozen.'

196

Her gaze rested back on Robert as he folded away his instruments. 'I'll be sorry to leave her.'

'I'm moving you to the hospital. You can see her and Ellen there,' Robert told her, wilfully misconstruing her meaning. Bridget's eyes didn't leave his face.

'You take my meaning, Doctor,' she said. 'I'm old and I can't pull my weight any more. I've become a burden on Ellen.'

'I know your daughter enough to know she'd roast you for saying that,' Robert said, bringing a ghost of a smile to Bridget's grey lips.

'Aye, that she would. But it's true. I had to let three of my regular washes go a month past. That lost us three shillings. And I can only do sewing repairs and not make a whole gown, so we'll lose more. That's why my Ellen has to sing in Paddy's Goose to make up my money,' Bridget crossed herself.

Josie came back up and replaced the cleaned pail beside Bridget. She sat up. 'Excuse me, sir, but I will have to–,' Robert stood up as Bridget grabbed the pail and retched into it.

There was a sound below and Robert heard Bulmer call up the stairs, announcing the arrival of the litter. Bridget had now sunk back in the bed and Josie was sponging her forehead and wiping her mouth.

'Get the litter ready, I'm bringing Mrs Shannahan down,' Robert shouted to the men below. With one swift movement he wrapped the blanket that covered her around her, scooped her up in his arms and carefully carried her down the narrow stairs. As he deposited her on the wicker litter, she looked up at him.

'You're fond of Ellen, Doctor Munroe,' she said, sending Robert's emotions soaring.

'I am,' Robert replied as levelly as he could.

'Go and fetch her from Paddy's Goose. My Ellie's too good for that godforsaken place, don't you think?'

Ellen gritted her teeth and stepped out onto the rickety stage. As the lights glared on her, Paddy Flanagan struck up a chord on the badly tuned piano at the side of the stage.

The commotion in the public bar continued and Ellen had to raise her voice to be heard over the guttural voices of sailors and the shrill giggles of the women. After the first verse, a drunk at the front lurched forward and grabbed for the hem of her gown but fell short and ended up kneeling against the stage. He gabbled something, then slumped unconscious to the floor. Ellen took a step back as she launched into the chorus which at least set some in the room swaying in time to the familiar rhythm.

Was the five shillings that Danny Donovan paid her to sing in Paddy's Goose twice a week really worth it, Ellen asked herself as she started the second verse. Unfortunately it was.

She had argued long and hard with herself before accepting Danny's offer to sing at the White Swan, but in the end necessity had made her take the job.

While their daily washing and sewing had earned them enough to live on, the money she made by singing in the Angel and Crown and the Town of

Ramsgate went straight into the penny bank for their passage to America. So far, Ellen had nine pounds two shillings. That was two pounds eighteen shillings short of the money they needed for passage and supplies for the arduous twenty to thirty-day crossing. But now that Bridget was unable to work as she had, some of Ellen's precious singing money was being used to supplement their living expenses. So as much as Ellen froze every time she walked into Paddy's Goose, she had to do it, otherwise they would never save the money for America and would be trapped in poverty for ever.

Taking a small bow at the end of the first song, she quickly gathered up the money thrown on the stage. It galled her pride to scramble on the dirt boards for pennies, but every coin given by an appreciative sailor was a penny more for the thrift bank. Some mauling sailor from Galway had pressed three shillings into her hand the week before because she had sung an old lullaby his mother used to croon to him. That went straight down to the bank the next day.

Ellen cleared her throat. 'Any requests?' she shouted over the drone of voices.

'"Old Mammy's Ram",' a man at the back shouted. This brought forth a number of shouts of agreement.

Ellen ignored the request. A rendition of the song about an energetic, over-sexed he-goat would only send the audience off in a lewd direction as they joined in the actions.

'Any others?' she asked, appealing to those in the back of the room by the bar.

'"My Darling Sweet Maid",' shouted a slurred woman's voice from the back.

'"The Singing Waters of the Liffey",' another woman called and a few around her agreed.

Ellen signalled for Paddy to start. He struck a chord and Ellen drew in a breath. There was a crash at the back of the room as a portly man stood up and shoved two tables aside sending the glasses and bottles on the top crashing to the floor.

With an inward shudder Ellen recognised Brian Hennessey, a boon companion of Danny Donovan's, stumbling towards her. The woman who had been on his lap was now sobbing noisily in a dishevelled heap on the sandy floor at his feet, while others around him were moving swiftly out of his way. Brian was not known for his forbearance.

'Sing "Old Mammy's Ram",' he demanded as he reached the bottom of the stage and peered belligerently up at Ellen. Her heart was in her mouth and pounding as if it was about to burst from her chest.

'Maybe aft–' she started, but, drunk though he was, Brian was swift. He leapt up on the stage and grabbed her by the throat with his brawny hand. They both swayed as he regained his foothold and then brought her close. Belching into her face he squeezed her throat slightly.

'Sing "Mammy's Ram",' he said, smiling menacingly and revealing a row of tobacco-stained teeth. He slid his arm around her waist, ramming her onto his crotch. 'We'll do the actions later.'

The audience roared at this and shouted possible actions that Brian might like to consider.

Ellen's mind was numb. It was well known that Brian would slash a full-grown man for gain-saying him. How was she going to escape from his iron grip? His hands were already fumbling with her skirt, hauling it up over her bottom as best he could.

There was a sudden stillness in the audience that Ellen couldn't account for. Were they waiting to see or what? Suddenly, Brian's hand around her throat lost its strength and he was slipping onto the floor in front of her. As he went down with a crash into the dirt at her feet Ellen looked in disbelief at the figure who had taken Brian's place on the stage. Relief flooded through Ellen as she saw Doctor Munroe.

He tucked the walking cane with which he had pole-axed Brian under his arm and offered her his hand. 'May I have the pleasure of accompanying you home, Mrs O'Casey?'

In a wink she grabbed hold of his hand, her nails digging into his palm. He could feel her shaking and took the opportunity to put his arm around her waist to lead her through the crowd of gawping onlookers. After the first few steps she stumbled. Robert squeezed her waist and made her look up at him. The fear was still simmering in her eyes.

'It's all right, Ellen,' he said, holding her closer and enjoying the feel of her hip against his thigh. 'I'm here and no one will hurt you now. I promise.'

'Oh, Doctor Munroe,' was all she could manage but it was enough. All her desire and love were in those three words and Robert's heart fixed for all time on Ellen. Taking his coat off, he put it around her shoulders and steered her towards the door.

As they reached halfway across the floor their path was blocked by a bull of a man with dark red, curly hair. Two piggy eyes stared belligerently at them out of his bloated face. By the way he stood chewing a fat cigar out of the side of his mouth and blocking their way Robert guessed he was the landlord.

'Out of my way,' commanded Robert.

The man stood his ground. 'I'm Henry Forster and who the feck are you, when your mother knows you?' he said, squaring up to Robert.

Despite being taller than most, Robert was eye to eye with Forster, and although as broad, he judged he was several pounds lighter.

'I am Doctor Munroe. I take it that you are the landlord here,' he said, casting his eye around the room.

'I've heard of you. You're the doctor that's been poking his nose in where he's no business to.'

'Have you?'

Forster swallowed, then jabbed his index finger at Robert. 'Now, see here, doctor or no, you have just laid one of my best customers flat. I'll have to call the constable.'

'Please do. I'm sure they would be most interested to see the type of house you keep here.' He glanced casually towards where a woman with her skirts up her legs was rocking back and forth on a sailor's lap.

Forster's eyes darted uncertainly to the sailor, then back to his face. 'Even so, where the feck do you think you're taking Ellen? She's booked for

202

the evening and has only done one song.'

'Step aside.'

Forster, however, still stood in front of them blocking their exit.

'And what if I don't?' he said sneeringly.

'I am asking you for the final time to step aside,' Robert said in an ice-cold voice, 'or you will have Inspector Jackson and his men from Wapping swarming over these premises by morning. I doubt Danny Donovan would thank you for that.'

For a few seconds their eyes locked, then Henry Forster stepped aside, spitting the now soggy cigar in Robert's path. Leading Ellen gently, Robert walked past the landlord and towards the door.

'Mr Donovan will have something to say about this, Ellen,' Forster called after them. Robert felt Ellen quake at the mention of Danny's name.

Robert half-turned as he reached the door. 'If Danny Donovan has anything to say, he can say it to me,' Robert informed everyone within earshot as he put his hand to the brass plate on the door and pushed it open.

After the oppressive, smoke-filled atmosphere of the White Swan's main drinking room the cool air, even with the smell from the Thames close by, was refreshing. Silently they made their way along Ratcliffe Highway. After a few moments Ellen stopped and started to shake again. Swiftly Robert took her in his arms and held her. He allowed himself the luxury of letting his lips rest briefly on her hair. He held her closer to still her fears, relishing the feel of her head on his chest and her soft breasts pressed into his chest.

'It's over, Ellen, you're safe, my love,' he said,

liberated by saying her name out loud.

The shaking subsided and Ellen pushed away from him slightly. To his satisfaction she did it to look up at him and not to free herself from his embrace. The temptation to kiss her was almost too much, but he held back.

'Why on earth were you in Paddy's Goose?' she asked with a confused expression on her face.

'Ellen. It's your mother.'

Bridget lay, ghostly pale, on the clean sheets of one of the beds in the cholera hospital. Ellen and Josie sat beside her, huddled together in a large wooden chair. Around them the two night nurses moved quietly amongst the patients, seeing to their needs and offering a word of comfort as they went. Of the sixteen beds only ten were occupied. The rest were neatly made, waiting, like cool marble slabs, for the next sufferer to be laid on their pristine surfaces.

Since Robert Munroe had materialised at Paddy's Goose, the evening had taken on an unreal quality for Ellen. She had gone from terror to joy at his appearance, from fear of what Forster might do to him to ecstasy as he held her tenderly in his arms, and finally to dread as he told her of her mother's condition. Her emotions were now completely unravelled and scattered around her.

Ellen had given up all pretence of being merely fond of Robert; when he appeared on the stage in the White Swan and rescued her from Hennessey, she knew that she loved him.

She had diligently guarded her heart against love since Michael had died, only to find that it was now taken by a man who could never be hers before God.

Ellen gazed at her mother, who was breathing peacefully. Next to her Josie had nodded off to sleep. Ellen adjusted her position and eased Josie under her arm. Her daughter stirred, but did not wake.

After they arrived, Robert had led her to Bridget and left her and Josie. But Ellen knew that he would stay as long as she needed him.

Knowing that he cared, that he cherished her, warmed her from within. She gazed at him as he stood next to a bed at the far end of the ward and spoke to the attending nurse. He had opened his waistcoat and loosened his cravat, his hair was tousled and there was a dark shadow on his cheeks and chin where his night beard was beginning to grow through. He turned towards her and their eyes met. He said something to the nurse and walked over. Ellen eased Josie onto the chair and covered her with a blanket.

'Has your mother opened her eyes?' he asked in a whisper. Josie stirred and muttered in her sleep, so he took gentle hold of Ellen's arm and moved her away into the corner.

'No, but she is peaceful,' Ellen replied, feeling the strength of his presence wash over her. He left Ellen and went back to Bridget's side. Taking her limp wrist and sliding out his gold hunter, Robert took her pulse. His mouth drew into a tight line and he lifted the covers from her mother's feet, pressing the pad of his thumb firmly into her flesh. Bridget didn't stir. Robert regarded her legs for a second or two, then covered them again. He picked up his stethoscope from the table next to the bed and listened to Bridget's chest. He replaced the stethoscope and returned to Ellen's side.

'Is something wrong?'

He took hold of her hand, his fingers caressing her gently. 'I'm afraid there is,' he said, his troubled eyes looking deep into Ellen's. 'Your mother is very ill indeed.'

Ellen staggered back and Robert's arm circled her waist. 'But you said that she was only in the early stages of the disease and with proper care she had a good chance of recovering.'

'And that is true, but your mother has had a problem with her breathing, has she not?' Ellen nodded. 'Your mother's heart has been failing for some time.'

Ellen's world crashed around her. Her mother, who had rocked her on her knee, kissed away the scratches and scrapes of life, was dying. She let out a quiet sob and Robert took her in his arms and held her close. She did not resist, just rested against him and allowed her tattered emotions to flow through her and over him.

Tears shuddered from her and Robert held her tighter. 'Ellen.' His hand left her back and went to her head, stroking his fingers lovingly through her hair and kissing her head softly.

'I am so sorry, my love,' he said, as his lips moved down to her forehead. She felt the firmness of them on her brow. 'I wish there was something else I could do.'

My love. His love.

Wonderful though it was holding Ellen so close, he had to stop. They were at her dying mother's bedside.

'Let me sit with you a while,' he said, breaking away.

She nodded. 'Thank you, Doctor Munroe. That is kind of you.' She smiled and walked with him over to her mother's bed. Pulling up a bench he sat her beside her mother. Ellen gently took hold of Bridget's hand and smiled down at her. Robert slipped onto the bench on the other side of her. Although he wanted to take Ellen's hand, with the staff walking back and forth, it would have been unwise, so he contented himself with resting his leg against Ellen's as they sat.

'How old were you when you married, Ellen?' he asked quietly, as the nurse settled at the table at the far end of the ward.

'Fifteen,' she answered, still looking at her mother.

Fifteen! 'That's young,' Robert said, as she turned her large green eyes on him and smiled a haunted smile.

'It is. But the priest allowed it because I was with child.' Ellen's mouth twitched at the corner. 'Are you shocked?'

'No ... not as such, but...'

'But?'

'It's just that I was at school, sitting exams, at that age,' he said, remembering his days as a gangly senior at Stirling Academy. 'I didn't even know how to kiss a girl properly at fifteen.'

'The young men around here don't have exams to worry about, so they start on the other things

207

of life much earlier,' Ellen said with a hint of irony in her voice.

'Was that Josie?' he asked. She nodded. 'How did your husband die?'

'He was crushed between a ship and the dockside. Josie was three at the time,' she said simply, glancing over at her sleeping daughter.

A sad smile flitted across her face. 'I met Michael when I was no more than Josie's age. He was two years older, as I said, and working on the ships bringing coal from Newcastle to London,' she told him in a low voice. 'He was a handsome lad so he was, tall and straight and with a mass of black curly hair.'

Robert's heart lurched with jealousy of Ellen's long-dead husband. Ellen's smile disappeared and she shrugged. 'Anyhow, he was earning good money and he started courting me. Pappy got wind of it and forbade me to see him. He said I was too young, which I suppose I was. I tried to obey me pappy.' Robert heard a little sob in her voice as she said her father's name. 'But I fancied myself in love with Michael.'

Ellen stopped for a moment and Robert all but felt the pain of the old wound torn open again by recounting the story. She let out a harsh laugh. 'All sweetness and soft words was Michael, telling me he loved me like no other and how desperately he wanted to marry me.' She cast a rueful smile at Robert. 'And I, blind fool that I was, believed him. He was a real charmer was Michael O'Casey when he wanted to be.' Her face darkened. 'Then he changed. I should have realised of course that it was part of his game.'

'Game?' he asked, although it was obvious. It had been practised on many a young girl down the centuries.

'Game to seduce me,' Ellen replied. 'Michael was always taking liberties. He said as we were to be married what was the harm? But,' she paused and looked at Robert from under her lashes, 'as much as I wanted to, I wouldn't let him.'

Anger had replaced jealousy in Robert's chest as he pictured the young, innocent Ellen, so trusting and so in love with such a bastard.

'What happened then?' he asked in a low voice.

'When he stopped coming by I was heartbroken. When I heard he'd taken up with a girl from Limehouse, I cried myself to sleep for a week. Then Michael appeared again and was his old charming self. He said that he thought I did not love him because I was saving myself for someone better than him.' Ellen smiled sardonically. 'I swore I loved him and to prove it I ... I let him have his way with me.'

'So you became pregnant and he married you,' Robert said, moving nearer to her.

Ellen gave another short laugh. 'I became pregnant and his feet never touched the cobbles as he made for his ship.'

'So how–'

'My pappy...' She stopped for a second. 'My pappy made him.' She looked up at Robert and he swore he felt his heartstrings tighten. 'Mammy guessed first. She found me retching into the soil hole in the yard. She knew it was Michael.' Ellen bent over and kissed the dying woman's hand. A distant smile crossed her face. 'She didn't rant or rave like some would. She didn't call me names or threaten to throw me out. She just hugged me,' Ellen said, still looking at her mother.

Robert felt the love that encompassed the two women and he envied it. He loved his mother, of course. He tried to imagine what she would do if his sister Hermione came home pregnant. He doubted it would be to hug her.

'We kept it a secret as long as we could, but eventually we had to tell Pappy.' Ellen turned to him, raw pain etched on her face. 'It almost cut his heart out. He had great hopes for me. He taught me to read, write and calculate.' Ellen shrugged, and tucked the pain of her father's disappointment back deep inside. 'Anyhow, he raised hue and cry in the parish and when Michael returned, he had the priest waiting for him. We were married two weeks later, two months short of my sixteenth birthday. Josie was born four months after that.'

'Were you happy?' Robert asked.

'I suppose I was. I soon had Josie and for that alone I am thankful to Michael. He also taught me a great deal, too.'

'Taught you?'

'He taught me that when you're knocked to the ground you should roll into a ball and stay there.'

Robert was appalled. During his work he had seen many women who had suffered from his own sex's brutality. Even so-called respectable men felt they had the God-given right to assault the women in their care, but as a vision of Ellen cowering and beaten by this brute of a husband formed in his mind, blind rage surged through him.

Bridget moaned and Ellen leant close to her

mother. Robert looked closer at his patient too. Her breathing was becoming slower. The texture of her pale face had already begun to take on the waxy sheen of a corpse. Bridget would be fortunate to see dawn. The dying woman's eyes flickered open.

'Ellie,' she whispered.

'I'm here, Mammy, I'm here. So is Josie,' Ellen answered, shaking her daughter awake.

Bridget's gaze focused on her daughter and her blue lips curled slightly at the edges.

'Dr ... Munroe ... got you ... fro–'

'Save your strength, Mammy,' Ellen said, kissing her mother's hand again.

'He's a ... fine ... looking man, so ... so ... he is,' Bridget said breathlessly. She let her eyes rest briefly on Robert.

Robert saw Ellen's cheeks glow pink at her mother's words. 'Aye, he is a fine doctor.'

'Don't ... give ... me ... that ... Ellen ... Marie ...Shannahan,' her mother continued, struggling with each word. 'It's a ... man ... like ... Doctor Munroe you ... deserve ... my girl... I know ... you're right fond–'

'*Mammy!* Please, you're embarrassing Doctor Munroe,' Ellen said.

Ellen was fond of him! Please God, she was more than that.

Bridget waved her hand in a dismissive gesture, letting it fall back on the cover, and with a last effort, said, 'I but ... speak ... the truth. It's the right of the dying ... to say what they like.'

'Mammy,' Ellen whispered with a quiver in her voice. A tear swelled in her right eye and rolled

211

slowly unhindered down her cheek.

'Sing "The Soft Soft Rain ... of Morning",' Bridget said.

A lump formed in Robert's throat as Ellen took up the strains of the old Irish ballad. Although she sang faultlessly as always, there was a tremor of emotion in her voice. Josie awoke and came around to join Ellen. Robert gave up his seat to her and she sat holding her grandmother's hand tightly. He stood back and a lump came to his throat.

Death came to everyone in time of course, and Robert had seen more than his fair share. Like Kitty with her innards perforated, dying in agony, or the stevedore who screamed for days after having his skull crushed beneath a crate, or the woman who just gave up after trying to expel a dead baby for three days.

After witnessing such deaths he knew there was no easy way for the soul to depart the body, but if he could choose how he would leave this world it would be the way Bridget was facing the afterlife now, with Ellen's sweet voice surrounding him.

Fourteen

Danny eyed the men in the low-ceilinged bar, who shuffled uneasily under his unrelenting gaze. Uneasy? They ought to be shitting themselves.

'One week I'm away,' he said glaring around him. 'One fecking week, seeing Shamrock Lad

212

race at Newmarket, and I come back to this.' He spat on the sandy floorboards.

Black Mike stood calmly beside him, waiting for orders. Beside him his two cousins, Milo and Wag, lounged against the table of the empty bar room. Wag was cleaning his dirty nails with the end of a large knife and Milo was twisting the rings on his right hand and cracking his knuckles.

Danny jabbed a finger at Henry Forster. 'Just so's I know that I'm hearing aright, you're telling me that Doctor Munroe walked into the Goose's bar, floored Bull Hennessey with one blow and walked out with Ellen and no one stopped him?'

Henry Forster nodded. Danny rubbed his finger across his chin and turned his mouth up to one side, still looking at his bully boys ranged before him.

'And what did Munroe say?'

Henry Forster stole a gaze at the men flanking him. None met his eye. 'Doctor Munroe said, "If you have anything to say, you can say it to me".'

A caricature of a smile spread over Danny's face, making it a picture of artless good humour. He beamed at Forster, Black Mike and his two cousins Wag and Milo. 'Is that so?'

'Th ... that's what he said,' Forster stuttered, looking to the others for support. None was forthcoming.

Danny puffed out his chest and sauntered around the desk. He put his thumbs in the armhole of his waistcoat, pushing open his blue-striped frock coat. 'Well, that's mighty civil of him, don't you think, boys? What a kind gentleman our Doctor Munroe is.' He was inviting

213

them all to agree with him, but no one moved a muscle and only the squeak from the lamp fixture above cut through the silence.

'Rescuing the fair Ellen from ol' Bull Hennessey's clutches and stealing her off into the night. I might just have a word or two to say to him, don't you know.'

'He threatened us with the police, he did,' Henry interjected. 'I didn't think with all the – er – you know in the cellar, you would want...' He didn't complete the sentence.

Danny's face lost its congenial expression and was replaced by a look of pure venom. He struck Henry swiftly across the face with his new walking cane, opening up a deep gash on his cheek with its silver tip.

'I only said–' Another blow found its mark and silenced the landlord.

'Of course I don't want the fecking police anywhere near the Swan,' Danny said, towering over Henry. Out of the corner of his eye he saw Black Mike step forward. Danny took hold of Henry and the other men in the room stood back. Henry, although bigger than the average man, dangled like a captured rabbit in Danny's huge fists.

'Haven't you got a brain in that thick head of yours?' He shook Henry, who tried to say something, but Danny let him go with one hand and smashed into his face with the other, splitting his nose in an instant. Blood splattered over Henry's white shirt and over Danny's hand. He ignored it and continued to shake the now almost insensible man. 'Couldn't you have sent the lads after him?'

Henry's mouth was working but no sound was

coming out. His right eye was all but closed by a rapidly swelling and discolouring eyelid.

Danny stared at Henry for a second, imagining Robert Munroe hanging limp from his grip instead. In his mind's eye he could see him walking into the taproom and taking Ellen away. His stomach twisted as he imagined the soft smile Ellen had bestowed on her rescuer. The blood in his head pumped harder.

He focused again on the man in his grasp and threw him from him. Henry landed in a crumpled mess on the floor and Danny kicked him where he lay. Henry murmured, but lay still. Danny then swung around and pointed at Mike.

'That bastard'll pay for this,' he said, and no one was in any doubt as to which bastard he was referring.

'Comes here full of his do-gooder ideas,' Danny continued to no one in particular, 'poking his nose into others' business and costing me money with his repairs orders and investigations into the workhouse supplies.' He glared at Mike, Wag and Milo. 'God Almighty, if that's not bad enough, he's now looking to me business at the Swan.' The cane between his hands started to bend. 'And to top it all, he's after stealing my singer from under my very nose.' The cane snapped. He threw it behind him. 'And you.' He glared at Henry for a second then landed him another kick, square in his chest. 'You fecking well let him.'

Mike, Wag and Milo stood still and there was a long silence.

'Do you want me to cut him like?' Wag asked, sliding his knife across the pad of his thumb.

For a long moment Danny stood with his fists clenched, then a smile crept across his face. He tapped the side of his nose with his finger. 'Gentle now, me boys, gentle. Do you think you could pop around to Ol' Bull for me and tell him I'd like a few moments of his time?'

Unsuccessfully trying to stifle a yawn, Josie took the hot cup of tea from her mother. She sipped it and cupped it in her hands. Although it was not Friday night there was a large sugary bun on the plate at her elbow.

Taking up her own cup of tea, Ellen took the chair on the other side of the fire. She looked tired, with dark smudges under her eyes. It was hardly surprising that neither of them had slept much in the last two days.

'It was a grand send-off, though, wasn't it, Ma?' Josie said, taking another hot mouthful of tea.

Ellen gave a ghost of a smile. 'It certainly was. Just like back home.' The smile broadened a little. 'It's a shame your Gran wasn't here. She would have enjoyed it.'

'Well, she could have been if we hadn't had to bury her,' Josie retorted, which brought a further smile to her mother's face. 'When old man Ryan died last year he was in the middle of the room the whole time dressed in his dapper best.'

In truth it hadn't mattered. Despite the absence of Bridget's body, their small house had been open for the long night of vigil and neighbours came from the surrounding streets to pay their respects to Bridget and to 'keen and cry' with Josie and her mother.

'You know why we couldn't have her lying out for a week. Doctor Mun ... Munroe explained about the risk of catching cholera and why she had to be buried so quickly, didn't he?' her mother told her. Josie gave her a sharp look. There was something in the way her mother said Doctor Munroe's name that was different somehow. She wondered if she said Patrick's name in the same soft way and if her mother's sharp ears heard

'He did,' she conceded, but it still didn't seem right to have a wake without a body.

'I'm sure Gran would have understood.'

Yes, she would have. Gran always did. She understood when Josie was given the birch at school for punching Marjory Swallow. Gran understood when she told her about Patrick and how she thought he was the handsomest lad in the streets for miles around. Patrick had come to Gran's wake.

'Still it was a grand seeing-off for all that,' the young girl went on. 'The fiddlers were sharp and played every tune anyone asked them for, and everyone danced until they dropped. Even Mrs Munny from over the road was jigging around and she's never got a smile on her face for any.'

Her mother gave her daughter a long, considered look. 'You were on your feet all night, that's why you're so tired now,' she said, as Josie completed another yawn. 'And don't think I didn't see you dancing with Patrick Nolan.'

Josie nibbled at her bun, pointedly ignoring her mother's remark. She had danced with Patrick on three occasions, and wonderful it had been too.

'It's a shame that we had no relative here who

217

could have come,' she said, changing the subject and hoping her mother would do the same.

'I wish Joe could have been here and Aunt Mary, but it'll be weeks before she gets my letter in Munster and months before Joe hears the news in America.'

'Uncle Joe has another child on the way, hasn't he? That'll make five cousins, won't it, with the two older boys' two girls,' Josie said, her eyes bright in spite of their lack of sleep. 'I suppose we will be off to America sooner now there is just you and me.'

Ellen put her cup down very carefully and smoothed her skirt. 'There's no rush.'

'But if we book passage now, in the sailing season, we'll make swift passage. Patrick says that we might make it in eight weeks or less at this time of year.'

'There are peop ... things we need to see – er – do here ... before we join Uncle Joe,' her mother said in a tight voice.

A long strand of hair had come loose from the bun at the nape of Ellen's neck, and Josie watched the familiar action of her mother rewinding it into place. A little stab of pain shot through Josie's chest. What if it had been Ma, she thought. A great sense of emptiness swept over her. No Ma? But that's just what Ma was facing now. Life without *her* ma. In a swift movement Josie was out of her chair and hugging her mother.

'Oh, Ma,' she said simply. She was now crying as the thought of life without her mother overwhelmed her. She felt a reassuring pat on her arm as her mother disentangled herself.

'It's all right, Josie. She's with me pappy now. She'll be fine,' she said, her hand going back to her hair although it was all still in place.

Before she could stop it, Josie's mouth again opened wide in a yawn.

'Now then, young lady. Time for bed, don't you think?'

After her daughter had disappeared upstairs, Ellen sat back in the old chair by the range and sipped her tea. She had been pleased with her mother's wake. She had lost count of the number of times friends had said to her, 'I'm sorry for your trouble', and had spoken with affection of Bridget's kind heart and cheerful spirit. As she'd told Josie, Bridget really would have enjoyed the fiddle and the songs.

Talking to Josie had brought the emotions of the night Bridget passed away vividly back into her mind. And they centred on Doctor Munroe. For one moment, when her daughter mentioned going to America, panic had swept over her. Go away? Never see him again? No, she couldn't bear it.

Pushing away her thoughts, she turned back to the task she had set herself to complete that evening. With tears quivering on her lower lashes she tied the tablecloth around her mother's meagre bundle of clothes

There wasn't much. Three gowns, a couple of petticoats, a felt bonnet, a pair of shoes and a winter coat that had seen better days. Bridget's day-to-day working clothes were all but rags and it wouldn't be worth Ellen's while carrying them the two miles to Isaac Levy's second-hand clothes shop.

Ellen sighed and put the neatly tied bundle down on the table.

A warm glow spread through her as she remembered Doctor Munroe on the morning Bridget died. Utterly tired though he had been, he had stayed with her, taking the burden of the arrangements from her shoulders. For so long Ellen had been without the strong support of a man beside her, and she had forgotten how wonderful it felt. Even when he had finally taken his leave of her, as the cart bearing Bridget's coffin left the hospital, she continued to feel the warmth of his affection surrounding her.

Ellen's eyes rested on the bundle on the table. She should get six shillings for the lot, maybe more. Her thoughts went to the nine pounds three shillings that now sat in the Thrift Bank. She had calculated that she needed at least twelve pounds in total before she could book the passage, but that was before Bridget had died. Now, overnight, Ellen had the money for the fare to New York. But instead of making plans to book passage on the next ship leaving, Ellen found she didn't want to go to New York or anywhere else on earth if it meant leaving Robert.

She knew it was madness. How could they ever be together? Marriage would be impossible and she had sworn never to be any man's mistress.

Putting the cup down, Ellen stood up, trimmed the wick of the oil lamp and drew the curtains. It was the first day she had left off her black dress and she had opted to wear her dark green cotton. It was old, but its slim lines suited her. Taking up her brush from the shelf she turned the mirror that had been set against the wall during the past week, and unpinned her hair.

In the soft reflection of the lamp, Ellen looked at herself as she brushed out her long auburn hair. She should go up to bed soon. It would save oil and she had an early start in the morning, but now, with Bridget gone, the bed seemed large and lonely even with Josie beside her.

Ellen picked up a book and, tucking her feet underneath her, snuggled into the chair. She realised she must have dozed off because she was woken by a sharp rap on the front door. Thinking it must be someone who might have just heard about Bridget's death coming to pay their respects, Ellen got up.

Her heart leapt in her chest as she cautiously opened the door and found Robert Munroe standing there.

He removed his hat and bowed. 'Good evening, Mrs O'Casey.' His eyes took in her unbound hair. Ellen looked past him down the street.

'May I come in, or are you expecting someone?' he asked. There was a tightness in his voice as he posed the question.

'I'm sorry, do come in, I'm not expecting anyone. I just thought that you were on your way somewhere and must have a coach waiting.'

'I'm not on my way anywhere. I have come particularly to see you,' he replied as he stepped into the parlour.

He put his hat down on the table beside the bundle of clothes and waited.

'Oh, please sit down,' she said, indicating the

221

chair on the other side of the range.

'I'll stand if you don't mind,' he replied, his mouth turning up slightly at one end. 'But please sit yourself.'

She settled herself into the chair, this time taking up a more formal posture with both feet on the floor and looked up. Robert clasped his hands behind his back.

'I hear the wake for your mother went well.'

'Yes, very well,' she said, smiling at him.

He smiled back. 'I would have paid my respects, but I didn't want to intrude on your grief, with all your close friends around. It must be difficult for Josie and she was obviously fond of her grandmother,' Robert said, his eyes glancing towards the closed stairs to the upper room. 'Is she here?'

'She's upstairs asleep,' Ellen replied. 'It's very good of you to call to give your condolences, Doctor Munroe.'

'I didn't come just for that, I have something to tell you.'

Was he leaving? Had he come to say goodbye? Maybe he was going tell her he was getting married... Her heart thudded painfully in her chest. Maybe he was here to ask her to put aside her scruples and become his mistress after all? Surely not.

I'll never be any man's mistress. How many times had she said that over the past five years? She had meant it, and she still did.

But then she had welcomed his advances at the fair. Whatever had she been thinking of, flirting with him at the fair and then letting him hold her in the corner of the hospital? Did Doctor Munroe think that just because she had lost Bridget's small income she would alter her resolve on the matter?

Doctor Munroe took a step forward and took her hand.

'Ellen.' His fingers smoothed over her roughened palms. 'My dearest Ellen. You are the most beautiful woman I have ever met and what I have come to tell you is – I love you.' He lifted her hand to his mouth and kissed her fingers lightly. 'I love you totally.'

His arm slid around her waist and he drew her to him. The part of her mind that had vowed to be no man's mistress tried to assert itself, but Robert was here, holding her, telling of his love and nothing, nothing else on earth, mattered.

'I love you too, Robert,' she replied softly.

Her hand encircled his neck and he held her tighter. He looked into her upturned face for a moment longer, then did what he had wanted to do since the day of the fair: he kissed her.

'Ellen, will you–'

Become your mistress?

'Yes, Robert.'

'Ellen, will you marry me?'

Yes, Yes.

There was a long pause.

'No. I can't.'

Robert felt as if the air had been sucked out of his lungs, and for a second he thought he had misheard.

He put her at arm's length. 'Can't? You're a widow, and free to marry anyone you choose. I am not attached. Why can't you marry me? Is there another man?' he asked, knowing that she was admired by many who frequented the public houses where she sang. 'Don't you love me?'

Pain crossed Ellen's face and she grabbed hold of his upper arms. 'Don't I love you?' she said in a strangled voice. 'I love you like no other and will do until I'm lowered into my grave.'

Relief swamped him. She loved him. He let out a breath he didn't know he was holding. 'Then marry me.'

She shook her head, but stayed in his arms. Robert held her tighter to him and kissed her head. He felt her lean into his body and lay her head between his neck and shoulder. With both hands on his chest she looked up at him.

'It's because I love you that I *can't* marry you,' she said, breaking free of his embrace and going to stand a pace or two away from him. He took a step toward her but she matched it, keeping the distance between them.

He stifled his impatience. He didn't want her over there, facing him; he wanted her here in his arms. He would soon put an end to her reluctance and get her to answer 'Yes' to him.

'What nons–'

'I can't marry you,' she said, interrupting him, 'because it would ruin you. You're the senior medical doctor in the hospital. You're a member of the Royal College of Physicians, are you not?'

'I am,' he answered. 'But–'

'How do you think they would regard you if you married me?'

He didn't answer. There would be some scandal no doubt, for a year or two. Not that the

Society would be so crass as to say as much.

'And your family? What would they say if you returned home with an Irish Catholic wife?'

Robert couldn't even begin to tell Ellen the furore that would cause. To Robert's father, the Pope was the Antichrist and those who followed him were condemned to everlasting damnation. A Catholic daughter-in-law would probably burst every vein in his head.

'My father and I long ago agreed to differ over religious matters.'

Ellen gave him a sad look and shook her head.

'And your mother? What would she say if you told her that your wife and possibly the mother of your children...'

Children!

'...earned her living by singing in a public house?'

'Don't be ridiculous, Ellen,' Robert said sharply. 'You are the most respectable woman I know.'

'I doubt your mother would call me so.'

She was right, but Robert didn't care.

'Ellen,' he stepped towards her, and this time she stayed where she was. 'My dear Ellen,' he repeated, a warm smile spreading across his face. 'What you say may be true. But none of that matters to me. I want you as my wife.'

'But it matters to me,' Ellen said. 'It matters to me very much.' She placed a hand lightly on his arm. 'I can't destroy all you have worked for,' she said, looking up at him. She ran her hand up Robert's arm and around his neck. Her expressive green eyes gazed up at him. Automatically his arm encircled her waist tightly. 'But I will be

225

your wife in all but name,' she whispered pressing herself closely to him.

He kissed her deeply for a long moment then drew back.

'Ellen, Ellen,' he said.

She smiled up at him. 'Love me, Robert.'

His hand reached up and cupped one of her breasts. Her hand went to his coat buttons, undoing them in an instant. Although her slim hand sliding over the shirt on his back fired him with desire, Robert disentangled himself from her arms.

'No, Ellen,' he said 'I want you for my wife and will settle for nothing less.'

'Don't you want to make love to me?' she said, taking hold of the back of the chair and standing somewhat unsteadily.

'I want nothing more, but I want to love you as my wife, not as my mistress.'

Ellen gave a half laugh. 'I am offering to give myself to you and you are saying *no?*'

Within him, Robert's baser instincts were arguing furiously with his morals, asking him what difference a piece of paper and a few words would make. What was the harm in it? Physical intimacy would bind Ellen to him and he would be able to persuade her to marry him later. But his morals wouldn't budge.

'I am,' he told her.

She pulled herself up and smoothed her hair back into place. 'Well, I love you too much to marry you.'

'And I love you too much to make you my mistress.' He had to leave because, strong though his resolve was, with Ellen within an arm's length and willing, Robert wasn't sure that he could remain firm if he didn't remove temptation soon. He snatched up his hat and cane and bowed.

Ellen met his gaze levelly. 'It would seem that there is nothing left for us to say, is there, Doctor Munroe? You don't love me enough to make love to me.'

'And you don't love me enough to marry me,' he replied in the same controlled manner.

For a timeless moment their eyes locked. Then Robert re-buttoned his jacket.

'I'll wish you a good evening, Mrs O'Casey,' Robert said, spinning on his heels and heading for the door.

Ellen put her hand out to him. 'Robert,' she said, in low whisper.

He had to go, because if she had actually touched him again he would have been unable to control himself. He pulled open the front door and, without looking at Ellen again, he left.

Fifteen

The late afternoon summer sun streamed through the dimpled windows of the dispensary catching particles of dust in its beams. Robert looked up from his ledger and watched Thomas, his assistant, put the jars back on the shelves. He could have left an hour ago, but since Ellen had refused his offer of marriage Robert had taken to staying late in his rooms in Chapman Street. He had a reputation for single-minded dedication amongst his fellow doctors, so this extension of his day when the area was in the grip of a cholera epidemic seemed nothing out of the ordinary.

Despite vowing not to seek her out, Robert was drawn like a compass needle to the Angel and Crown each night he knew she was singing there, but seeing her there was bitter-sweet. She would look at him with deep longing in her eyes and he would call himself a fool. Being morally right didn't help him sleep at night.

He ached to see her, to talk to her, but knew that that if she threw herself into his arms again and begged him to love her, his willpower would evaporate. So, staying at work gave him some respite from the torture of loving Ellen. Work kept his mind occupied, and the long hours were spent in the hope that he would sleep instead of staring at the ceiling with pictures of making love to Ellen dancing in his head.

Thomas started to sing softly as he polished the jars. The contorted reflection of his thin face showed in the bulbous containers. Beside him were a small burner and sealing wax which he used to seal some of the more easily spoilt substances. The smell of hot wax drifted across the room from time to time as the stoppers received their overnight seals. Robert turned back to the letter in his hand. Thomas stopped polishing and came back to Robert's desk, taking a pile of papers to store away.

'Leave the letter on the top, Weaver, I have yet to answer it,' Robert said.

228

Thomas tapped the papers into a neat bundle and walked over to the drawers where they were stored. 'I saw your letter in *The Times* supporting the call to improve living conditions for the poor, sir. Have you considered standing for parliament? Lord Ashley is set to–'

An ear-splitting crash cut him off and, as Robert, turned towards the window, an oil lamp burst though the glass, shattering the panes.

As they watched, the lamp sailed in an arc across the dispensary and landed with an explosion of flames on the slate floor. Oil slithered across the floor and tendrils of flames leapt towards the storage cabinet, shelves, bookcase and the long curtains, igniting everything as they progressed. As Robert sprang to his feet another missile was propelled through the broken window and shattered on the stone floor. More lamp-oil gushed forth, sending up a wall of flame and setting the wallpaper and prints around the room ablaze. He shielded his eyes against the scorching heat and gathered the papers on his desk into one pile.

Arson! Strangely he wasn't surprised. It was clear that he had upset those who didn't want their sordid activities looked into too closely. In short, Danny Donovan. Because although someone else had no doubt lobbed the lamp through the window, it was Danny's hand which had instigated the attack. Robert blinked hard to moisten his eyes.

Thomas was stamping frantically on the flames nearest to the shelf of storage jars. Robert went to join him. If the spirits and alcohol contained in the jars were overheated or touched by flame

229

they would explode like gunpowder.

Through a heat haze Robert saw passers-by attempting to organise help. He tried to shout to them, but a wall of flame fuelled by the papers and notes on the low bookcase blocked him in. The chintz curtains were now ablaze and overhead some of the plaster was smouldering.

His records! He had to get his records.

Glowing wisps of wallpaper were falling from the walls like seared cherry blossom. He shielded his face as best he could with his arm and glanced towards his office behind the consulting room.

The whole room was ablaze now and the ceiling was in danger of collapsing. Above him, where the plaster had fallen away, flames were now taking hold of the support beams above.

He waved frantically at Thomas. 'Get out, man. Now!'

A shrill screech from outside caught Robert's attention. Peering through the sheet of flame into the street Robert saw onlookers pointing desperately to either side of the dispensary.

The lodging houses! Please God, don't let the lodging houses go up, he prayed earnestly, thinking of the impoverished families crammed into them.

Thomas started making his way towards the front door. Seeing him stepping carefully through the debris, Robert turned to his office. The doorframe leading to his study was on fire and the wood surround was already charred black. A quick glance at the office ceiling showed smoke coming from the corner joists but it was not glowing like the consulting room. He had to get those papers.

'You go, Weaver, I'll get my papers, and then get out of the back door.'

His apprentice raised a hand in acknowledgement and resumed his path to the door. All around Robert plaster and charred wood were falling from above. Suddenly there was a loud groaning sound and the rain of sparks and ash increased. Then with one almighty roar the whole ceiling crashed to the floor. Thomas howled as the large support beam landed on him pinning him underneath.

'Thomas!' Robert called, as he tried to get to where his apprentice lay inert beneath the blazing beam.

The heat on Robert's face was almost unbearable, and try as he might he could not go forward to help the fallen man. Another beam crashed down, sending sparks upwards in a pretty spray of red and yellow. Thomas was not moving and his eyes stared lifelessly at the ceiling. Anger and sorrow rose in Robert's chest.

Sickened by the sweet smell of burning flesh, Robert turned back to the office. Quickly scooping up all the leather-bound files with his reports, Robert headed to the back door in the small scullery. The smoke from the room beyond was now filtering into the back room and Robert started to cough. Grabbing the handle he tried to open the door. It would not budge. He tried again with all his might, but still there was no movement. He was trapped. Whoever had thrown that oil lamp through the window wasn't intent on just frightening him, but on killing him.

Robert pushed the door one last time knowing

it was useless even before he jammed his shoulder against it. Unless he got out of this inferno within the next few moments he was a dead man. He looked back into the dispensary's main room to see that it was now a mass of flames and thick black smoke. The fire was sapping the air and Robert was struggling to breathe.

Quickly scanning the rapidly igniting scullery Robert spied two large buckets of water in the corner by the sluice. Without a second thought he picked up the first and poured it over himself, then repeated the process with the second. Drenched to the skin Robert turned up his collar to protect his ears and neck as much as he could, tucking his head down and shielding his eyes with his arm. He secured the files under his other arm and dashed back into the smoke and heat of the blazing dispensary.

The heat hit his lungs like a wall as he re-entered the room. He could smell his hair singeing in the heat and the wool of his coat smouldering. Jumping over the prone figure of Thomas and the beam that straddled him, Robert sped towards the window with its jagged teeth of glass sticking out of the frame. He moved forward into the room and the heat beat him back.

But the window was his only hope.

A vision of Ellen floated into Robert's mind, spurring him forward through the heat, flames and choking smoke. He was going to get out of here because he refused to die without loving her.

Judging the height of the sill, Robert launched himself sideways at the window and sailed through it. As he did, he heard the explosion as the flames reached the spirits and chemicals on the storage shelves and a mighty whoosh as the roof followed the upper floors of the house to the ground.

Robert landed with a thump on the hard cobbles and instinctively rolled to extinguish any flames that had caught hold of his clothing. Coming to a halt he was immediately surrounded by a crowd of people. Staggering to his feet, Robert glanced down. His clothes were soot black and burnt in places. He ran his hands over his face and head, feeling the wiry texture of burnt hair.

'Praise be to the Blessed Virgin,' a woman said, as she dusted him down.

She was right. Praise be. Other than a few cuts, bruises and the odd blister Robert appeared to be unscathed. He took a deep breath.

In contrast to the heat of the dispensary the evening air was cool and fresh. He glanced around and then the full horror of what had happened washed over him. The dispensary he had only just escaped from was now no more than a blackened hulk. The roof had collapsed, leaving only the charred brick walls standing. But that wasn't all. Not only were his offices and workroom razed, but the two lodging houses on either side were now becoming engulfed in the flames as well. He stood aghast and watched as men and women dashed back and forth with buckets of water in a vain attempt to stem the blaze. To one side a group of women stood, their shawls tight around their heads and their eyes red with tears, while men desperately tried to reach those still trapped inside.

The house to the right was still standing for the most part, and in the upper windows a woman with two children could be seen imploring those below to help. Men were shouting for her to throw the children down and, lifting an infant up, the distraught mother did just that. All, including Robert, held their breath as the small child travelled though the air towards the pavement below. Two strong arms caught it and it was swiftly taken by a woman bystander who tried to soothe its screams.

The men below called for the other child. The mother was in the process of lifting it to follow the first when there was an almighty sound of creaking timbers. The mother screamed once, then disappeared as the floor she was standing on collapsed. There was a deathly silence broken only by the crackle of flames.

The fire had been intended to kill him, but he had survived while others – Thomas, the mother at the window and others – had died.

He breathed deeply, sucking in life. Yes, he was alive and he wanted Ellen.

After saying goodbye to Maisy Turner, the ribbon and lace seller opposite the Bell foundry, Ellen left the market with her basket on her arm. She smiled at friends and acquaintances as they passed her by, exchanging the odd word and smile. But behind Ellen's cheerful exterior, she sobbed. She sobbed as one who has lost everything in the world that she has lived for. She had lost Robert Munroe.

A vision of him leaning on the rail at the Angel and Crown took shape in her mind. No, she hadn't lost him, she had refused him. And in doing so had ripped the hearts out of both of them.

She told herself during the long cheerless day that she had been right to refuse his offer of marriage. She loved Robert Munroe too much to ruin him, his career and his future happiness. But by the time she stumbled into bed, exhausted after battling with heart and body all day, Ellen had failed to convince herself. She then spent hours staring up at the ceiling.

Who had ever heard of a man refusing to make love to the woman he professed to love? A grudging smile crossed her lips as she stepped over the stream of sewage babbling along in the centre of the street. God, he was stubborn, as stubborn as she, and she loved him for it. What had he said? *I want you for my wife, nothing less.*

What love!

Repositioning the basket that held the evening meal, Ellen crossed into New Road. In contrast to Whitechapel the thoroughfare to Wapping was quiet, with just a few barrows being taken back to their night storage and weary-looking souls shuffling home after a back-breaking day's work in a sweatshop.

As she started down Cannon Street Road, Ellen's attention was caught by a large pool of black smoke rising above the closely packed houses. She judged it to be be somewhere near to Chapman Street. She hurried on. Others now joined her as she turned into Cable Street and headed home and towards the fire. People were shouting and running to assist.

There were calls for the police and a hue and cry of outrage as men dashed past her with buckets in their hands. Now she could smell the acrid wood smoke in her nostrils. Running on down Cable Street and into Chapman Street, she was caught in a crowd and had to push forward. People seemed to be rushing with buckets full of water along to the other end.

Robert's dispensary was at that end of the street. A cold hand clutched at Ellen's heart and, dropping her basket on the pavement, she lifted her skirts and tore down the street. Forcing her way through the crowds of women, she stood and gasped at the sight before her. Where the dispensary once stood was now a gaping hole with only fragments of wall, like rotten teeth, where the house used to be. The charred beams that had crashed down jutted out at acute angles.

Sweet mother!

Her eyes fixed on the wreck of the dispensary. Was Robert lying dead under the rubble? A scream rose in her throat. How would she live without him? Did she want to? She stood frozen for a moment, then forced herself to action.

Ellen looked more closely at the scene. It wasn't just the dispensary that had been consumed by the inferno but the lodging houses on either side which were now also mere charred rubble. How many people had been trapped in there, she wondered. She stood back as men carrying full buckets and shouting for more shoved past the group of women. The hiss of water turning to steam could be heard as bucket after bucket of water was thrown onto the fire.

'They have taken three bodies out so far,' a woman's voice said behind Ellen. 'One of 'em a bundle no more than its first birthday.' She spun her head around to see who was addressing her. An old woman swathed in a dun-coloured shawl looked up at her with watery blue eyes.

The woman shook her head. 'They are saying that someone was seen running away, and that some draymen from the sugar refinery gave chase.'

Someone caught at Ellen's arm, and she looked down into the face of a young boy with an unruly mop of red hair. He tugged at her arm again, his thin fingers clutching at her arm.

'I heard as how someone saw Bull Hennessey hanging around a few moments before the doctor's gaff went up,' he said, wiping his nose on his dirty, ragged jacket sleeve. 'All knows 'ow 'e as a grudge against the doctor for somefink.'

'What about the doctor? Doctor Munroe?' Ellen's mind screamed at her and she managed to get her mouth to form words. 'Was he in the dispensary?'

'He was when I passed by an hour ago, saw him through the door, but where he is now and if he is under that lot,' the old woman nodded towards the rubble which rescuers were now climbing, 'I couldn't rightly tell you. Saint of a man so 'e was, and no argument to it.'

'That he is, missus.' The young lad was hopping from side to side on nimble bare feet to see past the spectators. 'I hopes as like 'e's not a goner.'

A bottomless pit opened up under Ellen's feet. I should have agreed to marry him, she thought bitterly. At least we could have had a brief time of love together. Now there was nothing, no memories and no future.

With her head spinning Ellen pushed through

237

the press of people. She caught hold of the arm of one of the men tearing blackened ceiling beams away. He turned from his task and looked at her, his weary eyes red with the sting of smoke and his face smeared black.

'Doctor Munroe,' she said, her heart now galloping uncontrollably in her chest. 'Is he...?'

'Doctor Munroe, God bless him, must have had the Angel Gabriel himself watching over him this afternoon, because I saw the doctor myself, black and singed, making his way to Wapping Police Station with the beat constable.'

Robert Munroe was alive. Ellen stumbled back clutching her chest. A wail went up from the crowd of women as another body was brought out. This one, from its size, clearly a child.

'How did it start?' she asked, as the man wiped the sweat from his brow with his forearm.

'It started in the dispensary and then swept through the houses either side before anyone could stop it.' He stood back as a beam crashed to the ground from the upper floor. 'I heard that something was thrown through the window, an oil lamp I expect, by the look of this.' He kicked a beam with his toe and a puff of ash rose from it. 'And the doctor's rooms went up like a powder keg, what with the spirit and stuff in there.'

Behind Ellen two bodies, contorted and almost unrecognisable as human beings, were being brought out. As she looked down at the two lifeless forms, the full horror of what had happened dawned on her. Robert was alive, but these poor souls and those carried out earlier weren't. Lifting her head, she gazed up at the walls of the three buildings. Both houses were three-storey lodgings with families in almost every room. How many people had died? Standing with her arms limp at her sides, Ellen saw men struggling to release two other doomed wretches from under a fallen beam.

As an icy chill ran the length of her spine Ellen knew that, although Hennessey was likely to have started the fire, it was Danny Donovan behind the deed.

With a hot meal and three brandies in his stomach Robert was beginning to feel better. He folded his silk dressing gown around him and prodded the logs on the fire with a poker. A few sparks illuminated the room for a second, then returned it to its soft, warm glow. Robert had set the lamps to low. He was warm and smoke-free after a soak in the hot tub and his hair was now clean, but still damp at the edges. He had put his trousers back on, but hadn't bothered with his shirt.

He had spent three hours in the Wapping Police Station with Inspector Jackson, giving an account of the disastrous events. In one respect, the fire at the dispensary might have brought Jackson a little nearer to getting that hard evidence, because Brian Hennessey had been apprehended a mile away with lamp oil spilled down his clothes. According to Jackson, when the draymen caught him, Hennessey was fighting drunk. They would have to wait until he sobered up before they could question him fully. Given the enormity of the criminal charges that awaited him, Jackson was hopeful that he might turn king's evidence.

Settled in his leather chair by the fire Robert

took another sip of warm brandy and thought of Ellen. She was his only thought when he desperately threw himself through the glass window of the dispensary and he had thought of her on and off for the rest of the day. He desperately wanted to see her and hold her – and he was still determined to marry her. But now, after coming so close to death, Robert wanted to live with Ellen, however that might be. First thing in the morning he would go to her.

The fire... A wave of sadness swept over him. He would organise a sum of money to be sent to Thomas's widowed mother in Shoreditch. But there had been not only Thomas, but the Chambers, the Harrises, the Moodys, and the other families who lived in the lodging houses on either side of his rooms – houses now just charred ruins. As a doctor he had seen many terrible things, but the sight of people desperately trying to escape through windows as the fire consumed them would haunt him for the rest of his days.

Letting his head fall back, he closed his eyes and thought of tomorrow. He would ask, nay, beg, Ellen to be his wife, but if she said no this time he would forget his principles and love her as she asked.

There was a faint knock on the door. Thinking it was Bulmer, Robert kept his eyes closed and called 'Enter'. He heard the door open and close then nothing. He opened his eyes.

Standing in the soft light of the dimmed lamp was Ellen. She was dressed in the same light-green dress in which he had first seen her, with a warm coat over it. Her hair was covered with her shawl, which obscured the lower part of her face, but it was her eyes that caught his heart. They stared at him with love brimming out of their dark-green depths. He rose slowly from the chair, his gaze taking in every last detail of her as she stood in his room.

They stared at each other for a second, then Robert reached out his hand. She shrugged off her shawl and coat as she came towards him, throwing herself into his embrace.

'Thank God,' she said, sobbing into his chest. Robert let his arms encircle her, pulling her close to him.

His large hand held her head tenderly as he kissed her hair over and over again. 'It's all right, my love. How did you get in?' he asked, not quite believing that she was actually in his arms.

'I caught Bulmer at the back door and told him I needed to see you.' She looked up at him with an amused smile on her face. 'Don't worry, I'm sure he is discreet.'

'I don't give a damn if he is or isn't, I am not ashamed of you or my love for you,' he said.

She didn't answer, just hugged him to her. 'When I saw your dispensary and thought you were dead in that rubble, I didn't want to live, Robert, not without you,' she said, tilting her face up towards his.

Her words spread though him, warming him with love as he gazed down into her beautiful face. He smiled at her. 'I love you so much.'

'I love you,' she said breathlessly, her arms sliding around him and holding him close.

'Then marry me,' he begged, her closeness

beginning to interfere with his thought processes.

She shook her head, a small regretful smile on her lips. 'Make love to me, Robert,' she answered, as her small hand reached around the back of his neck and pulled him to her.

'Please, Ellen,' he begged.

Again the small shake of her head. 'Robert, I want you,' she answered as her lips parted in readiness for his kiss.

Robert's senses were swamped with Ellen against him, imploring him to make love to her. He had fought with all the strength he could muster and he would win the war to make Ellen his wife, but for now he had to concede this battle to her. He was only a man and with the woman who held his heart begging him to make love to her, Robert had neither the will nor the inclination to fight any longer.

Ellen lay for a long while listening to Robert breathe. Behind the heavy drapes at the window the clock of St Mary's chimed twelve.

She had awakened just a few moments ago, wondering where she was, then snuggled back into Robert's warm body as she remembered. His arm had slid possessively around her in his sleep and remained there, his hand relaxed on her hip. She shifted up onto one elbow and gazed down at him in the dim light. He stirred as she moved, but did not wake.

Ellen knew that she would have to leave soon, but not quite yet. She wanted to watch the man she loved as he slept.

He was lying on his back, the arm furthest away

from Ellen behind his head. He had kicked the covers down and they now barely covered his hips. Ellen casually studied him in the half light. If she hadn't known better, she would have thought his profession was that of a labourer, not a doctor, as his physique was like one that had been honed by hard manual work. His broad chest was covered with a thick mass of hair that tapered down the centre of his stomach only to spread again as it travelled below his navel.

Her gaze wandered back to Robert's profile and to the night-time bristle now clearly visible across his cheek and over his chin. She lightly rested her hand on the delicate skin at the top of her breasts where those bristles had scraped her skin as Robert covered her with hot kisses...

Later, Ellen told herself, although the temptation to wake Robert now and make love to him nearly overwhelmed her. Her hand reached out and she rested it gently on his chest. His hand came back and covered it.

If you married Robert you wouldn't have to leave, a little voice inside her head said and for one brief moment Ellen allowed herself the luxury of imagining a world where she and Robert could be man and wife.

A tear caught her unexpectedly. There was no point wishing for the impossible, such a world didn't exist. All they had was this moment, and any happiness they could snatch in the future.

A cart on its way to market rattled over the cobbled street outside and Robert started up. He blinked twice, then looked across at her, and his face relaxed. He pulled her into his arms and

243

gazed down at her.

'Marry me, Ellen,' he said simply.

She gave him a bright smile. 'You know I can't.'

'I know no such thing,' he said, holding her tighter. 'All I know is I can't live without you and have no intention of doing so.'

Say yes, you fool! her mind and emotions told her. For one split second the word hovered on her lips. It would be so easy. One little word. Turning away from her own happiness she gave him a sad smile and shook her head.

'I won't give up,' he said fixing her with a penetrating look.

She struggled half-heartedly against him. 'It's just past midnight. I have to go,' she said, trying to twist out of his arms. His hand slid up her leg, over her hip bone and up to her breast.

'Not yet, Ellen, just an hour more.' He pulled her to him and slid his leg over hers.

What could she say? How could she refuse? Reaching up, Ellen moved the lock of unruly hair off his forehead. Robert smiled and gathered her under him once again.

Sixteen

'Doctor Munroe,' Jackson said taking Robert's hand in a firm grip and looking him in the eye.

Robert sat down again. 'Any news?'

Jackson sat back and crossed one massive leg over the other. 'Firstly, I am pleased to tell you that

Hennessey has agreed to turn king's evidence. He is faced with a charge of murder on twelve counts after his little escapade with the lamp.'

'Twelve!' Robert said, shocked at the enormity of it.

'Yes, twelve, and three of them minors,' Jackson said. 'I'll tell you, Hennessey's looking at a hanging and no mistake. He maintains that he never intended to kill anyone, just to get back at you.'

'That won't be much comfort to Weaver's mother,' Robert said, thinking of the letter he had to write later.

'No, indeed,' Jackson agreed. 'But at least we have him as a witness against Danny Donovan.'

'Splendid,' Robert said.

'I wish it were that simple.'

'Surely with Hennessey's evidence you are now able to make a case against Donovan?' Robert said, leaning forward. 'The Emergency Committee is only just uncovering the extent of Donovan's corruption. We have yet to get to the bottom of the accounts, but I know that the funds that should be going into the upkeep of the roads and drains are going straight into Donovan's back pocket. I have also uncovered details of a number of other women who had to attend the hospital's casual ward after a visit to Old Annie.'

Jackson sat back and shook his head. 'It's not enough. Danny Donovan might be a sadistic killer, a woman-hating pimp and an extortionist, but he is a clever one. Each time I have come close to linking him to a death or a burnt-out shop he slips through my fingers. Either he has got someone else, like Hennessey, to do his dirty work, or those who may have seen him perpetrate a crime or commit a murder are so afraid of his retribution that they won't come forward to give evidence.'

'But you have Hennessey,' Robert said.

'I have. But a good barrister,' he gave Robert a weary look, 'and, believe me Danny Donovan can afford the best, would demolish Hennessey's credibility as a witness in a moment by pointing to his own criminal associations and calling into question his motive for naming Donovan.' Jackson forcefully slammed a clenched fist into the palm of his other hand. 'What I need is firm evidence, in black and white, to link Donovan to his crimes. Then and only then will he be brought to justice. Although just to let you know that we have made some headway, between you and me, I will be paying Old Annie a visit soon.'

So many dead, Robert thought. He recalled the dying Kitty Henry, along with the lifeless face of Thomas, and the distraught mother at the lodging-house window. A steel band of fear suddenly gripped his heart as Ellen came into his mind. He wouldn't put it past Danny to maim her for the sheer pleasure of it if he found out about their relationship.

'You're right, Inspector. Until Donovan is convicted for his crimes none of us can go about our business without looking over our shoulders,' Robert said. 'I have contacts in the Cabinet. I have been in correspondence with Lord Melbourne, the Home Secretary, and Lord Ashley. I will ask them to speak to the Lord Chancellor.'

Jackson's mouth went into a tight line. 'I appreciate your help, Munroe. But as I said before, what

I want now is evidence, firm evidence, before any more innocents die because of Danny Donovan.'

Ellen sat in Robert's leather chair, wearing his silk dressing gown and with her feet tucked beneath her. Her hair was unbound and hung about her like a shimmering cloak while her bare skin tingled against the warm fabric that enveloped her. Across the room the fire crackled in the grate, warming the room and causing shadows to dance upon the wall of the study, whose heavy drapes were closed against the world outside. She sipped the sweet chocolate in the cup she held in her hand and watched Robert over the brim as he sat writing at his desk.

After settling Josie with Sarah Nolan and her lively brood for the night, Ellen had dashed to Robert's rooms. Not able to bear time apart from each other, they had fallen into each other's arms, but now they relaxed in Robert's comfortable study like a long-married couple. He scribbled his correspondence with a bold flourish of his quill and she quietly kept him company.

Oh, if it could only be, Ellen thought as a lump caught in her throat. She pushed the unhelpful dream away and turned her mind to her own correspondence. Two days after Bridget had died she had written to Joe in New York, telling him that she and Josie would be taking passage at the end of October and hoped to be with him, winter storms permitting, before Christmas. But now things, in the shape of Robert, had changed. And she was torn in two.

There was no possibility that she would ever be

able to give Josie better opportunities in life if she stayed in London. America was their only chance. But Robert!

After so nearly losing him, she could not think of leaving him for America without physical pain wrenching her heart in two. The domestic tranquillity of Robert's cosy study and rooms could not eliminate the brutal world outside.

She watched him as he concentrated on his letter, and her heart caught in her throat. He sat with his trousers and shirt on, but the latter was unbuttoned and gaped open. His hair was tousled and the wayward curl at the front hung forward over his eyes. The small muscles of his hands and fingers twitched the quill swiftly over the paper, making a soft scratching noise. He stopped for a moment and chewed the end of the feather for a second, then jabbed it back in the glass inkwell to replenish it.

Maybe they could be married, if they were discreet. But what about later when he was overlooked for a post? Would he still love her if she blighted his future? He might not think it now, but what about in a year or two's time? How would he feel about her then?

Not wanting to continue down the path her thoughts were leading her, Ellen uncurled herself and stood up. Slowly she strolled over to Robert, her bare feet making no sound on the Turkish carpet. He looked up and smiled warmly at her. He scraped the chair back and opened his lap for her to sit on. Ellen took up the invitation and flipped over the sealed letters at the top of his blotting paper.

'Do you know Viscount Melbourne?' Ellen asked in a hushed voice.

'I have met him a couple of times, though my acquaintance is with Lord Ashley,' Robert said, resting his hand lightly on her hip and stroking his fingers back and forth.

'*Lord Ashley?*' Ellen said in an astonished voice.

'Yes, he is the Member of Parliament for Woodstock and is interested in factory and living conditions of the poor.' Robert's hand slid up around her waist. 'It was he who suggested me for the post at the London Hospital after he had read my book.'

How would a lord and a viscount view Robert if he married a public house singer? Ellen doubted they would be corresponding.

'How did you get on at Wapping Police Station?'

'Jackson's after Danny Donovan, that's for sure. He has a file on him as thick as my thumb. That was before he caught Hennessey trying to burn me out.' His face darkened for a moment, and she guessed he was thinking of all those who had perished in the fire. 'A number of witnesses have come forward and *Hennessey* has turned king's evidence,' Robert continued in a serious voice. 'I said I would help in any way I could. That is why I am writing to the Home Secretary.'

A small shiver crept up Ellen's spine. She stood up and faced Robert, grabbing him forcefully by the shoulder and making him look at her. 'Robert, Danny didn't just burn you out. He tried to kill you.'

He fixed his eyes on her. 'I know that, Ellen. He has tried to silence me for weeks now. First, the visit to the hospit–'

'The hospital?' Ellen said, her eyes stretched wide as she looked down at Robert.

Robert lifted the side of his mouth in a mocking smile. 'Oh, yes. He and Black Mike came to have a *word* with me.'

Ellen's heart lurched uncomfortably in her chest and she felt herself start to tremble. Two-finger Sven had been dragged from the river a week ago after Danny had a *word* with him.

'Now, now what's this?' Robert said, his voice full of concern. He scooped her into his arms and held her tight to his chest. She felt his lips on her hair and the steady thump of his heart. Her own slowed a tad. Then a vision of Danny breaking a costermonger's arm because he had kept some of his takings back sprang into her mind.

Twisting in Robert's embrace, Ellen slid her arms around his neck. 'Be careful. Those who oppose Danny often meet a bloody end. Let Jackson catch him.'

'Ellen, my love,' he said in a light tone, starting to kiss her in a more purposeful way. 'I can look after myself. I learnt early in life that you need to confront bullies, and Jackson can't do it without help. Now, let's not talk about Danny any more. There are far more pleasant things for us to do.'

His hand slipped inside the front of the dressing gown and opened it. His eyes glided over her body. 'You're looking particularly lovely this evening.'

Ellen pulled herself from his embrace.

'You don't understand, Robert. This conflict between you and Danny is not a disagreement between gentlemen, with rules and courtesies,' she told him, gathering the open gown around her. She started to pace back and forth on the patterned carpet.

'Danny Donovan's a monster,' she said. 'He'll slash a girl's face if she won't pay him the money she's made working the streets, and you think you can look after yourself!' A sob burst from her. 'He'll kill you, Robert. He'll wait for you and slit your throat one dark night. He's done it before to others who have crossed him. You don't know how much he hates you for your interference in his business an ... and...' The words caught in her throat.

Robert stood up and drew her to him. 'You don't have to be afraid any more. Trust me. I will protect you and Josie.' He smoothed her hair away from her forehead. 'Jackson is very close to having what he needs to arrest him. All we need now is some hard and fast evidence that will link him to the many deaths and assaults and show the full extent of his web of dark dealings.'

'What sort of evidence?'

He took hold of her chin with his thumb and forefinger and tilted her head up and his lips descended on hers. 'Let's not talk about Danny Donovan any more.'

His hand smoothed over her stomach and around to her bottom.

'What sort of evidence?' Ellen asked.

'Names and dates of people who owe Danny or who are paying him for protection,' he said, kissing her neck below her ear and slipping the silk gown from her shoulders. 'Something in black and white.'

Seventeen

Danny Donovan sat at his table in the White Swan on Tuesday evening, scowling ferociously, with Black Mike lounging opposite him. He lifted the empty brandy bottle and shook it over his head and a nervous-looking waiter brought over another. Danny threw the bottle in his hand on the floor to join the other three he and Mike had consumed during the evening.

It was not his usual practice to have supper at the White Swan on Thursdays, but over the last few weeks Robert Munroe's investigations had brought the first crop of arrests.

After that snivelling bastard Hennessey turned king's evidence, Old Annie and Murphy were put away by the police and now Milo, second only to Black Mike, had been taken into custody.

The arrests had sent ripples of disquiet among many of Danny's business acquaintances. Some of those who had fallen over themselves to buy him a drink not a month ago were now avoiding him like he had the pox. If he had known the word, Danny would have called his situation humiliating.

He threw the last of the brandy down the back of his throat and poured another into his glass with a shaky hand. The comedian with a small dog dressed as a clown left the stage to grumbles and boos from the audience and Maggie, the new

252

singer Forster had engaged, stepped into the centre of the stage.

Danny pulled out the well-worn ledger and thumbed through it. The names underscored in red meant that Danny's men needed to have a *word* with them. There were others whose names had been scratched across once; in these cases, such a word had fallen on deaf ears, and the offenders now needed to be dealt with after which the name received a second line through it. Those names with double crossings-out were often the same names issued by the Wapping Police Station of people found dead in the gutters or washed up in the mud at high tide.

Danny looked at two names, Brown and Turlock, both of whom Wag was visiting that very night. He took out a stubby pencil and crossed the final line through both names with a bold stroke. Contemplating the imminent demise of the two unfortunates who had fallen foul of him, Danny's spirits rose a notch. He tapped on the page under another entry.

'Dirty Mary and China Rose both owe me a good number of sovereigns. I think we'll pay them a visit in an hour or two when their brothels are full of customers with their pricks up and their trousers down.'

Mike grinned. 'They'll soon cough up the coin.'

'They had better. They won't be able to charge their usual shilling if their noses are missing.'

Maggie almost hit a top C as she launched into another lively song.

'That there singer's got big tits and a fat arse, Danny,' Mike said, as customers around them winced. 'But, to be sure, doesn't she just murder every note that the good Lord ever invented?' Mike stretched his arms behind his head. 'Still, since Ellen's gone...'

'That bastard Munroe,' Danny said, narrowing his eyes as gnawing frustration started in his vitals again.

'Yeah, I don't s'pose that Doctor Munroe would be happy to have his fancy showing her ankles on the stage of the Angel.'

'Jumped-up madam,' Donovan spat out. He spotted a young lad collecting the glasses from the table. 'Mind your place, boy,' he said, and fetched the lad a stinging blow with the back of his hand. The boy staggered under the blow and scurried away.

'I'm surprised that Munroe hasn't set her up in some fancy house by now,' Mike said, filling both their glasses to the brim again. ''Tis a pity she's gone, though,' he continued, eyeing the young woman cavorting on the stage. 'She rolled in the pennies at the Angel and added a bit of class.'

'Class!' Danny spat out. 'Thinks herself above her class, does Ellen O'Casey. She's forgotten those who were good to her after that no-good, philandering husband of hers died. When it was the workhouse for her and her brat, she was pleased enough to sing for me, so she was. You'd think she would have shown her gratitude the usual way, but no. Tells me she's too fecking respectable for that.' He gripped his glass and his knuckles cracked. 'Respectable? Huh! So fecking respectable she opens her legs for Munroe after a couple of smiles. Haven't I always treated her well?'

Mike shrugged and cracked a flea from his beard between his finger and thumb.

Danny let out a loud belch. 'Yes. I treated her well. Did I force her? No,' he said, answering his own question. 'I behaved like the gentleman I am.' Mike raised an eyebrow and Danny waved it away. 'A light-hearted bit of hand work don't count.'

Hand work. Danny flexed his stubby fingers and gave Maggie a closer look. She was jigging on the stage as she sang. A lecherous grin crossed his face.

He enjoyed a bit of hand work with the girls. The more they resisted or tried to fend him off, the more he liked it. But Ellen had never cried or whimpered as the others did, just glared at him in outrage. Strangely, this had stopped him from going as far as he would have liked, and left him frustrated. An interesting image came into his head, of him ripping Ellen's clothes off and her begging him to stop. But he wouldn't stop, he never did.

His hand went inside his front flap and clutched hold of his half-erect penis. 'I'll promise you that, me fella me lad,' he said to his crotch, as he thought of Ellen sprawled on the floor, her clothes ripped from her body.

'Danny!' Mike said sharply, sitting up.

Danny stopped his rambling and followed the direction of Mike's gaze across the room.

His mouth dropped open as his eye came to rest on Ellen standing in front of the White Swan's main entrance.

Ellen's heart missed several beats and her knees shook as she pushed on the polished horn doorplate of the White Swan's public rooms.

She had dressed carefully for the evening in a lightweight calico gown of a floral print: red and blue flowers, little green leaves. To keep out the autumn chill she had thrown on an old velvet opera cloak that had been very tatty when she had bought it from Isaac Levy but, with a great deal of tucking and stitching by herself and Bridget, had been restored to some of its former glory.

Suppressing the almost overwhelming urge to turn tail and run, she stepped into the room and looked around. She didn't have to look far because there, in the corner of the room, sat Danny and Mike. From the debris of bottles on the floor around them, she guessed they had been there some time.

Squaring her shoulders, Ellen put on what she hoped was a relaxed, inviting smile and swayed through the tables towards Danny.

She let her eyes rest on him coolly and he glared back at her. Sitting open in front of him was his ledger of accounts and grudges. He snapped it shut as she stopped in front of him.

'What the feck do you want?' he snapped, his gaze running over her slowly.

Ellen breathed slowly to calm her raging pulse. Danny might be many things, but he was no fool.

'Do I have to want something to visit an old friend?' she asked, slipping the opera cape off her shoulders and letting it fall on a spare chair.

Danny studied her and Ellen forced herself not to move under his scrutiny. Although his posture was relaxed, his eyes had the all-too-familiar expression of lust clouding them.

He leant back and the chair creaked. 'All women want something.'

Mike sniggered and Danny's eyes glided over her again. He slid forward on the chair and straightened the front of his trousers. Ellen suppressed a shudder.

She stuck out her lower lip and looked seductively at him from under her lashes. His expression changed from lechery to disbelief, then back to lechery. Putting her hands on the table, Ellen leant forward. Danny's eyes rested on her breasts momentarily, then returned to her face.

'I'm not all women, Danny. You should know that,' Ellen said, smiling warmly at him.

Danny grabbed the coat on the chair behind him and slid the ledger into an inside pocket.

'What do you want?' he asked, trying to maintain his belligerent expression while his gaze continued to devour her breasts.

'Just a word, that's all.' Ellen glanced at Mike. 'In private.'

'Do you hear that Mike? Lady Ellen here wants a *private* word,' Danny said.

For one awful moment Ellen thought she would have to carry out her plan in full view of Danny's bully boy, but then Danny's lips became slack and he took Ellen's hand.

Remembering why she was standing in the White Swan a foot away from Danny Donovan, Ellen let her hand remain in his.

'If it's a private word you're being after, well then, I've been after that myself since I first set eyes on you,' he said, lifting her hand to his mouth and kissing it slowly.

With his eyes fixed to her face he drew her towards him until their legs touched, then ran his free hand up the outside of her thigh, ruffling up the fabric of her dress as he did so.

He watched for her reaction but Ellen remained unshaken by his fondling. Steeling herself to play the part she had to, Ellen rubbed her leg against Danny's stout knees. For one split second, as his expression registered total surprise at her actions, he actually looked boyish, then the venal expression returned.

'Get us another bottle, Mike, and don't rush back,' Danny told his man, without taking his eyes from Ellen's face.

Black Mike shrugged and ambled over to the bar.

Ellen slid onto the chair next to Danny and forced tears into her eyes. Laying her hand on his arm she looked beseechingly up at him.

'Oh, Danny,' she said, with a quiver in her voice.

Ellen didn't have to pretend to be afraid and shaking because so close to Danny, she was.

A tear rolled slowly down her right cheek. If he had looked surprised at her caressing his knee, he was positively astounded now. He had never seen her cry before. 'I've been such a fool,' she told him.

'You, and every other fecking woman I know,' he said, reaching up and tracing his index finger down her cheek.

Every bit of her wanted to dash for the door but Ellen shoved the urge aside.

'I should have listened to you. You were right about Rob ... Doctor Munroe,' she said, as Danny smoothed his finger over her jaw and down her neck. 'He promised me a house and an allowance, and I, soft-hearted fool that I am, believed him. But it seems he only wanted a...' She trailed off.

His first finger slid across her collarbone while his other fingers trailed across the top of her breast. If she didn't stop his hand travelling over her skin she would vomit so, shifting away, she drew a handkerchief from her sleeve and dabbed her eyes. 'I'm finding it a bit of a struggle at the moment. Josie's only young and she can't do the work Mammy could.'

'What's that to me?' Danny asked, in an indifferent tone that was belied by his heavy eyelids.

He placed his hand on her thigh and squeezed. Ellen gave him a shy smile and ran a finger around on the back of his hairy hand.

'I thought you had a soft spot for me, Danny,' she said, wondering if she had gone too far.

Loosing his hand from under hers, he moved it up to her hip and then around to her buttocks. The impulse to brush him off her as she had done many times before came over her, but knowing that she must, Ellen endured his roving fingers. He shuffled forward until his face was a mean inch or two from hers.

Up close, Ellen could see the little flecks of brown in Danny's pale eyes. She could also see the unruly way his eyebrows grew, smell the dankness of his sweat and the spirit on his breath.

A strange needy expression settled in his eyes. 'You're a grand, lovely woman so you are, Ellen

259

O'Casey,' he said. 'I would have made you my special gal long since but you thought yourself too good for the likes of me.'

'Oh, Danny,' Ellen said, dabbing her eyes again in an attempt to keep what little distance there was between them.

'It's oh, Danny, is it now,' he said, his eyes hardening to their usual pitiless expression. He took hold of the back of her head and forced her to look at him. 'I wasn't good enough before, but now this bastard Munroe's finished jiggy-jigging, you come back to good old, kind-hearted Danny, telling me things are a bit of a struggle?'

Holding herself rigid, Ellen held his gaze.

He shifted the chair and his coat, hanging over the chair, flapped back with the movement. Out of the corner of her eye Ellen saw Danny's ledger poking out from the inside pocket.

Taking a deep breath and praying her courage would hold, Ellen threw herself into Danny's arms.

'Please, Danny, can I have my job back?' she asked, looking at him imploringly.

'Maggie's replaced you,' he said, indicating the stage where the woman in question was bidding farewell to a disinterested crowd.

Swallowing hard, Ellen slid her arm around Danny's rotund figure. 'Please, Danny,' she said again in a low sensual voice. His eyes fastened on her and a shudder crawled along her spine.

She watched as he studied her, calculating the advantages of the situation to himself without warmth or compassion.

On the pretext of snuggling up to him, Ellen felt

along the silk lining of the jacket hanging on the back of the chair. Her fingertips touched the hard spine of the ledger but as she went to close her hand around it Danny dragged her across his lap.

One of his hands held her around the waist while the other fastened on her leg. 'Let's see how grateful you are.'

Flicking the frills of her skirt up, he placed his hand on her calf, then moved his hand up. Ellen squirmed, but his iron grip held her fast. His hand reached her drawers and he delved up her flimsy underwear. Ellen suffered his probing fingers while she searched through the coat pocket for the ledger.

Stay calm, stay calm, she ordered herself.

Just as she thought she could stand no more of Danny's violation Ellen felt the soft leather of the slim notebook. This time she grasped it firmly and, giggling, twisted out of Danny's arms.

Her palms were moist and she could feel beads of perspiration springing out on her forehead. If he saw she had his ledger, she was dead. She feigned a stumble against the chair where the heavy opera cloak lay and swiftly slid the ledger inside the velvet layers.

She staggered up and swept the cloak up and held it firmly to her. She wagged her finger playfully at Danny.

'*I've* shown how grateful I am prepared to be, now *you* let me have my job back,' she said, patting her hair back into place and tucking the cloak under her arm.

Danny rubbed his hand over his crotch and grinned. 'Aren't I known as a benevolent sort of a fellow, Mike?' he said to his henchman, who had returned carrying a fresh bottle of brandy.

'That you are, Danny, none more so,' Mike said, taking up his usual position behind his boss.

'Well, then, Ellen. Although many would call me soft in the head after the way you've treated me, you can have your old spot at the Angel on Thursday nights,' Danny said with a show of munificence.

'And right glad my ears will be to hear you again,' Mike added with some feeling.

Danny reached out for Ellen again. She stepped aside, but his hand grabbed her. 'Now get back on my lap and show your gratitude again.'

He dragged her towards him. If he took her in his arms, he would surely feel the ledger in the lining of her cloak and, even if he didn't, she could not take another minute of Danny clawing and jabbing at her.

'Dirty Mary and China Rose?' Mike said.

While Danny's attention was on Mike, Ellen twisted away from him.

'Tomorrow,' Danny snapped, looking hotly at Ellen.

'Tomorrow we is up west,' Mike reminded him.

Danny's face grew dark. He lurched forward and for one ghastly moment Ellen thought he was going to demand that she sit back on his lap. But, as if sent by heaven, a waiter brought another bottle of brandy and he turned his attention to the fresh spirit. He pulled the cork off with his teeth and spat it on the floor.

He sent Mike a curt nod and poured another drink.

'Until Thursday then, Ellen,' he said, watching her with calculating eyes. Planning, no doubt, what he would make her do to show her gratitude.

With a pleasant smile fixed on her face Ellen turned to the door. She looked at Danny over her shoulder. He and Mike were now sitting close with their heads together. Mike pulled out his knife and turned it in his hand as he spoke.

God help Dirty Mary and China Rose, whoever they are.

Shaking inwardly, her legs feeling as they were about to buckle beneath her, Ellen managed to get them working sufficiently to escape from the bar room. Hugging the cloak tight around her, she dashed along Shadwell High Street towards her home.

As the sounds of the White Swan faded behind her, she slowed her pace and stopped at the corner of Cannon and Cable Streets. Leaning on the rough stone wall of someone's backyard she took a deep breath. Forcing her fingers into action Ellen pulled out a sheet of waxed paper and a length of string from her bodice and hastily wrapped Danny's ledger in it. Then, taking another long breath, she stepped out from the shadow, tucked the parcel under her arm and dashed towards St George's church.

Although Mike was still talking, Danny turned his head and watched Ellen as she left the public room of the White Swan. Wiping his nose with his sleeve, he visualised squeezing the breath out of her by fixing her under him and ramming home.

'What did I tell you, Mike? They all come

crawling back,' he said.

Forgetting his planned nocturnal visit to the two madams in Neptune Street, Danny let his mind race on to extracting in full measure what Ellen owed his pride. His cock valiantly tried to rise to the occasion, but the three bottles of brandy had taken their toll.

Mike pulled out a large gold hunter from his waistcoat fob. 'We had better be on our way in a while, Danny,' he said, folding his knife closed and tucking it back inside his jacket.

'And so we shall, so we shall,' Danny said, biting off the end of the cigar and spitting the end on the floor. He grinned widely and leaned back on his groaning chair. 'I was just giving Mrs O'Casey a moment or two in my thoughts.'

'I can imagine,' Mike said, and inserted an index finger into a circle made with the finger and thumb of his other hand. With graphic lewdness, he pushed it back and forth.

Satisfaction puffed out Danny's chest. He wasn't used to waiting, but now—

He leered across at Mike. 'That would be the way, eventually. But I was thinking that, seeing she wants her job back so bad, she might want to show me how in other ways,' Danny replied, putting his index finger into his mouth.

'That's rare,' Mike said.

Both men adjusted the contents of their front-flaps.

Through the haze of cigar smoke Maggie tottered towards Danny and Mike with a coy expression on her flushed face. Mike's arm shot out and grabbed her across his lap. With a flourish of lace petticoats she made a half-hearted show of indignation.

'If you're busy with Ellen, you'll not mind me keeping Maggie company then,' he said, delving his hand down the front of her dress and fondling her breast. Maggie giggled.

'Not at all,' Danny said. 'But as you said a moment ago we have a couple of business visits to make before we can turn our minds to pleasure.'

Danny stood up and so did Mike, spilling Maggie off his lap in a dishevelled heap.

Danny shrugged on his jacket and put his hand in his pocket to fetch out his ledger. The pocket was empty. He tried the other pocket, but again, other than his red handkerchief, there was nothing. He stared around dumbly for a moment. It must be there. He had tucked it away not half an hour ago.

'What's the crack, Danny?'

'My ledger. It's gone.'

'It can't be gone,' Mike replied, now searching through Danny's breast pockets. 'It must have fallen on the floor.'

Mike kicked back the chair and started to search on the floor. Danny did the same. There was the usual debris but no ledger. Frantically, they scoured the floor either side of the table, pushing customers off their chairs in the process. Those around them were on their feet now and moved away as Danny searched the whole area around his table. But, despite clearing the entire floor, the slim, leather-bound ledger was nowhere in sight.

The full horror of the situation swept over Danny. All his debts were in there. The neat columns listed everyone who owed him money, showing who had paid and who had not. There was a list too of the various officers of the port who turned a blind eye to missing goods and what he paid them. All his interests in the highways, and the brothels that paid him, were noted. But most worrying of all were the names scrubbed out. What if the police got hold of the ledger?

Whoever has it will want money for it, Danny thought, and for one second was actually relieved. But who?

Then the vision of Ellen throwing herself on his lap floated into his mind and he knew. The ledger was not on the floor or anywhere else in the White Swan and no one would be trying to sell it back to him, because Ellen had slipped it away.

She had come to find him deliberately so as to get her hands on it. She knew what was in there and how it could damn him. She had sought him out, feigned regret and wriggled on his lap – for Munroe.

Danny's mind roared with fury. Ellen had stolen his ledger from under his very nose for the man who had sworn to expose him and who was working against him.

'The bitch,' he ground out, as those around him backed away.

'Ellen?' Mike asked in a voice of disbelief. 'Surely she wouldn't–'

At her name Danny exploded. 'She'd do anything for that bastard doctor.' He took hold of the bottle on the table and hurled it on the floor. It smashed and the contents spilled over the floor. No one moved. 'She never let me touch her before. Never. But she'd suffer me touching her just to get the ledger for *him*.'

Grabbing the table before him in his paw-like hands, Danny raised it over his head. A couple of women screamed, men left their drinks and made for the door. Henry Forster had come out from his parlour to see what the rumpus was about, but stood still by the bar watching, like everyone else, as Danny stood for a few seconds with the pine table aloft then heaved it towards the mirror that covered the wall behind him.

The table met the shiny surface of the glass, shattering it into hundreds of shards.

As the last tinkle of glass faded, Mike crunched over the wreckage towards Danny. 'You'll have to get it back off her, Danny,' he said in a tense voice. 'Or we'll swing.'

'I'll get it back, that I will,' Danny said, breathing hard, with flecks of spittle around his mouth and on his chin. 'Mike, go and see if she goes to Munroe and I'll go to her home.' His lips drew back into a demonic grimace. 'Seeing as our Ellen has a liking for doctors, the surgeons at Bart's Hospital can have her corpse when I'm done with her.'

Eighteen

Where is that girl? Ellen thought, as she ran into her small front parlour. She had told Josie specifically not to go out, to wait for her at home. Ellen put her hand on the stove. It was still warm but hadn't been attended to for an hour or so by her reckoning.

She bit her lip fearfully. So far everything had gone to plan. The ledger was safe and now she had to make sure she and Josie would be safe, too, by getting to Robert's rooms at the hospital as soon as possible. They needed to be out of Danny's reach because when he found his precious ledger was missing it wouldn't take him long to realise who had taken the slim book. And his fury would be deadly.

But now Josie was out somewhere and what if Danny found Josie?

Fear, panic and terror coursed through Ellen. *For the love of Mary, Josie, come home.*

Dashing upstairs, Ellen gathered together the bundle of her books, marriage lines and poor pieces of jewellery that she had packed in her old carpet bag before leaving for the White Swan two hours earlier. She returned downstairs hoping that Josie would appear.

Her hopes were dashed as she looked again around the deserted lower room.

She'll feel my hand when she does arrive, Ellen thought, as panic at her precarious situation swirled around her. She didn't have time to waste.

The front door rattled for a second, then the latch lifted up as the string outside was pulled. Relief swept over Ellen.

The front door opened, but it was Danny Donovan, not Josie, who stepped into the small front room.

He closed the door behind him and smiled artlessly at her.

'Ellen, me darling girl, I thought seeing as we were getting on so famously a little while back I'd pop by. It's not too late, I hope?' He spoke in a convivial tone and tilted his head to one side.

Although her heart was galloping in her chest, Ellen matched his smile. 'I thought you were out visiting with Mike,' she replied, noticing that despite her best efforts her hands plucked nervously at the fabric of her skirt.

He moved forward, his leather boot shedding slurry from the street outside onto her rag carpet. Ellen stepped back and found herself backed against the table. Danny stopped just in front of her and put his hands on both hips. His smile widened, crinkling the small lines around his eyes.

'He can handle the night's business by himself so I thought why wait until Thursday before I had you bouncing on my lap showing your, gratitude,' he said, winking at her.

Ellen relaxed a little.

When she had seen him in her doorway her heart had nearly jumped out of her mouth. She felt sure that he would have discovered the ledger was missing by now, but maybe he hadn't ... and he was, after all, just coming to get what she'd promised him in the Swan.

That was bad enough, but she might still be able to stall him. If Josie arrived home, as she should have done by now, Ellen still might be able to get them safely away from Danny.

Danny raised his hand slowly and Ellen only just stopped from flinching. He lifted a coil of hair sitting on her shoulder and turned it over between his fingers. He studied it in the dim light from the lamp then turned his attention back to her.

She forced herself to give a little laugh. 'Well, Danny. It's a bit late and' – she sent him a shy smile – 'you know, I'm not ... not prepar–'

He twisted the length of hair around his finger and his eyebrows rose up. 'Now, don't be bashful there, Ellen, me love. You were willing enough a while ago.'

A sorrowful expression formed itself on his face. 'You're not expecting anyone else, are you?'

'No. It's just that–'

'Like our esteemed Doctor Munroe,' he asked, cocking his head to one side.

Fear like ice, cut through Ellen, but she managed to summon up a confused expression. 'Why would he come here? I told you he's finished with me.'

With a lightning move, Danny grasped the back of her head and yanked her to him. 'So you can give him my ledger,' he snarled.

Her head throbbed where he tore at her hair but she held on to her perplexed look. 'Ledger? I don't–'

Danny twisted her hair and Ellen screamed.

'Where is it?'

Leaving Danny with a fistful of her hair, Ellen wrenched herself free of his grasp and jumped behind the table. 'I do ... don't know what you're talking about.'

'Don't fecking give me that,' he said, taking hold of the edge of the table. 'My ledger. Where is it?'

Ellen backed away. 'Honestly, Danny, I don't kn–'

Danny's balled fist smashed across her face. She felt her lip split as she staggered back, frantically clutching onto anything to stop herself falling. Her head landed against the small table at the side of the fire, knocking the cups and saucers on it to the stone floor with a crash.

He wagged his finger at her, a playful smile hovering on his lips. 'Now, don't you be playing games with me, Ellen. You fooled me for a moment there,' he said, 'I thought you had seen which field your harvest was in at last.' The ingenuous expression fell away and the sadistic one returned. 'Wriggling on my lap and letting me feel you up.' His hand shot out and took hold of her hair again. Twisting it around his fist he pulled her face up to him. 'I know you filched it for him. That bastard doctor of yours. Now where is it?'

He threw her away from him and Ellen staggered back.

'If you've lost your book, it's probably because you're too drunk to remember where you put it,' she said, keeping her voice as level as she could despite her swollen lip.

Danny dashed to the middle of the small room. Although he was a large man he could move swiftly enough if he needed to. He took hold of the table and tossed it aside as if it had been a milking stool. Then he went to the dresser where the crockery sat clean and neatly stacked.

With a great sweep of his arm Danny cleared the top, then crunched over the broken china towards the mantelshelf.

'Where is it?'

'I told you I haven't got it,' Ellen repeated.

271

He grabbed her small collection of books and started to tear them apart, throwing the torn pages behind him.

Ellen tried to slip behind him to the door but Danny caught her. His eyes roamed down to her breasts and his hateful expression changed to one of lust.

'He must have fecked you good, Ellen, if you're ready to cross me like this,' he said, as his free hand took hold of her breast. He fondled it for a few moments, then his hand closed painfully around it. 'Now give me that ledger or I'll be sending you to meet your old mother.'

'I told you I–'

Her words were cut short as he slapped her across her face again. Ellen's knees buckled and at the edges of her vision small stars appeared, then burst. Blackness crept over her mind, but she forced it away as Danny held her upright by the scruff of her neck and hair.

'Where is it, Ellen?' he said, as more blows rained down onto her. 'I'll find it anyhow.' Danny's foul breath assailed Ellen and nausea rose in her throat. 'But before that I'll teach you a lesson that you will never forget,' he said, putting his powerful hand around her neck and squeezing.

Ellen gasped for air as the vice-like grip of his fingers tightened.

I'm going to die, she thought, as jumbled images of Robert and Josie swam around in her mind.

With a guttural growl and a bone-shaking thump Danny let go of her and Ellen sank to the hard floor. She felt the roughness of the knotted rag rug against her cheek, felt air, struggling back

272

into her lungs. Lifting her head she saw the faded colours stained with bright red blood. Putting her fingers to her mouth Ellen felt sticky dampness.

'Bitch,' he said as spit flecked the side of his mouth. 'Where is it?'

Ellen's head pounded and her focus began to blur as the foot of the fire grate came level with her line of vision.

'Answer me, woman.'

As Danny's toe knocked the wind out of her she crumpled back onto the floor. Struggling for breath, she tried to roll into a ball to protect her vital organs. With a swift movement Danny's hand snatched up the poker and raised it over his head.

'For the last time, give me the ledger!' he screamed.

Ellen looked up at the man above her through her half-closed eyes. The iron taste of blood was in her mouth. She swallowed. Danny was now swaying above her with a murderous expression on his face. Ellen would never need to wonder what the devil looked like because in her small front room he was manifest in the person of Danny Donovan.

Stop the pain, her body shouted.

Her lips twisted painfully as she summoned the ghost of a smile. She was dead anyway, whether she gave him the ledger or not.

She didn't want to die, but more than that she didn't want those she loved, Robert and Josie, to live in the evil shadow of Danny Donovan.

With steely determination, Ellen looked into

Danny's cold, blue eyes.

'No,' she said in a surprisingly firm voice. 'And may the Virgin curse your black soul to hell.'

For one second she thought she was saved because Danny's face went purple and he started to tremble. His raised arm shook and the poker wavered.

God strike, Ellen prayed, as Danny's rasping breath tore around the small room.

Then with an animal bellow, Danny swung the poker in a wide arc and down on her.

Ellen's arm came up to shield her head and the narrow metal poker smashed into her forearm sending reverberations down her arm. She sank backwards under the blow and felt the poker break her collarbone.

A vision of Robert came to her mind. He was sitting on a riverbank and beckoning to her.

Robert.

Danny and the pain were receding and Robert was drawing ever closer. Then from somewhere a scream ripped through the scene and the river bank and Robert vanished and the pain returned.

Ellen braced herself for another blow, but now with neither pain nor Robert to focus on, the swirling blackness in her head engulfed her.

'Me mam'll be wild,' Josie said, as she saw the light flicker through the window of her front parlour. She had only been out an hour and had meant to be back before her mother returned.

'She might not be in yet,' Patrick Nolan said, as he gazed down at her.

'She's in. Look, the street door's ajar,' Josie

replied, pointing at the crack in the door.

'I'll come in and explain,' Patrick said drawing himself up to his full five feet ten inches.

Josie gave him an uncertain smile. 'She'll be mad enough at me for going out. Let alone returning with you.'

Patrick gave her a severe, very manly look as he gazed down at her, noticing the light of the windows above them. 'I would think that your mam would be grateful that I did the right thing and escorted you home.' He ran his hands back through his thick black hair.

'Any other day, perhaps. But she's been like a cat on hot cobbles all day,' Josie said, remembering Ellen's tension over their supper.

'Even so.' Patrick went to walk across the street, but Josie caught hold of his arm.

'I'm safe now,' she said, looking up at him. 'You go on home.'

'I'm sailing soon,' he said, with just a hint of a youthful warble in his voice. 'You'll come and see me off, won't you, Josie?'

'Try and stop me,' Josie said, forcing a smile. She heard a tremble in her voice. Proud though she was, her heart was near to breaking at the thought of his leaving.

He pulled his shoulders back. 'I'll be a captain one day, just you wait and see if I won't, and then I'll speak to your mammy,' he told her.

'I have to go, Pat—'

The sound of an almighty crash from inside her house. Josie glanced across and saw a large shadow against the curtains. Leaving Patrick, she dashed over and threw open the front door. It crashed against the wall.

To Josie's horror Danny Donovan stood in the middle of the room with a poker raised above his head.

Dumbly, Josie stared down at the inert body of her mother at his feet. The images before her tumbled around in her mind as she tried to make sense of what she was seeing.

This was her home, her cosy parlour where she and Ma lived. The kettle still swung on the chain over the fire from tea and the sewing box was still where Ellen had left it three hours before, on the window sill. Even Waisy still sat propped up in the corner of Gran's old chair, but surrounding the familiar items lay their few sticks of furniture in splinters on the floor, with the pages of Ma's books scattered around. Their shattered crockery spread across the rug and into the fire grate, just one solitary cup still hung on its peg untouched by the devastation in the room.

It wasn't real. It couldn't be. Danny wasn't real and her mother couldn't be lying like a bundle of bloody rags on the floor.

Josie blinked and her gaze rested back on Ellen. She lay curled on her side with dark blood oozing from her nose. There was a dull red weal across her forehead and her shoulder rested at an odd angle. Despite her wounds, Ellen's averted face was calm, almost peaceful, like Gran's had been when she passed over.

Suddenly, everything in her vision burst over her. Eyes fixed to her mother.

'Ma!' she whispered, as fear and emptiness engulfed her. Her ma, dead!

Please, please, please God, let Ma be all right, Josie prayed. *I promise I'll be good, I won't give her a lot of lip like I have, just, please God, let Ma live.*

Nausea surged up within her. She swallowed it down, hatred and anger surging up in her as she pointed at Danny. 'Murderer!' she screamed at the top of her lungs.

Danny swung around and glared at her.

Josie sucked in a breath then let out another earsplitting scream that hurt her throat, then dashed back into the street. People had already come out of their houses to see what the yelling was about.

'Murder!' she screamed again, as she heard Danny lumbering after her. 'Murder. Me ma's been murdered. Call the police.'

Others took up the cry. A rough hand took hold of Josie's hair.

'Come here, you little who—'

Danny's gruff voice stopped abruptly, as did the painful tension on her hair. The sound of the poker hitting the cobbled street rang out.

Turning around, Josie gazed down at the unconscious body of Danny Donovan lying on the wet street. Behind him stood Patrick, a broken wheel spoke in his hand.

Nineteen

Robert dashed down the polished oak floor corridors, scattering all before him. Taking the stairs two at a time he found his heart beating wildly – and not from exertion. It thundered at double speed because it was being ripped in two with every passing second.

Shoving open the half-glazed door to the women's ward, he strode in. He spotted Sister Adams at the far end behind the nurse's desk. She squeezed herself from behind it and glided towards him.

'I believe Mrs O'Casey has just been admitted to your care, Sister,' Robert said in a low voice, his eyes darting around the dimly lit ward.

Sister Adams nodded sharply. 'Mrs O'Casey's daughter said you would want to know.'

'Where is Josie?'

'She is having some tea in the ward kitchen with May, the night orderly. If you'll follow me, Doctor Munroe.'

She led Robert down the middle of the ward. 'Nurse Watson is with Mrs O'Casey.' She stopped outside the door of a side room. 'I am afraid Mrs O'Casey is very badly injured,' she told him, her hand hovering on the brass plate of the door.

'How badly?'

'It's a miracle she's still alive,' Sister Adams told him flatly.

Nurse Watson stood up when they entered the room. Robert didn't glance her way as his eyes fixed on the small form lying motionless in the centre of the bed.

The whole room receded from Robert's consciousness as he focused only on Ellen. Bile caught at the back of his throat and an iron hand gripped his chest leaving him gasping for breath. He tried to draw breath but it was as if he had suddenly stopped living, frozen between two beats of the wall clock as he stared down at her bloody and battered body.

Ellen was almost unrecognisable. Her face was black and swollen and one eye was completely closed. Blood all around her left ear had seeped into her hair, giving it an unnaturally red tinge. There was blood on her mouth and a gash through her bottom lip where her teeth had punctured it.

Rage, guilt and fear rose up in Robert. Rage because he knew that if they stood before him now, he would kill whoever had done this to Ellen with his own hands. Guilt because he had promised to keep her safe and he had not, and fear because there was a real possibility that at any moment Ellen would sigh out her last breath and he would lose her forever.

Utter desolation swept over him. A life without Ellen was no life at all and he wouldn't live it.

From what seemed like a great distance away he heard Nurse Watson speak.

'The poor woman looks as if she has been attacked by a wild animal, not a human being,' she said, her voice echoing around Robert's head.

He knew he should respond in some way but one word crowded out all others.

Danny.

Animal was right. Danny Donovan was nothing more than a dangerous, savage animal that should be put down. As Robert, distraught, gazed dawn at Ellen, his own voice in his head tormented him. *It's all my fault. I've known for a week the sort of lengths Donovan would go to in order to stop me from exposing his criminal activities, so how could I have left Ellen so unprotected?*

The iron hand started to close around his chest again but this time Robert forced his mind to take charge. If Ellen was to survive this murderous attack she needed him to care for her, and that was what he was determined to do.

Taking a firm hold of his emotions, he glanced at Ellen's arms, resting above the blankets. Along with the criss-cross of cuts and scratches there was one huge bruise on her forearm where, he guessed, she had raised it to stop a blow to her head.

Robert summoned up all his professionalism to save him losing all control. 'I'll have to examine her to find out the full extent of her injuries,' he said, noting the cracked tone in his voice.

'Of course, Doctor.' Sister Adams beckoned to Nurse Watson, who jumped forward.

Sitting down on the narrow bed next to his beloved, Robert looked at her more closely. She was breathing evenly and with no obvious noise or effort. Both legs were the same length and lying as they should, so they had not been broken in the attack. But what about Ellen's insides? A broken leg would mend, but certain internal injuries could prove to be fatal.

'Give me the lamp, nurse,' Robert said, holding his hand out.

He raised it to one side of Ellen and opened one of her eyes, looking closely at the pupil. It reduced sharply as the beam from the lamp fell on it. Robert did the same, with the other eye, noting the same reaction. He let out a breath. Thank God. He glanced up at the two nurses behind him.

'Both are brisk to light,' he said, giving a brief smile.

Handing the lamp back to Nurse Watson, Robert moved Ellen's hair out of the way and let his fingers gently feel around her skull. Images of Ellen in his arms washed through his mind as his fingers traced their path across the curvature of her head. He sighed. All seemed intact, with no soft or broken areas.

With equal gentleness Robert made his way around the back of her neck. The same soft, slender neck he had kissed up and down until she had shuddered in his arms with passion. He moved the joints slightly and felt no resistance. Thankfully, he noted that the blood on her ears came from external injury and not from within.

He traced professional fingers down her neck and over her shoulders and felt a movement under his right hand.

'The left clavicle is broken,' he said to the nurse. 'That will have to be strapped.'

His eyes fell on Ellen's chest, rising and falling steadily as she breathed. There was a rapidly blackening bruise across her left breast where the heavy instrument that had broken her collarbone had been halted in its path.

Horror swept over Robert. Where else was Ellen's beautiful body damaged?

'I am pretty sure that Mrs O'Casey has several broken ribs, but I will have to have her bodice and shift removed so I can be sure.'

'Of course, Doctor,' Sister Adams said.

As the nurse fussed, making her patient ready for his further examinations, Ellen moaned and shifted in the bed. She was responding to being touched. That was a good sign.

Taking the edge of the sheet Robert lifted it up and looked down at Ellen. As his eyes ran over her body, he slowly took in the full magnitude of what she had suffered at Donovan's hands.

With his emotions almost at breaking point Robert folded the sheet back, uncovering her to the waist. With the nurses watching, he ran his hands over Ellen's ribs. A badly bruised area on her right side gave way under the smallest amount of pressure from Robert's fingers.

'There are at least four broken ribs on this side,' he said, trying to keep his voice even. 'Probably a blow from a boot, judging by the shape of the bruise above them.'

He could hear his calm professional voice informing and teaching while inwardly his heart was breaking.

Ellen could have been killed. He could have lost her forever to Danny Donovan's rage. Robert forced this unhelpful train of thought away.

He held his breath and rolled Ellen slightly at her shoulders. She moaned again, almost under her breath, but her spine moved with ease as he manipulated it. He then put his hands on her stomach and probed across and around it. Though there was a great weal diagonally across her flesh, feeling no underlying swelling, Robert concluded this wound was superficial. A quick check of both hips told him they too were sound. To his utter relief, battered though she was, Ellen seemed to be a lot less seriously injured now that he had examined her thoroughly than she had appeared to be at first sight.

Robert's heart grew lighter and his racing pulse started to slow. Then his eyes drifted down to the area just below her navel, still just hidden by the sheet.

It was in this precious area of her body that he had hoped she would one day nurture his children. What damage had Danny done there?

It didn't matter. Nothing mattered except that Ellen should live.

Although not being able to have children of his own would be bitterly disappointing, Robert knew that he could accept it as long as he had Ellen.

Slowly he reached towards the folded edge of the sheet. As his fingers took hold of the starched linen they were shaking.

'For decency's sake, would you like me to examine Mrs O'Casey's private area, Doctor?' Sister Adams asked, clearing her throat.

'If you would, Sister,' Robert replied, thankful for the offer. He didn't think he would be able to control himself if Ellen had been wounded by Danny's brutality in her most private parts.

'If I think there is anything you should see,

Doctor, I'll–'

'Yes, of course.'

Silently, Sister Adams raised the sheet from Ellen's feet and Nurse Watson moved Ellen's legs apart.

It doesn't matter, it doesn't matter, Robert repeated to himself. *Just let Ellen live. Please God, just let her live.*

A picture of Danny Donovan striking Ellen came into Robert's mind. Punching Ellen. Kicking Ellen. Then finally an image almost too terrible to contemplate flashed into Robert's head.

If that brute beast has forced himself on her, I'll kill the bastard with my own hands. So help me.

The violence of Robert's pounding emotions caught him by surprise as he pictured himself squeezing the life out of Donovan. How quickly the educated doctor with a position in society fell away and the primitive man took over. At last Sister Adams spoke.

'There is a large bruise and a small superficial gash on Mrs O'Casey's right hip bone. She also has several marks on both legs but, as far as I can see, there are no wounds or...' she glanced up at Robert swiftly. 'Or carnal deposits around–'

'Thank you, Sister,' he said briskly, as the nurse repositioned the sheet.

He straightened up, and the tension in his shoulders begun to evaporate. He had treated many women who had been raped, and he knew that long after the physical scars had healed the emotional scars remained. At least Ellen wouldn't have to live with that memory.

'Um, if you have finished, Doctor Munroe, we

284

will wash Mrs O'Casey and put a nightgown on her,' Nurse Watson said, looking nervously at Sister Adams, who said, 'I understand Mrs O'Casey is a particular friend of yours, so I'm sure that you'll want her nursed in the side room, Doctor Munroe,' she said, looking down the length of her stubby nose at him.

Nurse Watson lowered her gaze to the floor.

He drew his brows together. 'I want Mrs O'Casey nursed in this side room because her condition dictates it,' he said in a hard tone.

'Yes ... yes of course, Doctor.'

Robert stood up abruptly. 'I am going to see Mrs O'Casey's daughter. Call me immediately if there are any changes.'

St Mary's clock was sounding out two o'clock as Robert re-entered the small side room. Ellen was still lying peacefully in the centre of the bed while Josie sat beside her red-eyed and white-faced with tiredness. She gave him a weary smile as he crept into the room. He beckoned her over.

'Josie, my dear. I want you to go with Bulmer to Mr Cooper's house. I have sent him word and he is expecting you.' He lowered his voice and regarded Josie seriously. 'You'll be safe there.'

Josie shivered as she understood his meaning. 'I have sent word to Inspector Jackson that you are the only witness to your mother's assault and that you and your mother, when she awakes, are under my protection.'

Josie gave her mother a sorrowful look.

'Don't worry,' Robert said, following the young woman's eyes. 'I intend to stay by her side until

285

she wakes.' He heard the crack of raw emotion in his voice. He placed his hand on the young woman's shoulder. 'Now off you go. Mr Cooper has a couple of young daughters about your age, so I think you'll feel right at home there,' he added encouragingly. 'I'll be along later to fetch you back to your mother.'

As the door shut behind Josie and Bulmer, Robert settled himself in the chair beside Ellen and looked down at her in the soft amber glow of the oil lamp.

Although the wounds on her face were still livid, the two nurses had washed the surrounding blood off and now, battered though she was, Ellen looked more like herself. With his trained eye Robert noted that her breathing was regular and even. He took her hand and drew out his fob watch as he felt her pulse. The steady thump reassured him further.

He settled back and watched her.

Why had Danny beaten her? Ellen promised not to go anywhere near Danny or the White Swan again and he knew that she would not have gone back on that promise. Had Danny met her in the street and tried to force himself on her? Maybe he had followed her home.

Robert's head hurt. He had crashed through every emotion in his body over the last four hours. Bone-tired though he was he knew he wouldn't sleep until Ellen regained consciousness. His eyes ran over the slender form outlined under the quilted cover.

I am going to marry her, he vowed, his eyes on her bruised and swollen lips.

He had to marry her. There was no life for him without her. Now that the racing urgency of the past night had slowed to a bedside vigil, Robert allowed himself to sit and picture their life together.

It would be difficult, but society was changing. The House had debated the abolition of slavery and proper working conditions for the labouring classes. An image of his mother overseeing the local women's benevolent group flitted across Robert's mind. His mouth grew tight.

They could live in one of those new family houses in Tredegar Square in Bow – near enough to the hospital but in the country.

Family houses!

As the faint light of dawn crept under the shutters into the room, Robert allowed himself to think of the family that he and Ellen might have. Three, maybe four, children.

Up until now he had tried to avoid making Ellen pregnant, firstly by trying to control himself enough to withdraw at the crucial moment, and when that had proved impossible on several occasions he had resorted, much to Ellen's annoyance, to purchasing condoms. A smile stole over his face as he remembered her look of utter horror when he first produced the fine gut sheaths, but he had insisted. Not because he didn't want her to have his children but because he wanted her to agree to marry him, not be forced into it because she was pregnant as with her marriage to Michael.

But now he was not going to take no for an answer and they could consign the fiddly and unromantic condoms to the rubbish forever and let nature take its course.

Ellen gave a sigh and turned her head to one side. Robert leant forward and kissed her forehead. She sighed again, but didn't open her eyes. He felt her warm breath on his skin. How close he had come to losing this wonderful woman. He would never, never let her go.

As an angel kissed Ellen's brow her head exploded. She was surprised that in heaven – because that was where she surely was – you could still have a headache. And not just any old headache, but a headache to fair burn your brains out. She went to move her hand to her forehead and realised that in heaven you could also have pain like a nail driving through you as well.

She tried to open her eyes. A small glimmer of light stole in. She opened them again, only to realise that they were open already. Carefully, so as not to move her head which she was convinced would topple off her shoulders at any moment, Ellen looked around. She saw Robert, sitting in an old leather chair.

A small smile creased her lips, which she immediately regretted, as her jawbones ground together. She wasn't in heaven above, she was in heaven below and Robert was with her. Somehow, Danny had not killed her.

Ignoring the pain, Ellen gazed at Robert. She took a deep breath and her ribs groaned. She tried her hand again. This time the fingers moved against the quilting but felt too heavy to lift any distance. She left her hand where it was and returned to watching Robert.

I love him, she thought simply. After looking death in the face in the guise of Danny Donovan nothing else mattered but being with Robert.

Josie! Where was Josie? Panic gripped Ellen's chest. Forcing spit into her mouth and making her aching mouth work, Ellen forced out, 'Josie?'

Robert left the chair and sped to her side. His hand was cool on her forehead and his eyes calm as they looked down on her.

'She's safe,' he said, his fingers gently moving the damp hair from her forehead.

'Dann–'

'He is under lock and key in Wapping Police Station,' Robert assured her, as his lips kissed her forehead. Ellen closed her eyes and let Robert's love wash over her.

Sleep hovered, but Ellen forced herself to stay awake.

'Robert. Take Josie to–'

He kissed her lightly again. 'Shush, my love. I'll look after Josie.'

'No. Robert, it's very important.' She had to tell him where Danny's ledger was hidden because then, and only then, would Robert and Josie be safe.

'*You* are important at the moment.'

Ellen lifted her good hand and took hold of Robert's sleeve. The pain in her arm was almost overwhelming but she had stay conscious for just a few more moments.

'Take her to my mother's grave at St George's–' Robert opened his mouth to speak but Ellen hurried on. 'You'll find it under the wooden cross.'

'Find what?'

'Danny's ledger with all the names inside,' Ellen told him.

'Donovan's ledger?' Robert said.

Ellen let her hand drop back on the bed cover. 'Yes. I buried it there.'

Robert's face wore an expression of total puzzlement. 'How did you get it?'

'I ... I picked it–' she swallowed painfully.

'You took it from his person?' The raw anguish on his face now sobered Ellen. She could understand his horror. She had been shaking so much before she left the house she had had to have a brandy because she was so petrified of Danny.

'I had to,' she whispered, and sipped from a glass of water Robert held to her lips. 'Take Josie ... she knows which is Ma's grave,' Ellen said, as the darkness around her vision started to close in on her.

'I will.' Robert gathered her broken fingers and took them to his lips. 'But first, I want to tell you just how much I love you.' His lips brushed hers lightly. 'And ask once again, will you marry me?'

'Yes,' she whispered, just as unconsciousness enfolded her and soothed her pain again.

Twenty

The sun was just touching the horizon when Robert, Josie, and Inspector Jackson carrying a waterman's lamp entered St George's graveyard through the creaky iron gate. Although it was still dark, the sound of carts rattling along Ratcliffe Highway towards the City broke the silence. Around their legs wisps of early morning mist swirled as it hovered over the moist earth. They were not the only early morning visitors to the parish burial ground: the sexton and his assistant were already digging graves for today's crop of cholera victims. The bags of lime used to sprinkle on the corpses to hasten decomposition stood ready against the church wall.

Robert had left Ellen's bedside just before dawn but only after he was completely satisfied that she was out of danger. He then went back to his rooms, changed his shirt and dashed to the Wapping Police Station. He had arrived at 5.30, just in time to catch Inspector Jackson before he left at the end of what had been a long night shift.

He had explained to the inspector how Ellen had acquired Danny Donovan's account book as they made their way to the Coopers' house. Robert hadn't slept at all, neither had Inspector Jackson, and, by the look of the dark circles around Josie's eyes, nor had she. Thankfully, the chill of the early morning air helped to keep their tiredness at bay.

'Gran's grave is over by the back wall,' Josie said, gripping Robert's hand tightly. She hadn't let go of it since she left the Coopers' house half an hour before.

Carefully picking their way between the granite and marble slabs of the wealthier graves the three of them made their way to where the poor were laid to rest. Josie stopped in front of the last row in the far corner of the churchyard.

'That's Gran's,' she said, pointing to a mound of earth with a small posy of violets on top. Robert stared down at Mrs Shannahan's last resting place and thought of Ellen's mother. He wished she were still alive so he could tell her he was going to marry Ellen and that she didn't have to worry, about her daughter and granddaughter any more.

'Where did Mrs O'Casey say she hid Donovan's reckoning book?' Inspector Jackson asked, lifting the lamp higher to light the area before them.

'Under the cross,' Robert said, hunkering down and peering at the cross planted at the head of the grave.

'Patrick's da made the cross for us,' Josie said. She had let go of his hand but stood so close to him that Robert could feel her shaking.

He carefully picked up the violets and handed them to Josie. 'Hold these for me, would you?' She took them and held them to her chest.

Robert carefully moved the earth around the small cross. Ellen could only have spent a few moments in the graveyard and would not have had time to bury the ledger deeply but he didn't want to disturb the grave too much. As respectfully as he could, Robert dusted off the top layer of soil and then slowly inched his fingers deeper. To his great relief he felt something just under the surface. Hooking his finger around it, he teased it up.

'What is it?' Inspector Jackson asked, as Robert lifted a slim parcel free from the earth. He shook the dirt and insects off and unwrapped it.

'Bring the light nearer,' he said. Jackson did so, and the pale light from the oil lamp illuminated the ledger.

As Robert opened the pages and scanned the well-fingered pages his mouth grew dry. The hand that had written the entries was unschooled, like a child's writing, but they were clear enough.

'Well, man?' Inspector Jackson asked, craning his neck around to get a better view.

Robert stood up and closed the book. He smiled at the police inspector.

'It's all here. Names, dates month by month and columns of money paid. All Donovan's misdeeds and extortions are written here in black and white,' he said, holding the slim volume high.

Inspector Jackson's tired face suddenly became calm. 'Thank God,' he said simply.

Robert turned to Josie, who was still cradling the violets to her chest.

'We only came yesterday to put those flowers on Gran's grave,' Josie told him with a tremor in her voice. 'And now Ma's...' She started to cry softly. Robert took her in his arms and held her to him for a moment or two then she stood back and looked up at him.

Poor child, what she has gone through, Robert thought, smiling down at her tear-stained face. Josie would be his daughter soon, part of his family, and Robert found himself very pleased at the prospect.

'Josie, I promise you that your mother will be well again very soon.' Josie gave him a tight little smile. 'But thanks to her bravery, Inspector Jackson now has all the evidence he needs to send Danny Donovan and his gang to the gallows.'

Ellen remained in hospital for four weeks after Danny's murderous attack. For the first two weeks she suffered so much from headaches that Robert began to fear that there was some under-lying damage to her brain that he had missed. Much to his relief, these finally began to diminish and, over the last ten days, they had disappeared. Ellen's bruised flesh moved through the spectrum of colours from deep mauve to pale yellow, as it healed.

With a long look at her resting figure, Robert went back to his desk and picked up his quill pen.

Taking up the letter he was struggling to write he resumed chewing the ragged end of the feather. The letter was to his parents. He scanned the text again.

Dear Mama, Sir, I hope you are…

The first few paragraphs were fine, just the usual news about his work at the hospital and life in London. Nothing controversial there. But now he was on the fourth paragraph and the real reason why he was writing. Ellen.

Despite the onerous task before him Robert's face softened as he thought of the woman who had made his life complete. The woman who had put herself in mortal danger for him.

Every blasted letter his mother had ever written him since university had urged him to marry a good woman. He gave a wry smile.

Good women, as far as his mother was con-cerned, were not immigrant Irish women who had been pregnant and married at fifteen. They didn't keep themselves by taking in washing or singing on a stage. And they certainly weren't Roman Catholics.

I have good news. News that I had hoped to bring you myself, but I cannot, at present, leave London.

Now to the heart of the matter.

You will be pleased to hear, Mama, Sir, that I–

A loud knock on the door cut through Robert's thoughts. He shouted 'Come in!'. William strode into the room, his usual relaxed expression replaced by one of annoyance. He threw his top hat on the stand, where it swung wildly for a second or two then settled.

Robert smiled up at his friend. 'Cha–'

'Is it true?' William asked, leaning across the desk and glowering at Robert.

'Is what true?'

'This ridiculous rumour that you are going to *marry* Ellen O'Casey.'

Robert straightened up and glanced at the back of the leather chair. 'There is nothing ridiculous about me marrying Mrs O'Casey.'

'For heaven's sake, man,' William expostulated. 'I know you've been captivated by her since you set eyes on her, but I thought getting her in your bed would have sufficed.'

The chair scraped across the wooden floor as Robert rose to his feet. 'I love her.'

'For God's sake, man, what of your career?' They stood glaring at each other for a moment, then William let his gaze drop. 'A beautiful woman, I own,' he said with a heavy sigh.

The nails of Robert's fingers dug painfully into the palms of his hands. He and William had been friends a long time, but just at that moment

Robert had to hold back the urge to smash his fist into William's stern face. Ellen might have been asleep, but he doubted she was now.

'I am going to marry Ellen,' Robert said with cool deliberation.

William shook his head. 'Think, man, think. All your brilliance as a doctor, teacher and reformer will be lost if you marry Ellen.'

'You are exaggerating,' Robert said, spotting the top of Ellen's head over the high back of the chair.

'Have you got your invitation to the Annual Chief Physician's Address at the College yet?' William asked Robert with a tight smile.

'No. Not yet,' Robert answered.

'Davies has.' William crossed his arms across his chest. 'So has Sir William Lawrence from Bart's. Even St John, Young, Benthan and Maltravers had theirs delivered last week, so where is yours?'

'I expect it will arrive any day,' Robert said, sounding too defensive for his liking.

William raised his eyebrow. 'Has Viscount Wickford agreed to be the patron of your new dockland surgery yet?'

'I understand he has been engaged on his estates since he returned from Italy,' Robert replied. William raised his eyebrow higher and lifted one side of his mouth. 'What are you implying?' Robert went on.

'The rumours about your planned nuptials have reached beyond the hospital, Munroe. It'll be whispered in the salons of London soon and then in the corridors of Westminster.' William lifted both hands, palms upwards and shrugged.

'Quite simply, old man,' he looped his hat off its holding peg, 'you can argue all you like but if you marry Ellen O'Casey you'll be utterly ruined.'

Ellen had heard the heated exchanged between Robert and William. When she awoke and realised that it was William in the room she had almost made her presence known, but when she heard what he was saying, she remained still in her hiding place.

After being discharged as fit from the hospital, Ellen had followed Josie to Mr Cooper's house and now lodged with them. Robert was a frequent visitor but they were never alone. In order not to scandalise the Reverend and his family, Ellen came to Robert's room. Over the past weeks, after all the statements and interviews with the police, it had become a haven for them from the outside world. That world was now breaking in.

The door closed. Ellen swung her legs around and sat up.

Robert came around and took her hands. 'Ellen, I'm sorry.'

She forced a bright smile onto her face. 'I don't blame Mr Chafford. He is only saying the same things I've said all along.'

Robert rested his hand on the mantelshelf, scowling into the fire.

'Oh, Robert, I urged you to be discreet,' she said. She stood up and laid her hand gently on his arm. 'Didn't you notice the sly looks from your colleagues when they came into the room or the whispered gossip of the nurses who tended me?'

Robert gave her an indulgent smile. 'You're

being oversensitive,' he said turning away from the fireplace. 'A bit of hospital gossip...'

'It's more than "a bit of hospital gossip" if you are being snubbed by the College of Physicians.'

He waved the thought away airily. 'I am sure the invitation will be forthcoming.'

Although his tone was light Ellen could see that Mr Chafford's words had taken root.

'Mr Chafford is right. Have you really thought what our marrying will mean to you, to your work?' Ellen asked.

'Since I saw you lying as near to death as I ever want to see you, I have thought. I have thought constantly of what it would mean to me not to have you by my side,' he said drawing her to him.

'But if—'

He put his index finger onto her lips to stop her words.

'If?' he asked.

'When,' Ellen answered.

'I love you. God, how I love you.'

Forgetting William's words, Ellen surrendered to Robert's embrace.

As they lay exhausted in each other's arms, Ellen gently moved a stray lock of sweat-dampened hair from Robert's forehead. He hugged her then lay still, kissing her shoulders occasionally, but otherwise content to do nothing. His eyes were closed peacefully.

How could she not marry this man? She bit her lip.

But his work and position? Maybe there was another way. A small house where he could visit her. Maybe they could marry in secret?

298

Robert shifted up onto one elbow. He was silent for a long moment, then spoke.

'I can't lie to you, Ellen. William is right. I had started to believe society would judge a man by his achievements, not by who his father was.' He fell silent again for a moment. Where his body touched hers it was tense. Even in the soft light, the tight lines around Robert's mouth and his eyes were clearly visible. 'I am afraid that I have hoped for too much.'

An icy hand crept over Ellen's heart as she thought of his work. It had been his driving passion. It still was. But now he was on the brink of losing it all for love of her.

'Maybe you ask too much,' Ellen said softly.

He looked down at her and gave her a ghost of a smile. 'I don't think it is too much to ask of my peers that they regard a woman who has retained her virtue and dignity while battling against unbelievable poverty as a fitting wife for anyone.'

Ellen reached up and traced a finger along Robert's jaw. 'Maybe you ask too much for them to accept a Roman Catholic Irish immigrant who takes in washing and sings in a tavern as a fitting wife for one of the most eminent physicians in the land.'

'If society changes its regard for me, and some shut their doors on us after we marry, then so be it. I care nothing for their opinion. All I care about is having you as my wife.'

'Could we keep our plans to marry a secret?'

Robert's frown returned. 'Why?'

'Because of ... of ... because of the trial,' she said feebly.

The frown disappeared again. 'But what has that got to do with our marriage?'

'You are one of the main witnesses,' she said, lightheaded at her sudden inspiration. 'And you know that Danny's barrister will bring up your association with me as a way of discrediting you. But it won't be as bad for you, if I am portrayed as your mistress.'

'Ellen, I—'

'You having a mistress will not affect how the judge or the jury regard your evidence. After all, it is the way of things. I expect the judge and the barristers all have a little woman tucked away somewhere.'

Robert sat up. 'I won't have your good name dragged through the mud, Ellen.'

'Robert, my love, my heart, my life,' Ellen said, taking hold of his hand and kissing the tips of his fingers. 'Supper-room singers don't have a good name. But physicians with the ear of the Home Secretary do.'

Robert's mouth took on a hard, stubborn line as he glared at her. Ellen now sat up, pulling the sheet around her.

'Robert,' she said, in a voice she often used to Josie to make her see the truth of a matter. 'If you stand up in that court and tell the world that you intend to marry me there will be uproar. The judge and the jury will think you at best eccentric and at worst insane. All your evidence will be regarded in that light.'

She watched anxiously as her words sank in. He twirled a lock of her hair around his finger a couple of times. She held her breath. If Robert agreed to wait until after the trial before making their intention to marry public, it might stop some of the gossip that was already ruining his reputation. She waited.

'You're right. Any lawyer worth his sovereigns would have a field day with our relationship.' Another long pause. 'I have sworn to see Danny Donovan brought to justice and I will. And although I abhor the need for subterfuge, I agree.'

Ellen let out a heavy sigh.

Robert caught her chin gently with his thumb and forefinger and turned her head up to him. His dark eyes were warm as they gazed down at her. 'But understand this, when the trial is over, I am going to make you Mrs Robert Munroe, before the month is out and no argument. Agree?'

'Agree,' she answered.

How could she say otherwise? With Robert's love swamping her senses Ellen's mind gave up the struggle to argue. And as Robert rolled her over and covered her mouth and her body with his, she gave up thinking. She lost herself in Robert's arms and there was no reputation, no work, no society, only a woman and the man she loved.

Twenty-One

'Thank you Mrs O'Casey, those are all the questions I have,' Mr Hewitt, the prosecuting barrister, said as he returned to his seat.

Ellen moistened her lips with her tongue and

swallowed. She had stood already for an hour in the Number One court in the Old Bailey answering the questions of the prosecution while a hushed court hung on her every word. Now it was the turn of the defence.

All murmuring ceased as the jury, court officials and spectators waited for Mr Smyth-Hilton, the famous – some would say infamous – defence barrister to begin his cross-examination.

She had already laid her hand on the Bible and sworn to tell the truth, but as the gaunt man in the black gown and powdered wig approached, sweat trickled down Ellen's spine. Under the heat of the four brass candelabra that hung from the ceiling above, Ellen actually thought she was going to faint. With a small prayer for courage she squared her shoulders.

'Mrs O'Casey,' Mr Smyth-Hilton said, a condescending smile crossing his lips. 'Is that the kind of "Mrs" play actresses adopt?'

Several titters could be heard in the spectators' gallery. Robert sat among them. He had given evidence on day one when the charges of corruption and embezzlement were being heard and now, in his charcoal grey frock coat, that she had brushed and buttoned herself that morning, he sat giving her his love and support while she faced Mr Smyth-Hilton.

'No. I am a widow,' Ellen replied, her voice a-quiver with nerves.

All eyes in the body of the court and the spectator gallery were on her and to her left was Judge Beecham who, in his black gown and with his deeply etched face, looked more like a member

302

of the Spanish Inquisition than a dispenser of the King's justice.

'For how long?'

'Ten years.'

'Ten years,' Smyth-Hilton exclaimed, his thin eyebrows shooting up into his powdered wig. 'A pretty young woman like you a respectable widow? Has no other man in all those long years alone ever taken your fancy, Mrs O'Casey?' he asked, with a sly look at the jury.

'No,' Ellen said, as her mind went to Robert above her.

Again the incredulous look which included the jury. 'Never?'

'Objection,' Mr Hewitt barked, as he jumped to his feet.

'Sustained,' a voice boomed from the left. 'I fail to see what Mrs O'Casey's widowhood has to do with the case at hand, Mr Smyth-Hilton,' Judge Beecham said, looking down at the defence barrister below him.

Smyth-Hilton bowed.

'Mr Daniel Donovan is charged with attempting to murder you on the night of the fourteenth of September,' Smyth-Hilton stated.

Ellen stole a glance at Danny, who stood facing her behind an iron bar, shackled hand and foot between two sturdy-looking jailers. A mirror was placed to show every crease in his face to the jury. When he first entered the courtroom three days ago he was his usual swaggering self, waving to his supporters and acting the rough but honest businessman. He had acted outraged as the list of charges against him was read and emphatically pleaded not guilty to all of them. But now, after hearing witness after witness testify against him, he just stood there, his mouth twisted in a sneer of hatred, and his ice-blue eyes like dagger points as they fixed on Ellen. She shivered and looked back at the barrister questioning her.

'He did, and would have succeeded had not my daughter returned home,' Ellen said forcefully. Her nervousness had faded a little after Judge Beecham's intervention.

'Would you tell the jury what your connection with Danny Donovan is, Mrs O'Casey.'

'I sang in his supper rooms.'

'And where, pray, are these supper rooms?' the barrister asked, leaning back and looking at his fingernails.

'In the Angel and Crown, the Town of Ramsgate and occasionally at the White Swan.'

Smyth-Hilton stood up and his mouth dropped open. 'Are not the places you sing in public houses?'

'They are.'

'I understand they are also frequented by prostitutes looking for clients.'

Around the court tutting could be heard. In the gallery Ellen could see some smartly dressed women shake their heads and purse their lips.

'Yes,' Ellen said reluctantly, thinking of the poor women who earned a few coppers selling the only commodity they had.

'Mrs O'Casey,' Smyth-Hilton exclaimed in an astonished voice, looking around the court. 'You, a *respectable* widow, associating with prostitutes?'

Danny sniggered. Her cheeks now burned as

she saw the barrister look her up and down in a frank way.

'I had to earn a living,' she answered without thinking, then cursed herself for her hot temper. Inspector Jackson had warned her that Smyth-Hilton would try to make her angry. And he was certainly doing that.

'Of course. And Mr Donovan helped you earn a living, did he not?' Smyth-Hilton asked.

'Well, yes.'

'You came to him and asked him for a job singing.'

'Yes, yes, I'd–'

Smyth-Hilton moved into the middle of the court and asked. 'Had you ever sung on stage before?'

'No.'

'So although you had never sung before, Mr Donovan gave you a job. And you ask us to believe that this man, who had helped you out of the kindness of his heart, tried to murder you.'

'It wasn't out of the kindness of his heart he gave me a job,' Ellen said, again letting her tongue run away with her.

An expression of confusion creased the barrister's face. 'Why else would he give you a job?'

'He hoped that I would...'

'Would what, Mrs O'Casey?'

'Would...' Ellen lifted her head and looked at Danny opposite, 'would become his mistress.'

A loud shout went up from the court and the Judge brought down his gavel with a crack.

'Order, order,' he shouted and the noise subsided.

'What made you think that?' Smyth-Hilton asked, now with a sympathetic expression on his face.

It occurred to Ellen as she looked at him that, should Mr Smyth-Hilton ever be disbarred, with his repertoire of expressions he could make a fair living on the stage.

'Mr Donovan was always touching the girls who worked for hi–'

Smyth-Hilton cut in. 'Touching? Where?'

'Their breasts and between their legs,' Ellen said, remembering Danny's straying hand. The barrister said nothing, waiting for her to continue. 'And he was forever making lewd suggestions and forcing the girls' hands onto his male member.'

A murmur rose from the gallery as many strained forward to hear Ellen's words.

'And you allege he did this to you?'

'He did.'

Again the expression of incomprehension suffused Smyth-Hilton's face. 'But if this is the case why did you, being the respectable widow that you say you are, continue to sing in Mr Donovan's establishments?'

'As I said, I had to make a living,' Ellen replied.

'So do the whores on the dockside,' Smyth-Hilton slurred. There was a titter around the court, and Ellen felt her face burn again:

Hewitt rose to his feet again. 'Objection.'

Judge Beecham's voice cut across from the left. 'Sustained.'

Again Smyth-Hilton bowed in mock humility to the presiding judge. 'On the night of the assault I believe you went to find Danny Donovan in the

White Swan, did you not?'

'I did.'

'Is that your regular drinking house?'

'I don't *have* a drinking house,' she replied, glaring at the barrister. He wore a mildly amused expression.

Smyth-Hilton smirked. 'So you drink in any public house that takes your fancy?'

'Objection,' shouted Hewitt.

Smyth-Hilton bowed to his colleague then turned back to Ellen. 'But you had a drink with Mr Donovan and Michael Tooley that night?'

'Yes.'

'How many did you have before you arrived at the White Swan?' he asked. 'Remember you are on oath.'

'Two.'

'And why did you go to see Mr Donovan at the White Swan that night? You are on oath, remember.'

Drawing in a deep breath Ellen lifted her chin. 'I went to see Danny Donovan that night to get the ledger from him.'

The barrister put his hand to his chest and staggered back theatrically against the polished semicircular table in the centre of the court floor. 'You went to see the man who had given you your first job, who had treated you with affection, to *steal* property from him?'

'I–'

'And, despite your telling the jury how much you hated Mr Donovan's attentions, didn't you, Mrs O'Casey, a *respectable* widow, sit on Mr Donovan's lap that night and allow him to put his

307

hand up your skirt and feel your private area?'

Ellen clenched her fists together and breathed out hard through her nostrils. She could feel Robert's eyes boring into her. She had skirted around telling him how she had managed to slide the ledger from Danny's pocket, but he knew now, as did the whole court. She dared not look his way. Ellen raised her hand and jabbed her index finger at Danny across the room.

'Danny Donovan has lied, cheated and terrorised the people of Wapping for near on seven years. He and his gang regularly beat, maim and kill those who stand in his way.' She drew her breath and continued before the slimy Smyth-Hilton could interrupt her and make her lose her nerve. 'He ruins women and runs several brothels. The police have tried for years to catch Danny, but every time they found a witness that person was then found floating face down in the Thames.' She paused and turned to face the jury.

There was a gasp from the gallery and Ellen saw one elderly woman start to fan herself vigorously. She pulled back her shoulders and cast her eyes around the court, catching a blurred vision of Robert in the far corner of the spectators' gallery.

'I went to the White Swan that night to get Danny's ledger to put an end to his reign of terror. The police needed that ledger as evidence and I knew how to get it.'

She knew that other witnesses had given evidence about the entries in the ledger and Inspector Jackson had already shown how the names crossed out linked with dates and bodies found murdered.

She wondered at that moment, with the evidence stacked up against his client, why Mr Smyth-Hilton had questioned her as her evidence only added to the case against Danny.

The barrister came towards her, his long, white fingers stroking his chin thoughtfully.

'All very commendable, I'm sure. And you cast yourself in the role of a heroine of the common people?'

'I am no heroine, but someone had to get the evidence,' Ellen replied emphatically.

Smyth-Hilton's lower lip jutted out and his brow furrowed. Taking hold of both sides of his black barrister's gown, he strolled to where the jury sat.

'If I may, gentlemen of the jury, I would like to give you a different view of the events of that night and of Mrs O'Casey's role in them.' He spun around on his heels and pointed sharply at Ellen.

'Ellen O'Casey, who tells us that she is a respectable widow, is in fact the mistress of Doctor Robert Munroe.' There was a gasp from all in the courtroom. 'Do you deny that you are Doctor Robert Munroe's mistress, Mrs O'Casey?'

There was a gasp in the court and heads turned upwards to where Robert sat.

'No.' Ellen said, with as much dignity as she could muster.

'And rather than going to rob your long-time friend and benefactor, Mr Donovan, because you wanted to put an end to what you call his criminal activity, you did it to keep the affections of your lover.'

'That is not true,' Ellen said, raising her voice

so all could hear.

In their cramped corner of the courtroom, clerks from newspapers jabbed nibs into inkwells and scribbled furiously. Smyth-Hilton strode towards her.

'Didn't you tell Mr Donovan that night that Doctor Munroe had promised you a house, but it had not been forthcoming?'

'I did, but–'

Smyth-Hilton gave a knowing look at the men in the courtroom. 'Doctor Munroe sounds like a man who has got what he was after and is now cooling in his affections,' he said, and several heads in the jury nodded in agreement. Involuntarily, Ellen's eyes shot towards the back of the courtroom.

Around Robert, men were nudging each other, looking sideways to where he sat bolt upright. While the angular planes of his face were impassive, he had a tortured look in his eyes.

Snapping her head back to face Smyth-Hilton Ellen let out a strangled cry. 'No!'

'You thought that if you stole Mr Donovan's ledger it might warm Doctor Munroe to you a little longer.'

'No,' she said forcefully. But Smyth-Hilton continued as if she hadn't spoken.

'I also put it to you that before you met Doctor Munroe you had actually welcomed Mr Donovan's advances,' he jabbed his finger at Ellen's face. 'And had earned a few extra coppers for your troubles. As you did with a number of other wealthy gentleman and merchants who bought your services, like the other prostitutes in the

Angel and Crown and the White Swan–'

'That is untrue,' Ellen retorted hotly. 'I am not a pro–' Ellen trailed off, not able to say the word.

'But once you had caught the eye of Doctor Munroe, a man far above your station, Mr Donovan and all he had done for you was of no account.'

Ellen's mouth fell open.

'Knowing that your lover was out to ruin Mr Donovan's business, after drinking heavily, you–'

'I had two drinks,' Ellen interjected.

'After drinking heavily,' Smyth-Hilton repeated, 'you threw yourself into Mr Donovan's arms with the intention of stealing from him. You used your many allures to deceive this upright and honest businessman.'

'No.'

'Having offered yourself to Mr Donovan like a common whore, you picked from his pocket his business account book.'

'I took the ledger because–'

'Because you hoped to rekindle Doctor Munroe's cooling affections,' Smyth-Hilton said, completing Ellen's sentence. He turned back to the jury, who were on the edge of their seats, and gestured towards Danny.

'When Mr Donovan found out that his account book was missing, he was dismayed,' he said, addressing the jury like old friends. He let his gaze wander over the twelve men and true. 'But dismay turned to heartbreak when he realised that the only person who could have taken it was the very woman whom he had cherished for the past ten years.'

311

Cherished! Fumbled and snatched at, but never cherished.

'Being a reasonable man' – Ellen let out a sharp snort, at which Smyth-Hilton raised an arched brow – 'and not wanting to involve the police, Mr Donovan sought to get his property back by asking Mrs O'Casey, whom he regarded as a dear friend, to return it.'

'He beat me with a poker,' Ellen said, as the imaginative barrister drew breath.

Mr Smyth-Hilton turned his back on her, and focused on the jury. 'As Mr Donovan testified earlier, Mrs O'Casey had a tendency to violence when drunk and she turned aggressive that night. He also testified that he was reluctant to enter her home because she frequently took her clients there.'

Across the court Danny gave her a smug smile. Smyth-Hilton came and stood before her again, raising his voice so that the jury could hear him, and assuming an expression of poignant regret, 'Mr Donovan wants the court to know that it was only his anger at finding that he had nurtured a viper such as Mrs O'Casey at his bosom that made him strike out at her once, and then only in self-defence.'

Ellen laughed outright at this. 'I wonder if anyone in this courtroom is fool enough to believe that Danny Donovan, a six-foot, twenty-stone Irishman, with hands like shovels, would have to beat me senseless to defend himself?'

'Mr Donovan further stated in this court that any injuries you were found with must have been a result of your falling down drunk in the road as

you ran after him,' the barrister said. Ellen mar-
velled at his control over his features, because,
surely, even he could see the utter foolishness of
this statement.

'That,' Ellen said in a clear, ringing voice, 'is a
barefaced lie.'

Smyth-Hilton appeared to consider what she
said. 'A lie, you say.'

'I do.'

The barrister made a show of rolling his eyes in
a thoughtful manner then pulled his lips back in a
deathly grin. 'I wonder, Mrs O'Casey, if you can
distinguish between truth and lies. You tell us you
are a respectable widow, but then brazenly admit
that you are the mistress of Doctor Robert
Munroe. You tell us that you hated the attentions
of Mr Donovan, yet you admit that, in full view of
customers in the White Swan, you sat on Mr
Donovan's lap and let him take liberties with your
person that no *respectable* woman would allow.
Finally, you shamelessly admit that you stole Mr
Donovan's property. An offence which, I might
point out, in this court is a hanging offence.'

Ellen blanched and a roar went up.

'Objection,' Hewitt shouted over the noise as
he jumped to his feet again.

A sharp crack of wood on wood silenced the
crowded courtroom.

'Sustained. Might I remind you, Mr Smyth-
Hilton,' Judge Beecham said, placing his gavel
back in its rest and peering at Smyth-Hilton over
the rim of his half spectacles, 'that it is Mr Donovan who is on trial here for attempted murder,
not Mrs O'Casey. So I fail to see where this line

of questioning is leading.'

Ellen could have jumped up on the bench beside her and kissed the judge's sombre features.

Mr Smyth-Hilton sent the venerable judge a venomous look which was so swift Ellen thought she must have imagined it. His face styled itself into an expression of the utmost diffidence.

'Your pardon, my lord,' he said, inclining his head slightly to the judge's bench. 'I am just trying to establish how reliable a witness Mrs O'Casey is.'

He spun back to Ellen, his gown flying like a crow's wings around him. 'I submit, Mrs O'Casey, that on the night you allege Mr Donovan tried to kill you, you were too drunk to know what was happening, and that your injuries were caused by your falling drunk in the road and not at Mr Donovan's hand.' Ellen opened her mouth to protest, but Mr Smyth-Hilton continued. 'I am sure Doctor Munroe must have seen what a debauched woman you are, which is why, I suspect, he was trying to finish with you.'

'Objection,' shouted Mr Hewitt again.

Smyth-Hilton turned to the jury again. 'I am afraid that Doctor Munroe is just a man like the rest of us.' The jurymen muttered their agreement at this statement.

'Objection,' Ellen heard the prosecution barrister say again, but before the judge could lift his gavel Smyth-Hilton hurried on.

'And, given Mrs O'Casey's practised charms,' Smyth-Hilton ran his eyes up and down her in a suggestive manner to emphasise his words and then pointed a bony finger at her. 'It is hardly surprising that he should succumb.' Again the men of the jury indicated their agreement, a couple leering across the courtroom at her as he continued in a booming voice. 'Doctor Munroe seems to have come to his senses and was about to cast off Mrs O'Casey.'

Judge Beecham cracked down the gavel smartly. 'Mr Smyth-Hilton!'

Turning from the judge's bench, Danny's barrister raised his voice and looked across to where Robert sat.

'Doctor Munroe's judgement is sound, and his reputation beyond reproach. We can forgive his small lapse of judgement in his association with a skilled temptress like Mrs O'Casey.'

'Objection,' shouted Mr Hewitt at the top of his voice.

'Mr Smyth-Hilton!' Judge Beecham snapped. 'Desist, sir, desist.'

Mr Smyth-Hilton did not desist.

'But if he will not sully his good name with this woman, why should *we* believe her?'

'Mr Smyth-Hilton, I will hold you in contempt if you do not stop this line of questioning at once.'

With Mr Hewitt glaring at him, Smyth-Hilton finished and, with a flourish of his billowing sleeves, went back and sat behind the table.

A deathly hush prevailed for some moments, then all eyes left the pugnacious barrister and turned to Ellen.

'Have you any further questions for the witness, Mr Hewitt?' she heard Judge Beecham ask from a long way away.

The prosecuting barrister indicated with an

airy wave of his lace handkerchief that he did not. The judge turned to Ellen. 'You may leave the witness box, Mrs O'Casey,' he said.

Robert stood rooted to the spot as he heard Ellen give her testimony. He was unaware of the sly looks around him when it was revealed that he and Ellen were lovers, because he was so utterly appalled. Appalled at himself.

Ellen, the woman he loved and would love while there was breath in his body, had been almost beaten to death to protect him and now she was being beaten again verbally by the vile, unscrupulous Smyth-Hilton.

Watching what was left of Ellen's reputation being torn to shreds and trampled under the brass-heeled boot of Danny's barrister, Robert felt utter revulsion at his part in it.

He cursed himself roundly. It was his weakness that had held him back. William's words and the snub from the Royal College of Physician had unsettled him. Not that Robert thought for one moment that his marriage to Ellen would not cause tongues to wag. He had expected some of the fashionable homes in the city to scrub his name off their social list. But if he were brutally honest, he hadn't expected such a swift reaction from those he regarded as enlightened colleagues.

By keeping their love and their plans to marry a secret until after the trial, Robert now realised he had played right into Danny's hands.

As Ellen stumbled back from being publicly humiliated, Robert tried to move towards her, but now that the trial was drawing to a close the spectators' area was packed with those who wanted to hear the verdict and sentence.

The jury left and the court settled a little. All around, the spectators were arguing over the evidence. He heard Ellen's name mentioned a couple of times and was aware of furtive glances his way and the odd snigger. From where he stood Robert could see Ellen's cheeks were flushed and felt sure she was hearing the same coarse comments as he was. He had to go to her.

He tried to catch Ellen's eye but she had her face averted and was still looking at her feet. She sat at the far corner from him by the door.

In the light from the chandelier above, Robert caught a glimpse of unnatural brightness in her fixed gaze. He wasn't surprised. Being reviled the way she had been over the last hour would have brought a lesser woman than Ellen to tears.

There was a flurry of activity as, after only twenty minutes, the jury returned. Robert was hardly surprised that the twelve men didn't need time to consider their verdict. The evidence against Danny was overwhelming, and there could surely be only one verdict.

Judge Beecham rapped his gavel on its striking wood. 'Your verdict, if you please, sir.'

The voice of the foreman of the jury rang out. 'On the charge of embezzling parish funds we find the defendant guilty.'

A roar went up from the floor of the courthouse.

'On the charge of grand larceny we find the defendant guilty,' the stout foreman said, in a formal voice.

317

The crowd around Robert erupted again. Ellen was obscured from his view by the sea of waving arms.

'On the charge of the murder of...' the foreman listed the seven men who had been linked with the scrubbed out names in Danny's ledger. '...we find the defendant guilty.'

'On the charge of murder by arson, we find the defendant guilty,' the foreman continued above the noise of the courtroom.

'And, finally, on the charge of attempted murder of Mrs Ellen O'Casey...'

Robert glancing towards where Ellen sat straight-backed.

Although Ellen's good name had been thoroughly trodden into the mud, a guilty verdict would show clearly that Smyth-Hilton's oratory was a pack of lies.

'...we find the defendant not guilty.'

What! Robert couldn't believe his ears. A roar of outrage escaped him. Not guilty? Robert's mind conjured up the image of Ellen's beautiful body covered with the many bruises inflicted by Danny. He remembered having to ply Ellen with laudanum before he could manipulate her broken collarbone. She was like a piece of butchered meat when the bastard had finished with her.

Not guilty! It was outrageous.

Pandemonium erupted around him as people shouted and threw their hats in the air. Robert stood dumbly and stared ahead at Judge Beecham, who was now calling for the black hood to be brought to him.

While the judge pronounced the sentence of

318

death by hanging, Donovan's body then to be given for dissection, in Robert's mind the words 'not guilty' tumbled back and forth, adding fuel to his already burning emotions.

Having set the time and date when Danny Donovan would meet his Maker, Judge Beecham stood up and left the courtroom to wild applause. Not only was the shadow of the vicious Danny Donovan lifted from people's lives forever, but there was the spectacle of a public hanging to look forward to as well.

By the oak desk, Hewitt and his clerks were already being mobbed by well-wishers, and scribes from the daily newspapers were pressing forward to glean further information for their editors.

Robert stood on the balls of his feet and scanned over the heads of the crowd, but he couldn't see Ellen. He tried again to slide between the men around him. But he was held back. He pressed forward again, but to no avail. Turning towards the back of the court, he headed for the wall where there were fewer people and edged his way towards the main door.

He couldn't blame Ellen for fleeing from the furore that was now the Old Bailey's public entrance. The verdict of not guilty of attempting to murder her was tantamount to saying that Ellen was all the things Danny's barrister had accused her of and more.

The voices around him crashed in Robert's ears. The hard twang of the native East Londoners mingled with the well-rounded speech of the solicitors and barristers.

With a mighty shove, Robert got himself away

from the wall and plunged into the surging bodies around him. He lost his hat and let it go. He was pulled on all sides as people recognised him. Well-wishers slapped his back and blessed him. Robert fixed a bland smile on his face and pressed forward.

As he burst out of the courtroom, the cold November air took his breath for a second but it cleared his head. His eyes darted along the street towards Cheapside. Ellen was nowhere to be seen. People were collecting together by the back entrance of the court waiting for Danny Donovan to emerge on the prison cart for his short trip back to Newgate.

Turning north, Robert was about to walk briskly along the street when he heard his name called and a number of men rushed over to him.

'Doctor Munroe, can you tell the readers of *The Examiner* if you are satisfied now that Danny Donovan has been brought to justice?' a young man with a scrappy beard and ink-stained fingers asked him.

'Satisfied?' Robert answered. 'I am satisfied that an evil man has been judged as such, but I am not satisfied with the way that Mrs–'

'I'm from the *Standard*, Doctor Munroe. I understand that Earl Grey would welcome you into the House. Are you considering standing for Parliament?' a bald man with discoloured teeth asked.

Another rotund individual pushed to the front. 'Viscount Melbourne, the Home Secretary, is a close friend of yours, is he not?'

'I wouldn't say frie–'

'The readers of the *Weekly Visitor* would like to know when you and Mrs O'Casey first met,' a thin man with oiled hair plastered to his head asked, as he grinned at Robert.

'I have nothing to say,' Robert said abruptly, walking on.

'Will you be continuing to see Mrs O'Casey now that Danny Donovan has been convicted?' the grubby reporter from the *Weekly Visitor* enquired.

Robert spun around on his heels and gave the slovenly individual an icy look, but before he could give his biting retort, a shout went up from the mass of people gathered by the back gate as it slowly began to open.

A hellish howl rose around him as, under the bar of the gate, came a wooden cart drawn by two dray horses. It travelled over the cobbles and the occupants were forced to hold the rails to remain standing. The same two jailers who had stood next to Danny throughout the long trial now stood sentry while he took the short journey to Newgate, but Robert's eyes were riveted to the man in the front of the wagon with his hands shackled together in front of him.

All around Robert, rotten fruit and vegetables and dirt flew through the air. Some missiles splattered on the planks at the side of the cart while others, thrown by those with a truer aim, hit Danny Donovan as he stood erect and unmoved.

As if he knew Robert was there, Danny Donovan looked over to where he stood. Robert saw a small flicker of his old humour as the stout

Irishman held his gaze. For a long moment the two men stared at each other, then, just as the wagon turned the corner, Danny lifted his hands, touched his forelock at Robert and gave a wink.

Anger flooded over Robert. Was he satisfied, the reporter had asked. No, he bloody wasn't.

If it had been difficult for him to marry Ellen before, it now was near on impossible. Danny might be condemned to death, but he had condemned Robert and Ellen to another kind of death alongside him.

Josie should have been furious with her mother for forbidding her to attend the trial, but she wasn't. Although nearly everyone from the surrounding streets who was able to go was crowded into or around the Old Bailey, Patrick Nolan wasn't among them. That was because on the very day that the judge was making Danny Donovan an overdue appointment with the gallows, the *Jupiter*, Patrick's first ship, was sailing out of the Port of London bound for New York. Ellen's absence had allowed Josie to wave him goodbye without having to answer any awkward questions.

Sitting in the window looking out towards the river Josie hugged herself and gave a little smile. Despite her opposition to his choice of career, Patrick's mother had been on the dockside to see off her eldest son and, much to Josie's satisfaction, Mrs Nolan's presence hadn't stopped Patrick kissing her noisily just before he threw his seaman's sack over his shoulder and mounted the gangplank.

As the ropes were thrown off the ship and it

weighed anchor, Josie stood among the other seamen's women, sobbing as the sails unfurled and the wind filled them. She waited until the topsail had disappeared around the Woolwich reach and then she drifted back to Mr Cooper's snug house. Although she enjoyed the company of Mr Cooper's daughters, Elsie and Violet, she was pleased that they were both out. Repairing to the small room she shared with her mother, Josie took up a book and settled herself in the window. Her eyes skimmed over the page without seeing any of the words as she lost herself in dreaming of the future and her new life. The new life she would have when her mother married Doctor Munroe.

She pictured herself living in a house much like the one she had been staying in for the past twelve weeks. A snug house with oil lamps instead of tallow, where the tea was brewed with tea leaves that hadn't been used, dried and resold. A house with proper carpets on the floor, and a clock. No one she had known before had actually owned a clock, but Mr Cooper had three, and she was certain Doctor Munroe must have at least one or two. But more than that, she dreamed of a house that was a home, where she and her mother would be cared for. That was just what he had promised. Not in so many words, but in every action towards her mother. There was the same softness as they spoke each other's names and the same warmth as they looked at each other. It made Josie feel tender inside. She was just about to hug herself again when the door flew open and her mother appeared. She jumped off the sill and beamed at her, but there was no answering smile.

Ellen, who looked ashen, pushed past Josie and threw herself on her knees before the trunk under the window. Josie watched her scrabbling around for a few moments, then asked, 'Is the trial over?'

'Yes, and we are leaving,' Ellen answered, as she threw their few scraps of clothing into the middle of the candlewick counterpane.

'Leaving? Shouldn't we wait for Doctor Mu–'

'Now!' bellowed her mother. Josie started back in surprise at the sharpness in her mother's voice. A sad smile stole over Ellen's face. 'The trial went badly. We have to leave before Robert arrives. It is the only way.'

'But I don't...' Josie's face crumpled as she watched Ellen tying the corners of the bedspread together into a bundle. 'I don't want to leave. I want to stay. I want you and Doctor Munroe to be married–'

'That can never be now,' Ellen said in a strangled voice. She went back to her task, tugging and clawing the bundle to shape it. Then she started to sob. 'It's ... it's ... my ... fault. I ... I should ha ... have realised.'

The vision of the house with carpets and clocks began to fragment in Josie's mind as other, less pleasant thoughts crowded in. What had happened? Had Danny been found not guilty? Was he coming for them? Was that why they had to leave?

'But Ma–'

'It was doomed from the start,' her mother told her, tears coursing unchecked down her cheeks.

Josie couldn't bear the pain in her mother's voice. She caught hold of her. 'Ma?'

'I'm sorry, my sweetheart, so sorry,' Ellen said,

her hand resting lovingly on Josie's cheek. 'We have to go. I'll explain on the way. But be my good girl and do as I say now.'

What could she do? Her mother was now sobbing almost uncontrollably as she scraped together the last bits, and there would be no reasoning with her in the condition she was in. She hadn't been as bad as this when Gran died. Josie gave a heavy sigh, picked up her school books and tucked them under her arm.

She followed her mother down the servants' stairs of the Coopers' house, across Wellclose Square and out into the fading sunset of a cold autumn evening.

The sun was just touching the church spires of the city behind him when Robert burst into the hall of Mr Cooper's homely residence. He had run all the way from St Paul's, oblivious to the stares of amazement his sprint along Lower Thames Street caused. Twice he had nearly found himself under the wheels of a loaded cart fresh from the docks, but dodging all obstacles in his way he forced himself on. As the maid opened the front door Mrs Cooper came out of the parlour to greet him. She was still in her coat from her afternoon parish visiting.

'Doctor Munroe, how–' she began, with a welcoming smile, then froze where she stood.

Robert wasn't surprised. He probably looked as wild as he felt, but he didn't care. He didn't have time to exchange pleasantries. He had to find Ellen. His very life depended on it.

Almost knocking Mrs Cooper off her feet, he

dashed past her up the stairs to the small attic where Ellen and Josie were lodging. As his aching muscles propelled him up the final few steps he prayed silently that he would find Ellen waiting for him. Distraught yes, shaken yes, but waiting.

With the breath burning deep in his lungs he shoved open the door to find what he most feared, an empty room.

He stood for a second then let out an almighty howl and punched the wall to his side. There was an instant pain in his knuckles, but it was a pale imitation of the pain tearing through his body.

Behind him he could hear the sound of others in the house making their way up the stairs. Mrs Cooper's voice could be heard calling for her husband in a tone charged with concern, but it barely infiltrated his brain. All his mind could register was the vacant room.

He had to find her. There might be something that would give him an inkling of where she could have fled to. He scanned the room and spied a small travel chest under the window, then he exploded. He wrenched the lid open so forcefully that it hit the window sill and fell back, narrowly missing his hands. Robert lifted the lid and peered in.

Nothing.

Next he caught sight of a small chest of drawers against the back wall. He pulled open the top drawer in the small cabinet. It came out and clattered on the wooden floor, empty. He ripped out the drawer below. That was also empty and joined its fellow on the floor.

His gaze fell on the bed. She might have left

something under the mattress. Gripping the patchwork counterpane Robert wrenched it off and threw it behind him.

There was a scream in the room. It seemed to come from a long way away. Robert ignored it. He clutched hold of the mattress hurled it off the frame, exposing the slats underneath. Again there was nothing.

Blood was pounding in his ears and there was sweat on his brow. With his hands balled into fists Robert looked around the room. He saw Mrs Cooper in the doorway, her downstairs maid sobbing beside her. He spied the picture on the wall just above her head and reached for it. The maid let out a scream and fled back down the stairs. Robert didn't give her a second's thought, he just continued towards the picture. Maybe there was a note secreted behind it.

'Doctor Munroe,' he heard someone say in a distant voice. His fingers curled around the papier-mâché picture frame.

'Munroe!'

Robert stopped, picture in hand and surveyed the wreckage of Ellen's room. He blinked twice and stared at the Mr Cooper. He let the picture in his hand fall to the floor.

'Ellen ran from the court and I have to find her,' Robert told him. He picked up the bedlinen and started to pull it apart.

The minister gave his wife a small nod and she left the room. Mr Cooper took hold of the cane chair, one of the few pieces of furniture that had escaped Robert's attention, and sat down. Robert continued to sift through the debris on the floor.

327

'What happened?' the minister asked calmly.

'I have to find Ellen,' Robert repeated. He stopped his frantic upheaval of sheets and quilts and stood uneasily, shifting his weight from one foot to the other.

'And so you shall, but why don't you tell me first what happened at the trial,' Reverend Cooper continued in the same unruffled voice.

The thoughts and emotions racing around in Robert's brain started to slow. He relaxed his hands. He flipped the lid of the travel chest down and sat on it.

'Donovan *was* found guilty?' Mr Cooper asked.

'Oh yes. No jury could do otherwise. The evidence was overwhelming. With Danny and his gang in custody many have found the courage to come forward and testify. Jackson had two constables transcribing statements for the last week in readiness for the trial.'

'It's your pursuit of justice that has made that possible,' Mr Cooper told him. But Robert would not be flattered.

'Justice? I wasn't very just towards Mrs O'Casey, was I?' He dropped his head in his hands for a moment as the memories of the trial came back to him. 'What I let my poor Ellen suffer in court!' He shot a glance at the man opposite him. 'I hadn't mentioned it before because I didn't want to embarrass you and Mrs Cooper, but Mrs O'Casey and I are–'

'I think I understand the nature of your relationship with Mrs O'Casey. She is, after all, a handsome woman,' Mr Cooper said with just a trace of censure.

Robert pulled back his shoulders and, now, with his mind returned to its usual clarity he fixed the man opposite with a firm stare.

'I don't think you do,' he replied. 'I love Ellen and I intend to marry her as soon as I can.' Mr Cooper's shaggy eyebrows shot upwards. 'In fact I should have married her before the trial. That would have saved her from being mauled by Smyth-Hilton in the witness box.' Robert punched the palm of one hand with the fist of the other. 'In front of the whole court, including the press, he made her out to be a whore, a liar, a drunk and a thief.'

'I am sure no one who knows Mrs O'Casey would believe that,' the minister said.

'That is not the point. She should never have been made to suffer that. All those now so eager to give evidence against Donovan can only do so now because of Ellen's bravery.' Robert ran his hands through his hair. 'For the love of God, Cooper. You didn't see what she looked like when they brought her in to the hospital that night. It's a miracle, and I mean a true miracle, she wasn't killed. And after all that, I let Danny's greasy barrister abuse her in front of everyone.'

'I think you're being a little hard on yourself, Munroe,' Reverend Cooper argued.

'I don't. If it hadn't been for my own stupid pride, arrogance, self-importance, call it what you will, I would have done the honourable thing and married her as soon as she had recovered, what-ever the cost. She put herself in danger because she loved me and I should have protected her. Instead of which I allowed myself to be persuaded to keep our relationship a secret because of *my reputation.*' Self-loathing swept over him again. '*My* reputation! Huh! As if I should give a damm about it, compared with what Ellen did.'

He stood up and Mr Cooper looked alarmed. Robert put out his hand and patted the air. 'Don't worry, I am myself again.' He glanced around the room and lifted the corner of his mouth slightly. 'Please send my apologies to Mrs Cooper and tell her I am sorry for the disruption to her household,' he said, indicating the ruins of the small room. 'I will, of course, make good any damage. If you would excuse me. You'll understand that I have to press on because I will not rest until I have found Mrs O'Casey and done what I should have done weeks ago, and make her my wife.'

With her breath nearly gone Ellen collapsed against number fourteen Cinnamon Court. She grasped hold of the wooden knocker and pounded on the faded brown door. Several dogs barked warningly at the sound and glimpses of light showed in windows. Pulling the shawl closer around her head, she hid her face as curtains across the street were pulled back. Josie stood rigid beside her. In their dash from Wellclose Square she and Josie had passed not a word. They didn't need to. Her daughter's protest at their flight was written in every angle of her unyielding posture.

Just as she was about to knock again the door opened and Sarah Nolan stood with a raised pan above her head.

'Oh, it's you, Ellen,' she said, lowering her weapon and letting them into the small hallway.

'And Josie too. What's the to-do?'

Josie stepped into the hall but didn't follow as the two women started down towards the scullery at the back. Taking firm hold of her daughter Ellen dragged her along with her.

'I don't understand why we are running away like this,' she hissed at her mother.

'I do, and that's all you need to know,' Ellen replied tersely.

With Josie lagging behind her Ellen entered Sarah's scullery. Sarah and Patrick Nolan and their seven children lived in only the lower half of the house. Mr and Mrs Strazskoski, the Polish tailor, his wife and their four children lived above.

In the crowded scullery Josie's school friend Matte stood at the sink, up to her elbows in dirty water, washing the supper plates, while around a scrubbed table sat ten-year-old Anna, the snotty-faced seven-year-old Katie and an equally snotty-nosed four-year-old Fergus Nolan. Sitting together on a rug in front of the black iron range sat the year-old twins, Peter and Paul. Pat Nolan, the head of the family, sat by the fire in the only armchair, smoking a pipe. He acknowledged Ellen and Josie with a wink as they came in, but continued to draw on his pipe, a glass of dark beer at his elbow. For a second Ellen wondered where Patrick was, then remembered Josie saying that his ship was sailing that very morning.

Sarah pulled Ellen aside while her children continued their supper of potatoes and tripe stew.

'I'm surprised to see you here,' she said, pouring a small glass of beer from a jug on the mantelshelf and handing it to her. 'The word is that Danny's

331

goin' to swing. I thought you'd have somewhere cosier to be tonight than here. I thought you and the Doctor would be–' She stopped and gave Josie a quick glance. 'You know.'

Ellen took the drink and found that her hands were shaking. 'I ... I...' she started, then began sobbing.

Sarah clapped her hands sharply and the children looked up. 'Come on, finish your supper,' she commanded. 'Matte. Get the young 'uns to bed.'

Matte wiped her hands on her apron and gave Josie a little smile.

'I'll give you a hand,' Josie said, picking up one of the twins from the rug while Anna struggled to get the other one on her hip.

At their mother's instruction the children around the table slurped down the last of their supper and headed for the door. Ellen stood, unable to stem her flow of tears, as the children left the table.

Sarah came over and placed a brawny arm around Ellen's shoulders. She gave her husband a fierce look and jerked her head to one side a couple of times.

With a sigh, Patrick knocked out the embers of his pipe on the grate and stood up. 'I'll be away to the Grapes to settle the dust then,' he said, reaching for the tweed coat slung across the back of his chair. 'Ellen,' he said, nodding at her as he passed.

She couldn't answer. She just stood there like an idiot, blubbering. Sarah led her to the chair that Patrick had just vacated and sat her down. She turned back to her husband as he was about to leave the scullery.

'Don't you be buying that Dermot Ryan more than one drink without him returning the favour, you hear?' she called after Patrick. He raised his hand, but didn't turn.

Sarah turned to Ellen. 'Now, do you mind telling me what has caused you to be standing at my front door at this time of night greeting loud enough to summon the dead from their rest?'

So Ellen did.

For the first ten minutes she blabbered on incoherently, but after a shot of Irish whiskey from Patrick's precious store, she explained everything. It took a full hour of coaxing and crying, but finally Ellen managed to recount the whole story of the court, Smyth-Hilton, Danny and Robert.

'So that's why Josie and I are here. I need somewhere to stay until I can buy us passage on the first ship to New York. Do you see?'

'No. No, I don't. There is plenty of quality, King Billy for one, who have had women who played on the stage and they in *breeches* no less. At least you never paraded around like that. So what difference will it make to Doctor Munroe if a couple of stuffy toffs don't talk to him? To the devil with them, that's what I say. You're as good as any and better than most.'

'That's what I told her,' Josie piped up as she came back into the room. 'Doctor Munroe would have found us gone by now, Ma, and it must have fair broke his heart,' her daughter said, looking at her hard.

Ellen felt Robert's name like a blow in the pit of her stomach.

'For the love of the saints, Ellen, why can't you

333

marry the poor man? Sure everyone knows he's like a man with a spell on him,' Sarah said, uncorking the whiskey bottle again. She poured herself a drink and topped up Ellen's glass.

For one moment Ellen let herself think of a world where it might just be possible to do as her heart was begging her and marry Robert. For a moment she saw a home full of love and children and Robert. Then she shut it away.

It would never be. All she had now were the memories of their too-short time together. She would call them back and live on their warmth for the rest of her life, but just now she needed all her strength to do what she had to do. Not for herself, but for Robert.

There were spots dancing before her eyes and a red fuzzy line on the right of her vision. She had the strength left to argue but she barely had enough to stand. Putting her hand up to shade her eyes from the light of the spluttering tallow lamp, she spoke again.

'Will you give us board, Sarah, or do I have to go back through your door?'

It had taken him a week, but Robert had finally tracked down Patrick Nolan's dwelling place. It was sheer chance that he overheard a lumper with a gash across his hand mention a Patrick Nolan. At first, like others, the lumper had been less than forthcoming in answering Robert's questions, but finally in gratitude for saving the use of his hand, he gave him Patrick's address. It had been a stroke of luck for Robert, and he had needed it.

That was two hours ago and now, at eight-thirty,

after handing over the running of the casual ward to Benthan, Robert stood before the poor dwelling house with his heart pounding in his chest.

He uttered the same prayer that had been on his lips for the past seven days. *Please let her be here,* and then waited.

The door with brown paint peeling from it opened a fraction. The unshaven face of a man in his middle forties looked him up and down.

'I am looking for Patrick Nolan,' Robert said, his doctor's gaze noting the too-florid complexion and thread veins in the whites of his eyes.

'You've found him,' he was informed.

Despair washed over Robert. Nolan was a common name and he had sought out the wrong Patrick Nolan. But no. He had described young Patrick to the injured man and he had agreed it was the same lad he sought.

'The Patrick Nolan I am seeking is younger, sixteen or seventeen,' he said, encouraged that the door hadn't already been closed on him.

A stranger, especially a well-dressed stranger, asking for someone by name was treated with a great deal of suspicion in the Irish quarter of the neighbourhood.

'I think you'll be after our eldest, Patrick, named after the blessed saint and his old father,' Pat Nolan told him, looking warily at him but unable to conceal a swell of paternal pride.

Robert gave a weary nod. 'It is. I have been looking for him for days. I only found out an hour ago where he lived. I am Doctor Robert Munroe from—'

Patrick Nolan senior's demeanour changed

instantly. He wiped his soot-covered hand down his workaday trousers.

'Let me shake you by the hand,' he said, taking hold of Robert's hand in a fierce grip. 'It was a good day when God in His mercy sent you to see an end to Danny Donovan.' He continued to pump Robert's hand. 'Already the work tokens are easier to come by from the dock gaffers and I hear that there is an East India Company inspector due at the tally office to look into the weight scales and such matters. And it is all due to you.'

From somewhere Robert mustered up a smile. 'Thank you. May I come in?'

'What sort of a man would I be letting a fine doctor such as yourself stand on the doorstep like the rent man,' Pat said, flinging open the door.

Robert dipped his head and stepped inside the narrow passageway. Before he took a second step, the door to his left that led to the small front room was wrenched open and a kindly-looking woman slipped through it. She sent him a brief smile but then caught her lower lip with her teeth. She stood with her back to the door, her hands holding the door closed behind her. He guessed that it led to the family's sleeping area.

'This is me wife, Sarah,' Pat said, swinging his arm as wide as he could in the confined corridor.

Sarah bobbed a little curtsy but held fast to the door handle. 'I've seen you outside your surgery in Chapman Street.' She gave her husband a sharp glance. 'We are not up for company,' she explained with a small smile.

'I am not looking to inconvenience you. I just want a word with Patrick.'

'If you would follow me, sir,' Pat said, flourishing his hand towards the end of the cramped hallway.

Robert trailed after Pat, and Sarah Nolan, who had finally relinquished the door handle, followed behind him. Young Patrick would surely know where Ellen and Josie were hiding. Even before the day's end he could find Ellen and put an end to this living nightmare.

'Your son, Patrick, may I speak with him?' Robert asked, his nerves stretched to snapping point.

'You could, if he were here. He sailed for America on the *Jupiter*. You're a week late,' Pat told him.

Gone! Why could he not have found young Patrick last week? Why could the ship not have set sail tomorrow?

The cloud that had hovered around him for the past seven days descended. Would he ever find Ellen?

After his disgraceful behaviour at the Coopers' house, his logical mind had taken control again and told him that that it wouldn't be hard to find her in the close-packed houses of Wapping and Shadwell. How wrong he had been.

In truth he would have found Ellen without trouble if she had wanted to be found, but after the first day of encountering a wall of silence when he asked about her, Robert's optimism began to fade. Now, after a week of fruitless searching, his despair had returned.

Gripping the mantelshelf with both hands Robert let his head hang. Apart from the fire crackling in the grate there was silence in the room. After a long pause he turned.

'Do either of you know where Mrs O'Casey and Josie O'Casey are?' he asked.

Pat Nolan's face cracked in an ingenuous smile. 'Why bless my soul, she–'

Sarah stepped in front of her husband. 'She came here after the trial but left soon after.'

Beside her Pat Nolan's face took on an bewildered expression. His mouth gaped open then it clamped shut.

Robert's mind was a riot of emotions. She had been here but had gone somewhere else. He looked back at the Nolans.

'Where did she go?' he blurted out, taking a step towards Sarah.

'I can't say as how I know, sir,' she answered, smoothing the front of her apron in slow deliberation.

'Didn't she say anything? Give any hint as to where she might be heading?'

'Not that I know of,' Sarah replied in a firm voice. Beside her her husband was staring at a point just above Robert's left shoulder with a closed expression.

Robert remembered Bridget talking about her other grandchildren in various places but could never remember Ellen talking about any of them. But then in their precious moments together they spent most of it loving each other, not talking.

'Has she family anywhere she might have gone to?' Robert asked.

Pat swallowed visibly and looked as if he was about to speak, but again Sarah answered.

'She didn't say. Er ... um... Look, Doctor,

338

maybe it's better if you forget about Ellen,' she said, looking at him with eyes full of sympathy.

'Did she say that? Is there someone else in the area she might have gone to?' Robert asked, hearing the desperation in his voice.

'Well–' Pat Nolan started.

His wife cut across him.

'We don't know where she is.' Sarah Nolan smoothed her apron again but he saw the slight tremor of her hand.

'It is of the utmost importance that I find Mrs O'Casey. I ask you again. Do you know where she is?' he asked, looking her squarely in the eye.

'No,' Sarah Nolan replied, matching his forthright stare.

He saw her hand make a slight move and he knew that she was itching to make the sign of the cross to absolve herself from such a blatant lie. But what could he do? Fury, impotence and frustration boiled within him. He took a deep breath. He didn't want to lose his temper and demolish another room.

He glanced around the room, looking for he didn't quite know what. A clue, a sign of something that would give him the smallest hope of finding Ellen. There was nothing, just the usual chipped cups, unmatched plates and battered iron pans. He pushed his hands through his hair, then picked up his hat.

'Thank you for your time, Mr Nolan,' he said, forcing a smile and stretching out his hand.

Pat grasped it again. 'I'm mad I couldn't help you more, sir,' he said. 'And you're always welcome to call *here* at...'

Sarah's eyes flickered in her husband's direction and he trailed off mid sentence.

Robert lowered his head, re-entered the narrow passageway and made his way to the front door after his host, Sarah following behind. The Irishman stopped beside the door that his wife had emerged from on his arrival. He took hold of Robert's hand again.

'I wish you well in your search for Ellen O'Casey, Doctor Munroe.' He leaned his head to one side and raised his tone. 'If you would be asking my opinion, then I would tell you that Ellen O'Casey is a *fool,* yes, a blessed *fool,* to be hiding from a man such as yourself.'

Robert could almost feel Sarah Nolan's eyes boring into her husband. It was a pity that Patrick Nolan hadn't been alone. Robert was sure he would have been more forthcoming if his formidable wife had been absent. No matter. He would just continue his search and call back in a day or two when Sarah was out, although he wasn't hopeful of getting more information out of Patrick. His wife was the type of woman whose rules were observed even when she was physically absent, much like his mother.

Tapping his hat on his head Robert turned and trudged towards the end of the cobblestone passage. After a couple of paces he stopped and looked back to number fourteen Cinnamon Court. Yawning emptiness engulfed him. He had come to the Nolans with such high hopes of ending his quest, only to be further away from finding Ellen than ever. Idly he watched Sarah

Nolan shut the faded brown door. A draught moved the curtains in the small front window. *For the love of God, Ellen, where are you?*

Twenty-Two

Icy fog swirled around Ellen. She tugged the knitted shawl tighter over her head and covered the lower half of her face with a corner of it. As she and Josie made their way down New Gravel Lane towards London Docks the only other person to see them pass was the hollow-eyed night watchman.

Chilled to the bone, Ellen put down the bundle she carried and blew on her hands. She turned to Josie who dragged along behind her. She gave Ellen a sullen look.

'Won't be long, sweetie, and we'll be on board,' Ellen said with false jollity. Josie shrugged and looked away.

'You'll have to talk to me before we get to Uncle Joe's,' she said. Josie adjusted her bundle and glared at her mother with her lips firmly pressed together.

Ellen gathered up her bundle and carried on her trudge over the wet cobbles. The low boom of empty coal barges nudging into each other grew louder as Ellen and Josie approached London Docks.

Listening to her daughter's feet tapping on the cobbles behind her, Ellen's face drew into a frown.

341

Does she think I want to go? It's my heart that's ripped to shreds, Ellen thought, as the tall masts of the ships moored in the docks became visible in the fog. She didn't want to flee her home. But she had to.

Her resolve had been sorely tested when she peered out of the window and saw him standing on the Nolans' doorstep. Even in the gathering gloom he looked as hollow-eyed and wretched as ever she was. It was only her iron determination that rooted her to the floor and stopped her flying into his arms.

Banishing these unsettling thoughts, Ellen braced her shoulders and joined the small huddle of people who stood waiting to board the S.S. *Kentish Man.*

'It'll be a cold crossing,' the woman beside them, with three small children around her, said to Ellen as they waited. 'You off to relatives?'

Ellen nodded. 'My brother in New York,' she replied, hearing Josie snort beside her.

'Me too, to join me sister and her man,' the woman informed her. One of the children started to whimper. She soothed it with a soft word.

She, like Ellen, was dressed in warm clothes, and the children clinging to her legs looked to be wearing every piece of clothing they possessed. She sniffed and shook her head. 'There's snow in the air.'

'That there is, Mrs...' Ellen agreed, thankful for someone to talk to.

'Anne Collins,' the woman said with a smile, her breath visible in the cold November air.

'I'm Ellen, Ellen ... Shannahan,' Ellen said and

342

felt Josie's hot stare at her.

'We'll have many a day at sea, so it's as well to be friendly,' Anne said as the gangplank was lowered and the crowd surged forward.

'Get to the back in the middle,' Anne said. 'That's where the best berths are.'

With Josie at her side, Ellen scrambled onto the ship. Finding themselves a corner between the stout upright beams, Ellen and Josie staked their claim to a small area that would be their home for the next eight or so weeks. Around them others did the same. Fretful children were wrapped in ragged blankets and settled. The air below deck was warmer, but still cold. In the corner, some of the men amongst the passengers had lit the small stove at one end. When the hatch was closed they would be warm enough.

Below deck there were some sixty people crammed together; the rest of the cargo was tightly packed below in the lower holds. Untying her bundle, Ellen took out a warm blanket and fashioned it into a bed. Josie made a show of doing the same next to her.

Josie gave her a sideways glance. 'You do know he has been searching for you like a man possessed?' she said. 'He has been to Mr Cooper's house three times already this week in case there was news of you. Sophie Cooper told me Doctor Munroe cried when her father told him no one could find you.'

Ellen spun around. 'Do you think I *want* to leave him?' she said in a low voice to Josie as she wedged herself against the wooden beam.

'Then why, for the love of God, are we on this

343

stinking ship?' Josie asked.

'Because I love Robert Munroe too much to ruin him,' Ellen said with a sob.

Josie scrambled over and hugged her mother. 'But surely he should be the judge of what will ruin him or not?'

Ellen tried for a brave smile, but it would not come. Another tear trickled down her cheek. 'I wish it were so. But he'll insist on marriage.'

'So?'

For one blissful moment Ellen considered the possibility that it could be so. She only had to stand up, get off the ship and walk the two or so miles to the London Hospital to where Robert and her heart were. Then reality settled back as she remembered the lurid penny sheet sold by the hustlers in the markets and bought by those eager to read about Danny Donovan's trial. The details of her relationship to Danny and the fact that she was Robert's mistress had been seized upon and told and re-told with increasing embellishment for the last two weeks.

'It can't be. You'll understand when you grow more,' Ellen said, trying to get more comfortable on the wooden planks of the deck.

'But you love him and he loves you. Why is that so wrong?' Josie asked, her face a picture of puzzlement.

The world was so simple when you were thirteen. A sob escaped Ellen.

'But I hate to see you like this, Ma, after you being so happy and all,' Josie told her. 'Even Mrs Nolan said she'd never seen a body weep so this side of hell.'

She wasn't this side of hell. She was in hell.

'I'll be all right when we get to Pat's,' Ellen said without any real conviction in her voice.

Josie settled herself into the small space. 'You know Doctor Munroe will come looking for you? I nearly went to find him myself.'

Hope and fear collided together in Ellen's head. 'Josie?'

'Don't worry, Ma, I didn't,' her daughter said. 'Although seeing you like this, I wish I had.'

If Josie had gone, would Robert have come for her? Of course he would. Nothing would have stopped him. That's why she had been hiding like a felon in Sarah's front room these past weeks.

Get off the ship! her emotions screamed at her. *Go to him.*

A wave of nausea swept over her and her head spun. With a swift movement Ellen grabbed a handkerchief from her sleeve and put it over her mouth.

'Are you all right, Ma?' Josie asked sitting up and laying a hand gently on her shoulder.

Ellen waved away her concern. 'It's the ship moving.' Josie looked around at the solid deck. 'It will wear off in a couple of days, I expect, when we get used to the pitch and roll.' She tried to give Josie a smile, but had to reach for their slop bucket.

'Ma, are you sure you're all right?' Josie asked again.

Ellen snuggled down next to Josie and the low, wooden ceiling above her stopped spinning. 'I'm just tired and my nerves are frayed. I'll be fine after a good rest,' Ellen said.

345

Josie sighed and tugged her blanket around her, wedging her bottom against Ellen's hip. It was a comforting presence. Ellen lay in the darkness like those around her. St George's clock chimed four. They would be sailing on the morning tide in less than an hour. In the quiet, Ellen's mind returned to Robert.

Stop! Ellen all but shouted out aloud. She would have to put those thoughts from her before the grey waters of the Atlantic and everlasting life started to look too inviting.

The ship swayed and nausea swept over her again. She tasted bile in the back of her throat. In the dark she took deep breaths.

It's seasickness, she thought, as the nausea subsided.

Are you sure? A little voice asked.

The deck around them was becoming still as people settled. Many had walked miles, from Essex and beyond, to take passage to a new life in America. New life. No life. There would be no life without Robert.

Ellen rearranged the covers over her and thought of her brother and his family. In his last letter Pat had written that Mary had had another baby...

Without thinking Ellen's hand went to her stomach. In the same instant there was a scraping of wood on wood from above her and men shouting. The deck she lay on pitched slightly and rolled as the ship left its berth. Within a moment, the last tether ropes splashed into the river as the *Kentish Man* began its long voyage to New York.

With his head hard against the rough stonework of

346

the wall, Danny idly watched a large rat scamper across the other end of the damp cell. The rat was so used to sharing its habitat with men in shackles that, even as Danny moved and scraped the heavy iron fetters across the stone floor, the rodent continued its foraging without pausing. It was Danny's only companion now that the last of his visitors had departed. Dripping water sounded. It had rained yesterday and the far corner of the cell had filled with water. This had drained away now, but a pool of stagnant slurry marked where it had been. Although he had been kept apart from the rest of Newgate's population, he could hear the moans and whimpers of the prison's other inmates echoing around the arched stone corridors outside his cell day and night.

Disappointment crept over him. Very few of his old drinking and business acquaintances had visited him in Newgate.

Old Annie had been sentenced to transportation, although at her age he doubted she would survive the journey. After investigation of the East India Company books, Captain Merton had been thrown into the Fleet prison for embezzlement. From there, in a month or two, he was going to Botany Bay and, being the calculating bastard Danny knew him to be, would make a fortune out of his fellow exiles along the way. Milo and Wag, the parish constables, were being held somewhere nearby, but Danny hadn't seen them. They, too, probably had a long sea journey before them.

As a reward for his cooperation, Hennessey, too, had started his slow journey to the penal

347

colony on the other side of the world as punishment for the murder of the families killed in the Chapman Street fire. But he, Danny Donovan, and Black Mike were to keep their appointment with the noose in a few hours' time.

He had had a hope, albeit a slim one, that he could have had his sentence commuted to transportation, but the law demanded that someone die and he and Black Mike were those 'someones'.

Through the open grate above his head, the sky had become a lighter grey, hinting at the sunrise an hour away. He could already hear the sound of the gathering crowd outside, staking out the best position for today's main event. He planned to give them a show.

He had been a spectator himself on many occasions and knew what the crowd were waiting for. They wanted to see a man facing the rope cry for his mother and beg for mercy. Well, he couldn't remember the woman who'd given birth to him and he'd never begged in his life. So if that's what the mob wanted of Danny Donovan, then they'd be sore disappointed.

He looked around the narrow cell and wondered how Mike was faring. He'd seen him yesterday in the Prison chapel. They and their fellow death-cell prisoners had sat around the central table on which a coffin rested. He supposed it was there to remind them, as if they could forget, that they were under the noose. He and Mike had sat for a full two hours listening to an overblown parson with an ill-fitting wig call them to repentance. Wouldn't it be a mercy not to make the poor souls condemned to die at the end of a

348

rope suffer such a sermon on their last full day on earth? Still, it was a respite from the sameness of your own company.

After the service the prisoners stumbled back to their cells, shackles dragging on their arms and legs. He nodded to Mike before he was thrown back in the cell four doors down from his own. All prisoners sentenced to die were held in the condemned holds alongside Newgate Street. This gave them the added diversion, in their last days, of seeing the scaffold being made ready for use.

A small trapdoor squeaked open and a tin plate and cup were shoved through. Danny ignored it. His cell companion didn't. The rat scurried over and started helping himself to Danny's last breakfast this side of eternity. He watched the rat idly as his mind ran on.

Would Munroe be in the crowd? Would he come to see the completion of his work as Danny mounted the scaffold? He doubted it. Too fine a gentleman to stand and gawp with the rest of London.

He smiled. He'd seen to Doctor Munroe good and proper, that he had.

In fact, his revenge on Munroe was more complete than if he'd slit his throat as he'd thought to do. A man loses his life in a moment and then it's over, whereas Munroe now had to live with the loss of his reputation and Ellen for the rest of his natural.

Forster, one of his few cell visitors, did at least tell him of Ellen's disappearance and Munroe's frantic attempts to find her. It had given Danny the only scrap of satisfaction in an otherwise bleak two weeks.

He sat there thinking of everything and nothing until the cell was fully illuminated by the dawn light. The chief turnkey, Ebenezer Winkworth, entered. Danny's jailer was a man of about his own age and build, and one with whom he instantly knew he would be able to do business. Five shillings the old bugger had got out of him, but it was worth it. Danny didn't want to go to his Maker in Newgate rags. Winkworth carried a bucket of water in one hand and Danny's folded clothes and shoes in the other.

As Danny dressed he could hear the crowd outside become restless. Pulling his waistcoat down he faced the jailer. His neck felt strangely exposed – his cravat would not be needed. A shiver rippled through him. He pushed thoughts of his bare neck aside.

'Lead on, Winkworth,' he said, putting on his most artless smile. 'The good people of London have things to attend to other than seeing this old Irish neck of mine stretch.'

The shiver rippled up his spine again. Danny stepped forward, almost pushing the turnkey out of the door.

Outside, he felt the freshness of the morning air on his face. He stopped and lifted his head. Above the high walls of the yard a crisp autumn morning was in full splendour. Two pigeons perched on the wall were cooing. In the chapel yard several other condemned men were shuffling about in dirty rags. He spotted Mike. They stared at each other.

There was a jingling of metal as the manacles were taken off and, as the jailers sorted them into some semblance of order, Danny made his way over to his right-hand man.

'Morning to you, Mike,' he said with forced lightness. The shiver in his spine was now playing around his innards.

'I suppose we are overdue this meeting,' Mike said flatly. 'Some we knew have taken this trip long ago.'

Images of boys' faces long forgotten flashed into Danny's mind. Spike, Ten, Poo and others, all young and all dead. Lads like Mike and himself who had been born and raised in squalor and only able to eat if they could flitch enough to sell to a fence.

The shiver was now spiking his spine and mangling his guts. 'God, I could murder a drink,' he said, nudging Mike in the ribs and willing him to retort with banter.

Mike said nothing. Sweat broke out on Danny's brow and top lip. Unceremoniously, they were pushed and shoved into place, two abreast. He and Mike were in the centre of the column.

Winkworth marched along the side of the condemned men looking them up and down. He eyed Danny and Mike for a long moment then pointed at Danny with the end of his baton.

'You, Paddy. You and your sweetheart there look dapper enough to head up this parade. Move to the front.' Several of the guards snickered.

Sending the turnkey murderous looks, Danny and Mike stepped to the front of the column of prisoners and faced the main gate. Staring at the heavy oak gates with spikes across the top Danny's heart started to thump in his chest and his mouth grew dry. Someone in the yard whistled, and the mournful bells of St Sepulchre started to ring. A roar went up on the other side of the gates. Then they started to creak open.

'Move on!' Winkworth shouted,

The prisoners shuffled forward, Danny at the front with Mike a few paces behind. As they were spotted the noise from the jeering crowd grew.

They marched forward, the crowd pressing on them on all sides and the jailers struggling to keep them back.

All around a sea of faces grinned, screamed, laughed and made merry. Across the street, crammed into windows, were those spectators able to pay the three shillings to have an uninterrupted view of the hanging. Others perched on the stonework of houses in order to see clearly. Making their way through the milling crowds were street vendors selling oranges, penny twists and sheets recounting the trials of the condemned. At the front eager, wide-eyed faces watched the condemned men make their last journey to the gallows. Behind them was the raised platform of the gallows itself.

Missiles started to fly through the air from every direction. A slimy piece of fruit that had once been an apple hit Danny on the side of his face. A coil of dog dirt splattered across his chest sending up a stomach-churning odour. A clump of mud hit Mike, then some more rotting matter fell on him. All around them the crowd screamed with one voice. Someone dashed out of the crowd, spat in his face and told him that was for Sarah. He couldn't remember a Sarah or what he had done to her – there were probably a hundred or so Sarahs that he never knew, but who had been made to pay for displeasing him in some way. Now their friends and families were arming themselves with shit and decomposing vegetation to sling at him.

The execution party made slow progress through the screaming throng, but finally Danny reached the steps. On the other side of the platform were two carts, their cargo of open coffins clearly visible. With no family to claim his body Danny would occupy one of those caskets only as far as the journey to the surgeon's dissecting room. He looked up.

Above him the sky was blue and dotted with light clouds. His gaze lowered onto the men on the platform. The prison priest, the hangman and his two assistants. The steps up were only wide enough for two men so Danny and the jailer who had led the column the hundred or so yards along the Old Bailey began to climb. With feet like lead Danny plodded up the seven steps to the top.

Bracing himself on the uneven planks he looked around. The shiver on his spine was travelling both ways now and his guts felt as if there was a docker's hook twisting them. The sound of the crowd was almost drowned out by the blood crashing in his ears. He tried to swallow, but found he had no spit. His eyes darted around and fixed on the upright structure with the looped rope dangling from it.

He heard his name shouted by a multitude of voices, but his gaze remained riveted to the loop of rope swinging ever so slightly in the breeze.

Those now on the platform behind him pushed him forwards, towards the noose. He shoved them back and cursed roundly. His fellow prisoners muttered and one of the jailers poked him with his baton to move him on. Danny stumbled forward, his eyes not leaving the loop of rope.

From somewhere in the crowd a child called 'Mother'. It seemed to be coming from a long way away. Danny's head whipped around. About three rows back, being held on his father's shoulders was a small boy, bright-faced with a mop of fair hair.

Danny stared at the child, seeing as if for the first time the innocence of a child's smile. A noise started in his head as he noticed a red shawl to his left and the sweep of a feather in a woman's hat. All around him colours came at him, startlingly vivid in the clear morning light. Then sounds collected in his ear. A laugh, the bark of a small dog, the cry of a street trader. Suddenly his whole head was full of sounds and colours. Then he noticed his hands. He clasped them together feeling the coarse skin and the raised veins on the backs. He raised both hands and ran them over the surface of his face and over his head. He felt the scrape of the bristles on his chin and the coarseness of his hair as if he had never felt them before. He looked back at his hands. The black square nails would carry on growing after he was dead, as would the fine hair that covered his knuckles. Suddenly his breath failed him. His hands went to his neck, his bare neck, while his eyes were dragged back to the rope hanging patiently for him.

Behind him someone was trying to move him

forward towards that cursed noose. A dam of thoughts broke in his head. Why was he just standing here like a thick Paddy? He was Danny Donovan, not some gutter scum. Somehow he had regained his ability to breathe and now he was dragging in breath noisily. His head was roaring and his vision seemed to have a sharpness like never before.

He went from frozen to animated in a heartbeat and lurched forward. Strong hands caught him from both sides. He shook them off. At the end of the platform the parson who had bored the ears off them the day before stood, Bible open, reading passages in a uninterested voice.

He'll show the fecking, Protestant bastard what he thought about repentance, damnation, sinners and fecking eternity.

Danny stumbled towards him, avoiding the outstretched hands trying to hold him back. A whistle sounded and a truncheon crashed across his shoulder. He barely felt the pain and continued towards the black-robed parson. Other blows followed, but after a lifetime of street fighting his body ignored them and let his mind pursue its goal.

Seeing Danny approach, the priest let the Bible drop from his hands. It fell like a wounded bird at his feet. Someone got their arm around Danny's neck, choking off his air. With a swift backwards flick of his head, his skull connected with a sickening crunch against his assailant's nose. The grip loosened and, crouching momentarily, Danny launched himself at the white-faced chaplain.

With all his senses bursting within him and

competing for attention, Danny grasped the unfortunate man around the throat in a murderous hold. He tried to speak, but only guttural sounds came forth. No matter. The fear in the priest's eyes showed he clearly understood Danny's meaning. Something hit the side of Danny's head. It resounded in his skull and his hands lost their strength. As he shook his head to clear the sudden fogginess that was gathering, another further blow descended. Danny staggered back, the fog swirling all around in his head now. Hands grabbed him and something rough passed over his face and tightened around his throat.

He looked around and through his darkening vision saw Black Mike sobbing like a baby. He wanted to say something to him but his mouth wouldn't work. Something propelled him forward and the rope scraped painfully on his Adam's apple. The mist in his head was almost complete now, all sounds and colours were slowly fading.

For one dreamlike moment an eerie silence descended, the sound of metal scraping metal carried over the stillness. Then Danny's feet were without support, instinctively he flailed, trying to find a footing. There was a sudden jolt, a loud crack and then an abrupt nothing.

There was a light rap on the door. Robert didn't answer. There was another light tap and then the brass handle turned. Robert continued to gaze at the glass of brandy in his hand.

'I've brought you the special edition,' William Chafford said, slapping the newspaper down beside him.

Robert didn't look at it.

'The report makes chilling reading. Donovan nearly killed Newgate's senior chaplain on the gallows before they managed to bundle the noose around his neck and loose the trapdoor. It was a mercy there wasn't a riot.'

Robert took another long sip of brandy as William settled in the chair opposite him.

'No news then?'

Placing the glass on the table beside him, Robert leant forward and hung his head in his hands.

'But it's been two weeks, Robert. Surely someone knows where she is,' William said.

Robert's haggard face formed into a painful half-smile. 'I'm sure they do. But no one will tell me.'

Looking up, he could see William's face was etched with concern. He couldn't blame him. If he looked as bad as he felt, he must be a dreadful sight.

He hadn't slept properly for days and, when he did, he dreamed the nightmare of arriving at Cooper's house and finding Ellen gone. For a few seconds Robert watched as the red and orange flames of his fire formed into pictures of Ellen. He spun around and gave a hard laugh.

'I stupidly thought that I would find her. She couldn't have gone far,' Robert said, thinking of the hours spent walking through the streets and markets of East London looking for her. He snatched up a newspaper and flourished it in the air. 'After this rag had thoroughly dragged Ellen through the mire I couldn't even get a "good morning" from most of her neighbours,' he said,

357

screwing the newspaper up and hurling it into the fire. 'I should have married her before the trial.'

'You'll find her, Robert,' William said.

Robert dragged his eyes from the jumping flames in the grate. 'I have to, but Ellen has brothers in Ireland and America and cousins in Liverpool, Manchester, Bristol *and* Ireland. And there have been ships leaving the docks for each destination over the past two weeks.'

Only the crackle from the fire sounded in the quiet study for a few moments, then William spoke again.

'What will you do?' he asked.

'Continue to search for her until I find her,' Robert replied, remembering how only two nights ago he had come as near to ending his life as he had ever wanted to by throwing himself into the fast-moving Thames. 'I have also booked a seat at the Black Swan on the Edinburgh coach next week.'

'A trip home is just what you need.' William gave a forced laugh. 'Time in the bosom of your family will help you, I am sure.'

Making a monumental effort at good cheer, Robert stood up. 'Another brandy?'

'Thank you, no. I'm my way to supper at the Saracen's Head with Benthan,' William said, also standing. 'Why don't you join us?'

Robert shook his head.

William hesitated for a few moments then retrieved his hat from the hatstand. 'Give your mother my regards, won't you.'

Robert watched the door close, then turned back to the window. He stared unseeing over the scrubland at the back of the hospital.

The emptiness of his life without Ellen swept over him. He needed her like he needed breath. Without her love surrounding him, he was an empty shell, a husk of a man. But he would find her. Ireland? Liverpool? America? Wherever she was, even if it took him a lifetime, he *would* find her – and make her his wife.

Twenty-Three

The clock on the mantelshelf struck the melodious quarter of the hour as Robert joined his parents in the drawing room. It was as if he had last entered the room only the day before. Nothing whatsoever had changed. The old dark-oak dresser, the tables and the wheelback chairs that had been crafted at least two generations ago still dominated the room. Even the light from the sash windows still struggled to illuminate the sombrely furnished interior where the same paintings hung on the walls. Silhouette sketches of deceased relatives from both sides of the family faced each other in their oval ebony frames. An oil painting of a Highland house with shaggy cattle in the foreground was of his mother's ancestral home in Huntly; and on its usual wall, opposite the fireplace, standing alone in his bright red captain's uniform, was Captain Robert Fraser, his long dead uncle whom he resembled so strongly.

The leather-bound Munroe family Bible lay

open on its table. It had been there for as long as Robert could remember. His father would solemnly turn a gold-leafed page each evening and read the text to the children before they were put to bed by their nursemaid. He wondered idly if his father still turned the pages each night, or if the Bible had remained open at the same page since the last of them left the nursery.

He had arrived at Trinity Church manse yesterday and been welcomed into the bosom of his family, as William put it. In fact his welcome was warmer than he'd expected, mainly because his sisters Hermione and Margot were there. After greeting him formally under the watchful eye of their mother, they drew him aside into the old nursery and quizzed him at length about what the fashionable hostesses in London were wearing. He gathered that since neither of his sisters mentioned the court case, his mother had been her usual vigilant self and kept the scandal outside the manse.

His mother and father were not quite as delighted at his return. Since his arrival, the Reverend George Munroe had been shut away almost continuously in his study, writing his treatise on Paul's Epistle to the Romans, and his mother had been involved with the local Temperance Trust committee all morning. Even in the brief conversation over breakfast there had been no mention of his role in Danny Donovan's trial or of his relationship to Ellen. That was why he was going to grasp the opportunity of his parents' afternoon tea ritual to talk to them. Thankfully his sisters were engaged with their music tutor and would not interrupt what was likely to be a difficult conversation.

Unusually, his mother and father sat next to each other on the button-backed sofa. Robert took his place on the chair opposite and crossed one leg casually over the other. As they waited for Mrs Manners to bring in the tray, Robert studied them.

His mother was much the same as when he'd seen her in the summer, but her usual calm exterior was disturbed now and then by a sudden nervous twitch of her fingers as they lay across her charcoal grey skirt.

His father, in contrast, looked even more sombre than when Robert had last seen him. Although he had always been a solemn individual, Robert couldn't remember the lines tracking down his cheeks ever being so deep or the bones of his face so prominent. He was dressed in his black clerical garb, the white flaps of his collar making a stark contrast with his sinewy neck.

Mrs Manners came in and left the tea tray beside his mother. As she started to pour the tea, Robert decided to speak.

'I understand Danny Donovan's trial was reported at some length in *The Scotsman*.'

His father fixed him with a granite stare.

'It was,' he said, in a voice that sounded like a tolling bell. He patted his wife's hand in a rare show of affection. 'And it made terrible reading for your family and your Kirk.'

This interview had all the signs of being even bleaker than Robert had imagined.

'You realise that there was a great deal of

exaggeration in the reporting of the trial.'

'Did it exaggerate your liaison with an *actress?*' his father asked, sounding the word 'actress' as one would say dog excrement.

'Mrs O'Casey is not an actress. She is a singer,' Robert answered, taking the cup of tea his mother handed him.

His father's face formed itself into a sneer. 'I understand that both terms are used in London and elsewhere in the realm as an alternative word for a woman of loose morals.'

'If you knew Mrs O'Casey, you would know that is not the case,' he replied in an even tone.

His father blinked rapidly. 'I ... I say it is the case.' He put his cup in the saucer and it started to jiggle in his hand. 'I am astonished that you see fit to dispute this matter. Have you forgotten the fifth commandment?'

'Mrs O'Casey is not as you describe her,' Robert replied simply, refusing to debate further.

A flush splashed up his father's neck, then he turned his head and stared blankly at the wall.

Robert continued. 'Mrs O'Casey is a brave woman and a respectable widow, and I have great affection for her,' he said in a firm tone.

'So all of Edinburgh read,' his father replied, not turning his head.

'Now, husband,' his mother said. 'If Robert tells us that this Mrs ... Casey is a respectable widow, then I for one believe my own son over some sensationalist newspaper report.'

His father left his contemplation of the dull wallpaper and looked at his wife. 'I'd hardly call *The Scotsman* sensationalist.'

'Mr Munroe!' his mother said in a rare show of annoyance. The stain on his father's neck deepened as he slammed his cup down on the table beside him.

'Very well.' He fixed Robert with a razor-sharp stare. 'But, respectable or not, your liaison with this woman was of an intimate nature and now all of London and Edinburgh and beyond knows it.'

He resumed his study of the wall.

'I am not ashamed of my association with Ellen O'Casey,' Robert said calmly to his father's averted face.

'You should be,' his father retorted, sending his son a contemptuous look. 'What kind of example do you set the lesser orders, cavorting with a woman who earns her living displaying herself for all who have a penny or two to see?'

Robert put down his cup down carefully on the tea tray, placed his hands on his crossed knee and held his father's gaze. They all sat in silence for several long moments.

Then his mother spoke. 'It does not matter. Men are forever men. Not all of them have your iron will to fight temptation,' she said, looking to both of them to accept her olive branch.

For one fleeting moment Robert tried to imagine any situation that might tempt a man such as his father. He couldn't.

'It will all be forgotten when Robert marries,' continued Mrs Munroe.

'Marry?'

'When you marry Caroline, of course,' she beamed at him. 'That's why you've come back, isn't it? To marry Caroline?'

'Caroline?' Robert said, furrows appearing across his brow.

An indulgent smile crossed his mother's face. 'I have it from her own lips that she is willing to forgive and forget all about your association with Mrs O'Casey. I explained to her that men can be led astray, and a man needs a good wife who will settle his needs.' She patted his father's hand.

His father nodded ponderously. 'I am sure you're right, my dear. Miss Sinclair, who I have always found a little capricious, shows a great deal of charity in her willingness to forgive Robert.'

He stood up and rested with his elbow on the granite fireplace. Looking around the room for a second, he took hold of his jacket lapels and stretched his chin forward.

'This young woman has given us a Christian example which we would be wise to follow,' he said, addressing his wife and son as if they were a congregation.

'I have no intention of marrying Caroline Sinclair, or anyone else for that matter. I don't know where Mrs O'Casey is' – a heavy lump settled on Robert's chest – 'or if I will ever see her again, but I'll tell you this. While there is breath left in my body I will never, never stop searching for her. And when I find her, be in no doubt that I intend to marry her,' he told them firmly, before his father could launch into an impromptu sermon.

His mother's face drained of colour and his father fixed him with a bellicose stare.

'O'Casey is an Irish name, is it not?'

'It is,' Robert replied.

'Then would Mrs O'Casey be a *papist* by any chance?' asked the Reverend Munroe, spiritual leader of the largest Presbyterian church in Edinburgh.

'She has been raised in the Roman Church,' Robert agreed.

There was an icy silence.

'If you persist in this madness of marrying a follower of the Antichrist, then you are no longer my son. Do you hear? I'll disown you. You will be no part of this family. You have to choose between your family or your paramour. You can't have both,' his father said.

Robert sat very still for a moment. The clock, as if aware of the heavy silence, struck the half-hour. A shaft of light that had pierced through the heavy lace hangings at the window fell across the room, showing particles of dust dancing in its light.

An image of Ellen sitting in his rooms reading a book, her hair loose around her shoulders, came into Robert's mind. She looked up and smiled at him. His father's voice cut through his thoughts.

'You find this amusing, do you?'

Robert realised that he must have been smiling at Ellen in his head.

'See if you find it amusing when I cut you out of my will.'

There was another long, drawn-out silence.

'I do understand that your position in the Church makes my decision particularly difficult for you, Father,' Robert said, meeting his father's unswerving gaze.

Mr Munroe strode abruptly to the door. Robert

stood up.

'You may stay overnight, but be gone by midday tomorrow,' the Reverend said, pausing at the door. 'Unless, of course, you come to your senses and repent in the meantime.'

Robert's mother let out a little cry as the door slammed behind her husband. She turned and faced Robert. Her skirt swished on the wooden floor as she came towards him.

'For goodness' sake, Rob, if you find her why can't you just set her up in a house somewhere and stop all this marriage nonsense? Women in her situation always ask for marriage but I am sure she will settle for a properly drawn-up settlement.'

Robert gave a dry laugh. 'I am sure she would.'

His mother's shoulders relaxed. 'Well, then...'

'But I will not.' Robert smiled sadly at her. 'The truth is I have asked her, pleaded with her and begged her to marry me on many occasions and she has always said no. Then after she was all but killed by Danny Donovan, she relented. If I'd been half the man I should have been, she would be my wife by now. But I'll tell you this, Mother. Nothing will stop me marrying Ellen O'Casey.' He gave her an apologetic smile. 'I'll be gone in an hour.'

He turned and strode across the faded Indian carpet, his mind already on catching the first coach back to London.

'Robert.' He turned. 'Don't leave. I'll plead with him, and if you just tell him you'll consider his words, I'm sure he'll relent.'

'I'm sorry.'

He crossed the space between them and took hold of her shoulders. As he kissed her on both cheeks, a sudden rush of affection for his mother swept over him. Looking down at her, he thought she seemed suddenly old. She might not lavish affection on him, and perhaps there was still lingering disappointment that he hadn't followed her brother into the army, but she did love him in her own way.

Ignoring the emotional restraint that his mother always insisted on, he drew her to him and hugged her. He kissed her springy grey hair and hugged her again. He felt her resistance, then she put her arms around him.

He held her away from him and mother and son stared at each other just for a second.

'I'll write to you at the Association's offices, Mother,' he said, giving her a brief smile.

Then he turned and strode from the room.

Twenty-Four

Holding her school books tight to her chest Josie made her way up the Bowery on her way home. Alongside her, chatting and giggling, were Katie O'Malley and Mary Reardon, her two new friends from the Swartz Elementary school.

Her mother had tried to find her a school north of where they lived in the Vauxhall Garden area of the expanding town, but found the day fees were too expensive, so she had to settle for a school in Chambers Street run by a Russian professor. Josie had been somewhat apprehensive about attending a new school, wondering if she would be able to keep up with the lessons. To her surprise, she found she was one of the school's best pupils, so much so that she had already moved up a class.

She didn't really miss Wapping much, mainly because she had gained a whole new family, but she did wonder from time to time how Doctor Munroe was faring and where Patrick Nolan was.

She did miss Patrick. Twice in the past week the class teacher had caught her gazing out of the window, daydreaming that Patrick, having been promoted to Captain Nolan, would arrive at Uncle Pat's and whisk her away to be his wife. She had left a letter with his mother before she and Ellen sailed, telling him Uncle Pat's address in New York. A little lump caught in her throat as she thought about him. Maybe he'd forgotten her.

From the time in the middle of an Atlantic gale when she found out her mother was carrying Doctor Munroe's child, Josie had kicked herself daily that she hadn't gone and told him where her mother had been hiding. She had tried to talk to her mother about Doctor Munroe since they arrived but it only started her mother weeping. Aunt Mary said that wasn't good for the baby so she stopped mentioning his name, but that didn't mean she stopped thinking about him or Patrick.

'Look, there's Brian Clancy,' Mary said, turning to Josie and breaking out in a froth of giggles. 'And he's with Feggy Smith and Ernie Potter the b'hoys.'

Josie looked towards the three young men lounging outside a general store smoking. They looked a disparate group. Stubby Brian with his freckles and red hair, Feggy thin and dark, and Ernie blond and bony. Although they were as different as three boys could be, they all wore black trousers and frock coats with bright, almost garish waistcoats beneath, and hobnail boots. Each had their long hair oiled, and tied at the back. Ernie and Feggy each sported a tall silk hat, while Brian had on an oversized cap.

Katie lowered her head toward Josie and Mary. 'Don't they look fine?' she said, casting the three lads a sideways glance. 'Isn't Brian Clancy just a darling of a man?'

Singularly unimpressed, Josie cast her eyes over them, thinking that not one of them could hold a candle to Patrick.

Brian and his gang, their stance casual but their eyes narrowed, watched Josie and her friends pass. Much to Josie's annoyance, Mary arched her neck and smiled at the three young men, who then peeled themselves from the wall supporting them and sauntered over to the three girls.

'Good day to you all,' Brian said, as the youths fell into step around the girls.

Josie felt a trickle of sweat between her shoulder blades. Her ma wouldn't like her dawdling on her way home, especially not in the Five Points area of the town and especially not with Brian and his gang. They had a reputation for wildness that they were forever trying to add to, and were already well known to the ward constables for all the wrong reasons.

Ignoring the unwanted company and looking straight ahead, Josie quickened her pace, but

Mary and Katie had slowed down. The boys followed in their wake, and Katie simpered at Brian as if he were some sort of hero of old rather than a ginger Irishman only an inch or two taller then herself. Feggy came alongside Josie.

'Hi, there my pretty Miss Josie,' he said.

'Don't you be calling me your anything,' she told him.

A roar went up around her.

'Mind yourself, Feggy,' Brian said, slipping his arm around Katie's waist. 'Young Josie's got claws and no mistake.'

Feggy spat out his cigarette and gave a wide grin, revealing a missing canine tooth. 'I like my women with a bit of fire.'

Mary and Katie giggled.

'Give her a kiss, Feggy, that'll soon stop her fighting you,' Mary said, sending Josie a spiteful look.

Another time that remark would have earned Mary a bloody nose and pulled hair, but Josie decided to save her revenge for a more convenient moment and picked up her pace.

They had reached the Bull's Head tavern. Josie weaved her way through the milling crowd, hoping to lose the spectre of Feggy from her side. If she dashed down Hester Street and then along Essex Street she could get back to Uncle Pat's. Her mother didn't like her going down the side streets with their looming tenements, but Josie thought them preferable to fending off Feggy Smith all the way home.

Gathering up her skirts she dashed over the road. A male voice called her name but Josie pressed on as she caught sight of Feggy following after her.

Stretching her legs and dodging a milk cart she headed across the street. Just as she got to the corner of Hester Street she felt her books begin to slip out of her grasp. Before she could reposition them they plummeted to the floor, their white pages flapping in the wind. Irritated by the delay, Josie gathered them up and was just about to continue when someone caught her arm.

'Josie–'

She whirled around and brought the flat of her hand hard against her assailant's face. The crack of palm on cheek echoed around the narrow street.

'Take your filthy hands off me, Feggy Smith, before I take your eyes out,' she said showering the young man behind her with slaps and punches.

He curled away from her blows. 'Josie–'

'How is it you think you have leave to call me by my name?' she screamed, her hair loose and her books again on the damp cobbles. She started to punch lower. If he turned towards her a bit she would knee him right where it hurt. 'My Uncle Pat will have the constable on yer, if you lay so much as a hand on me.'

The young man she was so aggressively pummelling managed to take a step back and straighten up. Josie's head spun and she dropped her arms by her side.

She couldn't believe it. He looked the same yet different, and it wasn't just the barely healed scar crossing the chin. He must have grown an inch a day because he was now close to six foot. He had filled out in a muscular way, but the dark curly hair and the softness in his green eyes were still the same.

The widest of smiles spread across Josie's face as she leapt up and clasped her arms tight around her assailant's neck. 'Patrick!'

Her basket on her arm, Ellen made her way down Seventh Street towards her brother's small house at the end. She put her free hand to her back and stretched and the ache eased a little. She smoothed her hand over her swollen stomach and smiled.

By the fifth day out from London, just as they reached the swells of the Atlantic Ocean proper, Ellen stopped pretending to herself that she was suffering from seasickness and accepted the fact that she was with child. She had sobbed for a full day with a mixture of joy and regret as deeply held memories came back to her, memories of Josie's brother, a child cold and lifeless in her arms; memories of making love with Robert. She prayed that his child would not share the fate of her son.

She had spent a great deal of time on the voyage in wondering what her brother Joe would say when she arrived carrying a child but with no husband alongside. He was six years her senior and had always been very much her older brother. The memory of him, standing with a docker's hook in his hand, next to her father as he demanded that Michael O'Casey do the right thing by her, replayed in her mind each night.

It had been over twelve years since the newly married Joe and his wife Mary had sailed for

America. She had carried Josie down to the docks to see them off. Their family and Mary's had even held a wake for them as no one ever thought to see them again in this life. But when he dashed towards her on the quayside in New York and enveloped her in a bear hug, Ellen knew that she was home, and from that day to this no word of reproach had passed his lips.

The baby moved and Ellen's heart ached. If only she had known before they set sail... How many times had she lain awake listening to the creak of the boat and asking herself that very question.

Sometimes she wished she had known, then she could have given in to her heart and gone to Robert, salving her conscience with the excuse that she was doing it for the child's sake. Oh, Robert would have married her, but then what? She knew. She knew the consequences for Robert, and it was those very consequences that had forced her to leave him. At other times during those long empty nights, she was glad she hadn't known she was carrying Robert's child until it was too late, because she did know that her resolve to leave him would never have held.

On reaching the newly painted green door Ellen pulled on the latch and opened the door. Two small bodies dashed past her.

'Mind there, you two hooligans,' her sister-in-law Mary shouted, looking up from her baking. 'You'll knock your Aunt Ellen into the middle of next week.'

Ellen entered the small scullery and placed the basket on the table. She sat down heavily on the chair opposite Mary. Taking up a towel, Mary wiped the flour from her stout forearms.

'Now there, my love, let me get you a mug of tea,' she said, putting a solicitous hand on Ellen's head. 'You can't have long now, no more than a week or two, I am sure.'

'I think you're right,' Ellen said, sipping at the tea Mary set before her. 'I must have been three months when I sailed and Josie and I have been here near on five months.' She gave Mary a small smile. 'So any day.'

Mary went back to her task and Ellen relaxed in the solid wood chair with the patchwork cushions and let the heat from the china mug warm her hands.

There was a movement again and looking down Ellen could see the child she carried stir under the woollen gown she wore.

Robert's child. Ellen let the familiar ache for the man she loved come over her. She couldn't have him there, with her, to love, but she would have his child upon which to shower love. She loved it even now.

She took another sip of tea as Mary shovelled the family bread into the side oven with a long paddle.

Her brother had done well for himself and his family. They lived in a comfortable house at the quieter end of Seventh Street, away from the grog shops and bars. His ship's chandlery business in Rivington Street next to the varnish factory was going well. So well, in fact, that Joe was already talking about buying a piece of farmland to the north in the Bronx.

To Ellen's surprise, New York was very like Wapping or Shadwell. There were docks and sailors, prostitutes and slums. Because the Lower East Side of Manhattan was very much like the East End of London, she and Josie slipped into their new life without trouble. Even the multitude of accents along the waterfront of New York was the same as could be heard any night in the White Swan or the Bunch of Grapes. On a Saturday night, with ships in the harbour, Water Street could have been taken for the Ratcliffe Highway.

After his initial reaction, her brother had done well by her too. Ellen had eventually told Joe and Mary about Robert. Mary, kind-hearted soul that she was, cried for her.

Ellen placed the cup down and started up from the chair. 'Let me help you, Mary.'

'Put your rear straight back on that chair, Ellen O'Casey, and give that poor child you're carrying some rest. All day you'll be jigging him and jogging him. Fair tires me to see you dashing about from here to there and singing all night in the Shamrock bar.'

'It's not the Shamrock any more, Mary, and well you know it,' Ellen said with a crooked smile. 'It's the Well and it's a supper room.' Ellen moved herself and felt a pull in her back. Robert's baby will be here soon, she thought as she shifted in the chair. 'Mr Hermanshaw's attracts a much better class of customer than any other supper room. There are even rich customers coming from up-town since he redecorated.'

Mary leant with her fists on the table and gave Ellen a hard look. 'Joe's business is picking up with all the work from the docks,' she said. 'I don't see why you want to prance about the stage twice a week singing to all.'

'You know I haven't been there for months now,' Ellen said.

'But you'll go back,' Mary said as a statement rather than a question.

'Yes, I will.' She saw her sister-in-law's mouth take on a disapproving line. 'Look, Mary. I'm pleased that Joe's business is growing. It should be, the way he works. But you've your own mouths to feed.' Mary's mouth turned up slightly at the corners as she smoothed the floury apron over her still flat stomach. 'So I'm just making a contribu–' Ellen let out a gasp as another sharp pain reached her back.

'Ellen!' Mary cried, leaving her task and dashing to her side. 'Is it the baby?'

Ellen nodded. 'I think so. Josie was early and it looks like this one will be the same.'

The door behind the two women opened and Josie burst in. Her face was bright as she let her school books fall on the chair.

'Ma, Ma. You'll never guess who I met on the way back from school today,' Josie said, her pigtails bouncing. Her cheeks were flushed and her eyes sparkled with excitement and anticipation. 'Go on, Ma, guess,' Josie exclaimed jumping on the spot.

Hope and fear crashed through Ellen as her head swirled.

Robert?

But it could never be. She knew that. Ellen placed her hand on her tight stomach. A band of pain encircled her, stopping her breath and thoughts.

The pain around her middle gathered again as Ellen stood up. The tight band pulled again and Ellen felt something give. On the insides of her legs she felt a warm wetness.

Mary left what she was doing, crossed the room and stood beside Ellen. Ellen reached out and took her sister-in-law's hand, gripping it tightly as another wave of pain closed around her middle.

Josie threw down her school books on the kitchen table. 'He would have come back but his ship sails on–'

'Josie, fetch Bridie Murphy from around the corner,' Mary said, as she held Ellen around the shoulders. 'Your brother or sister is about to be born.'

Ellen lay back exhausted but utterly happy, her eyes fixed on the small bundle of humanity that she held against her breast. Robert's daughter. Love surged over her. His child was in her arms as her father could not be. Across the small bedroom Josie was making the crib ready for her new sister. The baby sneezed and Josie came over and sat on the bed.

'Aunt Mary said you were very quick. Only four hours,' Josie said, taking a tiny hand in hers and peering down at the infant in Ellen's arms. 'What are you going to call her?'

'Robina,' Ellen said. Her heart ached for him to be here with her to share this moment. What a father he would have made.

'She looks like him,' Josie said softly.

Tears started in Ellen's eyes and she blinked them away.

Josie lifted one small hand with her index finger. 'She is so small. Look at her tiny fingers.'

'She is bigger than you were,' Ellen told her. She kissed the soft down of the baby's blonde hair, then looked up at her daughter. 'I remember holding you like this when you were born.'

Josie looked astonished. 'Do you?'

'I do. And I loved you the moment I set eyes on you,' Ellen told her.

'Can I hold her?'

'After I've fed her.'

Carefully easing herself up on the pillows, Ellen offered the baby her breast. A hungry mouth rubbed over the nipple a couple of times, then latched on. Contentment swept over Ellen as she felt her newborn child work for her nourishment.

Then she remembered something. 'Who did you meet on the way home from school today, Josie?'

Josie raised her eyebrows in a cool, uninterested way and continued to play with the small hand resting on her finger.

'Oh.' Her gaze flickered over her mother's face and the corners of her mouth turned up a little. 'Just an old friend,' she said, letting go of Robina's hand and fussing around with the pillows behind Ellen's head.

'But you seemed—'

'There,' Josie interrupted, as she patted the white cotton pillowslip a couple of times. She reached out for the now sated baby. 'Let me take Bobbie so you can get some sleep.'

Sleep! At the word Ellen's body remembered just why childbirth was called labour. She yawned.

How foolish, she thought as sleep overtook her. *It couldn't have been Robert. If it had been him, he would surely have come home with Josie. And how would he know we were here?*

Would he come if he did know? She didn't know and couldn't bear to speculate as it would only tear her heart further into shreds. She felt her eyelids droop.

With one deft movement Josie scooped the infant from her mother and wrapped her in a crochet shawl from the bed. Ellen watched her two daughters head towards the door. Just before she left Ellen to rest, Josie lowered her head and kissed the soft brow of her baby sister. Looking back at Ellen she suddenly seemed very amused about something. For no reason that Ellen could see she suddenly threw her head back and laughed, an abandoned, joyful laugh and hugged the bundle in her arms to her again. Ellen caught her gaiety and smiled broadly.

'Who did you meet?' Ellen asked again, as sleep began to take her thoughts away.

'Come on, Bobbie,' Josie said to the infant sleeping in her arms. 'Let's leave Ma to rest while I introduce you to your cousins.'

'Your sister's name is Robina,' Ellen told her, putting her hand over her mouth.

Josie sent Ellen a saucy smile. 'Of course it is. Just like mine is Josephine.'

Although life without Ellen made emptiness his constant companion, Robert had forced himself to get out of bed again and live yet another desolate day. With a heavy sigh he turned his attention

379

to the unopened envelopes beside his plate. There was a knock at the door and Bulmer ushered Chafford in.

'One more for breakfast, if you please, Bulmer,' Robert said, as his friend settled himself in the chair opposite.

'I thought I'd drop in for a coffee and ask how your trip to Liverpool went,' Chafford said drawing his chair up to the table.

'Well enough. They have the same problems with overcrowding and poor sanitation that we have here in the capital,' Robert replied.

Chafford sipped his coffee and regarded Robert thoughtfully. 'I'm sorry to say it, Munroe, but you look dreadful. Still not sleeping?'

'I don't think I have had a full night's sleep since...'

Chafford gave him a sympathetic look. 'No sign of Ellen or her family in Liverpool then?'

Robert shook his head. 'There are so many Shannahans and O'Caseys in Liverpool I scarcely knew where to look, but I found none of them had any knowledge of Ellen.'

'It was a long shot,' his friend said in a quiet voice.

He'd known that, but even so, the fact that there might be the smallest chance of finding her was enough to keep him trailing through Irish churches in the area and peering into the local records until his eyes burned. He would do the same in Dublin when he got there at the end of the month.

Not wishing to follow the train of thought that any stray mention of Ellen always started, Robert picked up his correspondence.

'Anything from your family, Munroe?' William asked after a couple of moments.

Robert shook his head. 'I wrote to Mother about my trip to Liverpool, but I haven't had anything back from her yet.'

Her reply would probably be awaiting him on his return from Ireland. Please God his next letter would tell her that he had found Ellen. She had written a month previously telling him that his father had not relented in his decision. Robert hadn't expected him to and he certainly wouldn't once he and Ellen were married.

He ripped open the top letter and scanned it. 'Lord Ashley tells me that he has high hopes that this time the Anti-Slavery Bill will be passed.' He read on. 'He also invites me to spend a week with him and Lady Ashley on his estate in August to shoot.'

'You should go, Munroe. You've been working yourself too hard,' William said encouragingly.

'There is a great deal of work to do.'

'Yes, but–'

'The Home Secretary has asked me to speak at a dinner at the Mansion House,' Robert interrupted, before William could launch into his speech about putting the past behind him. He didn't want to. He *wanted* to live in the past, because Ellen was in the past, and without her he had no future. He laid the crisp, white paper aside.

'Well, if you have to work yourself to death, at least your reputation has recovered from...'

Robert's eyes flashed up at his friend.

'Recovered! It has been positively enhanced,' he

said bitterly. 'I am lauded throughout society for my bravery in tackling Donovan and my cunning in using his mistress to do it.' He slammed down his cup in the saucer and it snapped in two.

'Munroe–'

'I have society hostesses sending provocative glances and flirting with me because I'm a "dark horse" and have an "air of danger" about me.'

'And you're complaining?' William said, his sandy eyebrows high on his forehead.

'I am complaining, because it is these same people who would never have accepted Ellen as my wife, who see nothing wrong with me keeping her as my mistress.'

Robert stood up and began to get ready for the day ahead. There was a light tap at the door and Bulmer entered.

'What is it, Bulmer?' he asked smoothing down the cuffs of his shirt and buttoning them.

'Sorry to interrupt you, Doctor Munroe, but there's a young man who says he must see you urgently,' Bulmer said.

'Can't it wait?'

'He says not and that his name is Patrick Nolan.'

Ellen peered through the heavy, velvet curtains and scrutinised the audience.

'A bit busier than the usual Friday night,' the fresh-faced Harry said.

Ellen let the curtain fall. The Well was only a little better than the Angel and Crown but she was paid more and Mr Hermanshaw didn't take liberties. Mrs Hermanshaw saw to that.

In truth Ellen had come up in the world. She might still be singing in a supper room, but The Well was one of the most respectable drinking houses in the city. And New York was a growing city, with wealth and opportunity. Although the cramped house she shared with Joe and his growing family was only slightly wider than number two Anthony Street, it did at least have three floors, and they would be moving north at the end of the month.

As she watched the smoke from pipes and cigars curl up through the house lights, Ellen sent up a silent prayer that it would not be too long before she could stop spending the nights in a smoky hall and stay at home with her two daughters. Josie was making good progress in school and Bobbie was growing fast. In a few months, she would be crawling around and would soon be getting under everyone's feet.

But when Bobbie started walking she didn't want Robert's daughter's first steps to be in the alleys and lanes of New York's Bowery district. The area was becoming more crowded by the day as hundreds disembarked at the dock, full of little else but hope, to start a new life. The area around Coulter's brewery was fast becoming as impoverished as Flower and Dean Streets in Whitechapel.

'Ma.' Ellen turned around to find Josie, holding Bobbie, behind her.

'We have just been to see Hetty. She made a doll for Bobbie. Hasn't she, Bobbie?'

Bobbie looked up at her mother and smiled. Ellen reached out and took the wriggly child who every day looked more and more like her father. She had his hair, light brown with a dash of gold, and his frown. And she had Robert's impatient nature. But most of all – and that was what stopped Ellen's heart on a daily basis – Robert's dark, expressive brown eyes looked at her from her daughter's pretty face.

Many a night since she left London Ellen had awakened, her body on fire after dreaming of those dark brown eyes; dreaming of how Robert's eyes would grow soft when he looked at her and how they flashed with passion as he made love to her. She saw Robert's face in her dreams and wept. Bobbie snuggled against her.

'What shall we call your dolly?' Ellen said. The baby blew a soft raspberry.

From where she stood in the wings of the stage, Ellen heard the opening bars of her first tune.

'I have to go,' she said, handing Bobbie back to Josie. 'She shouldn't need feeding until I'm finished. I'll be done in half an hour or so.'

Leaving her two daughters, Ellen made her way onto the middle of the stage just as the plush dark-blue curtains were drawn back. Enthusiastic applause rose from the audience as she took centre stage.

As the majority of the audience was Irish she started, as she usually did, with a traditional Irish ballad. Looking out through the haze of cigar smoke Ellen could see that after the first chorus the audience were singing along with her. At the end of the song she looked round as she took a sweeping bow.

She launched into her second song, which again

was well received. As she swayed across the stage, Ellen spotted a man in his early thirties with light-brown hair smiling broadly and tapping his foot in time to the tune. The way he lounged back with his legs extended under the table brought a vision of Robert as she had first seen him and, despite the jollity of the house, an aching sadness over-whelmed her

She had planned to sing 'My Old Hillside Home' next, but with Robert's memory like a ghost hovering over her, she doubted she could make it to the third line without tears.

She signalled to Mr Levy, the conductor of the small orchestra, that she wanted 'Run to the Fair'. The orchestra struck up. She sang two more ballads which brought her to her last song.

What shall 1 sing?

Sensing her indecision, members of the audience started to shout.

'Sing "Come and Hear the Piper",' a woman's voice called from the back.

'Sing "A Sweet Maid Went A-Walking",' a gruff male voice with a heavy Donegal accent shouted.

There was a hush as the audience waited for Ellen to decide.

'Sing "The Soft, Soft Rain of Morning" for me, Ellen,' the strong, vibrant voice of her dreams called from the back of the room. Ellen's head spun.

It couldn't be...

Ellen raised her eyes to where the voice had come from. Stepping from the back of the house and into the light was Robert. He came towards her.

Ellen staggered back, clasping her chest. Her eyes ran over his tall frame which towered over those sitting around him. He was dressed with his usual understated elegance in a chocolate brown frock coat and buff trousers. With his hat in his hand, his rebellious light brown hair had its way and fell over his forehead just as she remembered. Her gaze took in the much-loved angles and planes of his handsome face and then she looked into the brown eyes. The same, yes, that had looked at her in passion and caused her bones to melt. They were now fixed on her.

It was Robert! Here! He was here.

Inside her the hurt, pain and regret were swept away. How could she have ever left him? Gazing across the smoky room at him now, she didn't know. She only knew that he was here.

'Robert! Robert!' she sobbed across the heads of the crowd.

He closed the space between them in two heartbeats and leapt onto the stage. In one swift movement he had taken her in his arms. Ellen felt their strength and she pressed herself further into his embrace. She clung onto him with both arms, her hands clutching at the wool of his jacket until it scraped her knuckles.

The crowd in the Well roared its approval.

'Ellen,' he said simply as his lips pressed onto her hair. 'Thank God.'

Hearing the rapid thump of Robert's heart beneath her ear Ellen shut her eyes and savoured the feel of the man she loved and who had traversed the ocean to find her.

Tilting her head, she gazed up at Robert. Her

eyes locked with his and he gave her a weary smile. 'Sing your *last* song, Ellen. Then I am taking you home.' He let her go and stood back against the curtain.

Wiping tears from her eyes, Ellen signalled to Mr Levy.

As Ellen sang the old Irish ballad there wasn't a dry eye in the house. The ballad itself could cause strong men to sob, but with the added drama of Ellen and Robert's reunion to fuel them, the audience were visibly wiping their eyes after the first few chords.

Ellen sang as she always did, clear and true, but with a tremor of emotion in her voice that had been absent since she had left Robert nearly a year before.

With his ardent eyes on her, Ellen's heart was near to bursting with joy. Robert had found her. He had found her and, judging by the look in his eyes and the firm way he had enfolded her in his arms, he would never let her go again.

She finished to rapturous applause. Robert took her hand and led her off the stage. As they ducked behind the heavy curtain his arm went out again and pulled her to him hard.

'I'm sorr–' Ellen began, but her words were cut short as Robert's mouth met hers in a forceful kiss. She could feel his emotion course through him, making her light-headed with the power of it. Her knees buckled and she felt Robert tighten his grip to support her.

'It doesn't matter,' he said, releasing her lips, but proceeding to kiss her cheeks and forehead. 'Nothing matters, now that I've found you.'

'But how?' Ellen asked, her hands on the flat of his chest and looking up at him. She couldn't take her eyes off his face. He looked tired, but otherwise the face that had haunted her night and day for almost a year was much the same.

Robert's here, her mind said over and over again.

'Doctor Munroe! Doctor Munroe,' an excited voice behind them shouted. 'You came. You came.'

Before she could turn around to face her daughter, Ellen was shoved aside as Josie threw herself at Robert, jumping up and down on the spot as she hugged him. 'You came. I knew you would.'

Josie grabbed her mother's hands. 'I knew when Doctor Munroe got my message from Pat he would come after you.' Josie clasped her hands together and looked heavenwards. 'It's just like–'

Ellen's head was already spinning. 'Message? Pat?'

'Patrick Nolan. I met him on my way home on the day you had...'

Bobbie!

Josie gave her mother a quick look and caught her lower lip in her teeth. 'I ... I wanted to bring him back but he was sailing on the evening tide and couldn't, but I made him promise to go to Doctor Munroe and tell him where we were.'

'You did the right thing, Josie,' Robert told her, with his eyes fixed on Ellen's face.

Bobbie! What would he say?

'Could you go and tell Mr Hermanshaw I'll be going home a little early tonight,' she said to her daughter. 'Er ... take your time. We'll be in my dressing room.'

Robert stepped forward and took hold of Ellen

388

again, catching her to him and forcing her to look up at him. 'Lead the way,' he said, his hand firmly around her waist.

Within a minute of dodging through the props and scenery in the wings, they reached Ellen's dressing-room door. With one swift movement Robert pulled her into the room, encircled her in his embrace and captured her lips in a hard, demanding kiss.

All of Ellen burst into life in Robert's arms. She kissed him back fervently, caressing his face and shoulders as if to reassure herself that he was truly here.

She tore her lips from his. 'Robert,' she said breathlessly. 'There is something you–'

Her words were cut short as Robert, taking hold of her head, pressed his lips onto hers again.

There was a muffled sneeze and a small cry. Robert's brow creased for a second, then he glanced around the room and spotted the basket on the floor with a small hand waving above its rim. He looked back at her.

'Ellen?'

Twisting herself out of his arms, Ellen went over and picked up the still sleepy Bobbie. The baby hiccuped and sneezed again.

Ellen held her out for Robert to see. 'This is Robina, your daughter.'

Robert's mouth dropped and his eyes fixed on the infant Ellen held. He came over and placed his index finger in Bobbie's small hand. He gave Ellen a stupefied look and she saw tears in his eyes.

'I have a daughter,' he said, his voice full of

wonder. He ran his hands lightly over the soft red-gold down on her head. His head snapped up. 'Did you know–'

'No, no. I was halfway across the Atlantic before I realised.' She laid her hand on his arm and gazed up at him. 'If I had even thought I was with child, I would never have left, Robert, I swear it.'

Robert's face remained sober for a second longer then a proud smile spread across his face and Ellen let out the breath she was holding.

'I know, Ellen,' he said, putting his arm around her shoulders and pulling her to him, his lips pressing onto her hair. 'I know.'

He enfolded Ellen and Bobbie in his arms and held them to him tenderly then, carefully wrapping the shawl around Bobbie, he took hold of her and sent Ellen a heart-melting smile.

'My love,' he said, emotion cracking his deep voice. 'You don't know how I have dreamed of this moment.' Settling his daughter in his arms he kissed her head and beamed back at Ellen. 'Now that we have a daughter, you'll have to marry me.'

Ellen thought her heart must surely stop at any moment as it couldn't stand much more happiness.

She let her head fall back and she sent out a peal of joyous laughter. 'I will marry you, whenever and wherever you say,' she said, and Robert joined in her merriment.

There was a tap at the door and Josie peered around the door.

'Come in, come in, Josie,' Robert called, as he saw her. 'Come and join the rest of your family.'

Bobbie, who had until now been quite content,

stared up at the tall stranger who held her tenderly in his arms and suddenly started to fret. Ellen held out her arms for her.

'I'll have to feed her,' she said, taking the child from Robert and settling down on the chair. Robert pulled up the chair and sat beside her as Josie scrabbled onto the large dressing chest and sat cross-legged. Robert watched Ellen offer their baby her breast and again she saw tears in his eyes.

'When did you arrive, Doctor Munroe?' Josie asked, as Bobbie suckled hungrily.

Robert took out his gold watch and glanced at it. 'Six hours ago. The ship tied up at ten this morning,' he said 'I dropped my bags at Mr Tappen's house in Rose Street just before tea.'

'Are you staying there?' Josie interrupted.

'I am. Mr Tappen is in correspondence with Lord Ashley and he gave me a letter of introduction,' Robert answered, his eyes resting briefly on Bobbie. He looked back to Josie.

'So, after a bite to eat, I changed my clothes and set about finding you. I reached your brother's at six where I introduced myself and asked your whereabouts.' Robert smiled at Ellen. 'Your brother looks like your mother, doesn't he?'

Ellen nodded. 'That he does.'

Robert let out a short laugh. 'He greeted me warmly and told me he was "right pleased" to see me.' He smiled as Bobbie was tucked onto Ellen's other breast. 'I can understand why now. Anyhow, after freeing myself from their hospitality, I took a brisk walk to the Well.'

'Are we going back to London, Doctor Munroe?' Josie asked.

'I hadn't planned to. I quite like the thought that we might stay here for a year or two.'

Robert stood up and went over to the young girl perched on the pine chest. Lifting her off, he stood her in front of him. 'And you'll have to call me something other than Doctor Munroe if I'm to be your stepfather,' he said.

Josie jumped up and hugged him around the neck, making him stagger back as her weight lunged against him.

'I can't think of anyone I'd rather call Pa than you, Pa,' she said, giving him a noisy kiss on the cheek. She dashed over to her mother, hugging her in turn. 'Can I go and tell Hetty, Ma?'

'If you like, Josie,' Ellen said, almost too happy to speak.

With the door slamming behind the exuberant Josie, Robert came back to Ellen and took the sleeping child from her. Deftly he wrapped her in a warm shawl and tucked her in the crook of his arm. Ellen stood up and shrugged on her coat and bonnet. She stood for a moment looking at Robert, standing holding his daughter in his strong arms. He was almost grey with tiredness and already the shadow of his beard was showing in the lamplight, but he had an air of peace about him that Ellen guessed reflected just how she felt too.

He gave her the weariest and happiest of smiles and the love that she had denied and stifled for the past months burst within her. He reached out his free hand.

'Let's go home.'

392

Twenty-Five

Josie nearly floored both Ellen and Robert as he unlocked the front door of number forty-five Cranberry Street. They stood back and let Josie have the run of her new home for a few moments. Robert slid his arm around Ellen's waist and hugged her to him.

'How do you like your new home, Mrs Munroe?' he asked, as they looked down the hill towards the East River.

Mrs Munroe. She had never thought she would ever be that, not after Danny's trial and her flight to America. But now she was.

Wearing a pale apple-green silk gown edged with Belgian lace covered with a deep green velvet spencer – the grandest outfit she had ever owned – she had walked down the aisle of the Mott Street Welsh Chapel on her brother's arm to stand beside Robert. So, after a simple ceremony in the presence of Josie and Bobbie and her brother's family, she had become what she had never thought she could possibly be: Robert's wife.

Unexpectedly, but much to Josie's delight, Patrick Nolan's ship had arrived back in New York two days before, so he was able to be part of the wedding party. Seeing Patrick again brought back memories of Bridget, and Ellen wished her mother could have lived long enough to see her married to Robert. But she had to look forward and put the past – Danny, the Angel and Crown, her old life doing other people's laundry in Wapping, all of it – behind her.

Following a recommendation from Henry Davies, his erstwhile medical officer at the London Hospital, Robert had been appointed Senior Physician at the New York Hospital. Although he intended to work in the poorest area of New York, he was adamant that his family would have the benefits of clean open countryside as they grew. Although there seemed to be new houses springing up all around them, the overall impression of Brooklyn Heights was one of a small rural town. Ellen turned and looked at the house Robert had rented for them.

'I love it,' she answered. Adjusting Robina on her hip she took a deep breath. The fragrance of freshly mown grass and spring flowers assailed her senses.

Robert beamed, giving her a glimpse of the boy he must have been. 'There's a stable and outbuilding at the back, and a chicken coop and pig pen already set for stock. I have already arranged for a fresh pail of milk to be delivered each day from the Connell farm down the road and I've also taken on his eldest daughter, Liza, to help you in the house.'

Fresh laid eggs and milk every day – and help! She looked again at the house that was now their home. It was timber-clad and whitewashed and stood in its own plot of land. It had steps up to a front porch which ran the length of the house and two good-sized rooms on either side of the front door with sash windows. Of course they hadn't enough furniture yet to fill the two rooms, but, as Robert had told her, now he had bought a practice in Grand Street it wouldn't be long before they could take a trip across the river to buy whatever she wanted for the house. They had already furnished the upstairs rooms with some comfort: a massive iron bedstead for them, a spindle four-poster with delicate drapes for Josie, a carved cradle for Bobbie. The living area downstairs was rapidly becoming a snug family home too, with woven rugs, sofas and a deep-buttoned chair for Robert.

'Are you sure you want to stay in America, Robert?' she asked, as she thought briefly about the home they had both left.

Robert lowered his head and kissed her hard.

'I'd be happy to live in America, London, anywhere else as long as we are together. It is you, Ellen, only you, that matters to me and nothing, nothing else.' He held her to him again for a long moment. Bobbie wriggled in protest at being squashed between her parents. Robert gave her a swift kiss on her baby curls. She smiled up at her father and grabbed his nose. 'It might not be forever. Society won't accept us as a married couple for a few years but things are changing.'

'What about your family? How do you think your mother will react when your letter arrives about Bobbie?' she asked, as a cart full of vegetables heading for New York trundled along the dusty road in front of their house towards the ferry.

'I am certain she will be pleased,' he replied, tickling his daughter under the chin and making her laugh. His face grew sombre. 'I can't say I have the same hope of my father.'

'Oh Robert.'

He had told her of his visit to Edinburgh and how his father had reacted. Much as she would dearly like to, she couldn't change what had happened, she could only love Robert and help deal with the hurt.

He looked intently at her. 'You, Bobbie and Josie are my family now,' he said in a firm tone. He raised one eyebrow and gave her a crooked smile. 'Besides, my skills as a physician are as sorely needed here in the Five Points and the Bowery as ever they were in Wapping and Shadwell.'

Ellen picked up his lighter mood and gave a deep sigh. 'I suppose that means that I haven't heard the end of drains and pumps then.'

Robert puffed out his chest. 'I should think not. In fact I plan to follow up my successful publication of *Observations on the Diseases Manifest Amongst the Poor, with the Effects on Health of Sanitation and Overcrowded Living Conditions*. I have already written the first few chapters.' He raised his eyebrows high and looked down at her. 'Did I tell you the surgeons' library in the hospital has two copies of *Observations?*'

Ellen let out a bubbly laugh. 'I think you mentioned it once or twice.'

Robert joined her laughter.

'Josie,' Robert called, as his excited stepdaughter poked her nose out of the window beside them.

Josie reappeared on the front porch. 'Ma, there's a bath in a room all by itself up there.'

'Take Bobbie from your mother,' he said, lifting Robina from Ellen's arms. He puffed in an exaggerated fashion. 'I swear this child gets heavier by the day.'

'I think you're right. I'll *have to stop* carrying her soon,' Ellen said sending Robert a meaningful glance.

He didn't notice her change of tone as he was struggling to stop Bobbie from wriggling out of his arms. For all that she had inherited her father's serious ways of investigating her dolls and bricks, she was as lively as her sister ever was.

Ellen smiled to herself. It was early yet, she had only just missed one monthly flow. But her breasts were tender and she had been unable to eat breakfast for the last three days. That would cause a stir, especially if Robert's next child arrived a little early. They had only been married six weeks.

'Now let's do this properly, shall we,' he said scooping Ellen off her feet and holding her effortlessly in his arms. Ellen flung her arms around his neck although she was in no fear of falling. Josie squealed, which set Bobbie off giggling.

'Welcome to your new home, Mrs Munroe,' Robert said, stepping over the threshold and into the hall. She laid her head on his shoulder, knowing she was truly home and safe. She felt his lips on her hair.

Robert carried her into the front parlour where the settee and side table looked lost in the vastness of the room. He stood in the middle, holding Ellen aloft.

'I don't know about Bobbie getting heavier, you seem to be too, my dear,' he said, his eyes twinkling at her. 'It's probably that little Munroe you have tucked under your skirt.'

'Robert, how–'

'For goodness' sake, Ellen. I'm a doctor.' He gave a quick look to where Josie had set Bobbie down and lowered his voice. 'Besides, my new scientific study is watching you undress each night.'

She looked up into the deep-brown eyes that would hold her heart captive until her dying day. 'Robert, I love you,' she said simply.

'And I love you,' he replied. He set her on her feet but held onto her, taking her to the window. Holding her against him he looked deep into her eyes. 'Do you know, my love, I used to dream about finding cures for diseases, and, who knows, one day I might succeed. But there is one thing I will never find a cure for. Love. Because I know there is no cure for love.'

The publishers hope that this book has given you enjoyable reading. Large Print Books are especially designed to be as easy to see and hold as possible. If you wish a complete list of our books please ask at your local library or write directly to:

Magna Large Print Books
Magna House, Long Preston,
Skipton, North Yorkshire.
BD23 4ND

This Large Print Book for the partially sighted, who cannot read normal print, is published under the auspices of

THE ULVERSCROFT FOUNDATION